Pictures of You

'90s Coming of Age
Book 1

LETA BLAKE

An Original Publication from Leta Blake Books

Pictures of You ('90s Coming of Age Book 1)
Written and published by Leta Blake
Cover by Dar Albert
Formatted by BB eBooks

Copyright 1ˢᵗ Edition © 2016 by Leta Blake Books
Revised Edition 2022

First Edition, 2016

Print Edition
ISBN: 979-8-88841-016-5

Other Books by Leta Blake

Contemporary

Will & Patrick Wake Up Married
Will & Patrick's Endless Honeymoon
Cowboy Seeks Husband
The Difference Between
Bring on Forever
Stay Lucky

Sports

The River Leith

The Training Season Series
Training Season
Training Complex

Musicians

Smoky Mountain Dreams
Vespertine

New Adult

Punching the V-Card

'90s Coming of Age Series
Pictures of You
You Are Not Me

Winter Holidays

North's Pole

The Mr. Christmas Series
Mr. Frosty Pants
Mr. Naughty List
Mr. Jingle Bells

A Boy for All Seasons
My December Daddy

Fantasy

Any Given Lifetime

Reimagined Fairy Tales

Flight
Levity

Paranormal & Shifters

Angel Undone
Omega Mine

Horror

Raise Up Heart

Omegaverse

Heat of Love Series
Slow Heat
Alpha Heat
Slow Birth
Bitter Heat

Gay Romance Newsletter

Leta's newsletter will keep you up to date on her latest releases, sales and deals, future writing plans, and more from the world of M/M romance. Join Leta's mailing list today.

Leta Blake on Patreon

Become part of Leta Blake's Patreon community to support her indie publishing expenses and to access exclusive content, deleted scenes, extras, and interviews.

Preface and Acknowledgments
Second Edition

It's been nearly twenty years since Peter first came into my life.

Unlike many of my other characters, he didn't appear fully formed with a story to tell, nor did he feel "downloaded" into my brain as an already complete being. Rather, Peter started out as the vague answer to a "what if?" question, and he grew slowly over many, *many* years. Perhaps it was because he was my very first character, or perhaps it was just indicative of his somewhat meek nature to come across slowly, but from the very beginning he made me work to know him.

The fact that it took him fourteen years to give me the first two parts of his story (*Pictures of You* and *You Are Not Me*) and almost another six to give me the last part (*Only You*) is very on brand for him. In some ways it seems impossible that Peter's role in my life is finished, and yet it is a relief and a joy to be able to finally hand him over to the world. His story has been the work of my heart; he's been both my love and my albatross.

For me, reading these books is like taking a walk back through time. I recall working on Peter's first book before my grown daughter was even conceived, and now she has participated as a beta reader and editor on the final stages of *Only You*. Unbelievable that Peter took as long to become an adult as she did. My daughter tells me that, having heard me talk about these books her whole life, she'd always felt as if Peter were a friend she'd never met. Now, after reading the books, she *has* met him, and she loves him passionately.

Truth be told, I'd nearly given up on ever finishing this series. There were so many roadblocks that prevented me from completing

Peter's story over the years: finances, lack of inspiration, depression, terrible first drafts, worse second drafts, silent characters, overly patient characters, wrong directions, story diversions, lack of needed skill, and so much more.

But in the spring of 2022, I was preparing to set out on a writing retreat in order to work on a different book altogether, when the television show *Heartstopper* was released on Netflix. The Friday before I was supposed to leave, I watched the show, and I saw parts of Peter in the character of Charlie. As I clicked the television off, I felt Peter wake from his long sleep. He rose to the surface of my mind in a hot rage.

"When do I get *my* happy ending? I've been waiting forever!"

"You'll get it when you tell me your story."

"I'll tell you then."

"Do it. I'll wait."

I thought he wouldn't because he'd teased me too many times over the years. I imagined he'd flail about some and then disappear again. But as I broke out the very-bad-horrible-no-good draft of the next book, Peter was loud and clear in a way he'd never been before.

"Cut that part. Write him out. Get rid of that. She never existed. Cut it. Rework it. Rewrite it. Burn it with fire. Add this here. Give me that instead."

He was clear, he was loud, and he was determined.

I spent the entirety of that spring's writing retreat, as well as the months after, finishing up the first draft of *Only You*, which I then recognized would be the third and final book in this series.

As I mentioned above, I had almost given up on finishing Peter's journey. I had a vague plan to make a deeply apologetic announcement in December of 2022 declaring that I would *not* be finishing the series, and then I planned to permanently unpublish Peter's first two books.

I'd been considering doing it since 2019 when I stood in front of Michelangelo's unfinished statues The Prisoners in the Galleria dell'Accademia. There, with his David in the room just ahead of me, I pondered these trapped men and thought, "That's Peter. He's a prisoner, too. Forever."

I asked myself then, if Peter was trapped unfinished for eternity, had he been worth writing and publishing at all? Would people still love the potential and forgive the lack of completion?

It amazes me even now that isn't the outcome for Peter after all. He *did* come through, and the final installment of his story, *Only You*, is beautiful and powerful.

I'm fiercely proud of these books. I wrestled with them longer and harder than any other book or series I've written, but, just as they say, the outcome is all the sweeter for the difficulty. I hope you feel the same.

For those of you who are new to Peter and his story, I hope you put aside all your expectations and just let yourself go on this Coming-of-Age/Romance journey with him. In these pages there's love, friendship, heartbreak, and heart-healing, and at the end of *Only You* there's a happy ending to swoon over.

Thank you to every reader who waited (not so) patiently for Peter to tell his tale. Thank you for the amazing reviews and love that have been poured out over these books during the last many years.

I'm going to leave my original thanks and Author's Note intact as well because those thoughts at that gratitude still applies. If you don't see your name here, please read the pages ahead. Hopefully I haven't missed anyone, but after twenty years, I fear someone is bound to slip through.

Thank you to the following:

My patrons at Patreon for loving Peter and rousingly supporting his story at every turn.

Brooke for her wonderful cottage where I go to find peace and quiet for writing.

Willow for the fantastic copyedits, and Mel for the excellent proofing.

Mia, Anne-Marie, Cecily, Amy, and Sharon for the sensationally helpful beta reads.

Dar Albert for the wonderful cover revisions.

Keira Andrews for handholding and developmental edits.

My daughter and husband for believing in me, and for always telling me that I could and would finish this trilogy.

Most of all, thank you to Peter for finally showing up. I'm going to miss you, dude, but I'm glad you're finally free.

Acknowledgments
First Edition

After fourteen years of writing this series, scrapping it entirely, rewriting entire sections, and spending untold hours on this work, it's hard to know where to start with the acknowledgments.

There have been so many people over the years who've held my hand, talked me through issues, and supported the completion of this series. If I leave out a name, I apologize deeply.

Ragna Kristjánsdóttir was Peter's first fan. Nancy Silberstein, Brigid Kelly, and Nisha-Anne D'Souza were also early adopters of Peter's story. Rachel Koteen supported this series by giving me a quiet place to stay whenever I needed time to concentrate on Peter's shenanigans. Jacyn Stewart has offered encouragement and generous advice. Jed Edwards has listened patiently for over a decade to my nattering about Peter's problems and has lovingly offered up advice, suggestions, and support. Liza Hinton has loved and encouraged me always. Keira Andrews has held my hand throughout the wrapping of these books.

Thank you to Erika for her readership and advice. Thank you to Kim Venable for her steadfast encouragement and last-minute proofing skills. Thank you to Skylar Cates, Anne-Marie, Alice, Jodie, Clay, Heidi, Sharon, Random, and Aimee for the beta reading.

Especially Aimee.

Thank you to the LiveJournal community that nurtured me.

Thank you to my parents, my husband, and child for giving me the opportunity to write. Thank you to my own Dr. L. Thank you to Mark, David, Morrie, and Lester for inspiration.

Thank you to my readers who take this journey with me. It's been a long time coming.

Author's Note
First Edition

Before September 11, 2001, it might not have been easy to be of Middle Eastern descent in the Christian South, but in liberal communities, like Knoxville, TN, it wasn't as fraught as it has become in the years following. For that reason, the treatment of Middle Eastern characters by non-Middle Eastern characters in this story may seem idealistic.

Dedicated to Aimee for loving Peter the most

Part I

August, 1990

Chapter One

I CARRIED MY Leica M6 as I did almost all the time. The camera was my baby, topped by an even more expensive Summilux lens. Both had been purchased with tediously saved allowance and mowing money. I loved the feel of the worn shutter button under my index finger and the tension in my wrist when I focused the lens. Usually its subtle weight around my neck was a comfort, but at the moment it chafed against my collarbones and hung too heavily. I tugged at the hem of my green polo shirt and rubbed my sweaty palms against my cargo shorts.

I was attending Kingsley High's orientation day for new kids. Most of the small crowd gathered around on the campus lawn were freshmen, but older transfer students were scattered in too. Some came from other states, hunched over with crossed arms and angry scowls, forced into new lives when their parents accepted jobs at Oak Ridge National Laboratory or TVA, but others, like me, were there by choice.

My mother stood next to me on the outskirts of the small crowd, her shoulder-length dark hair and dusty-rose printed sundress fluttering in the breeze as she rifled through her purse looking for Chapstick. I couldn't decide if I should stand closer to her, or farther away. I looked for some guidance from the rest of the group milling about but couldn't draw any definitive conclusions.

The campus was set up like a small college, with four short

brown-bricked buildings spread over the fields and the rolling hills, ending on all sides with a wooded area marking the boundaries. The grounds were dotted with leafy green trees and shady areas, as well as benches for students to sit on while studying or talking. It was a massive change from my prior high school: a large, prison-like structure, teeming with teenagers and no landscaping to speak of. Anxiety spiked as I tried to imagine myself walking between these buildings, going from class to class amongst strangers.

I wanted the first month of school to have passed and for me to already be settled into whatever place I fit in at Kingsley. I knew enough to realize it would be somewhere near the bottom, given my too-young face and vertically-challenged stature.

I sighed, ran my hands through my mess of dark curls which always frizzed in the Southern summer humidity, and pushed my glasses up on my nose. Quick inspection revealed that even some of the freshmen were bigger than me, and none of them seemed to know what to do about their parents either.

That's when I saw him. He had to be a senior transfer student too. He was tall enough his head rose above the rest of the crowd, hair shining a deep, red-tinged brown in the sunlight. His broad shoulders filled out a plain gray T-shirt, and his hands were shoved deep into his jeans pockets. He turned, smiling with an unselfconscious ease. His white, even teeth shone in the summer sun.

I lifted my Leica, pointed it in his direction, and snapped a picture.

The shutter snicked on him smirking in my direction, and again as he started to move toward me, and a fourth time as his eyeball peered, hazel, close-up, into my lens.

"Hey, Mr. Paparazzi, why're you taking my picture?"

Adrenaline zipped up my spine and my stomach dropped. "I'm a photographer?" I gestured at the camera as proof.

He smiled and stuck out his hand. It was larger than mine and not sweaty at all as we shook. "I'm Adam Algedi, and that—" he jerked his thumb over his shoulder at a tall, dark-haired girl, wearing a black, lightweight sundress, and staring at us with a mixture of curiosity and annoyance "—is my sister, Sarah."

"Peter Mandel," I choked out, happy my voice didn't crack.

"We're transferring from the American school in Jordan." Adam stuffed his hands in his pockets again, and my attention focused on his crotch. I quickly went back to fiddling with my camera's settings.

Adam went on. "It's a little country near Kuwait." When I looked up he winked at me. "We've been living there for the last two years."

"I know Jordan. On a globe. I've never been there or anything."

Adam smiled broadly. "Most people haven't." He motioned for his sister to come over and then returned his attention to me. "Where are you transferring from?"

"Um, just from here. Knoxville. From a public school."

"Ah, I see." Adam tossed his arm over his sister's shoulders. "Why the switch?"

I hoped my mother would jump in and save me, but she hung back, leaving it to me. "Um, I guess I needed a change."

"Change is good. Sare-Bear and I know all about change. We've moved around a lot, haven't we?" He gazed fondly at her. "But this is the first time we'll be staying for any length of time in the States since we were what? Eight?"

Sarah, even more intimidating up close, murmured, "Don't call me that."

Adam just smiled at me and Mom again. "So, what year are you in school, Peter?"

"Senior."

"Cool! Sarah and I are seniors too. Maybe we'll have some classes together."

"And your parents are…?" Mom asked, looking around to introduce herself.

"Oh, they couldn't make it," Adam said, shrugging. Sarah grabbed his wrist and threw his arm off her shoulders.

Before I could ask him what brought him from Jordan to Knoxville of all places, the headmaster—a squat, bald man in a cheap-looking jacket—burst through the main doors of the school. He called over his shoulder, "Follow me, follow me! This way. We'll head down to the auditorium and start our tour from there."

Adam fell into step next to me, lifting his head to the sky as though to soak up the sun. Sarah followed him closely. Her eyes burned hot paths across the landscape, like she might set the grass on fire with her gaze. Adam, on the other hand, sauntered along next to me as if he were quite at home already.

The auditorium was dark, musty, and less than half the size of the one at my public school. I turned around slowly, taking in the banners and the red stage curtain that blocked off the heart of the theater.

The headmaster grasped the sides of the podium. "Welcome to Kingsley. I'm Mr. Waverly."

Adam pressed his knee into mine, offering a stick of gum.

"Thanks."

"No problem."

Mr. Waverly spoke about the history of the school, the goals of the administration, and made Kingsley out to be an absolute paragon of education. For the price my parents were paying, the school had better live up to his promises.

"Each of you will be responsible for giving at least one speech per year to the entire student body. These speeches will be given during morning assembly." Mr. Waverly lifted his chin. "As we've pledged to your parents, Kingsley is an institution dedicated to the sole purpose of providing an excellent college preparatory education. Also, since this question was raised just this morning, let me reassure you, religious tolerance is, and will always be, guaranteed at Kingsley."

I suppressed a snort. Well, maybe as religiously tolerant as an institution could get and still be in the South. I leaned back in my seat and glanced over at Adam. Once classes started and he realized I was just a lame-o faggot geek, he would see his mistake in being friendly to me today. He'd probably go on to join the ranks of popular jocks, while I carried on in the usual way—alone.

Mr. Waverly ended his remarks, and we followed him out of the auditorium, looking around dutifully when he motioned toward the cafeteria and the hallway leading to the library. Exiting the main structure and drifting up the hill, he pointed out the buildings where we would attend the majority of our classes.

In a month, the halls would be filled with kids, but now, with just our small orientation group, the campus was peaceful, like the school was sleeping. We entered the shadowy interior of the main building and passed through into a central courtyard. Mr. Waverly stopped to discuss the sports teams, indicating the football field off to the left.

Adam walked with his hands in his pockets, chin up, and a half-asleep smile on his face. "Taking notes for me, Sare-Bear?"

Sarah, who still hadn't said a word to either Mom or me, grunted and tucked a thick hank of black hair behind her ear. "No. It's all bullshit, anyway. We won't be here long."

"Mom said the whole year. May as well get used to it."

"Mom can kiss my ass."

Adam tsked. I looked over at my mother to catch her reaction, but, as usual, she wasn't paying attention. Instead, she was making a grocery list on the back of a receipt while walking.

"Mom will be very sorry to hear you said that, Sarah."

"Fine, I'll tell her about—" Sara broke off, looking at me pointedly. "You know."

Adam laughed. "Oooh. Scary. Yeah, she'll be traumatized I'm making friends." He threw his arm around her again. "I'm sorry you're not happy with our fate, but you know what? Shit happens."

"I don't understand why they're suddenly so worried about our safety. We've been through a lot worse."

"Exactly." Adam pulled her close so their hips bumped with each step. "Mom doesn't want to go through that again, and you aren't being fair to her with your attitude."

"Sure. Whatever. *You* don't have to sleep across from Mo's room. I hear *things*."

"You could always move into the basement. I told you I'd paint it for you."

"Whatever."

Just as easily as Adam had pulled Sarah close, he clutched her shoulder and with a deft move shoved her away. He chuckled as she stumbled and whirled around to punch him in the gut before striding ahead of us both.

"She's pretty," I said.

Adam's eyebrows went up. "Stay away from her, because she's also a vicious bitch."

"Don't worry. Your sister's safe from me."

"I wasn't worried about my sister." Adam laughed. "She can take care of herself. So, tell me about Knoxville. What's there to do here?"

I chewed the gum he'd given me, stumped as always for a good answer to that question. "Well, it depends on what you like to do. There're mountains if you like to hike or do the nature thing." I glanced his way and Adam shrugged. "There're, uh, like four dance clubs in town and, if you can get in, I've heard they don't suck so much now."

Adam laughed. "Yeah? Don't suck *so* much?"

"Knoxville is kind of lame, really." I shrugged, aiming for non-chalance and probably coming across as embarrassed.

Adam frowned. "Don't say that. I've got to live here at least a year. Surely there's something to do that's fun."

I shook my head.

"Then how do you entertain yourself?"

I indicated my camera.

Adam lifted his eyes to the mountains and hills hemming us in. "Knoxville reminds me of Italy."

"Really?"

"Yeah. Italy in summer. Just a little. I think it's the lushness of the landscape and the way the mountains clutch at you. It seems like a dream, or—" Adam stopped himself. "Sorry. I'm a writer. I like words." He shrugged, like what he was saying didn't matter.

I touched his arm, just a friendly brush. "That's cool."

When the orientation tour ended, Adam and I found that by some strange serendipity we lived in the same neighborhood.

"Excellent! Let's get together before classes start. What's your phone number? I'll give you a call."

For a moment, I couldn't remember what it was, even though I'd lived in the same house and had the same number since I was three years old. I asked Mom for a pen and paper, and she handed me yet another receipt from the mess in her purse. I didn't ask for his, thinking he was probably just being polite. It turned out I didn't have to—he ripped the receipt in half and scribbled down his number too.

Sarah waited by their Mercedes with the passenger door open, her eyes still blazing as she glared at the entire Kingsley campus.

"Give me a call." Adam grinned. "You can show me what there is to do around here."

"I already told you. There's nothing."

"Then we can go do nothing."

My mother looked very pleased.

"Sure. Nothing sounds good." My heart pounded in my ears.

Adam shook my mom's hand. "Nice to meet you, Mrs. Mandel. I hope to see more of you both." He jumped in the car, and Sarah climbed in too.

Adam waved as they pulled away, and I stared after his car a lot longer than a straight guy would.

Chapter Two

I HAUNTED THE kitchen for the next twenty-four hours. We only had one phone because my mother resented the regular calls from telemarketers. She seemed to think if we just had one extension, we'd receive fewer of them. I was pretty sure her logic didn't work.

I ate grapes. I did the crossword puzzle. I made some spaghetti. I flipped through catalogs and read my photography magazine at the kitchen counter, as I sat hoping, wanting, waiting for the phone to ring. My dog, Harry, an old terrier mix, stirred his bones from his bed in the corner to sit at my feet and beg for food.

Adam's was the ninth call of the day. Mom was right, there were far too many telemarketers.

"May I speak to Peter?"

The stool at the counter was luckily close, and I dropped onto it as my knees went weak. "This is Peter."

"Hi! It's Adam from the Kingsley orientation."

"Oh, hey!" I tried to sound like I'd totally forgotten who he was and had only been reminded because he told me his name.

"I was wondering if maybe you wanted to meet me at the pool? I was going to head over that way in a few minutes."

I glanced out the window. The late summer light glowed invitingly. "Sure. Yeah. I've got to do a few things first, but then, yeah."

"Cool. I'll meet you there. Take your time. I can entertain myself for a while."

I grew uncomfortably warm suddenly imagining Adam "entertaining himself." I ran a hand over my face. "Okay. Sounds good."

I disconnected the call before resting my forehead against the cool surface of the counter. I lifted my head slightly and let it fall, again and again, whispering, "Stupid, stupid, stupid." I knew better than this.

"Stupid is hitting your head on a countertop," Mom said, gliding past me. She threw open the refrigerator door, pulled out a carton of orange juice, poured it into a glass, and then left without a second glance.

I regretted agreeing to meet Adam at the pool as soon as I put on my swim trunks. Since I hadn't hit my growth spurt yet, Mom and Dad thought it was perfectly acceptable for me to keep wearing trunks from several years ago. Trunks with a terrible, bright floral print.

I stared at my scrawny self in the mirror, noticing that my gray eyes looked wild and large. I straightened my glasses and squared my shoulders. If I stood tall, maybe Adam wouldn't notice my lack of muscles.

He's straight, idiot. He wouldn't notice if you had them anyway.

I smeared sunscreen on, because my skin was fair enough to burn even in late afternoon light, left my Leica safely on my desk, grabbed a beach towel, and jogged most of the distance.

The neighborhood pool, mossy and old, had been built in the nineteen-sixties. It only took me a moment to spot Adam at a concrete table with a huge green umbrella blooming out of its center, reading a book. His dark brown hair glittered reddish in the sunlight, and his skin glowed a warm, even light brown. He wore a pair of black, obviously new swim trunks, and nothing else.

Adam must have sensed my presence because he looked right at me, breaking into a grin. "Hey!"

I weaved my way between moms applying suntan oil and kids sporting floaties on their arms. The low sun glinted on the water and I figured we had two more weeks of summer before they closed down the pool.

"Hey." I dropped onto the concrete bench across from him, trying really hard to seem like I didn't care if I was wearing outdated swimwear and hadn't been in the sun shirtless for over a year. I shoved my glasses up the bridge of my nose. "What're you reading?"

Adam tilted the dog-eared, beaten-up book so I could see the title.

"Is it good?"

He stretched a little and I couldn't help but notice his nipples were raised in the subtle breeze flowing over his skin and through his sparse chest hair. Adam tapped the cover. "Have you read anything by Nabokov?"

"Nope." I wished I could say I had. I didn't want him to think I was an uneducated hick.

"Nabokov's work is the best thing since sliced bread."

"Since sliced bread? Is that still hip slang in Jordan?"

Adam wrinkled his nose in mock offense. "No. I'm just cool."

"Not."

As he laughed and sat the book aside, his gaze traveled over my body for a long, uncomfortable moment. I didn't know what to do with his attention, so I slid *Lolita* across the table and pretended to be interested. I moved my eyes over the summary on the back and flipped it over to look at the front cover. A girl with a lollipop stared up at me seductively.

Adam said, "So, tell me what winter is like here. Sarah's worried about it. She's been muttering about shoveling snow and Mo, our brother, is just egging her on."

"It hardly ever snows," I said, reassuringly.

"That's what I told her. Mo loves to freak her out."

A huge splash drew my gaze. A kid with a plastic raft flopped around trying to climb aboard. Adam pulled his book out of my hands and flipped through some pages, searching for his place.

"So, are we getting in?" I gestured toward the pool.

Adam shook his head. "Too cold. I dipped a foot in earlier. It's not worth it."

"Yeah, they'll shut down for the season soon."

Adam closed his book and tossed it onto the table. "Hey, you know how you said there was nothing to do around here? Well, I saw in the local paper there's a drag show at a club in town. Want to go?"

I laughed.

"No, I'm serious. Let's go."

"To a drag show? I didn't have you pegged for being into that kind of thing."

"Because you know me so well?" Adam's tone went a little cold. "It sounded like something to do. If you don't want to, that's cool."

I swallowed hard. Embarrassment slithered into my stomach at losing Adam's esteem so soon. "Why do you want to go?"

"It'll be fun. You're the one who told me about the clubs and how they don't suck 'so much.'" He raised a brow at me.

I cleared my throat. "I think you have to be twenty-one for most of them. They probably check at the door. And we're in high school."

"So?"

"I'm only eighteen." I wanted him to understand I had real reasons for not wanting to go, and me being lame wasn't one of them.

Adam didn't blink an eye. "Okay. If you want to let a little thing like us being only eighteen stop you."

I rested my elbows on the table and tried to look tough. A trickle of moisture dripped down the side of my face, and beads of sweat on the bridge of my nose made my glasses slide down half an inch. "Are you calling me a coward?"

"Maybe."

I narrowed my eyes and righted my glasses. "I'm not."

Adam didn't look convinced. "It's no big deal if you don't want to go, Peter." He picked up his book again.

I leaned forward to whisper, "I just didn't think you were into that sort of thing. You know—gay stuff."

Adam leaned forward too, saying teasingly, "Gay stuff? Is that what they call it here in Knoxville?"

"Are you?"

"Am I…?" Adam let it trail off as though he had no clue what I could possibly be referring to.

"Are you, you know, gay?"

Adam shrugged off the question. "Wanting to have fun in a town with limited options doesn't make me gay."

I swallowed back my disappointment. "I don't think we can get in, but if you want to try, I'm game."

Adam's smile wiped out most of my concern for my sanity. "We'll go on Friday," he said, grabbing up his book. "Want to head back to my place since we aren't going to swim?"

Adam's house was a split-level in the ranch-style. Immediately upon entering, we were confronted by two sets of steps, one leading up to the main floor and the other down to the basement. It felt weirdly unsettled.

Adam tossed his towel down the steps toward the lower level, not noticing when it only made it halfway to the bottom. I followed him as he took the stairs up two at a time.

Shirtless, clutching my beach towel in one hand and crossing my arms, I shivered in the air-conditioned house. At the pool, Adam had thrown on a worn Duran Duran T-shirt, and I'd cursed myself for not bringing a shirt too.

"Mo and Sarah went to the movies," he called over his shoulder. "Bummer."

Adam laughed. "It's for the best, really. If you think Sarah's got an attitude—" Adam whistled and shook his head, entering the kitchen and throwing open the refrigerator. "Mo's an asshole. I'm not even sure *I* like him."

Adam pulled out two beers and popped them open before I could protest. He dropped down at the sticky-looking, wooden kitchen table and gestured for me to follow. I shivered as I took the cold bottle from his hand. *Bass Ale*, not the light-colored stuff my parents drank. I hesitated before taking a swallow. It tasted vaguely like dirt.

"Why'd your parents move here?" I asked.

"They didn't. They're in Jordan right now, but they didn't think it was safe for me and Sarah to stay there with them anymore. So they sent us to live with Mo."

"Oh?"

"Yeah, my dad works for the UN, and we get transferred all over the place. I wouldn't mind settling down somewhere, actually. It gets old after a while." He paused and took another drag on his beer. "Sarah likes moving around though."

"You and Sarah, you're twins, right?"

"How'd you guess?"

"You're both seniors," I pointed out, sipping from my bottle and hoping he didn't figure out I'd never had a beer before.

"Yeah, that's right. I already told you—though what I should've said was Sarah's just stupid and got held back a ton of years so you could spread rumors about her when school starts. That would piss her off so much."

He laughed, and I smiled, wondering who I'd even have to tell.

"Anyway, so there've been some serious things happening over there. You know, general unrest in the Middle East and stuff."

I nodded.

"Mom decided she wanted us back in the States. She's American. Dad's from Iran originally, but he's an American citizen now too."

"So, are you Muslim?" I knew that could prove tricky in the South. Not that people would say much or do anything, but there was always a definite line between the Christians and the *others*.

"Nope. We're nothing. Condition of the marriage. Mom said she'd marry him if the kids weren't raised Muslim, and Dad said so long as we weren't raised Christian—so, we're nothing."

"I understand that. Dad's Jewish, and my mom's Christian. We just don't talk about it, but, you know, growing up here in the South, I probably know as much about Baptists as John did."

"John who?"

"John the Baptist?"

"Is he a famous preacher around here or something?"

I stared at him.

Adam grinned. "No, I'm kidding. Your face is hilarious, though. I'm not all that up on the Bible and stuff, but I'm not that dumb."

I laughed and took another long drink from my beer, trying to cool the heat in my cheeks. "So your brother's old enough to, what, be your guardian?"

Adam laughed. "Don't let him hear you say that, he'll lord it over us. He's old enough legally to take on our care, but mentally? I don't know. Mom and Dad think so."

"They must trust him a lot."

Adam shrugged.

"Why didn't your mom stay here with you?"

"My dad depends on her," he said vaguely.

"But why Knoxville?"

"Mom's from Maryville, but she prefers Knoxville. It's a pocket of liberalism with the university, TVA, and the nuclear physicists from Oak Ridge."

"That's important to her?"

"Yeah. Ever since the Iran hostage crisis, some communities are weird about Arab-Americans."

"Really? I've never seen that around here."

"That's why Mo and Mom looked at UT for school. When Mo got a journalism scholarship, and when Mom and Dad figured out the cost of living here was cheap as hell, they decided to buy a house for him. It makes more sense than renting in the long run." Adam took a pull from his beer. "So, Mo's been here…" He counted on his fingers. "I guess three years now. He likes it. He's actually managed to make a few friends, and believe me, that's saying something when it comes to Mo."

I shivered again, wishing for a shirt. "Mo is—twenty-one? Twenty-two?"

"Twenty-five. He took some time off after high school, traveled Asia a little." Adam wrinkled his nose. "I'm not big on Asia. Or rather I *am* big in Asia. The people are shorter than me usually, and I feel like a giant."

"Wow. You've really traveled a lot, huh?"

"What about you?" he asked. "Why did you want to transfer to Kingsley? Don't you want to graduate with the rest of your friends?"

I took yet another swig from the beer to postpone answering. I didn't want to tell him the truth. I couldn't say I'd been tormented by a group of jocks who'd pegged me as gay back in eighth grade, and my only friends consisted of a few girls who didn't know what to make of me either. "It's complicated," I said.

Adam's eyebrows lifted. "I get it. It was bad, huh?"

I wrapped my arms around my chest tightly, struck with another chill.

Adam noticed this time. "Let me get a T-shirt for you."

"Nah, that's—"

But Adam was already out of his chair and halfway down the hall. "Come on."

I left the unfinished beer on the table and followed him to the bedroom at the very end of the hall. There were two small windows, one on the wall directly above the bed, and the other next to his chest of drawers. It wasn't a big room, about the same size as mine, but it was pretty clean, which surprised me because the rest of the house looked like a bunch of college kids lived there.

Adam tossed a lightweight blue long-sleeve shirt to me. I pulled it on while he watched.

"You don't play sports, huh?" Adam asked.

"No," I answered quietly, adjusting the too-long sleeves of the soft shirt.

"Yeah, you're not built for it."

I kept my eyes on the floor, excruciatingly aware of the difference in our bodies. Adam stood tall and strong, well-muscled, and he looked like he worked out. I was skinny and so behind on my much-needed growth spurt it was humiliating.

My heart lurched when he stepped close and chucked up my chin.

"I didn't mean anything by that, you know. You look fine to me." His eyes were warm and he did an exaggerated once-over, as though pretending to check me out. He lifted a brow.

He was absolutely flirting with me. He had to be.

Blood pounding, I swallowed and smiled, hoping I was giving the right signals.

Adam waggled his eyebrows in an exaggerated leer before turning away and indicating a cardboard box with some silver-plated trophies sticking out of the top. "I'm going to go out for the swim team and soccer. Those are my sports."

"Cool."

He drank some more beer, and I wished I hadn't left mine behind, just to have something to do with my hands. As it was, I fiddled with the hem of the borrowed shirt and pushed my glasses up on my nose again.

Adam frowned suddenly. "Hey, where's your camera? I thought you were Mr. Paparazzi?"

"No cameras at the pool. They're too expensive to risk getting wet."

"Ah." Adam reached out and grasped my forearm, his thumb stroking the inside of my wrist. "Want to see some pictures of Italy? You can judge for yourself if you think it looks anything like here, *and* you can see what a crappy photographer I am."

I looked down at his hand and then up into his warm, hazel eyes. He held my gaze, and my mouth went dry, my tongue felt paralyzed, and I couldn't think of what to say.

"Come on."

I followed him out of the room, down a strangely blank hallway—no pictures of family on the wall, no ornamentation of any kind—and down the stairs to the musty basement. Cardboard boxes lined the room and it was dark despite the sunlight streaming in from the large sliding glass door leading to the green, slightly overgrown backyard.

"The pictures are around here somewhere." Adam dropped to his knees and rummaged through a big box of junk.

"Mom sent all this crap over here to be stored when Mo moved in." He pulled out a stack of *Playboys*. "It looks like he's been adding to it." He then withdrew a single shoebox. "Here. These are my pictures from when we lived in Italy."

I joined him on the decades-old, avocado green carpet. Between that, the musty smell, and the bazillion boxes of stuff, I could see why Sarah wasn't interested in moving down here.

Adam pulled out a handful of snapshots and passed them to me one by one. "That's me and my best friend from the American school in Rome. Marcus."

In the photo, Adam looked a lot younger, but he was still a handsome kid, even if he hadn't grown into his nose at that point. Marcus was a little shorter than Adam with red hair and glasses, and he had his arm around Adam's neck. They stood with the Pantheon as a backdrop.

"Nice. Looks nothing like Tennessee."

Adam laughed. "No, not Rome itself. The countryside. We'll get to a picture of that, hold on. Patience, Grasshopper." He passed me another picture of them and the Pantheon. "Marcus pissed on the side of it."

"On the side of what?"

"Pissed on the Pantheon." Adam passed another picture to me, and I saw a smaller version of Sarah staring up at me angrily. It looked like her attitude had always been hostile. "That's Sare-Bear outside the American school."

"Wait. Your friend pissed on the Pantheon? Isn't that, like, I don't know, illegal or something?"

"Well, he had to go. In Rome, you've gotta pay for a toilet, and we didn't have any change."

"So, he just—"

"Yup. I wrote a story about it. I'll show you sometime. The story is a little more exciting than what really happened. I added an encounter with the police to spice things up."

I couldn't help but laugh.

"You can get away with a lot of stuff as an American citizen overseas if you know what you're doing. I think some of the locals hated us more than they hated the tourists."

"Us?"

Adam passed a photo of a large woman with bleached-blond hair and thick glasses. "That's my mom in our flat in Rome. Yeah, us. The kids of American businessmen living overseas. Man, we really know how to push the limits."

"So can you speak Italian?"

"*Un poco*. A little. And a little Arabic, and a few other languages. But, you know, we mainly just hung around with each other. So we only learned enough to get by. Oh, here's the one I was looking for."

Adam handed me a clumsy photo of beautiful lush hills sweeping away into the distance, very green, very thick. I saw only a vague resemblance to the hills of Tennessee. I took my time looking at it, wanting to be polite, finally saying, "It's beautiful, but I don't really see it."

Adam frowned at the picture. "Yeah. I guess it was more the feeling I'd have when we drove along the roads, you know? The hills and mountains just sort of hang over you. Sometimes it's claustrophobic, sometimes it's comforting. You never know what's right around the corner, and all of it is so lush, green, and creeping in on you." He sounded far away, so I remained silent, looking at the picture. "Do you ever feel that way, Peter?"

"Yeah. I know what you're talking about." I smiled. "In fact, I've got some pictures of it."

Adam tossed his photos back in the shoebox. "Really? Wanna show me?"

"Sure. If you want—" I felt suddenly awkward. I knew I was a good photographer, but I didn't want to seem arrogant. "I mean, they're just pictures."

"No. I'd like to see."

"They're at my house. It's just down the street."

Mom was finished writing for the day and sat nibbling chips and salsa at the kitchen counter when we came in the back door. She wore jean shorts and a blousy white top she called her 'pirate shirt.' Her dark hair was up in a haphazard bun and her cheeks were a little flushed. Harry sat at her feet staring up at her, begging with all of his might.

"Well, hello!"

I cringed. Apparently, she'd been celebrating by having a few drinks as well. I recognized the somewhat lopsided grin.

"Hey, Mom. You remember Adam?"

"Couldn't forget a face like that." She winked and took a sip from her wine glass. "How're you doing, Adam?"

"Just great, Mrs. Mandel. Peter was going to show me his photographs."

"See you later," I said, hoping to get out of any prolonged interaction.

"Peter won first place for photography in his school art show last year, and he won second in the Southeastern Scholastic Art and Photography competition," Mom said.

I grabbed Adam's arm and tried to move him bodily toward the hallway and the stairs.

"Really? That's excellent. I bet you're really proud of him." Adam ignored my attempt to steer him along.

"We are. He's so talented." She gazed at me fondly, and I thought my head would explode from the rush of blood to my face.

I continued to tug on Adam, but he was larger than I was by far, and he was going to stay pretty much immobile until he wanted to move. "Great, Mom. Thanks. Come on, Adam."

Adam just grinned and held his ground. "What do you and Mr. Mandel do for a living?"

Oh, God, why was he doing this? Why was he talking to my mom? I didn't want him to know what she did yet. She always made it sound so sleazy.

"I'm surprised Peter hasn't mentioned it. What I do for a living is the bane of his existence."

"Oh, yeah?" Adam moved closer to her.

Mom nodded, her eyes glinting in amusement. "His father is a professor of religious studies at the University, and I'm an author. I write filthy romance novels."

I dropped Adam's arm and sighed. Why couldn't she tell people she wrote children's books, or science fiction, or fantasy novels about fairies and elves for Christ's sake?

"Awesome! I want to be a writer one day." Adam leaned against the counter opposite my mother and bent to scratch Harry behind the ear. "How old were you when you first got published?"

I sighed. This could take a while. I pulled a stool over and sat, thinking it should be some kind of consolation that my mother had already proven one thing to me over the years—it was impossible for me to die from embarrassment.

An hour later, Adam and I climbed the stairs to my room.

"Your mom is so cool!"

"She's crazy."

Adam laughed. "Well, that too. But in the coolest way, you know?"

"No. My mom is not crazy in a cool way. She's crazy in a really annoying way."

I wasn't about to tell him that she really wasn't healthy in the head and hadn't been since the "incident" with my uncle in the sixties.

Adam followed into my bedroom, glanced around, and sat on the edge of the bed, looking casual and at home. "Nice room."

I shrugged, just happy I'd convinced my mother to let me pull down and paint over the Strawberry Shortcake wallpaper border I'd picked out when I was six. And yet she somehow lived in absolute denial that I was gay. Given her past, I wasn't eager to bring it up with her, so we'd ignored the massive Strawberry-Shortcake-colored elephant in the room. My dad didn't know either.

After pulling my photography portfolio out of the closet and spreading it out over the bed, I knelt down on the floor and carefully handed Adam the first picture off the top. "Please hold it by the edges."

Adam took the photo carefully and examined it. "That's beautiful."

"I got that shot last Christmas. The red glow you see on the lake? That's actually some Christmas lights. Cool, huh?"

"Hell, yeah." Adam laid it aside carefully and took the next one I offered. "You're really good."

"Thanks." Praise from Adam was an entirely different thing than praise from my mother. It settled over me like a warm, glowing blanket.

What I was looking for was the fourth or fifth picture in the stack, and when I showed it to him, Adam said, "This is it! This is what I was talking about."

"Yeah. It's one of a series." I handed him three more shots that perfectly captured the snug fit of the Tennessee hills against the eye.

"I'm seriously impressed. Wow." Adam slid down to kneel next to me and we looked through the rest of the pictures in silence. He was almost reverent, and, in a way, I wished he hadn't taken my work so seriously. It just made me like him more.

Chapter Three

ADAM CALLED THE next day and invited me over to watch a movie, but we ended up talking the whole time about the political unrest in the Middle East, his favorite pubs in Rome, the color of the sunset off Cape Town, and the trinkets sold by the kids in Nairobi during his family's stay at the American Embassy there four years prior.

Adam talked a lot, more than most guys I knew, and that was fine, because I didn't mind listening. He seemed happy to have such a willing audience. And I was growing so enamored, I would have listened to him talk about anything: the periodic table, NASCAR, or even a recitation of algebraic equations would hold my attention coming from his mouth.

My crush wasn't helped by the fact that he was so handsome and allowed me to take tons of pictures of him without posing at all. I hated it when people froze and smiled for a camera. It always completely destroyed the beautiful moment I'd planned to capture. But Adam was so unselfconscious, he never flinched when I snapped shots of him.

We drank a few beers on the Algedi back porch, sitting in an easy silence as the sun went down. Our feet dangled over the edge of the second-story deck and our arms hooked over the railing as we listened to the dogs bark down the street.

I took a deep breath of the evening air and sighed.

Adam bumped my shoulder. "In Iceland, during winter, the sun never completely rises. It's eerie."

"You've lived in Iceland too?"

"No. Just visited."

"You've been everywhere."

"Not really." Adam bumped me again. "I like it here."

My heart fluttered, and I gulped my beer, still not used to the taste but pretending to enjoy it.

Adam leaned close enough I could smell his shampoo. "I like hanging out with you."

Heat rushed through me, and I swallowed hard. His gaze focused on my lips, so I licked them while butterflies cascaded in my stomach. Adam turned away, sipping at his beer again.

"Yeah, cool," I said. "Me too."

Drinking my beer in our renewed silence, I hummed under my breath and kicked my feet as I watched the shadows of the trees lengthen into darkness.

✧ ✧ ✧

THE NIGHT OF the drag show came quickly. I told my mom I'd be staying the night at Adam's and she shooed me off, her eyes never leaving her word processor.

Even though my stomach was knotted with nerves, I was excited. More than that, I was optimistic, and after the time we'd spent together over the week I was starting to believe maybe Adam wouldn't dump me as a friend as soon as school began.

When I arrived at Adam's, I was struck anew by how the Algedi home was so different from the quiet, but relatively normal, chaos of my own. There was no Dad stumbling in late trying to find something to eat, grunting greetings and jokes aimed at the dog. There was no Mom being alternately cloying or distant, disappearing for days on end to write and leaving me to fend for myself in my well-trained way.

There was just Mo.

Mo was caustic as hell and didn't have anything good to say to anybody. For his part, Adam usually avoided him, but Sarah wanted him dead. At least, that's what I gathered from how often I heard her scream, "I hope you die!" before slamming her bedroom door.

Adam ignored them both, locking the door to his room and sticking a chair under the knob for good measure. "You're lucky, Peter."

I shrugged. "Maybe I don't have any siblings, but I'm my parents' single great hope. I have a feeling they aren't going to get what they want out of me."

"What? No picket fence and two-point-four children? Shame on you. Selfish." He fumbled around in the back of his desk drawer as he teased. Triumphantly, he pulled out a small bag of greenish-gray organic material. Marijuana. "Shazzam!"

"I don't even know what to say about your vocabulary. Especially for a writer and all." I motioned at the marijuana he was still holding aloft. "Where did you get that anyway?"

"Mo's friend Sean sold it to me. Here, hand me the bowl." Adam gestured toward the apparatus on his bedside table.

"You realize keeping that out in plain view isn't exactly going stealth, genius? I don't think you're fooling anybody."

Adam laughed. "I don't hide the pot so they don't know. I hide it so Mo doesn't smoke it."

I flashed to a mental image of Mo on the couch, potato chips in hand, shirtless in his boxers, sucking down a huge hit from Adam's bowl. I couldn't help it—maybe I was giddy from the ongoing novelty of being Adam's friend—but I started to laugh and couldn't stop. I collapsed onto Adam's bed, covering my eyes with the crook of my elbow.

Adam plopped down beside me as I snuffled, snorted, and finally got myself under control. I peeked over to see him holding a lighter to the bowl, taking a long hit and holding it in. The pungent smoke curled around his head, drifting toward the ceiling. His eyes were closed and I watched as he slowly let out a hot, scented breath.

"It's good." He held the bong in my direction. "Your turn."

I shook my head, rolling onto my side and curling my arm as a pillow.

"What? You don't smoke?"

"Nope."

Adam smiled before taking another hit. "Your loss."

I shrugged. "Depends on how you look at it." I could tell it was good weed. I was already feeling the tingle of a secondhand high. "Mind if I open the window?"

"Shit. I meant to do that. Go right ahead." Adam rolled off the bed, cleared his desk and put the bowl in the middle of it as though in a place of honor.

I crawled up onto my knees, jerking open the window over the bed so summer-fresh air poured into the stuffy room. I sank down, flopping onto my back to stare at the ceiling. Random glow-in-the-dark stars dotted the white expanse, and I counted them lazily, content in our companionable silence. Adam dug around in his desk again and I looked over to see what he was up to.

He turned with a sudden grin and held up a dinky camera. He snapped a picture. "A photo of the photog," he announced and then tossed it into the desk drawer again before dropping casually on the mattress beside me.

"Does that piece of junk even take pictures? Did you even have film?"

Adam chuckled. "Guess you'll have to wait and see."

He turned onto his side and propped himself up on his elbow, peering down at me. His hazel eyes were serious, expressive. Like he was searching my face for a sign. My heart stopped and started again with a painful thump. I caught my breath, staring up at him, not sure what to expect, hoping, aching, thinking maybe—

Adam dropped onto his back again to stare at the ceiling. "You're a good friend, Peter."

I swallowed hard, biting back my disappointment. "I'm just a geek."

"You're not a geek. You're a genius. I've seen your photos." Adam sighed. "You really need your own darkroom. What did your parents say when you asked them?"

I laughed. "You think I actually asked? Adam—I know the answer and it is something along the lines of 'There isn't a good place,' or 'You'll make a mess of my nice guest bathroom,' or 'Those chemicals stink.' It's a no-go. No need to ask."

"You can't get something if you don't even ask, Peter."

"Yeah, well, you try growing up in my family."

"I'm afraid if I grew up in your family, I'd be in state custody."

"Huh?"

"I've seen the way your mom looks at me. I really don't think she's above seducing an eighteen-year-old, Peter." Adam shifted up on his elbow again to see my face and then cackled at whatever he saw there.

"Shut up." I punched him in the stomach with the right amount of strength to show I wasn't joking.

"Sensitive about having a hot mommy, are we?"

"Shut *up*."

Adam grew quiet. "Peter?"

"Yeah."

"I was kidding."

"I know." I sighed and rolled onto my side, facing Adam, watching the way his chest rose and fell gently with each breath.

Adam spoke even more quietly, "I'm not sure I'm really op- posed to being seduced, though. I mean, it depends on who's doing it."

I tried to laugh, but it came out weird.

Adam turned onto his side too, and then scooted down until we were face to face. He studied me and then touched my cheek, his palm warm, softer than I'd imagined. My chest squeezed, and I couldn't catch a breath. Maybe I'd never be able to catch a breath again.

His thumb brushed over my lips as he searched my eyes. "I'm sorry," he whispered. He shifted forward and kissed me. It was a chaste kiss, just a tender press of lips, and then he moved away, leaving a few inches between us.

I swallowed, stunned.

"It's okay I did that," Adam said softly. It wasn't a question—he stated it as though trying to convince us both.

I blinked, blood rushing in my ears.

"Friends kiss sometimes, you know." He stared at my mouth like he might kiss me again.

"They do?"

"Yeah. They do."

My throat went tight and my chest burned from the lack of oxygen reaching my lungs. "Okay."

Then he kissed me again. This time I opened my mouth and kissed him back. His hands came up and cradled my head, tangling into my hair. His stubble scraped against my cheek, startling and raw. His mouth was smoky-sweet with the taste of marijuana, and I grunted as he rolled over on top of me.

Floating between embarrassment and ecstasy, I held on tight. I'd never kissed anyone before, and he had to have figured that out, but he didn't stop, and he didn't pull back. When his hand came around to cup my ass, and he thrust his hips against my thighs, I gasped, shocked and amazed. His dick was hard—just as hard as mine.

"Open the goddamn door, Adam!" Sarah yelled.

I jumped, and Adam ran a soothing hand over my body, pulling his mouth away from mine enough to call out, "Go away, Sarah."

"Open up. Now." Sarah banged relentlessly, and Adam groaned, rolled off me, and charged to the door, jerking it open. "What?" He sounded pissed.

I sat up, shaky and wide-eyed, my dick throbbing.

Sarah glared at me around Adam's shoulder. I brought my hand up to wipe the back of it over my still-wet lips. Her eyes narrowed, and she gave Adam a cold glare. "I wanted a hit." Her voice was quiet, but hard-edged.

"Buy your own." Adam tried to shut the door in her face, but she thrust her way into the room, pushed Adam aside, and dropped down onto the edge of the bed next to me.

"Light it," she demanded.

Adam cast a glance my way before grabbing the bowl and doing as she said.

I tried to compose myself and get my racing pulse under control. I hoped I didn't look like I'd just had my first kiss. *My first kiss.* A frisson raced over my skin, rushing in hard waves like a tide, and even with Sarah's hostile eyes raking over me, it was impossible not to think about Adam's tongue, or the way he'd sucked on my lower lip, and those thoughts didn't extinguish the stubborn erection I sported under my long shirt.

I tried desperately to concentrate on Sarah in hopes of easing the pressure in my pants because it seemed like she was settling in to stay.

After staring at me while taking a hit, Sarah exhaled the smoke in my direction. "So, Peter. You're a native to this bullshit town. Am I going to like anyone at this fucking school?"

I waved the smoke away and blinked. Sarah always used strong language. I didn't know if it was an attempt to scare me, or if she just liked the way it sounded coming out of her mouth. Her husky voice was suited for curse words.

"I don't know. I don't know any of the girls who go to Kingsley. I guess you'll have to wait and see." I licked my lips and ignored Adam trying to catch my eye over Sarah's head. I could barely breathe with the taste of him still in my mouth.

Sarah interrogated me, asking me about my friends from public high school, rolling her eyes when I answered that I didn't have many.

I couldn't explain that most of my friends had dumped me when they realized the rumors about me were probably true, and I couldn't tell her I'd always been kind of a loner because I didn't want anyone to know I was gay. So I was relieved when she diverted her attention to pick a fight with Adam over whether or not it was rude of him and Mo to leave the toilet seat up.

Somehow, in that mysterious way of siblings, what seemed to me like a ridiculous conversation turned into a thirty-five-minute pissing match, and I was glad when it was time to go.

Chapter Four

Sarah didn't head out with us, although she did pull Adam aside before we left, whispering to him and flicking her eyes in my direction.

Adam shook his head and kissed her nose. "Later, Sare-Bear. Come on, Peter. Let's go."

I followed him out to the driveway and climbed into the Mercedes. It was a pastel Easter-egg green older model, a '76 Adam told me. I settled into the fancy leather upholstery and buckled up. Adam didn't strap on his seat belt at first, until I reminded him it was the law, and then he pulled it across his chest and snapped it in place, rolling his eyes.

As we left the neighborhood, I took stock of his car's three cassettes—The Smiths' *Strangeways, Here We Come*, The Cure's *Disintegration*, and Morrissey's *Viva Hate*—placed carefully in a holder between the passenger and driver seat. A totally empty garbage container rested at my feet, and the car was freshly vacuumed inside. I wondered what he'd think of the french-fry-strewn vehicles my parents drove.

"Should I apologize for earlier?" Adam asked, turning down the stereo.

"It isn't your fault she showed up."

Adam grinned at me. "I meant, should I apologize for the kiss, but I guess the answer is no."

I twitched nervously in my seat and took a deep breath. "I'm gay."

"No shit."

I stared. "What?"

"I mean, yeah. You're gay. I figured that out."

"So—" I stopped. "Wait. How?"

"I can always tell. I don't know how."

"But I thought you said you *weren't* gay."

"I never said that." Adam frowned. "Honestly, I don't know what I am."

My heart trip-hammered for a ton of reasons, but the scariest of them was hope. "What's the deal then? Uh, with us?"

"Us? We're friends. Like I said, friends kiss."

My hope settled into a knot of anxiety. "Then why hasn't a friend kissed me before?"

"I don't know. I mean, who wouldn't want to kiss you?"

To me, it was definitely more of a question of who *would* want to kiss me, and, more specifically, just exactly why he *had*. Especially when I knew how everyone else would view me once we got to school. Maybe living all over the world hadn't taught him the self-preservation skills required to make his way in a small city like Knoxville.

I decided to tell him. He really did deserve to know, and besides, if it was going to be an issue, I wanted to be hurt now, not later.

"I'm a huge loser, you know."

Adam glanced over at me like I was insane. "What?"

"I'm not popular. In school. In life. In anything." I turned my head and looked out the window, worrying at my lower lip. "I just thought you should know. I mean, you don't want to start out at a new school being friends with someone who's just going to drag you down."

Adam actually laughed. "You're crazy. Did you know that?"

My throat tightened. It hurt he wasn't taking me seriously. "I'm telling you why I'll understand when you decide we can't be friends anymore."

"Look, you haven't even started at this school, and you've already decided that as a friend you're not worth playing first-string? What's up with that?"

I shrugged. "I'm just being realistic. I mean—look at me."

In my peripheral vision I saw Adam do just that. He looked at me long enough that I worried about the car staying on the road. "Yeah. I'm looking. I still like what I see." He lifted his hand to the back of my neck and squeezed. "I'm serious."

A strange rush of emotion flooded my stomach and chest, and I wanted to tuck my face between my knees. Instead I just crossed my arms and frowned.

Adam brushed his fingers through my hair, catching in my frenzy of curls. It felt intimate and almost more real than the kiss. I shivered when he let go to grip the steering wheel again.

"But enough of that," he said sternly. "Get my book bag out of the back seat. I've got a surprise for you."

Happy to be leaving the uncomfortable topic of my gay dorkitude behind, I reached around and grabbed the blue nylon book bag.

"Open the front pocket."

I unzipped it, fished around, and pulled out a driver's license. It was Mo's, and I had to stifle a laugh at the typical bad license photo that made him look like a serial killer.

"I've got a fake ID that Sean got for me, but I liberated that one for you."

I tapped the picture. "You think this will get me into the club? I look nothing like your brother!"

"Don't be such a defeatist! You just hold your thumb over the picture when you show them your ID."

"Adam, that isn't going to work."

"We can always try," he said, lifting his shoulders dismissively.

"They'll confiscate the ID. How's Mo going to feel about having to get a new license made?"

That got through to him. "Oh. So, huh. I guess that won't work after all."

I snorted. "Uh, no."

Adam just smiled. "We'll figure something out."

"We could see what's going on at the under-twenty-one shows on The Strip."

"No. I want to go to Tilt-a-Whirl. I read it's the best gay bar in town and has, and I quote, 'the best drag queens in the area.'"

"If the area is East Tennessee, then yeah, it probably does. And why do you want to go to a gay bar so much? I mean, this is a small city. Word gets around."

Adam narrowed his eyes. "This last-minute resistance is futile, Padawan."

"Trek *and* Wars in the same breath. That is very wrong. Very, deeply, truly wrong."

"It is," Adam readily agreed.

"You're a total dork."

"Shh. It's a secret. Don't tell the jocks when school starts. I wouldn't want my nerdiness to drag us down and all." He rolled his eyes, poking fun at me.

I started to laugh, but stopped, struck by an uncomfortable thought. I picked at my blue jeans a little, toying with a loose thread, before asking quietly, "So the kiss is a secret?"

Adam looked over in obvious surprise. "Of course. I mean, like you said, this is a small city."

"And it's the South. And the Bible Belt. And generally homophobic, yeah."

I bit down on my lip. I didn't know what I was expecting. It wasn't like he was wrong. We couldn't be *boyfriends*—not here, not now. Not out in the open or anything. It was just that I wanted so much more already. And he'd *kissed* me.

Adam's hand clasped the back of my neck again. "Hey, listen. You're my friend. And you happen to kind of turn me on with your glasses, and your camera, and the way you walk." He gripped his fingers in my hair again and gave my head a little shake. "That's enough, isn't it?"

"Yeah. So—the drag show. How do we get in?" I hoped my voice sounded light because if in Adam's world friends kissed, I didn't want to do anything to ruin our friendship before I found out what else he thought friends might do.

✧　✧　✧

CHALKY 'N' JOE'S was an old dive serving greasy burgers and huge helpings of fries, and it leaned against the lopsided dance club known as Tilt-a-Whirl. We sat in a booth along the wall closest to the club and I could feel the vibration of the bass beat through the vinyl under my thighs.

Adam took a bite from his burger while I picked at my fries, watching the locals drift in and out. There were a few dirty-looking bearded men, maybe homeless, maybe not, and several gay guys who'd drifted over from the club, all wearing tight jeans and shirts, possibly cruising for an encounter, but none of them appeared to be together.

Then there were the typical college kids, mostly dressed in preppy clothes—khakis and tennis shoes—with their girlfriends sporting sorority T-shirts and bows in their hair. I watched, somewhat fascinated by the way the girls manipulated the guys with a small flash of their eyes and a flick of their ponytails.

I glanced at Adam. He smiled at me, warmth suffusing his face.

Yeah. He'd be able to manipulate me. I was sure of that. A week around him and I was already a goner.

I gestured toward the counter and the big, beefy, white-haired man behind it. "That's Chalky. He and Joe started this place in the fifties and it's been here ever since." I stabbed another fry into the ketchup I'd poured on the wax paper lining the plastic basket. "I know that doesn't seem long to someone who's lived in Rome and stuff, but in Knoxville, if it's been here longer than ten years, it's a historic landmark."

"That's not true. I've seen those Civil War houses and stuff."

"Why are you so bent on defending Knoxville against my much-deserved insults?" I asked, popping the fry into my mouth.

"Because I've been a lot of places and, despite what you keep telling me about how much it sucks, Knoxville isn't that bad. I like it. The people who live here all—"

"Care more about the Vols' football games than human rights? Are Christians who can't practice what they preach and spend all of their time judging each other? All—"

"All seem pretty nice, actually. They're pretty nice." Adam grabbed several of my fries and kept talking. "I've never met someone so willing to insult their hometown. Isn't that kind of like insulting your mother?"

I didn't reply. He had a good point. It probably said a lot about me that I was so uncomfortable with my roots. It was just that Adam reminded me of how big the world could be, and it made me feel pretty damn small. Besides, I *did* insult my mother. I just didn't want anyone else doing it.

"Hey, do you see those butch lezzies in the corner?" Adam made exaggerated eye movements to the left, indicating the general vicinity of the individuals in question. I turned my head to see two women in the corner holding hands.

"They scare me," Adam continued.

I choked. "What? Why?"

"You can just tell they'd rip you limb from limb if you looked at them wrong." Adam leaned forward as though sharing a secret. "Seriously. The other thing about lesbians, at least the ones I've known, is they don't really have any more female solidarity than the straight girls. A lesbian realizes she's bisexual? Decides she wants a big dick sometimes after all? Well—they go for the jugular. They rip her to shreds." Adam made gestures like an animal with claws tearing at the air.

I blinked at him, not sure if I should laugh or just what reaction was expected of me. "What lesbians have you known?"

Adam shrugged. "Well, okay, so I don't know any except for my mom's sister, and I don't really get to see her much now that she's out."

"Really?"

"Yeah, because of my dad. But before, when she was only *kind of* out, she told me all that stuff. Of course she was also bitter and angry at the time, since her lover left her for a guy. For the record, lesbians don't really scare me. I just wanted to see your face. You crack me up, Peter. You looked so mortified."

I ducked my head and shrugged. I was an easy mark; that was true enough. A few months back, my mother had told me that to get into Kingsley, I'd have to agree to a full physical, complete with photographic evidence that my body was "whole." I'd pitched a major teenaged temper fit, until she'd nearly fallen to the floor laughing.

"Hey, look—"

I followed his gaze, prepared to be turned into the butt of another joke. A young Black drag queen cruised in, dressed to the nines. He looked like he was in his late twenties, and with his dark brown flesh bunched, padded, and squeezed into that particular outfit, he really did manage to approximate a woman. The sway of his hips and the hand gestures rounded out the illusion.

I instinctively reached for my camera, disappointed when I remembered I hadn't brought it. "How long do you think it takes him to look that good?" I whispered.

"*Her*," Adam whispered back. "When someone's in drag, always say *her* and *she*."

I turned a little in my seat to watch. Her long fingernails pointed out the items on the menu. Chalky didn't even blink an eye.

"Unless it's a drag king, and then say he," Adam went on.

"I guess *she's* performing tonight. Too bad *we* won't get to see *her*." I kicked Adam a little under the table to emphasize my statement.

We'd been turned away from the Tilt-a-Whirl door earlier, and Adam hadn't come up with any decent plan to get us in. I wasn't really all that disappointed. I'd started to cultivate a ridiculous idea that I'd run into one of my father's fellow professors, or, possibly worse, one of his students, and somehow it would get back to my parents that I'd been in a gay club instead of safe and sound at Adam's.

Adam grinned mischievously. I realized with dread that Adam had a plan. I just hoped it was less lame than the fake IDs.

"I'll be right back."

"Adam—"

He ignored me and launched out of the booth, strolling toward the counter. I didn't know if I should follow or not, so I lingered, waiting for a cue.

"Hello, gorgeous. You're looking fabulous tonight." Adam smiled brightly and offered his hand. "Adam Algedi."

She smirked at him, lips curling up in amusement, as she took the tips of Adam's fingers like my grandmother shook hands, only much more coyly. "Adam, it's a pleasure. Renée DeShea."

"That's a beautiful name."

Renée glanced over at me. "And who's your sweetie?"

Adam smiled and beckoned for me to join him. I approached with some apprehension, no idea what Adam had up his sleeve.

Shaking her hand, I introduced myself. "Peter Mandel."

"As in the son of Abe Mandel?" Her carefully painted eyebrows lifted.

I groaned and looked at her pleadingly. "You know my dad?"

"No, but my father does. They work in the same department." She smiled slowly before she continued, "Don't worry, I'm not going to be telling Abe Mandel that his, what? Thirteen-year-old son? Was out with his boyfriend flattering the local drag queens. For one thing, I don't think my father would like to hear how I came by that bit of information."

"He's eighteen," Adam said.

"He looks young."

"He looks good to me," Adam stated firmly.

Renée had pointed out the obvious. I barely had any beard growing in. I looked like a kid. What did Adam want with me, anyway? Once school started he'd figure it out.

Chalky slammed Renée's order on the counter and yelled, "Number one-twenty-eight," quite needlessly since she was standing right there.

Adam grabbed her basket. "Come on, sit with us."

"Why?" Renée's eyes narrowed.

"Because I've got your food." Adam strode away as though *of course* Renée would follow. With an air of amused tolerance she did.

I sat down beside Adam, pulling my fries across the table to clear a space for Renée opposite. I jiggled my foot against the worn linoleum. I wasn't good with strangers. Adam had been a fluke. No, even in that case it'd been Adam who was good with me, not vice versa. So I cowered while he chatted up Renée, working his angle, trying to get us into the club.

"So, Tilt-a-Whirl. I guess there's a back entrance, huh?"

Renée lifted a lined eyebrow. "Ah. I see. You little virgins want into the club, huh? You think you can sweet-talk an old drag queen into letting you slip in the back way?"

Adam leaned in, suddenly intense. "You aren't old. You're gorgeous."

Renée tittered a little, obviously flattered. "How old do you think I am?"

"Twenty-three."

"Ha! Twenty-eight. You certainly know how to make a girl feel good, don't you?"

"Peter and I just want to dance someplace where people won't stare at us. You remember what it's like to be in high school, right? We just want to, you know, have some fun together without it being a scene." Adam blinked at her innocently.

I almost laughed, but I stuck a few fries in my mouth and chewed, trying to mirror his earnest expression.

Renée's face softened. She took a few bites out of her sandwich and studied us.

Adam threw his arm over my shoulder, twining his fingers into the curls at the back of my neck. I held very still, torn between feeling a little used in this whole manipulation, and ecstatic at the gentle way he was petting me, like he'd wanted to touch me all evening, and this was his excuse.

"How old are you?" she asked Adam.

"Eighteen," he said. "I've got a good enough fake ID I could use, but Peter doesn't, and I don't want to go in without him. We want to be together."

Renée considered. "All right. I'll get you in. But there are three conditions."

Adam pulled me close and kissed the top of my head. "Thanks, Renée. You're awesome."

"Don't jump to conclusions. The first condition is you can't tell anyone I sneaked you in. This is my only gig and I love it. I don't want to get into trouble with the management. The second condition is you don't drink anything. I won't be responsible for you killing someone while drunk-driving."

Adam raised two fingers and pledged, "Scout's honor."

He was such a dork. A sexy, gorgeous dork. I just nodded my head in agreement.

"Third, you have to help *me* out. I've got a portion of my act that involves another person, and he's backed out on me tonight. You agree to take his place, and you have a deal."

"Sure, fine. What would I have to do?"

Feeling oddly protective of Adam, I jumped in. "I'll do it."

Adam shook his head and squeezed my shoulder before letting me go. "No. I'll do it."

Renée's eyes sparkled with a glee that made my mouth go a little dry. "Well, during the break, before the second set, I have a little routine I go into. I tell a few jokes, that sort of thing. Then I call my collaborator out from backstage—he's always got to look young, it's important for the act—and then I put him over my knee and spank him."

Adam choked a little and then started to cackle. "You're serious?"

Renée nodded her head slowly, face set into a challenge, her drawn-on eyebrows up to her hairline and her bright red lips warped in amusement.

Adam squeezed my knee under the table. "Okay. I'll do it."

Chapter Five

TILT-A-WHIRL WAS LOUD, dark, and incredibly dense. I felt like I'd walked into a wall of cigarette smoke. Coughing, I paused in the doorway, but Adam grabbed my forearm and hauled me in after him.

Renée had given him instructions about his part of the show, where to meet, and exactly what he'd have to do. The show itself didn't start for forty minutes, and in the meantime, we could dance, or go upstairs to wait for it to begin.

Adam maneuvered our way through the crowd until we reached a far wall. Leaning in, he yelled in my ear, "What do you think?"

I shrugged, not sure what my response should be. I tried to get my bearings in the pulsing, throbbing room. The music was an assault on my ears, the heat from the throng of moving bodies was already making me feel sticky, and the darkness turned everyone either threatening or seductive. I gazed out to the dance floor and blinked.

It was sex.

The room was full of sex. Sexy guys with gorgeous bodies grinding and rubbing and moving together. My dick took notice of all the muscles and sweaty skin on display.

I looked up into Adam's shadowed face, trying to see him in the darkness. "I guess it's cool."

Adam laughed and cupped my face. He yelled, "God, you're

so—" Then he leaned in to brush his lips over mine. Just a small kiss. Pulling me toward the dance floor, he said, "Come on. You've got to dance with me."

I allowed myself to be dragged, but I was terrified. I'd never danced in public before. Adam moved like liquid grace, and I was clumsy and coltish. I just knew I'd look like a fool.

Adam pushed through the crowd until we were tangled, lost in the middle of a sea of bodies. He was already moving to the music, even as he walked. He finally stopped and turned to me. I stood stark still, staring at him.

Shaking his head, he yelled over the music, "Don't wuss out on me now."

He pulled my body against his, big hands on my hips, and forced me into rhythm with him. Adam was sweating, and I was too. It felt tropical, steamy, and the space between us filled with our hot breath, fogging up my glasses. Between the beautiful men all around and Adam pressed against me, it wasn't long before I was rock hard. Adam was too. I felt his erection shove against my hip every time we moved.

I closed my eyes, surprised when he kissed me. His lips were tender, offering slippery, sweaty kisses. It was a little while before I realized I was dancing on my own, pressed against him. I leaned my head against his chest and moved.

Letting myself go, letting myself trust him.

✧　✧　✧

EVENTUALLY, ADAM PULLED me toward the stairs. I couldn't see the risers very well in the dark, so I held on to his arm as we made our way up to the second floor. Once we entered the upper room, he kept a hand on my hip.

The atmosphere upstairs was more sedate. The room was nearly full—women and men talked in groups, most of them holding beers or liquor. Adam moved his hand to my back and pushed me ahead.

"Come on. Let's find Renée."

The tables closest to the stage were reserved for parties, but as we maneuvered around them, we located Renée easily. She stood across the room at the bar, flirting with a large, bald, Black man sporting piercings in his eyebrow and nose. He looked older than Renée but not by more than a few years. I pegged him as at most thirty-one.

Adam strode across the room. "Heya, gorgeous."

Renée tore her eyes away from the bartender and laughed. She'd obviously had a few drinks since we last saw her, and she pulled Adam close in an effusive hug. "Check it out, Barry. This is my naughty boy tonight."

Barry's voice was deep and thick. "That's a pretty one, but he looks kind of young."

"Ah, Barry, baby, we're just getting old, that's all. He's old enough."

"I doubt that." He eyed Adam and me. "How old are you?"

Adam smiled and said nothing, but Renée didn't seem to think there was anything to hide. "He's eighteen. And when I was sucking Rick off the other day—that's the owner," she clarified to us. "Didn't he tell me he's lowering the age of entry? I believe he did, Barry, baby. I believe he did."

"Yeah, well, that one doesn't even look close to eighteen."

"I am." My fists curled.

"Fine. I guess I'll pretend to believe that." He turned his attention back to Renée. "Don't let Rick find out. There's a reason it's not going into effect until next month. Legal doesn't have it all finalized yet."

"Legal schmegal. What's a few weeks early? Nothing, that's what." Renée grasped Adam's chin and tilted his head for Barry's benefit. "Look at that pretty face." She hummed her appreciation.

"Such a beautiful boy."

"Going to whip him hard?" Barry winked.

"So hard. He's going to love it."

Adam smiled brazenly, but I sensed strain beneath it.

Renée dropped Adam's chin in favor of her drink and took two long swallows, eyeing us both. She turned to Barry. "Two shots of Jack for my friends!"

I opened my mouth to remind her that she'd told us not to drink, but Adam jerked my arm, and I shut it again. I guessed if I were him, I'd want a drink too.

"This isn't a good idea," Barry said, but when Renée smiled at him, he just sighed, poured the amber liquor into the small glasses, and shoved them our way.

I'd never had a shot before. I watched Adam slam his and grimace. Mimicking him, I threw my head back and downed the dark liquor in one harsh, burning swallow. My throat nearly closed up, and I wheezed, eyes bulging. I heard Renée laughing in the background, calling out for two more while Adam slapped my back.

I'd barely recovered when Renée pressed another shot glass into my hand. I nearly declined it, but the next thing I knew I'd downed it too. The burn of the second shot was numbed by the lingering heat of the first, and I blinked back the sting of tears. The warmth in my stomach echoed the slick sweat covering my body from dancing, and I turned to Adam to find him staring at me with glazed eyes. He swallowed and licked his lips. Just that made me half-hard again.

He grabbed my neck and laid another kiss on me, rough and deep. I closed my eyes and kissed him back, the room spinning in the darkness behind my lids. It seemed unreal that Adam's mouth on mine was quickly becoming something I needed like blood in my veins.

"Young love. So cute, isn't it Barry?" Renée grabbed my shoulder and pulled me away from Adam. "You—go sit at that table in the front that's marked with an 'X.'" She shoved me in that direction. "And *you*, I'm going to take backstage to get ready."

I lingered, unwilling to leave Adam, especially when I was still anxious in the unfamiliar surroundings. He smiled nervously and nodded at me, allowing Renée to lead him away.

Renée shooed me with her long fingers. "Go on, you'll see your boyfriend later."

I sat alone at the table as the lights went down and tried not to panic. I could feel eyes on me, people from the shadows checking me out. I studied the tabletop, giving the grain of the wood undue attention and praying the show would start soon.

A drink plunked down on the table. I stared at it for a moment and then looked up at the tiny waitress who'd delivered it. She was sweet-looking with short, spiked black hair and a pixie face.

She winked at me. "I'm Krista and it's okay to drink this one. Renée sent it over. But if you get sent any others, and you don't want to, you know, be *bothered* by whoever sent it, you need to refuse it, okay?"

Gratefully, I nodded.

"If you need anything at all, or if anyone bothers you, just tell Barry." She pointed over at the bar, and Barry lifted his chin in my direction. Krista bent down low, actually pinching my cheek. "Renée says you're a virgin boy, and we need to treat you like a flower."

I might have been scared, and I might have been drunk, but I wasn't a child. I was in a gay bar, after all, with a guy who kept kissing me. I had it under control. "I'm okay."

"Sure. Right. Just drink that, and don't go into the bathroom alone."

I glanced around. The shadows with eyes all seemed to be looking at me. I licked my lips and squeezed my fingers into fists to combat my skittering heartbeat.

Krista patted my arm. "I was just fucking with you, kid. Chill out. It'll be okay."

I cleared my throat and hoped I sounded steadier than I felt. "How long until the show starts?"

"Just a few minutes."

I nodded and closed my eyes, determined to wait it out. I wasn't a coward. My mother would tell me to buck up and be a man. Actually, my mother would kill me if she knew where I was—but really, if it weren't for that, she'd tell me to buck up and be a man.

Just as Krista walked away, the lights went down and a spotlight shone on the red curtain. I leaned back in my chair as the familiar opening of Gloria Gaynor's "I Will Survive" began.

Renée twirled onto the stage, gyrating, dancing, and lip-syncing like she meant every word, her face contorted into what appeared to be a combination of ecstasy and pain. I had to bite down really hard on my lip to keep from laughing, and I took huge gulps from my drink in hopes that more alcohol might make Renée's performance more than hysterically unnerving.

I spared a thought for the fact that I'd consumed more illegal beverages in the time I'd known Adam than I ever had in my entire life up until that point. I wondered if that meant he was a bad influence. I'd never had one of those before.

I glanced around the club and chuckled into my drink. Who was I kidding by asking myself if Adam was a bad influence? Looking around, there was no question. Of course he was. And it was exciting. And kind of cool.

As the dancing became more heated, Renée began to rip off her clothes, made easy by Velcro holding on her skirt and blouse. Once she was down to a gold, glittery panty-like thing and a matching bra, Renée twirled feverishly as people lined up to stick dollar bills in the straps of her G-string.

I ducked my head to examine her crotch. Where the hell did she put it? It had to be there somewhere. But no, she was smooth. I took another long drink as I tried to imagine just how much strapping and taping went into that.

Four songs passed, and I took courage in my drink throughout. I didn't feel like laughing anymore, but the idea of crawling up to the stage and pushing dollar bills into Renée's panties didn't appeal to me either. I just sat and watched, averting my eyes whenever Renée looked directly at me. Being in the front row, I got a real gander at all of Renée's goods, like her little ass shaking around just three or four feet from my face. It was embarrassing and arousing.

After the song ended, Renée reached out toward the audience, and Barry walked up to hand her a microphone. She smoothed her hair a little and dabbed her face with a handkerchief someone tossed to her from the audience.

"Thank you, babies. Now, I've been kind and shown you my stuff, so break out the rest of your money, gentlemen and ladies! Mama needs some love!"

A smattering of laughter broke out in the crowd.

I wished I had another drink, and as if reading my mind, Renée looked over at my table, saying, "Krista, get this child a drink. He's looking parched." She was still breathing hard from her exertions, and every word she said into the microphone was followed by a violent puff of air. "Can't have my naughty boy's sweetie going without."

Krista showed up with another drink by the time Renée had started her mini stand-up routine. It was bad. Luckily, it was laughably bad, and so most of the crowd cracked up in the right places, and no one was rude enough to heckle or boo her.

I kept sipping whatever it was Krista had delivered to me, so I was starting to feel a little woozy by the time Renée called out, "Bring me the naughty boy. He needs a whipping."

The crowd cheered. Apparently, this part was a house favorite.

Adam's head stuck out from behind the curtain, face flushed and his hair kind of wild. He blinked against the spotlight and seemed to search the room, but from the way he was squinting, I didn't think he could really see anything.

"Get out here," Renée yelled, and Adam stepped through the curtains wearing a white robe and dragging a chair behind him. He continued to scan the audience until Renée grabbed his arm and pointed at me. "There he is. I told you he'd be okay."

Adam's face broke into a relieved grin when he saw me.

Renée took the chair and placed it in the middle of the stage, talking the whole time about how Adam was fresh meat, a little virgin boy, and all kinds of similar statements—whether to be funny, inflame, or incite, I wasn't sure.

I didn't feel too good. The alcohol seemed to be turning in my stomach, but I was emboldened enough to give Adam a long once-over. That's when I realized he didn't have any pants on—his ankles and feet were bare beneath the white material. But it wasn't until Renée took him over her knee and lifted up the back of his robe that I realized he didn't have *anything* on under there.

Adam was tall. To position his ass properly, he had to sprawl far over Renée's legs, and his head and hands rested on the ground. He managed to turn and look at me, grinning a little before a loud crack sounded through the room. Adam's eyes went wide and he jerked.

"That's for being bad. The next is for being dirty."

Crack.

Adam's face went a little slack, and I gripped the glass in my hand hard, wincing for him.

"This is for being easy."

Crack.

Adam looked over at me, eyes glazed and his cheeks flushed. I realized he was getting turned on, and my own body responded to the expression on his face. Unfortunately, feeling sweaty, sick, and turned on all at once wasn't really a good combination.

"This is for being pretty."

Crack.

"This is for being gay."

Crack.

It really was a perverted little show. Nearly everyone in the room seemed to get off on the spankings, and the reasons given for them. Each new item Renée listed was met with ever-increasing screams of approval.

"And this is for liking it up the ass!"

Crack.

Adam jerked hard, and his face crumpled a little. I wondered if he'd had an orgasm or if he finally couldn't take any more of the pain. My stomach churned, and the room became overly loud with the roaring appreciation of the crowd when Renée announced Adam had been sufficiently punished.

When he struggled up from her lap, I noticed he was breathing hard, and he beamed down at her with a silly expression. He waved at the crowd and then blew a kiss to me before rushing behind the curtain.

I stood, making my way toward the bar to wait for him. I felt clammy and verging on really sick as my legs went wobbly. I wanted to go home. I clutched at the edge of the bar when I felt my knees give out. Strong hands grabbed me, and I panicked, remembering what Krista had said about the bathroom. I struggled a little, but that brought vomit into my mouth, and I didn't know what to do. Then I recognized the voice. It was Barry.

"Easy, kiddo. Told her you shouldn't be drinking. She never listens."

Barry guided me toward the steps, calling out to someone behind him. "Tell the naughty boy I took this one outside. He's gonna be sick." I didn't want to go anywhere without Adam, but Barry had a grip on me. "If you puke in here, I swear to God—" I continued to struggle despite the vomit surging in my throat until he said, "You come with me, or I'll pick you up and carry you out of here, do you understand?"

The cooler night air did wonders for me, and I collapsed down to sit on the curb without throwing up. I buried my face in my hands, tucking down over my knees, squeezing my eyes shut.

Barry put his hand on my head. "It'll be all right, kid."

I kept my eyes closed, fighting the nausea. My thoughts focused solely on the repetition of *don't throw up. Don't throw up. Don't throw up.* My heart pounded dully, and my head throbbed.

"Is he okay?" Adam dropped down next to me, and I calmed under the soothing pressure of his hand on my back.

"He drank too much," Barry said. "He'd probably feel better if he just went ahead and puked."

"No," I moaned.

"It's okay, Peter." Adam rubbed circles on my back. I sneaked a glance and noticed he had his jeans and T-shirt back on. "Thanks, Barry. I've got him now. I'm just going to take him home."

"Better sober up first. Get some water into you. I don't want to turn on the news tomorrow and find out you got yourselves killed." Barry's voice was firm, and suddenly I was heaved up by both of them and dragged into the harsh light of Chalky 'N' Joe's.

The movement put my stomach on edge again, and I collapsed into the booth gratefully, pressing my forehead against the cool Formica tabletop. My glasses bit into the bridge of my nose a little. The sensation was grounding.

I vaguely heard Barry tell Adam goodnight, and then a chilled bottle was pressed into my hand. "Drink this, Peter. You'll feel better."

The last thing I wanted to do was drink anything at all ever again. I shook my head and Adam loomed in front of me. "Yes. Drink it."

He took the bottle and pressed it to my lips. I had to swallow or else it would run down my chin and over my neck. I took several large gulps, feeling the icy liquid race down my esophagus and chill my stomach. It was refreshing. Adam was right. I grasped the bottle, and he sat down next to me, rubbing the back of my neck.

"How much did you drink?"

I shrugged. "I dunno. Whatever Renée sent. I was—" I stopped short of saying I'd been afraid. I didn't want to seem like a big wuss so I just shrugged again.

Adam sighed. "I know. I'm sorry. I wasn't thinking when I made the deal. It didn't occur to me you'd be left out there by yourself."

I suddenly, and rather acutely, felt overwhelmingly alone. Melodramatic thoughts washed over me, and they made more sense than anything in the world. No one would ever love me. I was a big ball of faggotty freakiness and couldn't even handle something simple like drinking at a gay club by myself while my friend got spanked. I was a loser. Tears welled in my eyes. And now I was a crybaby.

Adam released a low sympathetic sound. "It's okay, Peter." He tossed his arm over my shoulder and whispered in my ear, "Just keep drinking the water, okay?"

I nodded, closing my eyes, horrified when two tears slid down my cheeks. Face burning, I stifled a small sob with a swig from the water bottle.

Adam murmured, "It's okay. You're just really drunk. You probably won't even remember this tomorrow."

I nodded, eager to believe my weakness would be something neither of us would have the awkwardness of facing in the sober light of day. After several more long swallows from my water bottle, I scrubbed the heel of my hand over my eyes and muttered, "Some first date, huh?"

Adam was silent.

I nearly sank through the booth in humiliation. I'd forgotten. I'd let my emotions get away from me. It wasn't a date. We were— friends. Or something.

"It's the best date I've had in a long time, Peter. I'm sorry I left you alone." Adam sounded sincere, and I turned slowly, lifting my eyes for the first time since we'd re-entered the greasy dive. I met his gaze, certain I'd see pity there.

But Adam's expression wasn't what I expected. He looked worried about me, but he also seemed deeply moved. His eyes were *tender*.

"Yeah?"

"Yeah. You feel any better?"

I nodded. My head seemed larger than normal, and my stomach wasn't eager to be introduced to solids, but I felt somewhat better. I needed to go to the bathroom, though, in an urgent and immediate way. All of those drinks, and now the water, had exceeded my saturation limits.

"Um—" I looked around the place, locating the door to the men's room.

Adam followed my gaze and quickly helped me out of the booth.

I waved him off. "I think I can handle it, man."

"I'm sure you can, but I'm not going to risk you passing out in there with the door locked."

"I'm not that drunk," I said, just before stumbling over a bit of perfectly flat floor that jumped up to trip me.

"Right."

Adam steered me into the men's room, a one-seater, and he

leaned against the door as I undid my jeans and pissed. It felt amazing, like I'd been waiting for *hours* when really the urge had only hit me minutes earlier. I sighed deeply, and Adam chuckled behind me. When I was finally able to zip up, I flushed and washed my hands while Adam took his turn.

"Don't you think people will think it's weird we're leaving the bathroom together?" I asked, drying my hands on my jeans.

Adam turned on the faucet and soaped up. "We're in a trashy diner next to *a gay club*. I doubt anyone will look twice."

I laughed and lost my balance a little, bumping into the wall before Adam took my arm and steadied me. His palm was wet and warm against my bicep. Our eyes caught and held. I licked my lips in a way I hoped was seductive, and whispered, "Maybe we should give them a reason to look twice?"

Adam smiled slowly.

My back slammed against the wall, and Adam's hands gripped in my hair as we pressed against one another and kissed hard. He wedged his thigh between my legs, and when I pulled my lips away to breathe, he moved down to suck a kiss onto my neck, thrusting against me. I was both there and not there. It was surreal, the alcohol fuzzing everything so I was in a place between waking and dreaming, a place where someone like Adam wanted me like this.

I closed my eyes, the curl of orgasm already beginning. It *was* dreamlike, and yet rutting against Adam, kissing his soft mouth and feeling his stubble scrape over my face, was visceral, a primal, overwhelming urge. I couldn't hold back a cry as I dug my fingers into his upper arms, jerking and coming all wet and messy in my jeans.

Adam slammed his body against me hard, rubbing off with tight hunches. Then he twitched, moaned, and obviously came too. I held him while he trembled, trying to catch my breath. He lifted his head from where he had fastened his mouth to my neck and looked into my eyes. He kissed me softly before pulling away to turn on the water tap again. "Let's clean up and then I'm taking you home."

Adam used paper towels to wipe the inside of his jeans the best he could before helping me clean up too. It felt sweet, like he was taking care of me. After making sure we were both zipped, buttoned, and properly tucked away, he gave me another gentle kiss before opening the bathroom door and walking out with his head held high.

I stumbled after him, ignoring the little looks from the other patrons, pretending I hadn't just had my first sexual experience ever in the bathroom of Chalky 'N' Joe's.

✧ ✧ ✧

THE ALGEDI HOUSE was dark when we pulled up. I teetered from the car, still not entirely steady on my feet, but definitely feeling better than I had before leaving the club. When we entered the door, Adam put his finger to his lips and pointed down at our shoes. We took them off to soften the thud of our footsteps on the wood floors.

The lights were out under both Mo's and Sarah's doors, and I didn't hear any noises from inside. I was relieved they were asleep. Somehow, I felt like Sarah would know what we'd done together in the bathroom at Chalky 'N' Joe's and be angry about it.

Adam locked the door to his bedroom, stuck the desk chair under the knob, and then carefully turned on his stereo until the music was loud enough to cover our voices but not loud enough to wake his siblings.

When he turned to me and beckoned me closer, a flock of butterflies went wild in my stomach.

Still, I padded to him slowly in my socked feet, fingers fiddling anxiously with the hem of my T-shirt, uncertain now of nearly everything on earth except for the growing erection straining my pants and the magnetic pull of Adam's eyes. I stopped less than a foot in front of him and swallowed down my fear.

"Hi," I whispered.

Adam smiled softly, reaching out to grasp my hips, pulling me closer. "Hi."

"I, um, haven't—"

"I know. It's okay."

Adam's hands sneaked up under my shirt and slowly pulled it over my head. He held me at arm's length and gazed at me, his eyes traveling over my stomach, my chest, up to my lips, and finally meeting my eyes. He touched the frames of my glasses, a question in his expression, and I nodded. He lifted them off of my face, and the world went hazy.

I blinked at the loss of focus before closing my eyes. He slid his hand down my neck and over my shoulders, fingers lightly tracing my nipples and making me shiver before reaching the top button of my pants. My dick jumped at the proximity of his hands.

I reached out to help him with his clothes, but he shoved my hands away. "Let me," he said. "Let me be in control, Peter."

I trembled at his words and let him do the work. My skin had never been more sensitive and never more alive than with his fingers skimming over me. His hot breath puffed against my stomach, and my gut curled, my balls ached, and I wanted to grab his head and beg him to lick me there. Instead, I held my breath and stood as still as possible, hoping he wouldn't just *stop*.

When he'd stripped me to nothing but my tented boxers, he pushed me down onto the bed, moving back to remove his own clothes. I wished for my glasses to see him better, to get a look at his cock.

Naked, he leaned over me, pressed me down, and his lips locked on to mine. I sighed into the kiss, feeling all my tension collapse into a massive hole of *need*, and I followed it down. I'd jerked off for years imagining a male body in my arms. But there'd always been a part of me that'd never believed I'd actually get to have it, especially with a guy like Adam.

I kissed his mouth, licked his neck, and bit the skin of his shoulder as he shoved my boxers down and got his cock against mine—velvet-hot length sliding against me where I needed it most.

I felt cored by the wanton desperation that shot through me. I clung to Adam's shoulders, digging my achingly hard cock up against his, reveling in the glow-in-the-dark stars on the ceiling giving off the only light.

The smooth sound of Morrissey's voice covered our groans as our mouths, hands, and thrusting hips collided. When Adam grabbed me close and shot wet, slick cum all over my cock and balls, I buried my face in his neck and came too.

Before I'd even caught my breath, he scooted down my body to lick the jizz off my stomach and cock. I squirmed and whimpered, shocked and thrilled as he sucked the head of my dick into his mouth. I stared, awed, and already aching for more even though I'd just had an orgasm. My body didn't care about refractory periods or sensitivity. It was ready to feel all of that again.

I spread my legs to give him more room.

"So good, Peter," he murmured.

I nodded, lost in a haze of lust and joy. I was having sex. With a boy. It was amazing. It was the best idea anyone had ever had. And I never wanted it to end. "Don't stop," I said when he let my dick fall out of his mouth.

"Not gonna," he slurred.

And then he sucked my cock in again, and I clenched my hands in the sheets. Blinded by pleasure and still a little drunk, I discovered the hole of need I'd tumbled into didn't have a bottom; it just went on and on.

Down I went, happy and heedless, eager and moaning, with my hands twisted into Adam's hair.

Chapter Six

I BLINKED AWAKE. My body felt like a wrung-out sponge, and my head ached painfully.

Adam held me close against him, an arm draped across my chest and a heavy thigh thrown over my own. I shifted and Adam gripped me more tightly. I could see the corner of his face tucked into the pillow, and I rolled onto my side to look at him.

We were both still naked. I closed my eyes as a small shiver ran through me at the memory of his lips on mine, his kiss on my neck, and his mouth on my dick. It'd been more amazing than I'd expected, and I'd expected it to be pretty damn amazing. I trembled again at the memory of the slick wet heat and the slightly rough feel of his tongue cradling the underside of my cock as he'd gone down on me, and the way I'd grabbed hold of his hair, crying out uncontrollably as I came.

And then I'd done it for him. I was proud that I'd figured out to move my hand up and down the shaft while I tongued his slit. I couldn't get him far into my mouth, but Adam didn't seem to care. And when he came, I swallowed. He'd tasted bitter and I'd choked but sucked it down anyway.

I shifted to press my now-hard cock against Adam's side. I wanted to wake him up, to roll on top of him and move against him, to slide down and blow him again. My body wanted more. My mind did too. After the week we'd spent as friends and after everything we'd done last night, from getting into Tilt-a-Whirl to sucking each other off, I felt like I *knew* him.

And somehow that made everything we'd done seem all right.

Except—I jerked a little at the realization. I hadn't asked the questions. The right ones the guidance counselors had drilled into me since I was in fifth grade. *What is your sexual history? How many sexual partners? Have you been tested for disease?* My heart fluttered, and I flung Adam's arm off to sit up, breathing hard.

"Peter?" Adam sounded groggy and a little worried. "You aren't going to freak out, are you?"

I didn't know the answer to that question. My mind raced, rushing through dozens of thoughts I couldn't keep up with. I'd known I was gay, had known with complete certainty since I started jerking off to photos of male underwear models in the Sears catalog when I was twelve, but what we'd done was something else entirely. It was undeniable proof I wasn't going to suddenly wake up and live a heterosexual life.

Shit. I'd had sex with a guy. With Adam. With a *friend*—well, a stranger really. Someone I actually knew relatively little about and who might have AIDS for all I knew. But we hadn't had anal sex. Sure, he'd come in my mouth, but I didn't have any sores in there, and—

I ran a hand through my hair, looking around desperately. "I need my glasses. Where are they?"

I sounded angry, but I was panicking and really didn't care. I slid out of the bed and groped around on the floor for my jeans and T-shirt.

"Peter—wait a second." Adam rolled up to standing, grabbed my arm, and pulled me close. His naked body against mine sent a shock of lust through me that nearly rivaled the panic. "Freaking out is normal, okay. Just calm down."

Freaking out was normal? How would he know that? How

many people had Adam done this with anyway?

"I just need my glasses."

Adam released me, and as I blindly yanked on my jeans, he snatched something from the desk and then placed my glasses on my face. I blinked in relief as the room and Adam's concerned expression came into clear focus.

"Peter—listen," he said, pulling on his boxer shorts. "I don't know what you're thinking in that strange head of yours, but—"

I tugged my shirt on over my head. It snagged on my glasses and my ears for a moment, but I forced it down and smoothed my hair. "I'm just thinking I need to get home and—" I broke off, suddenly angry.

"And?"

"And how many people have you done this with, anyway?"

Adam smiled sympathetically. "Oh, I get it. I see. Peter, listen, I don't have any diseases or anything. I promise."

"How many?"

Adam reached for my arm but I moved away. "I've been with two guys and four girls."

"Oh, so you're basically a sex addict."

Adam fought a smile. "Maybe. I don't think so, but, even if I was, that's not what this is about, Peter. I like you."

My heart pounded unsteadily, and I sank to the bed, trying to remember where my shoes had ended up after I'd carried them into the room last night. "You aren't using me?"

Adam laughed and ran his hand through my hair affectionately. "You're funny. One day you're convinced you're not someone I'd even be interested in, and the next I'm just using you for your hot body."

I glared at him. I didn't find that funny.

"Of course I'm not using you. I already told you last night—do I really need to tell you again?"

I looked up at him, seeing nothing but sincerity on his face. I took my glasses off and buried my face in my hands, feeling immature and unworldly.

"It's normal to freak out. I freaked out my first time with a guy." Adam sounded very patient.

I didn't know what to say. Maybe I should be prouder. After all, I wasn't so inexperienced now, and it'd been great, and it'd been Adam, and he said he didn't have any diseases, so why was I so upset?

He sat next to me, moving my glasses back to his bedside table.

"Hey, come on," he said and pried my hands off my face. He kissed my eyelids before pulling me back onto the bed and covering me with his body, all firm muscle, scratchy hair, and soft skin.

My dick took notice, and heat rushed through me as my body responded to him. I remembered the noises he'd made when he'd come the night before, and I wondered what his face had looked like. It was daylight now. I'd be able to see.

He whispered, "Are you ticklish?"

My breath caught in my throat, and I shook my head desperately.

"I don't believe you."

"Your sister—" I started.

"They're gone. They left hours ago. Sarah has an early dance class, and Mo goes up to campus. You're screwed."

I struggled in earnest but he used his greater body strength to hold me tight. His fingers unerringly sought and found my ticklish spots, and he only stopped when I was howling with laughter, tears threatening to spill from my eyes.

When he finally pulled away, I tried to catch my breath. He cuddled me close, murmuring in my ear as we spooned together, "See? It's okay."

His cock pushed against my hip, and I rolled him over, climbing up to straddle him. I was breathing hard from being tickled, but my dick pushed against my jeans and his tented his boxers.

"Wanna suck me again?" he asked, lifting his hips to get even more pressure on his erection. "God, thinking about it makes me almost come."

Lust shot through me hard enough to take my breath away. Knowing how awesome it was to have a thick dick in my mouth, resting on my tongue and gagging me, made my previously unfocused teenage hormones zero in on sucking cock as a necessity in my life. Now that I knew what it was like to touch a guy and be touched in return, it was going to be hard to give it up.

I pulled my shirt over my head and threw it to the side, bending to kiss Adam. His mouth was murky with morning breath and the taste of my cum from the night before. It should have been gross, but it just reminded me of how desperately I wanted to get my dick in between his lips again.

"Get your jeans off," he muttered, and I clambered off him, getting myself naked again. He threw me onto the bed, and I bounced against the mattress.

He turned around to kneel over me in the sixty-nine position, and when his mouth closed over the head of my cock, it felt so good my knees came up of their own volition, cradling his head with my thighs. Adam wrapped his arms around my hips, dragging my cock deeper into his throat. I writhed as he bobbed his head. Hot, sloppy spit ran down over my balls and into the crack of my ass.

I threw my head back and twisted my body up, desperate for more of the sweet, hot, slick feeling. Adam moved his hips, waving his cock in front of my face as a hint. Even though Adam's tongue flicking on the head of my dick made me feel like my cock was now the center of the known universe, I got it together enough to reciprocate.

I buried my face briefly in his scratchy, dark reddish-brown pubes, smelling his musk, and then opened my mouth, lapping at his salty pre-cum before sucking him in. He froze, dropped my cock, scrabbled at the bed, and then spurted into my mouth.

"Peter! God!" he cried out.

Desperately, I tried to swallow the cum flooding my mouth and gagging me.

Adam fell to sucking me again, strong, confident, hard pulls that made my toes curl. I moaned and whined around his softening cock, not wanting to let it go from my mouth yet, even though Adam twitched and groaned. But when the coil of orgasm in my balls grew overwhelming, I released him, afraid I'd bite down.

I turned my face to press against the inside of his hairy thigh and gritted my teeth. Grabbing him around the legs, holding on tight, I yelled as I shot into his mouth, my balls throbbing and my whole body singing in pleasure.

Adam swallowed my cum again, and I trembled, bucking against him as he sucked the last spurts from me. Releasing me, he flipped himself around and dropped down into the space between my arm and body. He pressed open-mouthed kisses to each of my nipples, nuzzled my throat and ear, and then breathed, "Thanks, Peter. That felt so good."

As for me, I was speechless and quivering. I curled against Adam, and he held me quietly until our breathing grew deep, and we both fell back to sleep.

✧　✧　✧

THE SECOND TIME I woke up, I was overly aware of the rancid taste in my mouth and the pretty offensive way I smelled. Adam had rolled onto his stomach, his face turned away from me. Flashes of the prior night and the morning slipped through my mind, the good and bad all jumbled together.

I glanced at the clock hanging over Adam's desk and slid out of the bed. Smoothing my hand over my hair, I squinted around the room looking for my glasses.

Item number one on my Christmas list—yes, I was kind of Jewish, but yes, we did the tree and Santa—would be to ask for contacts. Glasses were a pain in the ass. Finally locating them where Adam had placed them on the bedside table, I pulled on my socks, which I found under the bed, and tucked my shoes under my arm.

I turned to look at Adam. He was still asleep. I took some deep, steadying breaths. It would be okay. He'd said it would be okay. I had no reason not to believe him, even if I had no idea what "okay" meant.

I closed the door gently behind me and padded down the hallway in just my socks. The front door opened with a substantial creak of the seal and I cringed, not really knowing for sure why I needed to leave before Adam woke up. But I did. I needed to go home.

I slipped on my shoes and ran.

Sneaking into my house was a little more difficult than sneaking out of Adam's had been. My mom sat at the kitchen counter eating sticks of string cheese and reading over a manuscript. Seeing her through the back window, I considered trying to get in the front door and up to my room before she could call my name, but decided that would seem more suspicious than breezing in with a cheery hello.

I threw open the kitchen door, putting on my best face. "Hey, Mom!"

"Peter! Did you have a good time at Adam's?"

I smiled hugely. "Great time! The best!"

Mom frowned a little, and I realized belatedly I'd been overenthusiastic. Now she would ask questions.

"Really? What made it 'the best?'"

Thinking I should've tried the front door after all, I said, "Uh, we just—had a good time. That's all."

Mom shrugged. "Okay."

I waited for the next question, but instead Mom slid off the stool, opening the fridge to rummage around in one of the drawers.

"I'm going upstairs to shower and stuff."

Mom's muffled reply came from behind the refrigerator door, something about there being no more string cheese, and she was going to kill my dad for not buying some at the store like she'd asked. So long as she wasn't asking me any more questions, I was fine with that.

In the shower, my body felt strangely tender, like I'd come so hard the orgasms had bruised me. The hot water felt great on my muscles. I leaned my head back to wash my hair. The stench of secondhand smoke, alcohol, and sex washed away, swirling down the drain with the suds.

After toweling off, I studied myself in the mirror. Two red love bites on my collarbone, low enough I could easily cover them, were the only signs anything had changed. The only signs I'd had sex with another person.

I brushed my teeth, eager to get rid of the now-gross taste of old alcohol and semen. I put on my glasses with one hand while I combed some de-frizz gel my mom had picked up for me into my hair with the other. In my room, I threw on fresh jeans and an Oscar the Grouch T-shirt, grabbed my camera, and darted back into the bathroom. I shoved aside the neck of my shirt and used the mirror's reflection to document the bruises on my skin.

It was a little after one in the afternoon by that point, and I decided to go out with my Minolta Maxxum 7000. It wasn't as expensive as the Leica, so I felt more secure lugging it around the neighborhood. Figuring Adam would be waking up soon and that he'd probably call when he found me gone, I left the house quickly. I didn't feel up to talking to him yet.

Over the prior week, the wan late-summer light had failed to bring sufficient heat to keep the pool open, and they were busy draining it. I took some photos of the process, as well as the ass-crack of the guy bent over the pump.

I crossed the small field separating the pool from the neighborhood, heading toward the playground. It held a dilapidated set of equipment. I remembered climbing the monkey bars and playing inside the industrial-sized tire when I was a little kid. I took photos of the faded and peeling paint of the merry-go-round and a glowing penny sparkling in the grass.

"Hey."

I spun around, startled, my hand over my heart.

Adam lounged against the industrial tire, hands in his jeans pockets, and a lightweight blue sweater clinging to his chest in the breeze. Automatically, I lifted the Minolta again and took his picture.

"Hey," I replied.

"So, you were gone."

I shrugged and took a photo of my tennis shoes just to look busy. "Wanted to take some pictures before the sun went down. It's getting dark a little earlier now."

Adam nodded but didn't say anything.

I was grateful. It was only midday, and he knew there were still hours before nightfall. I took another picture of him with his brows slumped in concern, then dropped the camera lower to snap a shot of his neck.

"I could take a whole roll of you."

Adam's eyes crinkled into a smile, and I froze the frame before I slung the leather strap over my neck and walked toward him.

"I'm sorry."

He shook his head in confusion. "For what?"

"I don't know." I chuckled nervously.

"I liked what we did last night. Did you?"

I nodded.

"I want to do it again. Do you?"

"Yeah," I breathed, and looked into his eyes, before amending, "Um, except no more drag shows."

Adam laughed. "Deal. So, friends?"

My stomach clenched a little. Why wasn't there a better word for us than that? "Yeah. Friends."

Adam glanced around before angling in. Our noses bumped and our lips brushed together softly. I managed to twist the camera lens up and captured a photo of our kiss.

For some reason, I wanted proof.

Chapter Seven

A WEEK BEFORE school started, Adam sat at our kitchen table petting Harry, talking to him softly about the bunny rabbits and the birds outside, and wouldn't it be fun if they both went out and chased them a little? Catching my amused glance, he claimed they wouldn't hurt them; just toss them around for fun, maybe play catch with them, nothing truly terrible. Harry seemed to agree to his plan with a short, happy bark.

I fell more and more in love with Adam by the second, and I had to admit that to myself as I prepared a cheese, tomato, pepper, and mushroom omelet for us to share for dinner.

"I'm sorry about Sarah," Adam said softly, looking up at me with his most earnest expression.

"I know."

It wasn't that big a deal, but I understood why he was upset. Every time we made out or tried to blow each other at his house, Sarah found a way to interfere. The final straw for Adam had come that afternoon when she started pounding on the door while I was going down on him. I'd never seen him that angry with her before. He'd pulled his jeans back over his hips, threw the door open and yelled at her to leave us the fuck alone. She screamed right back that she was looking out for him, and he should know that by now. All the while I sat on the bed, wiping my wet mouth with my fist and not meeting her eyes.

"Really, though, I'll find a way to make her stop, okay?"

"In the meantime, we always have my house," I said.

Most parents of an only child monitor their kid's activities like seismologists monitor the California fault line. That wasn't the case for me. My mother didn't have the time or inclination to be a *mom*, being somewhat mentally ill and so wrapped up in her books she barely had time for her husband, much less her kid.

And my father was a typical academic. He couldn't pull his head out of his ass long enough to really get a good look at me. I knew he loved me, but he also really loved Mohammed, Buddha, Gandhi, the Knights Templar, Mary Magdalene, and the Greek Orthodox Church.

Dad hadn't even met Adam yet because he usually staggered in from the university at seven or eight o'clock at night, sometimes even later. Then he'd pour some Wild Turkey and Coke, and open the fridge in the vain hope there would be something good in there to eat. Usually, he'd resort to the freezer, zap a microwave dinner, and mutter to Harry things like, "You think we feed you just for being cute, Harry? I don't think so. Get off your duff and run the dishwasher now and again, you old mutt."

After that, Dad would venture to poke his head into my mother's office. Sometimes he'd disappear in there for a few hours, and other times he'd barely get out a word of greeting before she was barking at him that she was *writing* and couldn't she have any *privacy* and, "Really, Abe, what do I have to do? Lock the door? Weld it shut? Rent a studio somewhere? What?" That's when Dad would retreat to his own office, calling Harry to keep him company, and slam the door to research his next article.

So if my mom and dad didn't notice anything strange going on between me and Adam, well, it was because they didn't notice much of anything about me. And for the first time in my life, I was really damn happy about that.

Nearly every day, if we weren't at his house, Adam came over and we'd head upstairs, lock the door as a purely precautionary measure, and then his hands would be in my hair, beneath my shirt, under the waistband of my pants.

I took photo after photo of bite marks, scratches and hickeys, just to record that, yes, I really was having sex with the hottest, most charming guy on earth, and yes, he was so hot for me he left marks on my body. I really wanted to photograph Adam nude, but didn't know when I'd ever be able to develop the film, and I was still shy and afraid to ask.

"Tryouts for swim team are next week," Adam said. "I'm thinking about skipping it this year."

Just the thought of starting up at Kingsley made my stomach hurt. I wanted to ask Adam what would happen when school began, but I knew there was no way he could tell me for sure. Always, even as I was arching up in orgasm, shooting into Adam's throat, the doubt lingered in the back of my mind. Once school started, it would all be different. But I was going to take what I could get from Adam for as long as I could get it.

"I thought you liked swim team."

"I'm good at it," Adam said. "It's not the same thing."

I was about to ask more when my dad stumbled in relatively early from work. His wrinkled dress shirt was unbuttoned at the top, his khaki dress pants looked tired, and tufts of his brown curly hair, shot through with gray, stuck out everywhere. It looked like he'd had a rough day wrestling with sacred texts.

Dad sniffed at the air, not noticing Adam. "Ah, Petey-boy, I always knew you loved me. Look at you, making dinner for your dear old dad while your mom probably drinks the last of the decent beer in her little cave of depravity." He patted his small pot belly and clucked his tongue. "And the woman calls herself a Christian!"

He winked at me, his gray-blue eyes twinkling, and crossed over to put his hands on my shoulders, peering at what I was cooking.

He continued his spiel. I'd heard it a million times over the years. "Should've raised you right, Petey. Should've made you learn Hebrew and taught you about the holy days. You probably would've liked it. You've got the soul of a Jew, Pete." He paused, thinking. "Or maybe a Catholic."

Adam laughed, and Dad jumped, surprised.

"I agree on both counts, Mr. Mandel."

"My soul is perfectly atheist, thank you." I indicated Adam with my spatula. "And Dad, this is my friend, Adam Algedi. Adam, this is my dad."

Adam stood, abandoning Harry to dream of bunnies alone, and crossed the room to shake my dad's hand. "Mr. Mandel, it's a pleasure to meet you."

Dad smiled. "Algedi, eh? Any relation to Mohammed Algedi?"

Adam bit his lower lip and leaned casually against the counter. "Will I still get to hang out with your son if I admit he's my brother?"

Dad chuckled. "Mohammed is in my Tuesday-Thursday History of Islam class. Excellent student. A bit of lip on him, but there's always a place for that in a college classroom, if applied properly."

I pulled the omelet from the heat and turned off the stove, grabbing a couple of plates. "Really? I didn't know Mo was in your class."

"Well, considering you never ask me about my classes, that doesn't surprise me." Dad sighed. "You'd think with your diverse cultural background, you'd be more interested in the study of religious philosophy."

"Dad, I'm just interested in photography."

"Anyway..." Dad turned back to Adam. "Your brother is a very fine student. He told me recently he lived in our neighborhood, but I didn't realize he had any siblings."

"My sister and I just got dumped on him last month." Adam quickly explained his mom's choice to leave him and Sarah with their brother.

Dad seemed to agree with Mrs. Algedi's decision. "Things are messy over there."

"Mo's not thrilled about it. He claims we cramp his style, but I don't know how, since he's never had a date in his life."

Dad clucked softly. "Hard to get a date when you've got such a bad attitude toward life. I think girls are put off by someone as ill-tempered as Mo."

"Uh, Dad? Maybe that wasn't the most polite thing to say to Mo's *brother*."

Adam laughed. "It's true, Petey-boy."

"Don't call me that!" I glared at him and threatened to scrape his portion of omelet off into the doggie bowl.

Adam just waggled his eyebrows, obviously amused to have gotten a rise out of me.

"When Peter here was a little guy—"

"Dad—" I warned.

"—he had fat little legs and arms, big round cheeks. The little girls he played with called him 'Peter the Eater.' Then he grew out of it."

"*Dad!*"

Adam chuckled helplessly beside me, trying to hold in guffaws.

"Thanks for the flashback, Dad."

"Peter!" Dad's eyes twinkled. "I was attempting to indicate that people change, and perhaps Mohammed would grow out of being angry."

"Yeah, right. Sure, that's why you brought that old nickname up." I pushed by them both with our plates, setting them down on the table.

"When have I ever lied to you, Petey?"

"I've got five words for you: Jenny Goldfish. The Big Pond."

"Well, that was a small lie, and you were three. We were trying to save you some grief."

Turning to grab some glasses and a carton of juice, I said, "Sorry, Dad, but I think it's a microwave dinner again for you tonight."

THE DAY BEFORE school began, Sarah sat on guard at the Algedi house, curled in a chair reading while Adam and I played video games. She wore a red sweater that dipped low, showing off her developing bosom, and tight blue jeans that emphasized her slender thighs.

I wondered how long it would be once school started before she had a boyfriend. I also wondered if Adam would prowl around outside her bedroom door when she brought the guy home, banging and demanding to be let in if things were silent for too long. I glanced at Adam. Yeah, he probably would.

Adam's thumbs worked the Nintendo controller. "Peter, have you ever been into playing D&D?"

Sarah groaned from the corner. "No, Adam. No D&D. Why do you have to make things so hard for us?"

Adam ignored her, glancing from the television set over to me. "Have you?"

I shook my head. "No, I—" I didn't want to admit I'd thought the game sounded interesting, but with no real friends to play it with, it hadn't really been an option for me. "No."

Adam sighed. "I want to put together a group—"

"No, Adam!" Sarah growled.

"And I thought you might help me find some other people who might be interested when school starts."

"Okay, sure."

"Cool! It'll be so fun, you'll see."

Sarah stood and blocked the television screen. "No! Absolutely not!"

Adam frowned. "Get out of the way, Sare-Bear. You're being a bitch again."

"Well, someone has to think with something besides their geek brain and their horny dick! Jesus H. Christ, Adam! We've got problems enough without introducing the geek element."

"Sarah, what's the big deal? D&D is fun. It's just a game. I'm sure lots of people play it. Right, Peter?"

I shook my head, not very happy about being dragged into a Sarah-vs-Adam conflict. "I don't know. Don't ask me."

Mo spoke from the doorway to the kitchen, a carton of ice cream and a spoon in his hands, "Actually, Tad, it's considered to be the 'work of the devil' around here. Satanic and evil." He shrugged his dense shoulders. "Sarah's probably right on this one. At least until you get settled." He frowned. "Which hopefully you won't because hopefully Dad'll get transferred soon, and hopefully you'll both just *go the fuck away.*"

"Yeah, *Tad*, it's considered Satanic," Sarah taunted. Mo was the only one allowed to call Adam by his childhood nickname. Even so, it was cooler than Peter the Eater. "Guess you can't play after all. Courtesy of Mom and her overprotective streak."

"Shut up, *Sare-Bear.*"

Sarah made a face. "Somehow it loses its mocking potential when you call me that *all the time.*"

As always, I was a little lost during these family squabbles, never sure just how much was too much, and what might push it over into an all-out screaming match.

Mo plopped down on the sofa next to me, digging into his carton of ice cream. "Tad, scram. I want to watch porn."

I blinked, shocked and repulsed.

Sarah screamed and stalked off down the hall, slamming her

bedroom door after the obligatory, "I hate you!"

Adam shrugged, stood, and pulled me along with him. I followed him into his room, desperately trying to put the picture of Mo, ice cream, and porn out of my mind.

Adam locked the door behind us, stuffed a towel along the bottom, shoved his desk chair under the handle, and lifted the window above his bed without saying a word. He pulled open his desk drawer and fumbled around in the back, frowning.

"Son of a bitch!"

"What?" I asked, nervously.

Adam didn't reply. He thrust aside the chair and stormed down the hall, banging on Sarah's door, yelling, "Which one of you stole my stash?"

I watched from the doorway of Adam's room, heart pounding.

"What stash?" Mo yelled from the living room. "Have you been holding out on me?"

Adam kicked Sarah's door. "Open the fuck up, *Princess!*"

Sarah yelled from inside, "That's Princess Sare-Bear, to you!"

Mo lumbered down the hallway, grinning and still eating his ice cream. He squeezed by Adam and leaned against the wall next to me. "This'll be good. I love this shit. It's the only thing I miss when they aren't around."

Adam kicked harder and the door shook, making a splintering noise. "Give me my fucking stash!"

Sarah was silent, and I could hear rummaging in her room.

"Sarah," Adam called, warningly. "Don't make me kick your door in!"

Finally, Sarah flung the door open, eyes wild and angry. "Fuck you, I smoked it all!"

Adam shook his head. "Bullshit. Hand it over."

Sarah started to slam the door in his face, but he blocked it, shoving into her room.

Sarah yelled, "Get out!"

Mo chuckled and scooped more ice cream, pushing off the wall to peer into Sarah's room. I cautiously followed him.

Adam tore open her desk drawer, dumping the contents on the bed while Sarah screamed and kicked at him.

He turned to her vanity table, and Sarah started to beg, "Don't, Adam! Don't!"

He paused. "Then give it to me."

She looked torn, and her eyes cut back and forth between her closet and Adam. His focus narrowed, and he stalked toward the closet, threw it open, and thrust her clothes around, finally settling on her boxes of shoes.

Sarah sighed dramatically, obviously beaten, sinking down to the bed.

We all watched as Adam went through the boxes one by one, throwing the shoes around the room, until he came to a pair of boots. He thrust his hand inside one of them, pulling out a baggy containing marijuana and several already-rolled joints. He shook it in Sarah's face. "Mine. Understand? Unless I invite you to smoke with me, don't fucking touch it. You want some? Buy your own."

Adam shoved by me and Mo, pausing just long enough to slip a joint to Mo. Payoff, I guessed. He called, "Come on, Peter," over his shoulder.

I followed, trying not to tremble.

Adam kicked the door closed behind us, repeated the locking, towel, chair ritual, and dropped onto the bed.

"My family is so fucking—" He broke off and yelled wordlessly, banging his head on the pillow.

I took a deep breath, shifting anxiously from foot to foot. "Should I go home?" I asked when he'd stopped yelling.

Adam shook his head and reached out for me.

I shucked my shoes, crawled onto the mattress, and sat down

cross-legged by his head.

He patted my leg. "I'm sorry."

"Yeah, that was kind of—wow."

Adam laughed. "Well, get used to it. It happens a lot."

He rolled over to open his nightstand drawer and pulled out a lighter, took one of the joints and threw the baggy into the drawer. He lit up, flopping onto his back and staring up at the ceiling as he took a long drag. He patted the bed next to him and I slid down to lay in the curve of his arm, head on his shoulder.

I watched his chest rise and fall, the strong smell of marijuana permeating the air, soaking into his T-shirt, clinging to his skin. I knew when I kissed him I'd taste it on his lips, on the skin at his throat, smell it in his hair.

"Take a hit, Peter."

I shook my head, content with the lazy secondhand high, and with the simple wonder of touching him.

"Come on, one hit," he urged.

I frowned, the peace of the moment disturbed by his insistence. "Why?"

"I think you'd like it. Help you chill out."

"I'm chilled out."

"Yeah, I can tell by the way your hand is fisted in my shirt, and your entire body is tense."

I consciously let go of his shirt and tried to relax.

"Just once, Peter. If you don't like it, you never have to try it again."

"This is called peer pressure."

He smiled at me in a way that made me want to do whatever he asked, so I propped myself up on my elbow and reached for the joint. Adam's grin went even wider and that seemed reward enough for me.

"Just breathe in and hold it. Make sure to breathe deeply. If it just goes into your mouth, you won't feel it."

I closed my eyes and sucked scalding, thick air into my lungs, shocked by the burn and wanting to get it out of my body as quickly as possible.

I heard Adam say, "Hold it for a second—that's good."

I coughed, choking and spluttering, sitting up, trying to catch my breath.

Adam took the joint from me, snubbed it out on the small incense holder he had by the bed, and rubbed my back, soothingly. "It's okay. It's normal to cough the first time."

I glared at him, choking out in a raw voice, "Well, it's a good thing you always know what's normal for first times."

Adam sat up and wrapped his arms around me, rocking me and tucking my head into the crook of his neck as I gasped for breath.

After I calmed down, Adam eased me back to the bed and his hands crawled under my shirt. His mouth sought the sweet spot behind my ear, and the world seemed to flow seamlessly from one second to the next, one sensation to another.

I closed my eyes, riding the gentle tide, feeling my heart open, and it seemed as if light poured from it, coating everything with pure, golden love. I gasped as the wet trails from Adam's mouth cooled on my skin and left light blue streaks in the gold filling my vision.

"Adam, do you see the colors?"

Adam pulled away. "What?"

"The colors—should I see colors?"

Adam took off my glasses and set them on the night table, hand stroking through my hair. "Uh, well—sometimes, I guess maybe—"

I could tell by his tone that seeing colors was not a typical reaction, not even for first times. My heart began to ricochet in my chest, and the light that had been gold faded into black shadow, seeping from my heart, crawling over the furniture, up the walls—

"Adam?" I knew I sounded scared, but I didn't care.

"Peter, just stay calm."

I began to hyperventilate, suddenly absolutely sure I was dying, that the black shadow pouring out of me was death. I was the one person alive allergic to marijuana, and I would go into convulsions at any moment, my heart would stop, and I'd never get to tell Adam I loved him. My mom would probably have a huge wake instead of a funeral, with dancing and beer. Would she let Adam come, since it had been his marijuana that killed me? Would he want to?

"Peter?"

"I don't feel so good, Adam," I managed between shallow breaths.

"Breathe deeply, okay? You just need to calm down."

I nodded, trying to make my lungs inflate fully. They rebelled, obviously still angry with me for forcing hot poison into them. I closed my eyes so I wouldn't see the blackness anymore and tried to concentrate on Adam's soothing hands and voice.

"It's okay. Just relax. You're okay. I've got you."

My breath grew more even, and my heart slowed. I dared to open my eyes and found the darkness was gone, and the room was just a glowing, fuzzy version of its usual self.

Adam peered down at me, face creased in concern. He was so gorgeous, so sexy. I wanted to crawl inside him.

"I'm sorry, Peter. I'm a fucking idiot."

I reached up and pulled him down for a kiss, his mouth sweet and wet. I pushed his shirt up and released his lips long enough to get it over his head.

"You're so hot, Adam. You make me feel so incredibly, amazingly good. I can't believe you want me. When you suck me off, I just stare at you and think I'm dreaming. Did you know that?"

Adam's eyes were wide. "Peter—wow."

I kept talking, not sure where all of these words were coming from, a flood of them pouring from my mouth. "I want to take pictures of you all the time. Right now. I want a picture of you right this second. I want a picture of you naked, on the bed, in the shower, crawling toward me on the floor. I want a picture of your face when you come, because—" I licked my suddenly dry lips "—that's the hottest thing I've ever seen in my life."

"Um—Peter—" Adam shifted against me. "Whoa."

"Adam, I—" I swallowed. "I want you so much."

"Peter, you're chatty when you're high." Adam worked to pull off my shirt and started on the buttons of my jeans.

I pushed his hands away and tried to get them undone myself, muttering, "Stupid button fly."

Adam pulled off his pants, his erection bouncing up against his stomach. He slid back to the foot of the bed and helped me work my jeans down, pulling my socks off too. He kissed his way up my legs, sucking on my inner thighs, leaving red bite marks in his wake. As he climbed on top of me, I wrapped my legs around his hips and pressed his hardness against mine.

"Do it, Adam," I murmured against his mouth. "Fuck me."

Adam ground his hips down, shuddering. He tangled his hands in my hair, kissing my eyelids, my cheeks, my lips. "Peter, God, I want to—but not now."

"I want you so much."

Adam groaned.

I hitched my legs up, sliding our cocks together. "I want to know what it's like. I want it with you."

Adam rolled off me, taking my erection into his hand, jacking fast and hard. "I'm not going to do that, Peter. You're high. I'm high. I'm not ready."

"Adam—"

"I'll tell you about it, though. What it feels like. If you want—"

I nodded avidly, eyes fixed on Adam's hand around my cock.

"It can hurt. A lot. I mean, *a lot* the first time. It did for me, anyway. But if it's done right, it can feel incredible, like someone's stroking you inside and out. And if it's done *really right*, like your prostate is getting hit with almost every stroke, it feels like your whole body is lighting up with fireworks. It's so good. And some guys can have an orgasm from it and—"

My balls seized, and I started to come, the first spurt splashing my stomach.

Adam paused to kiss my forehead. "You're so damn *sweet*, Peter. You scare me."

I shook my head. I wanted to tell him I was just Peter, nothing here to fear, but I got caught in orgasm and lost my train of thought.

Adam whispered in my ear, "Now *I* want a picture of *that*."

Part II

September, 1990

Chapter Eight

"YOU LOOK LIKE such a nerd in that uniform," Sarah said bluntly as I slid into the back seat of their Mercedes.

It was the morning of the first day of school, and I was already nervous as hell. I'd been up half the night worrying about Kingsley and Adam and everything in between. Despite how much my self-esteem had grown in the light of Adam's regard over the last few weeks, Sarah's comment still hit me in the gut.

"Sarah," Adam scolded. He caught my eye in the rearview mirror and winked. "I think he looks good."

I was starting to think Adam had questionable taste.

Unlike me, he looked amazing in his uniform. The white collar of the oxford shirt was stark against his skin, far darker than mine due to his father's genes. His tie was loosely knotted so his Adam's apple was free to bob with each swallow. His shirt stretched nicely over his shoulders. Even his strong thighs looked good encased in navy wool pants.

Sarah continued to study me, and I turned my attention from Adam's appearance to wait for the inevitable. I'd been around her long enough to know when she was on the attack. Her long, almost-black hair framed her face and her hazel eyes sparkled as she dragged them over my entire body. She glanced over at my camera bag and frowned before turning back around in her seat. "You never take any pictures of me. Why?"

I caught Adam's smirk as he glanced to check his blind spot.

Sarah pulled down the passenger-side sunshade and gazed at me in the vanity mirror. She really would be an excellent subject to photograph. She reminded me of a tiger's-eye, all black and glittering brown. So why hadn't I taken her picture?

I shrugged. "You kind of scare me."

Adam laughed, and Sarah turned around to face me with a grin. It was the first time she'd ever really smiled at me like she meant it.

She reached out and patted my knee. "I like you, Peter. You're honest."

When we arrived at Kingsley campus, I climbed out of the car clutching my camera in one hand and my backpack in the other like two security blankets.

Sarah grabbed my arm, forcing me to stand still in front of her. As I shifted anxiously, she studied me for a minute with her hands on her hips.

Unsure of what her focused attention meant, I hid behind my camera and took my first picture of Sarah. I trained the lens on her sleek legs and the fringe of her kilt, her little white bobby socks and her saddle shoes.

Suddenly, she lunged at me, mussed my hair, and pulled the tail of my shirt so it was barely tucked in before loosening my tie. I tried to fight her off, but she was fast.

When she was done, she stood back, arms crossed, regarding me with a critical expression. Then she smiled at her handiwork, announcing, "Much better. Now you just look like an artsy photographer guy." She nodded firmly. "We can tell everyone you aren't *actually* a geek and…" She sighed. "Maybe they'll believe us."

Sarah grabbed her book bag from the car, turned on her heel, and started down to the main building.

I turned to Adam, bewildered. "S—so, I look cooler like this or something?"

Adam's eyes had gone glassy, and he swallowed. "Yeah. You look—" Breaking off, he turned away and ran a hand through his hair, his posture and attitude suddenly distant and cold. "Forget it. Come on, we'll be late to assembly."

As we followed Sarah toward the main building and entered the auditorium, teachers stood off to the side, ready to tell new students where their assigned assembly seats would be for the school year. I remembered Mr. Waverly had told us assembly would mainly consist of taking attendance, important school announcements, student government addresses, and student body annual speeches. My public school hadn't had a daily assembly. It'd been much too big for that.

My seat assignment was P12 and Adam's was B9. My heart twisted when I realized he was going to be seated fifteen rows down from me. In that moment, reality hit. I was alone in a new school with no friends and no Adam for most of the day.

I ducked into my seat, scrunching down as low as I could, watching as Adam dropped casually into his own, stretching his arms out over the empty chairs beside him. He didn't turn to look at me.

A girl with reddish-blond frizzy hair sat down to my right. When I glanced over, she smiled and put out her hand. "Welcome to Kingsley! I'm Susan Morris." She had a lisp, which was unfortunate given the number of "s" sounds in her name.

"Peter Mandel." I shook her hand.

"Where are you from?"

"Knoxville. I went to public school before."

"Oh. A transfer student." Susan's red-cheeked face took on a kind of dreamy quality. "What's public school like? Is it cool? Are there lots of weird people there?"

I frowned. "Um—" I didn't know how to answer that. "It's, uh—"

"Cool camera! Are you a photographer?"

That I could answer. "Yes."

"You know, except for the new people, I know every single person in this school and have since kindergarten. There's no excitement left, Peter. None whatsoever." She grinned. "Expect to be hit on by all the artsy girls just because you're new blood. You're not my type, so you're safe from me." She winked. "However, that total babe you walked in with—now *that's* my type. What's the story?"

Sarah stood beside my row, checked her seat number against the paper in her hand, and dropped into the chair beside Susan. "The story is he isn't fucking interested in lisping redheaded geeks."

I gasped. That was just—whoa. "Sarah!" I hissed.

She shrugged.

Susan turned scarlet and with a tight voice asked, "Who are you? His girlfriend?"

"No, his sister." Sarah shoved a long black lock behind her ear. "And believe me, while your admiration is only to be expected, it's entirely unwanted. So keep it in your diary where it belongs."

Susan stood up to push by me, muttering something about the bathroom. I watched her stumble a little going up the aisle. No one stopped to ask her if she was okay.

Adam had been right that first day: Sarah *was* a vicious bitch.

I turned to her. "That was mean."

"I don't want geeks glomming onto him. We've got enough baggage with you around."

I stared at her, wondering if I looked as hurt as I felt. I opened my mouth but nothing came out.

"Don't get me wrong, Peter. I like you. Adam obviously *really* likes you. And I love Adam. It's all good. But I'll be damned if I'm going to let his soft spot for the geeky and geekier get us any further on the wrong side of the social scene."

I shook my head in disbelief. "You don't even know her. Maybe she's the prom queen's best friend."

Sarah smirked. "Where do you think I've been for the last fifteen minutes? I've already scoped out the cool crowd, and *infiltration plan numero uno* has been launched."

My eyes bugged out of my head. Sarah was terrifying.

"Don't worry so much. God, you're part of the plan, okay? Adam wouldn't have it any other way, unfortunately."

She sighed dramatically as if Adam's bizarre affinity for me had made her ability to be cool at Kingsley exponentially more difficult, perhaps to a degree so large it would be impossible to overcome.

"I'm just glad I like you too. It's much easier this way." She suddenly broke into a grin and waved at someone behind me.

I didn't know what to say. "I thought you hated me. Constantly banging on the door when—"

"Shut. Up." Sarah was suddenly in my face, eyes glinting. "Don't talk about that here. Don't talk about that *ever*." Her smile was savage, dangerous. "Do you understand me, Peter?"

I nodded, swallowing hard.

Sarah leaned back, her face relaxing. "Good, I'm glad we understand each other." She reached out to touch my face. I recoiled, but she still managed to place her palm against my cheek. She leaned in close and whispered, "I'll even pretend to date you if I have to, Peter. But let's both hope it doesn't come to that."

"I'd never pretend—"

She lifted her eyebrows, saying slowly, "Oh, but I'm sure there's something you want that'd make it worth your while. But don't worry, that's highly unlikely. I'm just trying to explain to you—" She broke off smiling as a jock guy nearly tripped over my feet trying to make his way past me. He sat down next to Sarah and introduced himself.

"Mike Harris."

"Sarah Algedi." Sarah smiled sweetly at him, and she was so exquisitely beautiful I had to take a deep breath, because I was either in the presence of a demon or an angel. I really wasn't sure.

Mike looked at me in expectation, and I realized he was waiting for me to introduce myself. "Peter Mandel."

"You guys a couple?" Mike asked lightly, obviously referencing Sarah's seeming caress moments ago.

Sarah laughed. "Oh no, Peter is my brother's best friend." Sarah pointed out Adam, and then indicated me again. "Peter's artsy, but he's cool."

Mike grinned and asked her where she was from. I tuned out the particulars of Sarah's response. I'd already heard it all before and from lips that didn't make my blood run cold.

I gazed down the fifteen rows separating me from Adam, watching as the five girls within proximity to his assigned seat introduced themselves and vied for his attention. Just when I was starting to feel kind of sick to my stomach, because he was definitely flirting back with all of them, he turned and caught my eye.

I waved a little, and he smiled and shrugged. I dropped my hand as he turned his attention to the girl on his right.

The chattering voices all around sounded like birds, flocking to their friends, each person aware of what his position would be in the flight pattern. I sat alone and unsure. Susan Morris returned, but she didn't speak to me. Adam didn't look around again. The agony of uncertainty grew. The bell rang and assembly began.

✧　✧　✧

"YEAH, I FELT kind of bad because she wouldn't even look at me when she came back to her seat," I said.

Adam frowned and rolled his eyes. "Sarah can be cruel. She overplays situations sometimes."

I opened my notebook and pulled out a new pen, uncapped it,

and scribbled a little to get the ink flowing smoothly. My desk wobbled a bit, and I wadded up a piece of paper and stuck it under one leg. At least I'd grabbed the desk next to Adam.

Adam and I shared only one class together—English. Sarah and I shared two—Geometry and Spanish. The other classes I had to brave alone, and on that first day, it'd been hard to face rooms full of strangers.

"So, what are you going to do?"

Adam looked surprised. "About Sare-Bear? Stay out of her way until she gets herself established. That's what I always do."

"You don't even care she hurt that girl's feelings?"

"Of course I care. I just can't do anything about it. Sarah is—well, a bear. How do you think she got the nickname?"

"I don't think you're being fair to the bear with that comparison."

Adam laughed. "Really, Peter. There's nothing that can be said or done to stop her from scheming. She's a society diva, and she'll always be a society diva. Just stay out of her way."

"She threatened me."

Adam shifted uncomfortably. "What did she say?"

"That I shouldn't talk about—" I paused significantly. "You know. Ever. And then she pretty much implied the *or else*."

Adam wouldn't meet my eye. He shuffled his papers and stretched his long legs out in front of him before saying quietly, "She's right. Never talk about that."

I bit down on my tongue, turning my back on Adam to rifle around in my book bag. Getting out another pen, I faced forward again and stared at the blank page of my notebook. It swam suspiciously. I faked a sneeze and used the opportunity to wipe the moisture from my eyes.

"Peter—" Adam sounded worried.

I just shrugged and didn't look at him.

"We'll talk later."

What was there to talk about? His desire to keep our relationship a secret shouldn't upset me. After all, I knew better than he did the repercussions of being gay in a conservative, Southern city, but—there was some ridiculous part of me that'd wanted him to be proud of me, like I was proud of him.

Friends. The word slammed into my mind, and I shook my head at my own thoughts. We'd never been more than friends anyway. Not really. What was I thinking?

As the teacher walked into the room, I didn't need to look over to know Adam was stewing in his seat across the aisle.

Our teacher was a tall, thin man, slightly balding, with an aristocratic nose. He pulled an unoccupied student desk from the corner and climbed onto it backward, his butt on the writing table and his feet in the chair. The other students grew quiet and waited patiently as he stared out the window for a long, long moment.

Finally, a kid at the back of the room piped up, "Earth to Dr. Landry. Come in, Dr. Landry."

Dr. Landry turned pale blue eyes toward the back of the room and gave his greeting. "Hello, William Henry. How was your summer break?"

William Henry enthused, "It rocked!"

Dr. Landry nodded, as though fully considering the implications of that statement. "Excellent, excellent. Did you manage to finally learn the all-important truth that listening is a skill?"

"No, sir. I did not," William Henry answered proudly. I glanced back to see the daring young man and found him grinning like a wolf. His green eyes glowed and his blond hair swooped into his handsome face.

Dr. Landry smirked. "No, I wouldn't expect you would."

He turned his eyes onto the rest of the class. "Fatima, good to see you. Leslie, looking lovely and fresh as a ray of sunshine after the break. Mandy—ah, yes, Mandy—have you dumped that scoundrel of a boyfriend yet?"

Mandy shot a glance at William Henry across the room and giggled. "Nope. Still dating the jerk."

"Figures." Dr. Landry winked. "Okay, we've got some new folks too. Adam Algedi—" His eyes wandered back and forth between me and Adam. "That'd be you, I'd wager," he said, nodding at Adam.

"Yes, sir."

"So, you're from Jordan, my sources tell me."

"Actually, we're kind of from all over, sir. But yes, Jordan was the last place my father was assigned."

Dr. Landry nodded as though this information was only to be expected. I had the impression he would've nodded in just the same way if Adam had said he was a spy from Libya, hired to infiltrate the American school system for information on how we train our children.

Dr. Landry's eyes wandered over to me. "So, that leaves you as Mr. Peter Mandel. I'm assuming your father is Abe Mandel, the bright light of the university's religious studies department?"

"Yes, sir."

"And you're a local transfer student?"

"Yes, sir." I didn't know why I was so nervous, but I could feel everyone's eyes on me, and I broke into a fine sweat.

"I hope you find Kingsley to be a better environment for you than the public school system, Mr. Mandel. I see you've got a camera. Are you a photographer?"

"Yes, sir." I glanced down at my camera and asked, "May I take pictures of you, sir?"

"Snap away, Mr. Mandel."

Dr. Landry uncurled from the desk and crossed to the chalkboard. He wrote in scrawling letters across the top of the board

Favorite Words. He underlined it four times.

"That is the topic for today's journal entry, boys and girls. At the end of the week, you'll hand in to me no fewer than two pages per daily journal topic. Poems and stories count." Dr. Landry glanced at me. "Sadly, Mr. Mandel, since this is an English literature class, photos will not be allowed toward the completion of the assignment. But, let me assure you I understand how unfair that must seem. Photographs often speak when words are silent."

"What about drawings?" William Henry asked from the rear of the room.

Dr. Landry leaned against the chalkboard, smearing the writing with the back of his shirt. "Let me think—" He looked out the window for a long second and then met William Henry's eye. "No. You know, William Henry, beyond the concept of listening, in and of itself, it's often valuable for a student to learn to apply information given on one subject to another related subject. Keep that in mind."

William Henry laughed. "I'll make note of it, sir."

Watching Dr. Landry turn back to the chalkboard, I realized Kingsley truly was different. The students and teachers had a rapport. Hope rose that my life could be better than it'd been, and I might find a place here after all. Here with Adam.

Dr. Landry grabbed a book from his desk. "Now. Poetry—"

AS WE STOOD in the cafeteria line for food, Sarah chatted with two girls, one blond and one brunette, occasionally glancing over her shoulder to make sure I hadn't wandered off. She beckoned me closer, and I approached nervously, wary after the morning's interactions.

"This is Peter. Adam's best friend here in the States."

I saw immediately the effect Sarah's reminder that she wasn't exactly from around Knoxville seemed to have on the brunette. She shot her friend a glance and stood up straighter, trying to enhance her coolness quotient for the new girl.

Sarah went on, "Peter's a photographer."

The girls oohed, as though that was suddenly a huge selling point for claiming me as a friend.

"This is Allison Hart," Sarah said, indicating the brunette. "And this is Leslie Howard," indicating the blond. Sarah smiled at me and said pointedly, "They're on the cheerleading squad."

"Nice to meet you," I muttered.

I felt oddly on display like a puppy at the pet store. I could almost see the girls debating the pros and cons of purchasing me and taking me home.

"Are you from Jordan too?" Allison asked.

"No. I'm from here. Knoxville."

"Oh." Allison glanced at Leslie. "Local transfer."

I had a feeling that wasn't considered quite as good a thing.

Sarah jumped in and changed the topic. "So, what were you asking me earlier about my brother?"

"I can't wait to meet him. Leslie and I were talking, and you probably don't even know, because he's your brother, but he's hot!" Allison grinned.

My stomach knotted up.

"Aw, I hate to curb your enthusiasm, but Adam likes blonds." Sarah winked at Leslie, obviously implying *her* chances were better due to her hair color.

I shot Sarah an irritated glance. Adam liked *blonds?* Adam liked me and I sure wasn't blond. And I was damn sure Adam liked *cock*, given how often he put his mouth on mine. Unless Leslie had something unexpected beneath her skirt, I was sure she wasn't his type.

But he's been with four girls, remember?

My blood went cold.

"Besides, Allison, I think Van would say you're not available," Leslie reminded her.

"Stupid boyfriend. Gets in the way all the time." Allison pretended to pout, crossing her arms over her chest and throwing out a hip.

Sarah laughed. "Don't they always?"

"Who always whats?" Adam asked from behind me.

Relief welled in me at the sound of his voice. I turned to allow him entrance into the circle and he carefully held himself away from me. My heart stuttered at the subtle rejection. But what did I expect? That he'd put his arm around me?

"Boyfriends get in the way of going out with other people," Allison said coyly, batting her eyelashes.

"Depends on the boyfriend, doesn't it? Some don't mind sharing." Adam gave Allison a flirtatious once-over. "Does yours share?"

Some don't mind sharing. My mind turned those words over and over in the span of a heartbeat. *Adam prefers blonds. I'll pretend to date you if I have to.* Comments from the day slid into place, gelling into an implication I didn't want to admit. I suddenly wasn't in the mood to eat. Because if Adam Algedi thought I was the kind of boyfriend who didn't mind sharing—

But wait. I wasn't his boyfriend. We were just friends. We'd never committed to more, and if I'd let my heart get involved, that was my own fault, right?

I stepped out of line, muttering, "I forgot something in my locker."

Sarah frowned, and I bolted from the cafeteria without looking at Adam, my stomach churning, mind whirring. Adam was flirting with that girl like he didn't even care about me that way—and he didn't. I wasn't. We weren't. What the hell was I so upset about?

"Hey, Peter, wait up!" Adam called.

I slowed my steps but didn't turn, head bent and shoulders hunched up protectively. I burst out the doors of the main building, the cool air slapping me in the face as I started up the hill.

"Peter?" Adam fell into step next to me, hands pushed into his pockets, the Kingsley tie fluttering in the breeze.

"Yeah?"

"Are you—" Adam broke off. "Will you come back to eat?"

"I'm not hungry."

"Peter the Eater not hungry? Insanity!"

I didn't laugh at the joke.

"Bad first day?"

"Not so bad." I shrugged and kept my eyes down.

I'd been letting myself believe there was more between us than just friendship, and I couldn't afford for him to see the jealousy and fear in my eyes.

Adam trudged along next to me, silent.

"You'll miss lunch. Better go on back," I said quietly.

Adam ignored me and followed doggedly at my side. We entered the building and sighed in relief at the cool, shadowed inner hallway. Locating my locker, I spun the dial on the lock.

"What did you forget?" Adam asked.

I let my head fall forward, allowing the metal door to break the descent with a bang. I'd forgotten to protect my heart.

"Hey," Adam exclaimed. "What the hell?"

"I didn't forget anything, okay? I just can't—I don't know how—" I broke off and flung my locker open, rummaging aimlessly through the stack of books and notepads.

"Peter—" Adam leaned back against the locker. "It's always hard at a new school. Every time we move I think I can't do it, this time I can't make friends again. I'd rather be alone. But then I meet someone and we click and we're friends. This time it was you."

We were both silent for a long time, until I said, "I'm okay. I'll see you later, after History of Religious Philosophy."

Adam ran a hand through his hair. "Okay, then. I'm gonna have some lunch."

I smiled half-heartedly.

Adam walked away with one final glance over his shoulder before he exited into the blinding noon light and left me alone.

✧   ✧   ✧

LESLIE HOWARD SURPRISED me by sitting next to me in History of Religious Philosophy.

"So, what school did you go to before? Bearden? Farragut?" Leslie asked, smiling with a kind, open face.

I answered her in a soft voice, not wanting to draw attention to myself or my personal history.

Leslie said, "My cousin went to school there. Did you know him? Brent Ellwood?"

"No." Fidgeting with my notebook, I looked away. "You don't have to be nice to me just because you want to impress Sarah. She doesn't really care about me that much."

Leslie laughed, her nose wrinkling a little with her smile. "I don't even know Sarah, so who says I'm trying to impress her?" She turned to her books and arranged them on her desk. "I'm being nice to you because I'm a nice person. Go figure."

"Oh."

"Yeah, oh."

I slumped down in my chair.

Leslie turned her back to me and chatted with the girl on her left until the teacher, a Mrs. Parson, entered the room, issued a cheery hello to the class, and the class answered back.

I wondered where Adam was now and wished he were there to smooth over my mistake. He always made everything look so easy. I finally managed to look at Leslie again, but she didn't notice. Her attention was focused on Mrs. Parson. She chuckled softly, her eyebrows lifted in amused interest at the story Mrs. Parson told about her two-year-old granddaughter's visit during summer vacation.

When Mrs. Parson finished her anecdote, turning to her desk to grab a stack of papers to hand out to us, I gently tapped my pencil on Leslie's desk to get her attention and then mouthed, "Sorry."

Leslie shrugged and waved it off.

Mrs. Parson made her way to my row, and I took a packet from her. There were some photocopies of selected readings and a listing of books we should have by the end of the week. My father was the author of two of the titles, and I felt an odd mix of pride and annoyance. At least I wouldn't need to pay for those since my father kept copies of each at home.

As Mrs. Parson took a moment to write the syllabus on the chalkboard, Leslie leaned across and whispered, "Hey, it's your first day in a new school. I bet you're nervous."

I nodded.

"And Sarah? She's intense. So, I get it. No problem."

"Really?"

She smiled at me, and it was infectious. I smiled too, a sense of relief washing over me.

Mrs. Parson clapped her hands together lightly to get our attention. I pulled out my notebook and took notes about her policies on homework, missed quizzes and tests. I didn't want to get off on the wrong foot with my teachers any more than I wanted any problems with the other students.

After class, Leslie offered to help me find the chemistry room and I agreed, relieved I hadn't managed to get myself blacklisted on the first day of school.

I'd already discovered that Kingsley was full of attractive boys. Some guys were like me, too adolescent and gawky to pull off the uniform blazer and tie, but others were mature enough to fill out their shirts and pants in a way I found hard to ignore.

As we walked past a group of three guys all digging in their lockers, and all with asses like apples, I had to drag my eyes away, worried that someone would see how I stared. Remembering the time I'd gotten beaten up after gym class in my last school, I steeled myself. That day I hadn't even looked at anyone, but I couldn't convince the jocks of that.

"You okay?" Leslie asked. "You look kind of anxious."

I shrugged. "Why doesn't Kingsley have any P.E. requirements?"

"They let us get our credits with outside lessons. I'm a cheerleader and that counts too. What about you? Are you going to go out for a team to get your credits?"

"They took my gym credits from my last three years into account so I'm in the clear."

I was incredibly grateful for that. I'd hated the idea of trying out for a team and my folks couldn't afford lessons. Being a benchwarmer for a sport I didn't even like wasn't the way I wanted to spend my free time during my senior year in high school.

"Cool," Leslie said, pushing her hair behind her ear. "And here we are. Mr. Snyder's Chemistry class. Have fun with him."

"Is he good?"

"Good? Sure. Mean? Definitely. Just always have your homework and do well on the tests, and you'll be just fine."

Leslie patted my arm and waved as she continued down the hall to her classroom. I steeled myself and entered the room, trying not to look too sick with nerves at the sight of sixteen faces I didn't know.

The only way out was through, and I was over halfway through the day. If nothing else, I thought the odds were good I'd survive.

✧   ✧   ✧

ON THE RIDE home, Adam kept his hand on my knee while Sarah analyzed Kingsley's social system from the back seat.

"The popular crowd is a mix of smart jocks and theater nerds. It's not your regular American school situation," she said, taking out a notebook and actually referring to what appeared to be notes about the social hierarchy of the school. "Normally, I'd expect jocks and cheerleaders to reign supreme, but Kingsley is a prep school, and everyone had to test to get in. So, brains are important in a way sports aren't. And it seems artists—especially the theater crowd—have a place too."

Adam looked at me and rolled his eyes.

"Don't act like what I'm telling you isn't important, Adam." Sarah stabbed her pen in his direction. "You failed to go out for swim team and are acting disinterested in soccer, so it's a damn good thing sports aren't the end-all and be-all at this school, or we'd be doomed." She glanced at me. "Well, more doomed."

"It was all sports all the time at public school," I said.

"Yeah," Sarah said, "which is probably why you were chopped liver there. But at Kingsley you'll manage to be upper-to-mid lower echelon without too much of a problem."

"Gee thanks."

"You're welcome. We stand a chance of making this work, guys."

"Wow, listen to Sare-Bear, sounding all optimistic and stuff. Be careful. Wouldn't want you to feel happy or anything. It might cause your ice-cold heart to shatter into a million pieces."

Sarah scribbled something and then snapped her notebook shut. "Kiss off with your attitude, Tad, because for once you lucked out. Maybe your dick didn't make such a bad choice this time."

"My dick doesn't make choices, Sarah. I do."

"Right. Tell it to someone who didn't see what happened in

Rome."

I tried to sound nonchalant. "What's she talking about?"

Adam made a face to dismiss her comment.

Sarah kept on like I hadn't said a thing. "Peter will probably fit in just fine if he keeps his mouth shut and doesn't do anything lame. I mean aside from his usual weird lameness."

"I am sitting right here, you know," I said.

"I'm talking *to* you, geekster, so yeah, I know."

Adam squeezed my knee. "So how was your first day?"

"Could've been worse."

"Cool."

"Yeah, the most embarrassing thing that happened was raising my hand to ask for a hall pass. So, all in all, not too bad." I didn't want to tell him about Leslie—especially not in front of Sarah who would scream at me for being socially inept.

"How is that embarrassing?"

"Apparently they don't have them at Kingsley. If you need to go, you just *go*." After the virtual lockdown of my public school experience, the simple freedom of that was both exhilarating and alarming.

"I'm still not getting it."

"He basically announced to the whole class he had to piss," Sarah said.

"Actually…" I felt my cheeks get hot. "I was gone a while."

Adam started to laugh. "Everyone poops, Peter. Didn't you know? You're not alone."

I knocked his hand off my knee and crossed my arms. "Being teased by you both is what I need. Thanks."

"I wasn't teasing you," Sarah said. "I was serious. Everyone knows you took a shit."

"Shut up, Sarah," Adam said, swinging into my driveway. "And you can walk the rest of the way home. I'm going to hang out with

Peter."

She slammed her door, hitched her backpack higher onto her shoulder, and walked off without another word, her dark hair streaming behind her.

Adam smirked. "Good riddance. Now we can be *alone*."

As much as I liked that idea, I was still unnerved by the events of the day. Instead of racing up to my bedroom the way I knew Adam hoped, I swerved into the kitchen instead, putting together a snack of cheese and crackers for the two of us.

While Adam took a seat at the kitchen table, Harry heaved out of his bed to come whuffle at my ankles, hoping I'd drop a piece of cheddar. After making him work for it by commanding him to lie down, sit, and speak, I gave in and dropped him a slice.

"He's a good dog," Adam said, scratching behind Harry's ears as he licked his chops.

I sat down across from him and passed over a soda. "Yeah. He is."

"So, what's eating you? Aside from everyone in your class knowing you took a dump today. Is it what Sarah was saying in the car? Or how she acted this morning?"

"She's awful."

"She can be. But hey, this afternoon she was a whole lot more positive about everything. Take my word for it—Sarah's at her worst when she thinks she has nothing to lose. Now that she's got a handle on things, she'll lighten up, and you'll see she's not as bad as she wants you to think she is."

"Why would she want me to think she's awful?"

"Control."

We ate in silence for a few seconds and then Adam asked, "What else is eating you up inside?"

I sighed. "All those girls."

"What about them?"

"You can't tell me you didn't notice how they were circling like sharks around chum."

"I'm the chum in that analogy?"

"Adam."

"Peter, girls are girls. You're you. We don't need to worry about that right now. It's the first day of school. Come on, relax. Eat your cheese."

I turned over his meaningless words as I created a double-decker cheese and cracker sandwich and took a crunchy, tangy bite. I hadn't even realized just how hungry I was, but I'd skipped lunch after all. I wolfed down the rest and made another, inhaling it too.

Adam grinned. "There. Feeling better? Low blood sugar is known for making people paranoid."

"I'm not paranoid."

I could hear my mother's word processor from behind her closed office door. It was clacking like mad printing out a manuscript. I missed the sound of her typewriter from my childhood. The *thwack* as the typewriter hammers hit the page and the *bing* of the returning carriage had been my lullaby. The word processor just wasn't the same.

Adam cocked his head and shoved a piece of cheese in his mouth. "What now?"

I shrugged. "Nothing. So, how was *your* first day?"

"Great. Like I said earlier, everyone's really friendly. But there was one thing I didn't mention when Sarah was in the car."

"Yeah?"

"There's this really hot guy in one of my classes. Totally turns me on just looking at him."

Nausea rose in me, and my mouth went so dry I couldn't chew my cracker.

Adam's eyes twinkled at first but then flashed with frustration. "What the hell, Peter? I was talking about *you*. What's your problem today?"

I swallowed some soda quickly to get the cracker down before I choked. "I don't know. I'm tired, and I've never done this before. You do it all the time, right? It's stressful."

"Yeah, okay."

"Besides, how was I supposed to know you were talking about me? There are tons of hot guys at school!"

Adam's lips quirked like he was trying not to smile. "Oh yeah. Tons, huh? Should I be worried now?"

Worried about what? I wanted to ask. *Worried that your fuck buddy might get a real boyfriend? Or do you actually have feelings for me? Like I have for you?*

"Yeah, you should be worried. I'm going to hook up with some guy who doesn't have a crazy controlling sister and see how that works out for me."

Adam looked like he couldn't decide if that was funny or not. Instead of saying anything, he came around the table, grabbed the last cracker from my fingers, and tossed it to Harry.

"Come on. Let's go upstairs. I've got something I want to show you."

As lame as the line was, I was tired of my own angst, and so I went willingly.

With Adam's mouth on my cock, and his dick thrusting against my tongue, it was easy to let go of my fears and just be happy with what I had. I might not be able to tell all those girls at Kingsley to back off, nor could I claim Adam as my boyfriend, but this physical pleasure, this closeness—it was something that was mine.

Chapter Nine

QUICKLY, IT BECAME clear *infiltration plan numero uno*, as Sarah called it, had been a massive success. Every morning she tried to make me look cooler, and every day the Algedis' popularity grew. They were beautiful, charismatic, confident, and funny—of course, everyone wanted to be their friend.

Out of the people drawn in by Sarah's machinations, there was a core group that solidified quickly. Mike Harris, the handsome, sober, and good-natured quarterback was one. He'd asked Sarah to be his girlfriend that very first week. Adam said it was to get her locked in before any other guys could get their foot in the door, but it seemed like he actually liked her for some odd reason.

Allison Hart and her boyfriend, Van Wright—a couple who seemed to argue more than anything else—also became Algedi groupies. They hung around almost constantly, and I grew accustomed to their presence at school.

Van was always angry and sulky in a way that appealed to very base instincts in me. The frown lines between his eyebrows became masturbation material on more than one occasion—a fact I found both hilarious and shameful. My fantasy always ended with me coming on Van's sulky face while he frantically beat himself off. Even though Adam and I weren't a real couple, I still felt guilty afterward, like I'd cheated on him in my mind.

The final friend rounding out our group was Leslie Howard.

We'd bonded by making fun of Mrs. Parson's love for both the *New Yorker* and long knitted scarves. Leslie was forthright and cheerful, and, best of all, not intimidated by Sarah. I could breathe easier when she was around.

Amongst this group of beautiful, confident people, I fell into the role of the strange artsy guy everyone accepted because the cool new kids, Adam and Sarah, seemed to like him. For the first time in my life, I had people to hang out with at school and a guy I had feelings for and got to have actual sex with. Things weren't perfect, but I was the closest to happy I'd ever been.

✧   ✧   ✧

ONE DAY, ABOUT a month into school, Leslie and Allison's cheerleading practice was canceled because their coach's mother had passed away.

"She'll be back in time for the game, though," Allison said, gripping the flagpole next to the main building and using it to swing herself around.

"That's gotta be hard for her," Mike offered.

"Yeah, it's so sad. Her mom was only like sixty or something."

"Some old lady we don't know dies, and everyone acts all sad about it," Van muttered, sticking a piece of grass in his mouth and letting out a shrill whistle.

Leslie slapped at Van's arm until he stopped. "After school, let's all go down to Beans."

"What's Beans?" Adam asked.

"It's a cool coffee shop in the Old City." Seeing the confusion on Adam's face she went on, "It's the historic district of Knoxville, and they're trying to make it super cool for college students and teens. They've opened bars and clubs and this coffee shop. It's fun."

"And let's hit Swansea Station," Mike threw in.

"Hell yeah," Van agreed.

"I'll bite. What's Swansea Station?" Adam asked, laughing.

"A little underground convenience store with Playboys out of the plastic," Van said.

Mike nodded. "And last time there were some weird magazines with freaks covered in tattoos, and one had a hot naked chick with her tongue split in two."

"Just think what she can *do*," Van added.

"I'm in." Adam grabbed my shoulder and shook me. "And Eater's along for the ride."

I glared at him for using my old nickname, but he just smiled at me until my irritation dimmed.

Van and Mike waggled two fingers at each other, grinning like loons. "I mean, it'd be like two tongues on your dick. Think about it!"

"Two tongues!"

"On your dick!"

Allison and Leslie rolled their eyes and scooted closer to each other, whispering and laughing about something. Out of the corner of my eye, I saw Sarah approaching with a genuine smile on her face. It was weird enough to make me nervous.

"Hey, Sarah, we're going to Beans after school," Mike said. "You coming?"

"It's a coffee shop," Adam supplied.

"Sure."

"Why do you look happy?" Adam asked suspiciously.

"Guess."

"What?" Leslie asked.

"Coach left word before she left. Since Macy Lawhorn dropped off the team, I'm officially on the squad."

"That's my girl!" Mike gave her a highfive.

The girls' squeals and hugs seemed a bit over-the-top to me, but Sarah's eyes shone with joy at her success. Not only had she entered

Kingsley at the top of the social ladder, but she'd managed a major coup. She was now the girlfriend of the quarterback and an official cheerleader.

Go Sarah, rah-rah, I thought. If nothing else, her ambition was impressive.

RIDING THROUGH THE Old City in Mike's big brand-new SUV that could hold us all, we passed a new dance club none of us had seen before.

"Oh, hey. Is that one all-ages?" Adam asked. He was seated in the second back seat between me and Leslie, and directly behind Sarah.

"Nah, it's another gay club," Mike said matter-of-factly.

"Like they need a special club for fags," Van added. "It's mostly fags at *any* club, isn't it?"

Adam said nothing and a tense silence fell in the car.

Mike shifted in his seat as he pretended to be hunting for a parking spot.

"Paid parking's right up there, man," Van said, pointing the way.

Sarah coughed softly.

"You okay?" Mike asked her.

"Sure, it's just Van's bullshit fouling up my air."

Mike chuckled, and surprisingly so did Van. The tension broke, and everyone relaxed. Adam brushed his hand against my knee briefly. No one noticed, but the sensation of his touch lingered as I climbed from the SUV and walked down the street at the back of the group.

Coffee scented the air two blocks down from Beans, and when we stepped inside the small shop the comforting aroma swallowed me. I relaxed into it, surprised to find the place was virtually empty.

Adam put his arm around Sarah as they gazed up at the chalkboard menu. I stood next to them, having already decided on the caramel latte.

The barista was a guy in his thirties with salt-and-pepper hair. Wearing a white T-shirt and a towel over his shoulder, he smiled and asked with a deep Southern accent, "What can I do ya for?"

I put my order in first and then Adam asked for a coffee with a slice of chocolate cake. While we were waiting, Adam leaned against the counter and asked, "So, how's business?"

The barista glanced over to see if Adam was harassing him or asking seriously. Apparently finding Adam sincere and charming, he answered, "Great. It's quiet in the early afternoon, but come evening the university kids'll fill up the place. I'll be out of here by then. Got the evening off."

Mike and Van shoved some tables together to make room for all of us. We'd barely settled down with our coffees and baked goods when the door chimed and a guy with an acoustic guitar came in. "Hey, Heath. The usual," he called as he sat down at a table by the window, propped his feet up in the opposite chair, and began to play softly.

"This is kind of nice, don't you think, Sare-Bear?" Adam asked, looking at me, but addressing his sister.

"*Don't* call me that," Sarah replied.

"Sare-Bear," Mike said under his breath, like he was trying it out. "It's cute."

She glared, and he laughed softly, unfazed.

Adam pulled a small book of Rimbaud poems from his jacket pocket and began reading aloud in French to anyone who would listen, which was mainly just me, since Allison was gossiping to Leslie and Sarah about one of the girls at school who'd pierced her eyebrow and allegedly given a hand job to a gross guy in her neighborhood over the summer.

Van and Mike talked about whether or not Van would be able

to go out for the school play, since he was one of those oddballs Adam called "drama-jocks," meaning Van enjoyed both acting *and* tackling people on a cold, wet football field. I sipped my latte, listened to Adam read, and snapped the occasional picture of our group, enjoying a sense of amazement and gratitude that I was part of a group.

Not necessarily an integral part, of course. But Van or Mike asked me where I'd been if I missed lunch to develop photos, or if I didn't hang out at the flagpole during free period. Adam was still the only one I spent time alone with, though. Mike and Van didn't call me to go to the movies or to race go-karts with them. But that was okay with me. After all, I didn't want them to figure out I was gay and head-over-heels for Adam.

Between the acoustic guitar and the sense of belonging, sitting there in the coffee shop, I was pretty happy.

"What are you smiling about?" Adam asked, both sincere and teasing. "That poem was about murdering babies."

"No it wasn't," Sarah said over her shoulder before turning her attention back to Allison's gossip.

"No, but Peter wouldn't know that because he's taking *Spanish*," Adam said, bringing up an argument we'd had before school had even begun about my choice of foreign language.

"¿Cómo está?" Mike asked, clapping me on the shoulder. "¿Muy bien? Gracias. ¿Y tú? ¿Tengo un perro o un gato?"

"No sé. ¿Tienes un gato o un perro?" I answered, as the door chime announced new arrivals. Sarah and Leslie rested their heads together, dark hair twining with blond. I took a picture.

"Hi, faggot. Long time, no punch."

I stiffened, slowly lowering my camera to see a sneering, sunburned face backed up by a blue and white letterman jacket. Jason Huddleston—captain of my old school's football team, the ringleader of the group that'd harassed me, and the guy who'd broken my nose.

I cleared my throat, opened my mouth, but no sound came out.

"I wondered what happened to you, sissy boy."

Two more blue and white letterman jackets appeared behind Jason, but I couldn't look away from his eyes long enough to discern the identities attached to them.

"But my cousin, Eric Morgan—know him? Yeah, he's at Kingsley and he told me you'd shown up at his school. I guess your momma and daddy decided to send you where they cater to perverts. Eric tells me Kingsley's full of queers and queer-lovers."

"Who the fuck are you?" Adam asked, standing up, fists clenched.

Jason's eyes flared, turning his attention to Adam. "I think the question is who the fuck are *you?* His butt-buddy? Are you the little faggot's boyfriend?"

Mike stood up too, flanking Adam's side. When Van joined them, he effectively blocked Jason and his cronies from my line of sight.

I cleared my throat and tried to speak again. A strangled noise was all that came out.

The tension in the room grew. Out of the corner of my eye, I could see Leslie, Sarah, and Allison sitting frozen, their chests barely stirring with breath. Adam's hands were clenched into fists, and his stance left me with no doubt he'd throw a punch. Mike and Van looked ready too.

"I don't know who the fuck you think you are," Adam said softly, his voice like steel. "But if you don't leave my friend alone, you won't be playing in this week's game. Or next week's either."

Just then Heath, the barista, grabbed Jason by the jacket and shoved him toward the door. "Get out. These kids were behaving until you came along. I don't need you here stirring up trouble. Out, or I'll call the cops."

Terrified that an all-out brawl would start, I flinched back against the wall. But at the mention of the police, Jason and his friends left. Adam, Mike, and Van remained standing until they were gone.

Even once the immediate threat was over and the guys sat back down, I couldn't stop trembling. Leslie came and put her arm around my shoulders. "What assholes. No wonder you wanted to leave that school."

I nodded mutely.

"And calling you a...*fag?*" she added, whispering the word like it hurt her to say it. "Jerks. It's always the lowest common denominator with those types."

I saw Mike and Van exchange significant glances. Frightened by that, I met Adam's eyes and found them still full of rage.

The guy who'd been playing guitar stared at me over his coffee. It was a piercing stare, and I felt like he saw right through me. Starting to sweat, I swiped a hand over my forehead in response to an irrational terror that the word "fag" was somehow tattooed there.

Finally, I cleared my throat. "I guess you found out my secret." Trying to sound lighthearted, I added the punch line, "I wasn't exactly popular at my old school."

Allison laughed feebly while Mike and Van avoided my gaze and turned to their almost empty coffees.

Leslie grabbed my hand and smiled at me. "Ignore them, Peter. We like you just the way you are."

On the way back to Kingsley to drop Adam off for his car, the girls convinced Mike to take them to see *Ghost* again. Allison had seen it three times already, and while I agreed with her assessment that Patrick Swayze was dreamy, once had been enough for me.

Adam jumped out of Mike's SUV, dragging me out after him, and after terse goodbyes to our friends, he climbed into the Mercedes without another word. I got into the passenger seat, my heart in my throat and my hands still shaky.

Pulling onto the highway, Adam said, "Some friends you had at public school, Eater. So what happened? Did they beat you up? Is that why you left?"

I looked out the window, watching as buildings and trees flashed by.

"What do you think they've told Eric Morgan about you?" he asked.

"That I'm a fag. Funny, since I am and all."

Adam's jaw clenched. "So, they hurt you, didn't they?"

I shrugged.

"Didn't anyone stick up for you?"

I hated talking about this stuff, and just when I'd started to feel like less of a loser, of course my past showed up to ruin everything. "You know, I'm like Johnny Cash—a solitary man." Adam's eyes called me on my bullshit, and I groaned. "What do you want me to say?"

"Tell me why your friends didn't stick up for you."

I was quiet for a long time, but I finally said, "When I was a kid, my best friend was Ella Burstein. She lived next door, and we played Strawberry Shortcake together every day."

Adam lifted an eyebrow. "Strawberry Shortcake, Peter? Really?"

"The doll smelled good. Do you want to hear this or not?"

"Go on."

"Ella moved to Virginia when I was ten, and then I mainly played with these two girls from school."

I picked at the edge of my uniform tie, pulling a few threads. My mom would be annoyed if she had to buy me a new one. It wasn't like the uniforms were inexpensive.

"Somewhere along the way, I guess it was in middle school, they stopped inviting me to their slumber parties. Which makes sense, right? I mean, I'm a guy. I'm sure their parents saw me going through puberty—"

Adam snorted. "Well, they were wrong."

I gave him the finger. "I'm sure they thought I had no business at a slumber party with a bunch of girls. If they only knew, right?"

"Peter, you really don't come off as that gay, you know? I mean, if you did…then…" He shrugged.

My stomach ached. If I did then *what?* Then he wouldn't be with me? Why? Because he wasn't attracted to flamers, or because then everyone would know about him? I really wasn't sure what the deal-breaker was in that scenario.

"So, was that it?" Adam asked. "You didn't have any guys to be friends with?"

"I tried, I guess, but I sucked at sports—"

Adam made a noise of agreement, and I was getting really annoyed now. I glared at him and fought the lump stupidly rising in my throat. I didn't need this bullshit from him. Not now, not after the coffee shop.

"What?" he asked, like he wasn't being a dick.

"Nothing."

"You're not good at sports. That's nothing bad. You're good at a lot of other stuff."

"Like what? Sucking you off?"

Adam's eyes flashed angrily. "Like photography. Like being a great person. Come on, Peter, I'm not trying to pick on you. I just want to understand how it was, so I can figure out how we're going to deal with it, you know?"

Deal with it. What was there to deal with? The fact was, I was gay, and that was a dangerous, scary thing to be. A few hours ago, I'd been happy, maybe the happiest I'd ever been in my life, and then, just because I was gay, a few words from some dickwad made everything fall down around me.

"Everyone seemed to *know* I was different. Mostly guys avoided me. Until they started harassing and tormenting me. And then they beat me up."

Adam sucked in a breath like *he'd* been punched, and he put his hand in my hair, tugging at it a little.

"When they broke my nose, the principal called my parents to come get me. So they found out. They wanted to know what happened."

"What did you say?"

I took off my glasses and rubbed at my eyes. I felt bad about it even now. I didn't know what I was so afraid of—my dad was liberal-minded, but what if this was the one time he wasn't? I needed him. Especially since my mom was so unreliable, losing days to her writing and ignoring the reality of me with all of her might, avoiding the trauma that truly knowing me would remind her of. I loved them both, but I couldn't be honest with them. If my dad couldn't handle it, what would I have?

"I told them it was because I'm a Jew."

"Not really, though. Your mom's not a Jew."

"Don't even go there, Adam," I said irritably. "I'm a Jew, okay. I say I'm a Jew, so I'm a Jew."

"No, you say you're an atheist. And I don't think it works like that. I don't think you get to just decide if you're a Jew or not."

I threw my hands up. "I'm an atheist Jew. And I didn't just *decide*, okay? Leave it alone."

Adam's eyes took on a little heat the way they always did when I stood up for myself. He liked it when I was bossy, I could tell, but it wasn't a default setting of mine.

"So, you didn't tell them this guy Jason had it in for you because you're gay."

I put my glasses back on and gave a small shrug. "I told them Jason and his buddies *thought* I was gay."

"And what did they say?" Adam seemed deeply interested in my parents' response, and I wondered, not for the first time, what the situation was with his parents and what they might or might not know about Adam's sexuality.

"My dad was furious about the anti-Semitism, and scoffed at the idea I was a 'homosexual,' as he always puts it."

"Oh," Adam said quietly.

"Yeah." I shoved some of my curly hair off my forehead. I needed a haircut. "And Mom was just overwhelmed. 'We'll get him into Kingsley! This is unacceptable!' All that kind of stuff. She has a bad personal history with violence from when she was young. She freaked out when she saw my face."

Freaked out wasn't the half of it. Dad had needed to sedate her just to get her to calm down. She'd gone down the rabbit hole of bad memories, and it had taken a few days for her to resurface. I hadn't told Adam about my uncle, or about my mom's history with depression. I didn't see the point. Besides, no one had ever really told me about it either. I'd just picked it up over the years in bits and pieces from Dad, Mom, and overheard phone calls before my grandmother died.

"What'd you say when they mentioned Kingsley?"

I laughed, and it sounded kind of wounded to my own ears. "I just sat at the kitchen table with a tissue stuffed up my nose to stop the bleeding. I didn't say anything."

Adam pulled into my driveway, and he turned to me with a serious, intense look on his face. "Peter. No one will ever hit you again. Okay? Not on my watch."

My smile felt wobbly, and I took his hand. I wanted to kiss him, but we were in the car, and someone might see. I didn't know how he could keep a promise like that, but it touched me all the same.

✧ ✧ ✧

THE FOLLOWING FRIDAY afternoon, I sat outside by the flagpole with our group during our free period. Adam wasn't around. He and Leslie had both been in Dr. Landry's class with me, but I'd had to stay after to ask Dr. Landry a question about the reading material for the upcoming test. When I came out to join the gang, they were nowhere to be seen. It was nice, though, to not feel like I needed Adam to be there with me to feel welcome in the group.

I busied myself taking photos. Mike was being charming. He'd made Sarah a whimsical necklace of red and yellow leaves by twining the stems together. Sarah's soft expression when he'd found it too small to fit over her head and had instead dubbed it a crown for his most beautiful queen, was forever caught on film. I planned to develop the picture for Mike as a gift.

Allison wore her cheerleading uniform instead of her school kilt in preparation for the game that evening. As she rested with her head cushioned on Van's knee, she rolled her eyes at his sulky monologue. He'd landed the role of Danny for the school's production of *Grease*, but couldn't seem to enjoy his success, whining instead that it was going to be hard to do the play *and* play football.

I was waiting for Sarah to get fed up with Van and tell him to shut up, when out of the corner of my eye, I saw Adam walking our way with Leslie. He held her hand in his, laughing at something she said. She smiled broadly back up at him, and when they got close to the group, she lifted their joined hands in the air so everyone could see.

Allison squealed in celebration. Sarah clapped and whistled. They both rushed Leslie together, jumping up and down and hugging first her and then each other. My gut roiled, and I blinked at Adam, hoping there was some alternate interpretation I just hadn't reached yet.

"Aw, man, like no one could see that coming," Mike said, rolling his eyes at the antics of the girls.

Adam wrapped his arm around Leslie's shoulder and pulled her to his chest in a tight hug. He avoided my eyes.

My stomach crawled up my throat. I stood and walked away as quickly as I could, heading blindly across campus, not even sure where I was going.

Mike called after me, but I heard Sarah, ever the mastermind, say, "He told me earlier he was getting a migraine. He's probably going to take medicine. He'll be okay. We'll check on him later." And then to Adam, "So, you asked her finally, huh? It's about time!"

I nearly threw up before I got to the bathroom, but I made it. I stood in the stall after I'd puked, wiping at my eyes and trying to breathe, but each breath I took tore into me. I started to cry, which made me feel like throwing up all over again.

Mike's words echoed in my head. *Like no one could see that coming.*

I couldn't say I hadn't noticed *anything* at all—just two days prior, Adam had allowed Leslie to sit on his lap to play with his hair, putting little braids into the longer portions—but I'd thought it was just friendly. Because it had to be. Because *he was with me.*

Only, he wasn't. He'd never said any such thing. We were friends who gave each other orgasms. We cared about each other. But he'd never said it would ever be more than that. Hell, Adam wouldn't even say he was gay, and suddenly, in the face of his new relationship with Leslie, it occurred to me maybe he wasn't. Maybe he was bisexual. He told me he'd had sex with four girls, after all, and only two guys. Maybe he was bisexual and actually liked girls better.

I leaned sideways against the stall and pressed my cheek against the cool metal partition. After a long time, I finally stepped out, washed my face, and rinsed my mouth.

I looked at my reflection in the mirror. My glasses were a little crooked, and my hair was a mess. I smoothed my wet hands over that frizzy disaster, managing to get my hair to lie down a little, and then straightened my glasses. I looked presentable. I could walk out of the bathroom at least, and no one would suspect I'd been throwing up and crying in there.

I went to the school office and signed out as sick. I didn't go to Spanish and instead waited on the benches out in front of the main school entrance for my mom to come pick me up.

At home, Mom took my temperature, declared me fever-free, and gave me some Pepto-Bismol and a kiss on the cheek before disappearing into her office to write. Dad wasn't back from the university, and Harry was asleep in his dog bed. He hadn't even greeted me when Mom and I had come home.

I grabbed my coat and headed outside with my camera.

The trees were losing their leaves. Piles of yellow and orange were heaped over lawns. I walked along the edge of the road through the subdivision, heading for the woods behind it and my childhood hideout. It was an old storage building left over from the original farm the neighborhood had been built on. It'd been dilapidated when I was eight—now it was decrepit and barely standing.

I ducked inside, running my fingers over the splintering wood. I unpacked the folding tripod from my backpack to take slow-speed self-portraits on a timer. I huddled in a corner, curled in on myself, and swaddled my trench coat around me. I did a lot of poses, a lot of angles, and then spent time photographing the details of the building's decay before heading back to the house.

I was exhausted and certain Adam would call soon. I was also certain I'd need to be home when he did.

So I could tell my mom I didn't want to talk to him.

Chapter Ten

THE NEXT MORNING, I left a message with Mo to tell Adam I didn't need a ride to school. Instead, I had my father drop me off on his way to UT. It meant getting up really early, but I had a key to the darkroom and permission from the art teacher to use it any time the campus was open.

An hour before the assembly bell was due to ring, the batch of film from my hideout was turning out pretty well. I tilted my head back and forth, considering whether or not to mess around with the cropping, before jumping at a sharp rapping on the door.

"Just a minute!" I called, hastily canning the undeveloped rolls.

Adam stood outside. His hair was a mess and his eyes were glazed over like he hadn't slept. He didn't even look like he'd shaved. I just stared at him.

"Hey." His voice was soft and hopeful. "I, uh—hey."

"Hi." I didn't move to let him in.

"Don't be mad, Peter." He ran a hand through his hair and looked at me from under his lashes, sweet and gentle, like he hadn't been the one who'd shown up the day before with a *girlfriend*.

I crossed my arms.

"Peter—" Adam looked around. "Listen, can we talk?"

"Actually, no. We can't talk. I think Sarah said we weren't allowed to talk about it *ever*, and you concurred that she was, and I quote, 'right.'"

"What's your problem?" Adam narrowed his eyes and looked a hell of a lot like Sarah in that moment, angry and volatile. "I'm trying to *protect* you. Protect *us*."

"My problem? I'm afraid I can't talk about my *problem*."

He pushed me into the darkroom and locked the door behind him. I stared at him, angry, ready to fight. But he kissed me, pressing his body against mine and wrapping his arms around me tightly. He devoured my mouth, small bites and angry nips, rough licks and sweet sucking. I gasped, my hands clenching in his shirt as I pulled him closer.

Adam opened my belt buckle and unfastened my pants, pushed them off my hips, and got a fist around my cock, squeezing and jerking its length.

"I'm scared." Adam breathed, and then kissed my mouth, forestalling any comment from me. After plundering my mouth again, he broke away, pressing his forehead to mine. "I'm scared for you if people find out."

"Oh, and you're not at all scared for *you* and your precious reputation," I hissed, my hips bucking. My cock ached in his grip as my heart pounded.

"You make me crazy." Adam dropped to his knees, and I groaned as his mouth enveloped me, hot and wet, my knees going weak when he sucked hard.

He made *me* crazy too. He made me want to climb on top of the stupid Sunsphere downtown and scream, "I'm in love with Adam Algedi!" for the whole world to hear. He made me want to grab his head and fuck his mouth. He made me bang my head against the wall and stifle a cry when I came down his throat. He made me pull him up and kiss him blind afterward. He made me want to tell him I loved him when I didn't know what the hell was going on anymore.

With my head still spinning, I found myself on my knees returning the favor, one hand cupping Adam's balls, massaging gently, and the other grasping his ass. I loved the tender way he played with my hair when I did this for him, and when he finally came, he held me in place with fistfuls of my curls, as I almost choked on his cum.

I stood slowly, shaky and unsure, pushing my glasses back up the bridge of my nose. I zipped and buttoned my and Adam's pants while he caught his breath, and then he pulled me close, holding me tight.

He whispered, "This is the way it is, Peter. This is how things always *are,* how they have to be."

I asked, "How things always are? Did you do something like this in Jordan? In Rome?" Suddenly it struck me that in all likelihood, redheaded Marcus had been another me. "Did Marcus go along with it?"

Adam's hands were on my shoulders, and he tried to soothe me with languid strokes up and down my arms. "Of course he did."

Jealousy burned in my gut when I remembered the photos of Adam and Marcus at the Pantheon. Adam had called Marcus his *best friend.* I pulled away from him and smoothed my shirt, tucking it in to meet uniform regulations.

"Well, I'm not Marcus."

"No kidding." Adam laughed and grinned. "You're definitely not Marcus."

"Screw you."

Adam's eyebrows lowered. "Peter, I'm glad you're not Marcus. We were just friends."

"Funny, that's what you tell people about me too."

Adam ran his hands through his hair, frustrated. "What do you expect, Peter? It isn't safe. For either of us."

I was silent, because I didn't know the answer. I knew as well as he did we couldn't be honest about our relationship. Not now. Not unless we were both a whole lot braver—and kept handguns in our lockers to protect ourselves.

"Well?" Adam insisted on an answer.

"I don't want you dating other people. I don't think that's too much to ask. I want you to be with just me. Is that wrong?"

"No. But it isn't easy. People will talk. They already talk, Peter. I heard that asshole Eric Morgan making comments about you last month in calculus and now we know why. Plus there's that guy from your old school, the one from the coffee shop."

"Yeah." I swallowed.

"And we spend a lot of time together, you and me. This girl-friend thing will fix it so no one listens to Eric or thinks he's right."

Eric Morgan really was Kingsley's resident prick. Not only did he sneer at me whenever he walked past, but he'd spit in nerdy Stephen Layton's salad one day at lunch for laughs. Being Jason's cousin was the cherry on the Eric-is-a-dick sundae.

"Eric Morgan said something about me? You didn't tell me before."

"I didn't want you to know."

"Why? What did he say?"

"Don't make me repeat it."

"Tell me, Adam."

"He just said the same things that Jason guy said."

"Like what?"

Adam sighed and ran a hand over his face. "He said you were a fag, and I told him to shut up, and, true to form, he said I was a fag too."

"Aren't you?"

"No. I'm not." Adam's dark eyes pleaded for understanding.

"You sure suck cock like a fag," I spat out, a roaring rage grow-ing in me.

"Peter," Adam said, a note of pleading in his voice. "It's different. And listen, having a girlfriend will stop any trouble, okay? Take my word on it. It's a good plan."

It was *different?* In what way? In the way he refused to accept it, or in the way he was bisexual and not just flat-out gay like me? I really wanted to know, but no matter when or how I pushed him, Adam managed to evade answering me.

"I hate this. I hate you." I paused. "I really hate how this makes me feel."

"Peter?" Adam leaned over me then, eyes trained on mine.

"Yeah?"

"I love this." He ran his hand down my body, and I shivered under his touch. "I love you."

My heart stuttered in my chest and I couldn't breathe. "Yeah?"

"Yeah." Adam kissed me tenderly and pulled back to whisper against my lips. "I wish I didn't, but I really do."

"Oh." A wondering sense of happiness instantly drowned out the anger and fear. He loved me. We weren't just friends who had sex. He *loved* me.

"Oh," I said again, breathless and shocked. "I love you too."

Adam grinned and pulled me back into his arms, kissing me until I felt like the world ended and began in that little darkroom, and nothing else mattered.

✦   ✦   ✦

ON MONDAY, MILLAR Johansson, a small, hyper, straight-A type, and editor of the yearbook, approached me.

"Hey," he said, bouncing on his toes. "Adam Algedi told me to talk to you. He's signed up as a yearbook reporter and said you might help us out with the photography side of things?"

Adam had signed up for the yearbook? I wasn't too surprised since he *was* a writer, and I knew the guidance counselor had suggested he not rely on his extracurriculars from his previous years for his college applications. Especially since he hadn't even tried out for the swim or soccer teams.

I'd questioned him about that. I'd seen his swim trophies and knew he'd been pretty good, but he'd shrugged it off, saying he no longer saw the appeal of diving into freezing cold water first thing in the morning. I actually suspected something else—Adam wasn't very competitive, really. Not to mention, Kingsley's pool of prospects for each team was a lot bigger than the American school in Rome or Jordan, and against some of the more committed athletes, Adam didn't stand a chance. Yearbook was probably a better fit for him.

"What would I have to do? If I was in charge of the photography side of things?" I asked Millar.

"You'll be the one taking most of the pictures, of course. And you'd have the final say about which pictures get to go in the book. Well, Miss Patty has to approve it, but we know how Miss Patty is." Millar ran a hand through his fine blond hair, his sharp green eyes glowing. "You'll be required to attend all the yearbook meetings, but those are almost always fun. You can ask Adam about the rest."

I stuck out my bottom lip a little, thinking about the proposition.

"It's a big honor to be asked, Peter. This'll give you a great line on your college applications."

I shook his hand in acceptance and wondered just how this would result in me having orgasms with Adam more often. Because there was no doubt in my mind Adam would find a way to turn our positions on the yearbook staff into sexual gold mines, because Adam was always horny, always ready to go. He looked for every conceivable opportunity to get me alone with my cock out. He was a genius at finding opportunities.

I wasn't that different. I spent most of my waking hours *not* thinking about calculus, chemistry, or English literature, and instead trying to figure out when I could be on my knees with my mouth around Adam's dick again, or when his mouth could get around mine.

Needless to say, the girlfriend thing complicated matters in that regard.

Leslie and Adam had spent their first weekend together as a couple going to the mall on Saturday and a movie on Sunday. I'd spent that time at home wondering just what it meant for them to be alone. Even though Adam called me as soon as he got back to invite himself over, I was still wary of how this new thing with Leslie was going to cut into our time.

At the first meeting of the yearbook staff, Millar sipped coffee from a Giant Gulp cup, which he had filled from the pot in the teachers' lounge, and jiggled his knee in a frantic beat as he handed out assignments.

"Mandel, here's a list of the various school functions you'll want to attend to get pictures."

I looked over the list and sighed. I hadn't realized I was going to have to attend at least one football game, basketball game, volleyball game, tennis match, swim meet, and basically every other sport the school sponsored. But that was just the beginning—there was also chess club, drama club, geology club, and more.

"Do I have to actually go to the events? Can't we just have 'club picture day' or something?" I asked.

"Sure, if you want. But people are going to want to see themselves actually *doing* whatever-the-fuck, you know?"

"Sadie will definitely want a shot of herself moving that chess piece to victory," Adam said.

I shot him an annoyed glance, and he laughed.

"Algedi, here's a list of all the assignments for write-ups. We'll need one for each club and team, and then some independent stuff for the more candid shots Mandel takes."

Adam glanced over the list and nodded. "Not a problem."

"Oh, and definitely do a write-up about the Kingsley Pirates, okay? I want an interview with Mike and Van about it," Millar said, and then glanced at me. "Obviously, we'll need pictures."

He turned then to Darla Shields. She was in charge of rounding up corporate sponsors to reduce the out-of-pocket costs. "Have you talked to Mr. Riker about sponsoring a couple of full-page ads?"

Mr. Riker was Joy Riker's father, and he owned a chain of grocery stores in town, was richer than Midas, and generous to his daughter. If Darla could get Mr. Riker on board, then the money problems the yearbook committee faced every year would disappear.

Darla sighed heavily. "I don't know. I don't like him. He's, like, all into eating sprouts and vegetables and stuff."

Millar looked at her like she was an idiot. "So?"

Darla threw her hands in the air. "So, he farts a lot. I don't want to have to sit in the same room with him."

Adam and I cracked up, and Millar did too, followed by everyone else. I had to wonder if Joy was going to be pissed when this conversation got back to her.

"Fine, I'll meet with him myself."

"Take one for the team, Millar," Adam said.

The meeting lasted almost two hours, and when we broke away the school was basically empty. Adam said he had to stop by his locker to pick up something he'd forgotten, and I followed him, adjusting the straps of my backpack and fiddling with my camera, not paying much attention, too busy trying to decide how I was going to organize the club picture day.

I gasped when Adam grabbed my arm and pulled me around the corner into a dark custodial closet. It was pitch-black with the door closed and smelled like dirty mops.

"What are you doing?" I whispered, though I knew—his hands were all over me, his mouth already on my neck.

"I'm going to blow you."

"Here?"

He dropped to his knees as an answer, opening my pants and pulling out my dick.

"You're going to get us busted."

"Not if you're quiet."

Then I couldn't say anything more because he was sucking me off, and I had to use every single bit of effort not to moan or make any noise when I came.

Afterward, he didn't let me go down on him, saying he wanted to wait until we got home, but he wrapped his arms around me and shared my taste in a kiss.

"What was that all about?" I asked. "I didn't need it so bad that I couldn't wait."

"Yeah, you did," Adam whispered in my ear. "And I needed to do it to you, to remind you."

"I hadn't forgotten, Adam. I kind of live for it." I fumbled for the door handle, but Adam stilled my hand.

"I know, and that's why. Peter—I want you so bad. Even with everything else, I still want you all the time."

Everything else. That was code for Leslie. I thought of her kind smile and shoved away a surge of guilt.

I leaned against him and kissed his neck. "Okay, message received. Now, let's get the hell out of here before we get caught."

✦ ✦ ✦

ADAM TOOK TO spending every Friday night with Leslie, taking her to the movies, or dinner, or hanging out at her house. He said they were taking it slow and hadn't done more than kiss, and described their relationship as "glorified friends."

That was hard enough to take. Just the thought of him kissing her, or holding her the way he held me made me want to be sick, but I forced it from my mind. Instead, I focused on how to make *our* relationship even more special to him.

"I don't think it's a good idea," Adam said, kissing my inner thighs and rubbing his lips against my leg hair.

I was impaled on two of his twisting fingers and begging for him to fuck me. "Come on, Adam. I'm ready. I really am."

He sighed. "I know. But I'm not."

I groaned. He'd been saying that for a while now, telling me anal sex was something we couldn't take back, like I was going to regret it or something, and I couldn't get him to budge. Not even a little. Two fingers were all he'd put in, and he never wanted more than one of mine.

It was frustrating, because for as long as I'd been masturbating, I'd jerked off thinking of a cock in my ass. Adam had done it before with other guys. He'd done it with Marcus even. I couldn't understand, when he said he loved me, why he wasn't ready to do it with me.

I arched up as he pushed against my prostate, writhing, asking him just that.

"*Because* I love you. I'm scared enough as it is. If I fuck you, I'll want it all the time. I really will."

"So?" I countered. "Maybe I will too."

"Or maybe you won't. It's really intense, Peter. It's hard-core, and I want to wait."

He sucked my cock and began to milk my prostate in earnest, so all I could do was clutch his hair and try not to be too loud. It was so good, and I couldn't understand, if anal sex might be even better, why he didn't want to do it.

After we'd both come, Adam was lounging half-naked in my bed, still recovering from his own orgasm, when he said, "Peter, about Friday night, um, Leslie's friend Tina is going to go to the movies with the three of us, okay?"

"Why?" I tried to keep my tone free of any telltale signs of jealousy, but I was sure I didn't succeed. It was bad enough to be the third wheel on a date with Leslie, but to add another person in the mix meant I'd have even less of Adam's focus.

"Well, um…" Adam rolled up onto an elbow and looked down at me, hand already stroking soothingly over my stomach and chest. "I sort of set us up on a double date. Tina will be, you know, your date."

My eyes felt wider than Texas, wider than the Pacific Ocean. "What are you talking about? I'm gay. I don't date girls."

Adam frowned. "Peter, please. I know we try to ignore it, but people are saying things again."

I huffed in disbelief. "You told me this Leslie thing would fix it. You said it was the entire point of you getting a girlfriend."

"Yeah, well… They aren't talking about *me*."

I narrowed my eyes, sat up, grabbed his T-shirt, and tossed it his way. "Put that on."

Adam complied, rolling his eyes like I was being ridiculous to be upset about this. "Listen, the other night when we were at that football party getting that crap for the yearbook, I heard some guys talking about you, and it scared me."

"You're just afraid they'll think you're gay too."

Adam's expression darkened and he tensed. "I'm afraid the guy I'm in love with will get hurt by a bunch of assholes. That's what I'm afraid of, you prick."

I glared, trying to stay angry, but it was hard when he was looking at me like that, and part of me knew he was right.

"So, what, I go to this movie and that's it?"

"Yeah," Adam said. "Why not? And you might like her."

I knew Tina. She was a skinny strawberry-blond girl with a generous helping of freckles who hung around the group sometimes and laughed too hard at all of Sarah's jokes, desperate to fit in. Also, rumor had it she was kind of easy. Of course, it was just a rumor, but the gossip spread about me was true enough, maybe it was true about her too.

I suddenly understood the bigger picture.

"I'm not doing anything with her."

Adam looked a little uncomfortable. "A kiss wouldn't be that bad, Peter."

"Really? You're okay with me kissing some girl? What am I saying? Of course you are. *You* kiss some girl all the time and think *I* should be okay with it!"

Adam's jaw was tight. "First, Leslie isn't 'some girl,' she's a really good friend. And second, hell yeah I'll kiss her and ask you to kiss Tina if it means not giving this up." He gestured between us. "You mean that much to me, Peter."

I shook my head. I didn't get it. I could see being afraid for my safety or for his own, but he wouldn't lose me. Unless he was afraid someone might kill me. I bowed my head, defeated. It wasn't as though that was outside of the realm of possibilities.

"Fine," I said. "I'll go to the stupid movie. But I'm not kissing her."

"Hold her hand?" Adam asked.

I sighed and flung myself back on the pillow, staring at the ceiling. "I might hold her hand," I conceded. It was unfair, but then what had my father always told me? *Life isn't fair, Petey-boy. It's a bunch of lopsided bullshit.*

✦   ✦   ✦

DURING THE MOVIE, I held Tina's hand. It was cold and small, and I felt like an asshole. Adam and Leslie, however, kissed and cuddled, making lots of wet sounds with their mouths. I wanted to go home and die. I hated him, and I hated the entire universe.

Afterward, we dropped the girls off and Adam drove me home.

I planned to get out of the car, slam the door without a goodbye, and not invite him in. But he surprised me by saying, "Hey, I know that was hard. Thank you."

I snorted. "You're not welcome. And I'm not doing it again."

"I know. You don't have to. I was wrong. We'll keep you safe some other way."

I didn't know what to say to that. I wanted to ask if he'd been jealous seeing me holding Tina's hand, but I really didn't think he had been, and I'd feel stupid if I asked and he said no.

Mostly, I suspected he saw how bad I was at faking it, and decided exposing Tina, or any other girl, to my ineffectual attempts at pretending to be straight would more likely result in them discovering how very gay I was instead.

I opened the door and then hesitated. "You could spend the night."

Adam groaned and threw his head back. "God, I want to. But I have to get home. I promised Leslie I'd call her at ten. She has something she wants to ask me."

"Oh." My relief he'd let me off the hook with Tina turned bitter. "What do you think she wants?"

"I don't know. She wouldn't say."

"You could call her from here," I offered, wanting the reassurance of seeing his lips wrapped around my cock to wash away the image of those same lips kissing Leslie.

"I could. Would you mind? I might have to talk to her awhile. Like a good boyfriend."

I bit my bottom lip and fought with myself. The situation we were in was wrong. I knew that, and I felt unbearably guilty lying to Leslie. But I didn't know how to make it be any different.

"Come on," I said. "I can handle it."

✧　✧　✧

AROUND THAT TIME, the group started a new ritual. Friday night was "date night" and all the couples went out on their own, while those of us who were single sat around at home feeling like losers. Or, in my case, trying hard not to think about my boyfriend sucking face with his girlfriend.

But Saturday night was "party night."

Someone's parents were always out of town, or were going to be out late at a party themselves, and word would go around about where we were all supposed to meet up.

On this particular Saturday, we were at Van's house sitting in a circle on the floor with a Ouija board in the middle of the group. I sat cross-legged with my back to the wall, scratching at my arms beneath the new, itchy wool sweater my mother had bought for me. She'd said the gray-on-black design brought out my eyes and, vainly, I'd hoped Adam would think I looked good enough in it to ignore Leslie tonight. I'd been wrong again, as usual.

I straightened my glasses and watched Adam and Leslie across the board from me. They looked the picture of an adoring and adorable couple. Adam's skin glowed against the cream color of his soft sweater, and his jeans fit perfectly. Leslie was the epitome of cuteness in her Gap jeans and colorful Benetton sweater. She sat on his lap, snuggling close, and Adam's soft smile implied he was more than satisfied to let her. Guilt and jealousy clawed at my gut.

I pulled my gaze away toward Sarah and Mike. They shared a soft-looking brown-flecked afghan stretched over their shoulders. Mike wore a mischievous smile as he tapped at the edge of the Ouija board.

"Okay, first, an opening toke." Tina giggled, lighting the joint. She sat with her legs tucked under carefully, her blue, frilly so-called "baby doll" dress exposing plenty of thigh.

"Toke? Who says that anymore, Tina?" Van asked grumpily. He'd been in a bad mood all night, ever since he and Allison had returned from their little rendezvous upstairs.

"Me," Tina laughed proudly, passing the joint across to Allison.

Allison tossed her dark hair and took a long hit, careful not to let ash fall on her black lacy blouse.

"How do you say, 'wanna get high?' in Italian, Adam?" Leslie asked, playing with the inseam of his jeans.

"Facciamoci una canna?" Adam murmured, lumping her blond hair into three hanks and making a clumsy braid. She grabbed his hand and kissed the palm, smiling over her shoulder at him.

Van pressed the joint into my hand, and I turned to Sarah to pass it on.

"Oh, *come on*, Peter. Don't tell me you aren't going to smoke up." Van rolled his eyes as if this confirmed my utter lameness.

"No thanks," I answered quietly, hoping they'd just let it drop.

"But, Petey-sweetie, everyone has to be high, or it's no fun!" Tina said.

Leslie nodded vigorously, almost shaking out the braid Adam had made, and Allison added, "You have to, Peter!"

"Peter doesn't smoke pot," Adam said firmly.

"Yeah, but—" Tina started.

"He *doesn't smoke pot*. End of discussion." Adam accepted the joint from Mike and took a hit before passing it to Leslie.

Allison pushed a dark-brown lock of hair out of her eyes. "Have you ever tried it, Peter? It's really—"

Adam stood up, dumping Leslie on the floor. "I said he doesn't smoke. Leave him alone."

Van and Mike exchanged glances. Sarah shifted nervously.

"It's okay, Adam." I turned to Allison. "I had a bad experience, and I don't want a repeat." I motioned at Adam. "Sit down. Let's just play. It's not a big deal." I nodded at the Ouija board.

Adam glanced at Sarah and then slowly dropped down next to Leslie. "Sorry, I just get annoyed when people don't take no for an answer."

"*Yeah*, Van," Allison said teasingly, but that appeared to be the wrong thing to say, because he scooted farther away from her.

"Well, um, so—" I indicated the board again, eager to break the tension.

Tina, who'd been holding the joint limply, took a long drag and passed it on to Allison. "Okay, boys and girls," Tina said in an attempt at a spooky voice. "Last chance to just play spin the bottle."

"This is the lamest party I've been to in years, just so you know," Sarah said.

"Thanks for sharing. You say that every week," Tina countered.

"And every week it's true!"

"Okay, everyone has to put their finger on the triangle-thingy—and no pushing it!"

Sarah leaned forward, groaning and rolling her eyes. She placed her finger on the indicator. "Why don't we all just find a room and have sex?"

"Together?" Allison giggled, adding her finger. "All of us?"

Sarah wrinkled her nose. "Ew!"

Tina, Adam, and Leslie all added their fingers to the 'triangle-thingy,' as Tina called it, while Mike, Van, and I still held out.

"I'll just watch," I said.

"Petey-sweetie," Tina crooned. "You never do *anything*."

I added my finger. It was better than going through another scene over something stupid. I really hated the "Petey-sweetie" crap, but didn't know how to tell her to stop. Worse, the other girls had picked up the habit of calling me that too.

Sarah elbowed Mike, and he rolled his eyes, giving in, which left Van.

"I vote for the sex," Van quipped.

"Too bad! No sex for you!" Allison giggled and, again, it was the wrong thing to say, because Van stood.

"I'm getting more pizza," he said as he stalked into the kitchen.

Allison shrugged. "Whatever. Let's play."

Tina closed her eyes and took a deep breath. "Okay, everyone concentrate now."

We all took a deep breath too.

She said in a loud, firm voice, "Is there anyone there who wants to talk to us tonight?"

Slowly, slowly, slowly the triangle circled and then crawled over to the YES. Tina squealed and scooted closer to the board.

Sarah rolled her eyes and whispered to me, "This is so fucking *lame*. I seriously vote for the sex too."

I glanced at Mike to see if he'd heard her, and noticed he'd taken his hand off the pointer. He had it resting on her back, rubbing in slow circles.

Tina intoned, "What is your name, oh wandering spirit?"

Sarah cracked up and pulled her finger away, curling over herself. "Oh God, save me from this fucking hick town!"

The indicator swirled in circles before spelling out *ARATHAM*.

"Are you pushing it?" Tina asked. "Because I'm not pushing it."

We all shook our heads. Sarah snorted and sniffed, managing to stop laughing. She propped herself up with her elbows on her knees, watching.

"Will anyone in this room die this year?" Mike asked, doing a much better spooky-voice than Tina.

NO

"Is anyone in this room in love with anyone else in this room?" Tina asked wistfully. I knew she had hopes that Mike might have feelings for her, despite the fact that he was clearly wrapped around Sarah's finger.

YES

"Who?"

ADAM

Tina and Leslie smiled at each other. Leslie grabbed Adam and kissed him. "You pushed it didn't you?" she asked.

He glanced at me for a millisecond. "No. I didn't push it."

The indicator swirled and swirled and swirled, moving suddenly again with much more force and velocity to spell out another name.

PETER

I jerked my finger away. "Someone's pushing it."

Adam shook his head and I realized he didn't even have his finger on the indicator. Sarah didn't either. Who was pushing it?

Tina gasped and looked at me with wide, gooey eyes. "Who do you love, Peter?"

I stared blankly at her, confused and irritated. Then suddenly it hit me. She thought I had a secret thing for her. Oh, God.

I blurted, "I love…my mom."

"Sick, Peter," Allison commented.

"You thought it. Not Peter." Tina giggled. "Peter is too sweet to think sick things like that, aren't you, Petey-sweetie?"

I avoided Adam's eyes and shrugged. "I'm going to have some more pizza before Van eats it all."

Adam said, "Good thinking, Peter the Eater. I'll join you."

Sarah jumped up. "Me too."

"But guys," Tina whined. "You're ruining the game."

"The game was lame, Tina. I already told you," Sarah said, pulling Mike up off the floor and leading the way into the kitchen.

I thought I'd made it home free, but Tina tugged on my arm just as I reached the threshold into the kitchen.

"Peter, can I talk to you?"

I caught Adam's eye and he smirked, covering his mouth to

hide his laughter.

"Sure, Tina."

I let her guide me over to the fireplace and stood uncomfortably as she smiled sweetly, high as hell.

"Peter, I really like you. I'm so flattered you care for me."

I bit my cheek to keep from laughing at the absurdity of it. I glanced up and saw Sarah in the doorway, nodding her head and making a rolling hand gesture, mouthing, "Go with it!"

"Um, yeah. I'm glad you're, uh, flattered."

"I so am, Peter. I've wondered why you've never asked me out on another date, but maybe I just misunderstood your signals?"

I ran my hand over my face. "Well, actually, Tina, I'm not really able to date anyone right now, so—you know, you didn't misunderstand."

Tina looked confused. "Not able to date? Why not?"

"Because, I—" I looked to Sarah. She shook her head in disgust, turned on her heel and left me on my own. "Because I—"

Don't like girls. Because I like boys. Because I like tabs instead of slots? What the hell was I supposed to say?

"Are your parents really strict or something?"

"Yes!" I nodded in relief. "Yeah, uh, really, really strict. They don't even know I'm here tonight. They think I'm staying over at Adam's." True enough. "And they're really overprotective and stuff. They want me to get a scholarship. They don't think I have time to date," I babbled.

Adam stood in the doorway now, listening with an amused grin. He finally interrupted, saying, "Hey, Eater, what's the deal? I thought you wanted pizza?"

"Yeah, pizza." I put my hands on Tina's shoulders and moved her aside. "Thanks for being so understanding. I'm going to get pizza now. You're the best."

Adam snorted back a laugh.

"You suck," I whispered as I passed him.

"Later," was his soft reply.

✧　✧　✧

ADAM PICKED ME up first, kissing me quickly in the car before we pulled out of the driveway on our way to get Leslie. We were headed to the pep rally, Leslie for cheering purposes, and me and Adam for yearbook assignments.

Adam hummed happily along to a mixed tape of songs by The Cure. He looked at me and grinned. "I'm glad we're all going to this together."

I shrugged and looked out the window. Sometimes it unnerved me how easily Adam seemed to integrate me and Leslie both into his life, fitting her into the role of girlfriend, and me into the role of best friend. It wasn't so simple for me.

"How's your journal in Dr. Landry's class going?" Adam asked, changing the subject after my lack of response.

"Words hard. Me no like them."

Adam chuckled. "What did you write for yesterday's assignment?"

"I tried to describe some of the pictures I've taken of acorns and oak trees. It was sort of lame. I barely scraped two pages together."

Although that assignment had been easier than the one when Dr. Landry handed a nail to everyone in the class, saying, "That's a nail, boys and girls. Look at it long and hard, talk to it, ask it questions. Then tell me its story."

What was I supposed to do with that? In the end I'd free-associated for two pages. Dr. Landry had scribbled, "Excellent work, Mr. Mandel!" across the top of the page when he passed our journals back. I'd pretty much decided Dr. Landry was a total fruitcake.

"What did you write about?" I asked.

Adam turned the music down and put his hand on the back of my seat. "I talked about the acorn inside everyone. You know, the potential within us all, and how just like every oak tree is different, we're all different too. Only I was a lot more eloquent than that. Dr. Landry seemed to like it."

I grinned, happy that Adam was proud of himself. He was smart and talented. He deserved to feel good about what he accomplished.

Adam licked his lips, smiled at me, and then cleared his throat. "I'm going to take Leslie home with me tonight."

"What?"

Adam swallowed nervously, and I felt like I got whiplash from the sudden change of topic. "I just wanted you to know. I'm going to take her home and, well, her folks are out of town. She's going to spend the night. I'm going to maybe have sex with her."

"You're going to *what?*"

"I care about her, Peter. She's a good friend, and she cares about me too. It's perfect, really. Besides, it's just for this year, until I go away to college."

"So, you're just going to have sex with someone else for a year. That's all." If I sounded sarcastic, it couldn't be helped. How was this proposal something I could even process, much less accept?

Adam rubbed his eyes with his fingertips. "Why do you have to put it like that?"

My eyes bugged out. "Put it like what? I could put it like this, 'So, Adam, you're going to put your dick into your girlfriend's pussy, but still suck my cock most days after school, and still tell me you love me, and still kiss me with the same lips you use to suck her clit.' I *could* put it like *that.*"

Adam's mouth hung open in a mix of astonishment and rage. "Peter, shut up."

"You're going to *fuck her,* and you want me to *shut up?*"

He pulled the car over into a small park off Northshore. It was deserted except for a dark brown Cadillac parked near the rocks leading down to the lake.

Adam took long deep breaths, his hands shaking when he raised them to run through his hair. "Look, I've been dating her a few months now, and it's starting to look suspicious. She keeps…well, it's getting harder to say no."

"So you *want* to fuck her."

Adam groaned. "I don't know. I'm a guy, and she's hot."

"*What?*" I nearly screeched. "You're *gay!*"

"I keep telling you I'm not, and—"

"Fine, you're bi. I don't get it, but even if you're bi, you can say no."

"If you felt anything for girls then you'd know how hard that is when she's got her panties off and—"

"She's had her panties off? You told me you were just kissing. You said *just kissing!* You said glorified friends, remember?"

Adam flinched and hunched over the steering wheel, hiding his face.

"What have you done with her?" I said, my voice whispery but full of rage. "I want to know."

"Stuff," Adam said, barely audible where he had his head buried.

"What kind of 'stuff?'"

He didn't answer.

Sick to my stomach, I got out of the car. The cold air kept me from throwing up. I bit my lip to keep from crying, but even so my eyes filled with tears.

I'd believed him when he told me he'd only kissed her.

"Peter, get in the car," Adam said after a few minutes.

I ignored him. Five minutes or more passed and I finally got back in, buckling my seat belt and saying nothing.

Adam said with terrible calm, "We're going to go pick up Leslie now, and we're done with this conversation."

"Yeah, because you'd hate to have to talk about this. Then you'd have to think about it, and you'd hate yourself. We can't have that, can we?" I spat the words out, my arms crossed so hard on my chest that bruises formed on my biceps.

Adam started the car without another word, but I noticed his hands shook, and he bit his lip. When we pulled into Leslie's driveway he muttered, "You're right. I do hate myself," before he got out of the car. I moved into the back seat, my stomach roiling.

He told her I was suddenly sick with a migraine, and I knew I looked the part. Leslie clucked over me, but I kept my head down, buried in my hands, refusing to even look at her. I didn't want her to be nice to me. I wanted to hate her. But I couldn't, and that made it all so much worse.

Adam didn't say anything else as he drove me back home. Leslie's hand twined into his hair, and she leaned close, whispering in his ear. He nodded. I averted my eyes and tried to think of anything but them, anything but Leslie's hands all over Adam, about the *stuff* they'd done, about what he wanted to do with her.

My heart thudded painfully when Adam pulled up to my house, turned around and said in an odd voice, "Feel better, man."

Leslie said, "Yeah, feel better, Peter. We'll miss you tonight."

As I opened the car door and stepped out, I heard my voice saying, "Thanks. I will. Goodnight, Leslie. Have a good time."

My mom sat in the living room, flipping through a book. She looked up and smiled. "I thought you were going to a pep rally, baby?"

I felt the horrible press of tears in my throat and shrugged, heading for the stairs.

"Peter?"

I took the stairs two at a time.

"What happened?" she called after me, not getting up from the sofa.

"Nothing, Mom."

She called from below, "Okay, baby. You can tell me in the morning!"

I slammed my bedroom door and locked it, just in case she got curious. I fell onto the bed, burying my face in the pillow. I felt carved out and hollow.

I'd been lying there for what seemed like forever when there was a soft knock on the door.

"Peter? Adam's on the phone."

"Tell him I'm asleep." I took a deep breath. "And Mom?"

"Yeah?"

"I *don't* want to talk about it in the morning."

She was quiet. Finally she said, "All right. You know I love you?"

"Sure." And I loved her too. But she couldn't help me. She didn't even *know* me. And she didn't want to.

I heard her go back downstairs and made out the muffled sound of her voice as she delivered my message to Adam.

Chapter Eleven

AROUND SEVEN THE next evening, my mother knocked on the door and turned the handle, humming in surprise to find it locked. "Peter, honey, did you eat dinner?"

"Yes," I lied.

"Peter? Listen, open the door, okay? I want to talk with you."

"I said I didn't want to talk about it, Mom." I pulled the pillow over my head and tried to ignore the fact she hadn't moved away and was just standing there silently.

"Abe! Abe, come up here!"

My father clomped up the stairs and then his shadow joined my mother's at the crack under the door. I heard them whispering and hoped after all of these years they wouldn't turn into snoops now.

"Peter? Son? Open the door, please." Dad sounded gruff and nervous. He didn't like these kinds of things any more than Mom did, yet she always used her "fragile state" to get him to do the difficult work of raising me.

I just stayed in bed and pondered what would happen if I ignored them both.

"Peter?"

I flung off the covers and jerked open the door. "What? I'm trying to sleep."

Mom pushed my dad in my direction, and he used his larger size to get into the room and turn on the light. I sank to the bed and covered my face with my hands. God, why now? Why after all this time were they going to ask questions now?

"Jessica? Can you leave me and Peter alone?"

Mom went back downstairs and Dad sat on the bed next to me. He put his arm around my shoulder. "Your mom tells me you went out last night and came home upset, you haven't left your room today, and you aren't eating."

I was surprised she'd noticed.

"Is this about a girl?"

I laughed bitterly. "You could put it that way. Yeah."

"Do you want to talk about it?"

"Do I look or sound like I want to talk about it? I think I clearly told Mom I *didn't* want to talk about it." I sighed heavily. "And yet here you are."

"This isn't like you, Peter. This attitude."

"Well, I'm a teenager. Cut me some slack."

Dad was silent for a few minutes, and then he started rubbing my back softly. I relaxed a little under his gentle touch, remembering when I'd been sick as a kid and he'd sit by my bed and rub my back for what seemed like hours.

"So, can I try to guess what happened?"

I shrugged. He'd never guess. Not in a million years.

"Okay, then. I'm thinking there's someone you really like, and something happened last night that makes you think maybe you don't have a real shot."

That was close enough to the truth. I nodded.

Dad squeezed my shoulder. "I know it sounds terrible to say this right now, but there are plenty of fish in the sea, and there's going to be someone so much better, so much more wonderful, who will look at you and see what a terrific, kind, and giving person you are. And that'll be the right person for you."

I thought about it for a minute. "Maybe. Or maybe this is the right person for me, and I'm not the right one for them?"

Dad squeezed my shoulder again. "The black-and-white view-point of youth. The limited and yet limitless horizon. Ah, yes, I remember it well."

I stiffened against the patronizing tone, but Dad just hugged me closer.

I almost said it then. I almost said, *"Dad, it's Adam. I'm in love with him, and I'm gay."* Such a mix of anger, hurt, fear, and need churned inside me at that moment. I even opened my mouth to let it out, but then he asked, "Did you try to kiss her?"

Any thought of telling him the truth left my body with a rush of breath. I closed my eyes and pulled away. "No."

"Ah. I thought maybe that's when she shot you down."

"I think there's another guy she's interested in." Lies and more lies. What was another one at this point?

Dad sat in silence for a few more minutes and then said, "If you come downstairs, I'll make spaghetti for you. I bought Ragu. Your favorite."

I smiled at that. It was our joke. Other families had recipes for spaghetti sauce passed down through generations. We had Ragu. We didn't even like it much, but we ate it anyway. I didn't think my dad had ever bought another brand.

"Okay, you'll clean the dishes too?"

"Of course!" Dad snorted. "I mean, it isn't as if your mother is going to do it!"

✧   ✧   ✧

AS IT TURNED out, Ragu wasn't a cure for a broken heart. I tossed and turned all night, thinking about Adam fucking Leslie. I imagined him sinking into her wet pussy, his eyes rolled back and his body shaking with lust. I *knew* that was what he'd been waiting for. He liked pussy, not ass, and her sweet folds were the reason he'd never wanted to screw me. I fixated on that thought. Tortured myself with it.

I expected to hear from him on Saturday, but I didn't, and I started to despair. I wanted him to call me and say he hadn't fucked her. Or if he had, that it hadn't been good, and he was sorry. I wanted to hear that he never wanted to fuck her again. He only wanted me. But he didn't call. And he didn't come over.

I finally fell asleep thinking surely he'd call on Sunday. He'd told me he loved me, and I'd believed him. It couldn't be over. Not really. He'd break up with her now, wouldn't he? He'd proven what he needed to prove—he could do the deed with a girl. And fine, maybe he did really like it. But he liked me *more*. Didn't he? Why did he owe it to her to stay together now?

I was sick with myself for even thinking that. Leslie was a good person, a good friend. I knew exactly why he might stay with her.

The person knocking on my kitchen door on Sunday morning wasn't Adam, but Sarah. Dad had already left to go up to his office on campus, and Mom was, as usual, writing with the door shut. It was just me, Harry, and the cornflakes.

I opened the door and let Sarah inside. As she gazed around, taking in the place, her eyes softened. "It's like a real house where real people live."

"Um, yeah," I said, confused.

"It's not some stupid palace like everyone else at Kingsley has. And it's not like our place—it's not like some frat house."

Adam had told me Sarah missed living with her mom and having a regular home life, and despite acting like the queen bee at school, she was sometimes uncomfortable with the amount of wealth the other students had and took for granted. "*We've traveled the world,*" Adam had told me. "*We've seen poverty. Sarah's a bitch, but she's not actually stupid or heartless.*"

I gestured toward the box of cereal. "It's not much, but you're welcome to some if you want."

Sarah shook her head and dropped down in the seat next to mine, not removing her coat, as if she didn't intend to stay long. "Adam's upset."

I shrugged and dug into my cereal. *Adam* was upset? Good. I wanted him to be in at least as much pain as I was.

"He took Leslie home early yesterday morning, before I even got back from Allison's, and now he won't talk to me. And he won't leave his bedroom."

"Huh." I took a large bite of cereal and took my time chewing.

"Yeah. Peter—" Sarah bit her lip. "I'm not sure if I should tell you this or not. I'm not sure if it will just make things worse, but—" She met my eye squarely. "He had sex with her. And now he thinks you won't forgive him."

I gagged on my cereal and had to spit it out into my bowl. Sarah looked disgusted, but my heaving stomach didn't care. I stood. Hearing Sarah say the words made it even more true, and my mind supplied me with images of them fucking.

Sarah stood too, her face pale. For the first time since I'd met her, she looked unsure. "One of you had to..." She spread her hands in a pleading gesture. "I know you've never been in this kind of situation before. I know you don't understand how important it is to keep it a secret, but Peter, people were already talking about the two of you."

"I don't care." I felt like I'd been broken open.

Sarah shook her head. "Don't you understand? Think about how miserable you would be if it got out. Think about how you'd feel if no one would talk to you, if guys tried to beat you up all the time, if you were completely and totally snubbed by anyone that mattered. And that's just for starters. Just think about it, Peter."

I thought about it, and I was pretty sure I couldn't be any more miserable than I was at that moment. "You should leave and tell Adam not to call me. Tell him I'll get a ride to school with my dad from now on."

Sarah's eyes flew wide, and she looked frightened. "No, Peter. He'll be so mad at me for coming here. He'll think I did or said something to make you angrier."

"Sarah, if you think I give a shit right now about whether or not Adam is mad at you…" I strode to the kitchen door, shaking, and threw it open. "Get out."

Sarah shoved a lock of hair behind her ear and ducked her head. "I'm sorry, Peter," she whispered as I shut the door behind her.

✧　✧　✧

THAT AFTERNOON, I tried to cope by taking photos. I wallowed in misery, pressing myself into dark corners and seeking out the most corroded and corrupt things I could find to shoot. I twisted my body into contortions and came close to using a knife to carve some of the pain into my skin, thinking how nicely that would come out on film, but I didn't.

I rode to school with my father, who took my lie that Adam made the swim team and now had early practice in stride. I avoided everyone for most of the day, hiding out in the darkroom until I was late to assembly, and then ducking back into that welcoming refuge for lunch and free period.

But the hardest thing of all was avoiding looking at Adam when he sat next to me in English. He wouldn't leave me alone, trying to make eye contact with me constantly. The fact that I refused to talk to him didn't seem to make a difference.

History of Religious Philosophy sucked. I'd always sat in the front row next to Leslie, and now I couldn't deal with seeing her, or pretending nothing was going on, or trying to come up with some kind of explanation for anything.

Luckily, Leslie wasn't in the room when I arrived, so I sat at the back in a chair by the window overlooking the soccer fields. I kept my eyes on the muddy grass, nearly lifting my camera to take a shot of the dark lines of the trees against the gray sky, but I didn't want to draw attention to myself.

"So, why are we sitting in the back today?" Leslie asked as she slid into the seat next to me, the one usually occupied by Lyle Fredericks. She unzipped her backpack to pull out the text.

I glanced over and shrugged, sullen and frustrated. "I don't know. I felt like changing things, I guess."

Leslie's eyebrows quirked and she half smiled. "Look, I don't know what's going on, but you've been hiding out in the darkroom, which isn't unusual, except for the fact that it *is* when you miss lunch and free period, *and* Adam is sulking like he just lost his best friend." Leslie paused meaningfully. "Which would be *you*, by the way."

I shuffled my papers around on my desk before saying coldly, "Yeah, I suppose that's the role I'm playing in this story."

Leslie watched me as I found a fresh sheet in my pad for taking notes, flipped through the textbook, and found the reading we'd had the night before. I started to copy out sentences I'd already highlighted, just to pretend like I had something to do.

"Right," Leslie said, uncertainly. "Okay, so…" she trailed off, her head tilting as she examined me carefully.

I slammed my pen down. "What? Can't you see I'm working on this? I need to study. I'm behind on my work, okay? I don't have time to be…whatever I've been doing. I don't have time for it. I'm busy. Don't you understand?"

Leslie's eyebrows lifted in surprise, and hurt flashed over her features. "You don't have time to sit in the front of the class with me?" She spoke slowly, taking her time to enunciate each word, calling me out on my bullshit.

"Listen, I don't want to be his friend anymore. If you want to know *why*, then ask *him*. I don't want to be in the middle of it." I gathered up my stuff and walked out of class as Mrs. Parson walked in.

I headed toward the bathroom and ducked inside for nearly thirty minutes. I spent the time in one of the stalls trying not to cry and knocking my head against the metal partition to try to stop myself from thinking.

When I finally walked back into class, Leslie was sitting in the back still, so I took up my usual spot in the front row. Mrs. Parson looked at me with concern, obviously worried, but seemed to find my uncomfortable expression enough to forestall any embarrassing questions about what had taken me so long in the bathroom. I was there now and that seemed good enough for her.

I wished it had been good enough for everyone else too, but it seemed my "friends" still thought they were my friends, even though I didn't want them to be. The irony of this wasn't lost on me, but I just couldn't deal with anyone.

On Thursday, Mike caught up with me in the hallway next to my locker and punched my shoulder in greeting. "Hey, man, what's up?"

I held up the book I'd just retrieved. "Spanish," I said.

"Cool. So, where've you been?"

"At home. At school. Yearbook meetings. The darkroom. The usual."

Mike nodded, his expression a mix of confusion and relief. "Same old, same old, then." He punched my shoulder again. "Okay, well, there's a party tomorrow night at my place. The folks are in Meh-hee-co for a week. Be there."

I smiled faintly and waited until he was walking away to mumble, "Thanks, I think I'll be square instead."

Mike had only told me about it because he knew something was up between me and Adam. Or else he would've just told Adam to tell me, or assumed Adam would bring me along. In the past, there'd never been a need for a special invite.

I knew if I stayed out of his way, out of all of their ways, I'd be forgotten soon enough, and things would go back to the way they should've been all along.

✧ ✧ ✧

IT WASN'T AS easy as I'd imagined it would be to break things off with Adam. And not only because I found it hard to breathe through the pain, but also because I hadn't taken into account the way the rumor mill of a small school operates.

I was the center of more scrutiny than I'd been since the very first day. As I walked down the hall, girls whispered, growing silent and wide-eyed as I got closer. I had people I'd never talked to before try to befriend me to elicit confidences, asking me not-too-subtle questions about what was up between me and Adam directly after offering to share their notes or gum with me.

I didn't know what everyone was saying. I could guess, but I was so intent on avoiding everything and everyone, focusing completely on schoolwork and photography that I managed to tune out the details.

Three weeks into my return to a lonely life, Dr. Landry sat backward on his desk, scratching his chin and gazing out the window. We'd been reading some poems from the World War II era when he'd spaced out. He often faded away in the middle of class, sometimes for just a moment and sometimes for minutes on end. Today he seemed lost and not apt to return any time soon.

William Henry took the opportunity to pass a dirty magazine around in the back of the room, and Adam opened up his journal, scribbling away in silence. I got out my camera and trained it on Dr. Landry, wanting to capture his abstraction.

The sudden snick of the shutter caused Dr. Landry to jerk, and he turned to me with a strange look on his face. I was just about to apologize for surprising him when he spoke.

"Mr. Mandel, do you know what it's like to wake in the dark to the sound of machine guns firing and the smell of smoke?"

He paused, his eyes boring into mine. "Do you know what it's like to watch a man get filleted open by bullets from an automatic weapon? To know, even if you go home again to your wife and child, you aren't the man who left them? That they've killed all of the poetry in your soul and you will *never* get it back?"

I swallowed hard, feeling all eyes on me. The silence in the room was like molasses, heavy and thick. "No, sir."

Dr. Landry stared at me for a long, long moment and then stood slowly, moved over to his desk, and flipped through some items before settling on a sheet of paper. He dropped it onto my desk, saying quietly, "Oh, but I think you have a small idea, Mr. Mandel. Just a small one. God willing, you'll never have a bigger one."

I looked down at a copy of one of my recent photographs. Me at the old hideout, cold and alone, shirt off and wadded in a corner. I was curled in on myself, misery radiating from every line of my body, eyes hollow and tired.

"That's an expression of something deep, Mr. Mandel."

I looked up at him and met his eyes, biting my lip to keep my face free of expression, free of the despair.

"You dropped it when you were in here yesterday. It's lovely, though hideous work."

The people around me leaned in to see, so I slid the photo into my notebook to hide it.

Dr. Landry turned away and took a step back. "Journal topic— death of poetry, loss of soul. Class dismissed."

I took my time putting my stuff away, waiting for Adam to leave the room.

Dr. Landry caught my arm as I stood, and he studied my face. "If you ever find the words to go with that picture, Mr. Mandel, I'm here to talk. If you don't want to talk, you can put the words into your journal. And if the words never come, you can always share your pictures with me."

I nodded, throat tight.

"Your friend is waiting for you."

Adam stood in the doorway. I knew I wouldn't be able to put off talking to him any longer, so I followed him outside.

The wind swept over the football field. Autumn was dissolving into a vicious winter with temperatures already in the thirties. Adam led me to a hidden place underneath the bleachers and I stood against a pillar, trying to stay out of the chilly blasts. I watched him pace in front of me, hands ripping through his hair, breathing hard.

I'd refused to speak to him for nearly three weeks now. During that time, he'd tried everything from ambushing me at my front door, to calling and begging my mom to please make me talk to him.

Mom had thought that exchange rather bizarre, and she'd asked me, fear lining her face, if I thought Adam might like me as more than a friend.

I'd replied bitterly, "Definitely not."

It was the first time I noticed her giving me a considering look, as though she was thinking, *"Is he...could he be...?"* But even the idea had proved too much for her, and she'd taken a Valium and gone to bed.

I leaned my head back, willing Adam to just get on with it. Finally, he stopped in front of me, biting down hard on his lip until a white line appeared in the skin under his teeth.

"I love you," he said.

He said it like that was supposed to make up for everything, like that was supposed to negate the fact he was still dating and screwing Leslie.

"I do, Peter. I love you. Or maybe I'm obsessed with you. I don't know. I find myself outside your house at night, and I just want to be inside with you. I can't stop thinking about you and wanting you. I'll do anything. Anything at all."

I shook my head. I couldn't believe he still didn't get it. Maybe if he'd ended things with Leslie on his own, maybe then, but I wasn't going to voice the ultimatum that was implicit in every move I'd made since I'd gotten out of his car that night.

"Please, Peter. Just talk to me."

I took off my glasses, scrubbed a hand over my face, and resettled them so I could see. "What do you want me to say?"

Adam's face melted with relief at the sound of my voice. "I want you to say we can work this out."

"Adam, we can't. I'm not willing to stand aside while you screw Leslie just so no one thinks we're gay. Because you know what? I'm gay."

Adam scrunched up his face, obviously fighting for some kind of control, pain radiating from him. "Being away from you hurts."

"I know the feeling."

Adam moved toward me. I tried to step backward, but I'd trapped myself against the pillar.

I managed to whisper, "Wait," before his lips were on mine and his thigh pressed between my own, his body warm and hard, hands gripping my hips and pulling me into a full-body grind. My glasses ended up in the dirt and my sweater and button-up shirt shoved up so Adam could get his hands on my skin.

I gasped. Just a few more grinds and I was going to end up with a very sticky problem and a stain that'd be really hard to explain.

Adam cupped my face, searching my eyes. "Take me back. Please. I need you."

I wanted to say yes. I truly did. I took a deep breath, determined to be strong. "With or without Leslie?"

Adam kissed me again. His silence was the answer.

I pushed him aside and walked away without looking back.

Part III

December, 1990

Chapter Twelve

EVENTUALLY, WINTER BREAK scuttled onto the horizon. The girls drew Secret Santa names, and everyone discussed their plans. Despite avoiding the Algedis and the rest of their group, I still overheard the gossip about them. In fact, it seemed like people purposely talked about them in front of me just to see if I would react.

Rumor told me that for a while it wasn't clear if Adam and Sarah would be going to Jordan for Christmas or if their parents would be coming here. Then the news came that Mr. and Mrs. Algedi would be arriving at the Knoxville airport just a few days before the twenty-fifth and leaving in early January.

Even from afar, I could tell Sarah was ecstatic, the happiest I'd ever seen her. I imagined Mo was apathetic. It took a lot to get Mo excited about anything, anyway. But from what I could see, despite trying really hard not to look it, Adam was just as unhappy as before the news had come in.

The break couldn't come soon enough. Getting away from seeing Adam every day seemed like the solution to ending my misery, and yet also seemed like a death sentence of its own special kind.

I'd just finished my last exam for the semester and had turned in my final paper to Dr. Landry when the shit hit the fan.

I stood alone by the tennis courts, close to the parking lot where

Millar Johansson kept his car. I was distracted, taking a picture of one of the torn nets flapping in the wind, waiting for Millar to be done with his exams. He'd offered to take me home from school so I wouldn't have to hang out until my dad came to pick me up.

"Hey there, faggot."

The voice came out of the blue, but I knew who it belonged to. Eric Morgan approached me with clenched fists and five other guys at his heels. My breath caught and ice slid down my spine.

A small army of girls had followed Eric and his group over the hill, and Sarah was at the front of the pack. Her presence reassured me—she was so intimidating, surely no one would touch me when they knew I was her friend? *But am I still her friend?*

"What?" I asked with a hard tone, hoping I didn't sound scared. Bullies could smell fear.

"My cousin tells me you're a fucking queer."

The troop of girls gathered around, nervously shifting and whispering. Sarah stood at the front, her eyes glinting angrily. She watched me intently, as though she expected something from me, or perhaps feared I'd cave under pressure and expose Adam.

"Sarah, will you take my camera?" I asked, hoping to protect it in case they shoved me down and started kicking. "And my glasses?"

Sarah didn't move. She just stared at me. I noticed Leslie break away from the crowd and run up the hill, probably going to get a teacher.

"Please, Sarah. Take them."

Tina stepped forward. "I'll hold them, Peter." Her voice was small and terrified.

"Thank you." I handed off my glasses and then ducked my head to pull the camera strap over my head, missing the throw of the first punch. I only knew when it connected under my chin, snapping my teeth together and knocking my head back.

"More worried about your precious camera than your own skin, fudge-packer?"

Even though my head was spinning, I managed to get the camera strap from around my neck. I handed it off to Tina just in time to double over from a punch to my stomach, accompanied by a kick to my hip, which knocked me down.

Eric closed in and someone moved around behind me, picking me up, holding my arms behind my back. I couldn't hold in my cry as Eric kneed me in the stomach. I couldn't catch my breath, stunned as Eric's fist slammed into my cheek, and then I screamed, agony ripping through me as a foot connected with my balls.

I bent over, trying not to vomit, unable to process the pain as the hits kept coming. He threw another to my shoulder, a kick to my shins, and a punch to my stomach. At that point, everything was pain, everything hurt, and I retched, vomiting.

Suddenly, I was dropped to the ground. Still struggling for a breath, blood running down my throat from my nose and choking me, I braced myself for the onslaught of kicks I was sure was coming.

Instead, I heard Adam's voice and then there was the sound of a lot of scuffling. I looked up. Adam had grabbed Eric's jacket and shoved him against the fence surrounding the tennis court. A full five inches taller, Adam had to lift Eric up by his shirt to get in his face. "I'll fucking kill you, do you understand?"

Eric's nose bled freely and a black eye was already swelling. His hands scrabbled where Adam gripped his shirt, but he still had enough fire to say, "Why? You his boyfriend, cocksucker?"

Adam slammed Eric against the fence, whispering menacingly, "Don't fucking mess with him again or you'll wish to God you'd never heard the name Algedi." He kneed him in the balls and Eric screeched, his face going purple. Adam spit in his eyes before dropping him to the ground.

"Let's hear it," Adam ordered. "I want to hear you say it."

"I'm sorry!"

"And you won't bother him again."

"I won't bother him. No one will. I promise." Eric's voice was raspy.

Adam whirled around, and I watched as all the guys who'd accompanied Eric drew back. Adam's eyes glowed fiercely. I swallowed hard, still trying to breathe. I'd never seen him so angry.

"Any of you bother him, touch him, call him names, anything at all, and I will make you sorry in more ways than you can imagine."

I glanced around. Alliances shifted, some boys abandoning Eric for Adam's leadership, and others choosing to stick it out with the guy they'd known the longest.

Adam met each of their eyes solidly and then turned to his sister. I shuddered at the hot rage in his eyes as he glared at her.

Someone dropped down next to me and tried to help me to my feet. "Let's get you to the nurse."

It was Leslie. I groaned as I tried to stand up. Leslie threw both arms around my waist and helped support me as we moved toward the hill.

Adam stalked beside us, seething, his hand on my back.

The school nurse had already left for the holidays when we got to her office, but on later reflection, that was probably an act of providence. Otherwise, we might've been suspended for fighting.

My whole body ached, and I wanted nothing more than to crawl into bed and sleep for a week. Maybe I'd wake up and none of it would've happened after all.

Adam told Millar Johansson he had my ride home covered, and I didn't protest. Leslie got a ride with Allison, giving me a gentle squeeze before she left. I really wished she wasn't so freaking nice and that I didn't like her so much.

As Adam drove, rage poured off him. I took my camera out of

my backpack and began to document the bruises by using the reflection in the window and the small vanity mirror.

"What the fuck are you doing?" Adam asked.

"Taking pictures."

"Of your fucking face? Of the fucking bruises?"

"Yeah. Uh—" I shifted and swallowed. "Documentation. Kind of."

"Documentation of—" Adam slapped his hands against the steering wheel, yelling at me, "Why the hell did you just stand there, dammit?"

I shrugged and closed the sun visor, deciding I could wait to document the developing bruises until I got home.

"Answer me! Why did you just stand there and take it?"

"I would've punched back, but they held my arms." I knew it was a lame defense. I knew I really hadn't tried to protect myself. "Besides, it's not the first time. It's happened before. I'm used to it."

Adam slammed on the brakes, screeching over to the side of the road. Sarah made a small, fearful sound from the back seat, but Adam shot her such a look of anger she shut up immediately. He grabbed my shirt, getting in my face. "If I *ever* see you just stand there and take it again, I will personally kick your ass myself."

I swallowed and nodded.

Adam ran his hands through his hair, whispering, "Christ on a fucking pogo stick." He whipped around to Sarah. "And if you ever, *ever* just stand there while the guy I'm in love with gets his ass kicked, then I will fucking make your life a living hell. Do you understand me?"

"Yes." Sarah sounded strangely frightened, her normally strong voice very quiet.

Adam pulled back into traffic, still breathing hard. "Good. I'm glad we're all on the same page. Fucking morons. Both of you."

After Adam dropped me off at home, and I declined his offer to help me in, I stood in the bathroom with my shirt off, taking careful shots of my bruised and swollen face.

I wondered if I could bike over to the half-burned house on Lovell so I could get some pictures of myself there. It'd be a good backdrop. I composed the photo in my mind—the tripod would be set up *there* and I would be shirtless in the freezing air *there* and it would be shot on four hundred speed film, maybe a thousand speed—

"Peter? Jesus, you're a freak."

I jumped. Adam stood in the doorway, looking at me like I was insane.

"The back door was unlocked. I let myself in."

"Rude," I managed to say.

"I'm sick of being turned away. Besides, I needed to see you." His expression grew soft. "Make sure you're okay."

I didn't say anything to that. I felt fragile and tired, and mostly I just wanted him to hold me. In the face of Eric Morgan's fists and the assholes who'd helped him, Adam's relationship with Leslie seemed weirdly unimportant. My rage had simmered for weeks now, but suddenly I just didn't care. I wanted him. I didn't want to fight my feelings anymore. Not if I was going to end up bruised and beaten anyway.

Adam must have sensed the shift. Softly, he asked, "What else do you take pictures of?" He managed to put just enough emphasis on the question to leave me in no doubt he'd guessed my secret fetish of collecting photos of the marks he left on my body.

I lowered my eyes and then looked up at him again.

Adam leaned against the door. His soft green sweater clung to him in all the right places. He lifted his brows, and I took his picture.

"Take your sweater off," I murmured, suddenly wanting to leave marks of my own, the only marks I could—photographic ones.

Adam glanced over his shoulder, down the hallway to the stairs.

"She's in the throes of new-novel ecstasy. She won't be out for hours."

"Are you sure? Nothing's changed."

I swallowed and nodded. "I'm sure. I don't care anymore."

It was a half-truth that covered the fear and terror I'd felt and my need for comfort, my need for it to not matter that he was with Leslie, because I was so tired of hurting and not having what I wanted, of being punished for who I was even when I tried to do the right thing.

Adam's body lost its tension and sweetness filled his face. He pushed off the jamb and gracefully pulled his sweater over his head. I took four shots of that move alone. He stepped toward me, and while he unbuttoned my jeans and slid them off, I set the camera on automatic at thirty-second intervals. I placed it on the counter facing the mirror, carefully adjusting the focus as Adam slipped off my socks.

He was unbelievably tender with me. He covered me with kisses; every bruise was touched at least once by his lips, his tongue tracing over every inch of my skin.

"I was so scared," he whispered, nuzzling against my neck. "I wanted to kill them." And then he opened his mouth and sucked hard on my throat, leaving a large red bruise.

We were together, and the truth of us couldn't be denied by my skin, even though he could deny it with his actions in bed with Leslie. The camera snicked and snapped as he knelt and lapped at my ass, drew a line up my back with his tongue and sucked on my ear.

He had me incoherent, trembling with desire and need, all the blood in my body racing toward my groin. He kissed me again, his tongue oily, and he sucked on my lower lip as he scraped his stubble over the sensitive skin of my throat before latching on again, sucking until it hurt. My knees gave out, and I heard the camera snap as I slid down the wall, held up only by his grip on my hips, his mouth on my neck.

He took me to my bed, and the soft pads of his fingers tapped and rubbed my asshole, sliding inside and spreading me. When he pressed a third finger in, I realized he was preparing me, opening me. I started to shake. I'd wanted this for so long.

Adam fished a condom and a tube of lube from an inside pocket of his backpack by the bed. I tried not to think about why he kept those items there. He slicked his fingers, pushing and moving them inside of me until I was sweaty, until I begged him to give me more. He shoved my knees up to my chest and thrust a pillow under my hips. He kissed me and gazed down at my face, not saying anything at all, but he watched me carefully.

The first press was huge, overwhelming, and painful. I bit down on my lip to stifle my cry. I felt like I was being torn open. I knotted my hands in the sheets to keep from shoving him away and fought the urge to kick him off. Slow, burning heat accompanied the inexorable press of his dick. Adam's eyes darted between my face and where he was entering me, murmuring, "You're all right, you're okay, a little more, deep breaths."

I inhaled, long and shaky, keening as Adam slid deeper into me. He caressed my thighs soothingly, and I shook my head back and forth, not sure I could take any more.

"You can do it."

Adam pushed hard, and I arched up, crying out. He covered my mouth with his hand. It was too much, and I couldn't handle it. I shuddered and shook, feeling my anus spasm around him. It hurt so bad.

Adam murmured against my cheek, stubble scraping my lips, "You're okay, Eater. You feel so good."

Adam's eyes were hugely dilated, and his lips were open and swollen from biting them as he rocked in and out, slowly fucking me. I lost it. I felt like more than just my anus was being opened, and there was no way to keep him out of my body or my life. He was in. All the way in. The bruises ached and hurt with the pressure of his weight on me, and my balls throbbed, but somehow the pain grounded me and made the rest of it bearable.

Then he sped up his movements. It was too much. I wanted to tell him to stop, I couldn't take it, but he thrust harder, and I choked on the words. I was being fucked, there was no denying it. Irreversible, it was done, and it was happening, and I wanted it, but it hurt so badly tears ran down my cheeks.

Adam curled over me. "You're all right. It's intense, I know."

He kissed me, and I moved with him. Accepting him into me with an active movement of my own made the pain recede a little. I closed my eyes, trying to get myself back together.

Adam ran his hands over my thighs and down to clutch my hips. "Are you okay?"

I answered with a kiss, not wanting him to stop but not okay at all. Shock, pain, and a burning kind of pleasure spun through my body. My dick was soft, but the fuck was going smoother, better, and I thought I *might* one day be okay when doing this. But not now. I whimpered and held on tight as he rode me.

"You make me crazy, Peter." Adam kissed my eyelids, the pain of my bruises fading entirely in the face of the harsh, tight stretch of my asshole around his cock.

Suddenly Adam lifted up and locked his elbows, thrusting with hard, deep strokes. I tensed against the sharp pain, legs tucked tight against Adam's sides. He closed his eyes, groaning as his hips snapped in a seemingly helpless rhythm, shaking his head as though in denial that he was only moments from coming. With one final ramming thrust, his head fell back, and his face went slack as he jerked and shivered. The sensation of his cock pulsing in my ass startled me.

Adam collapsed to his elbows, eyes searching mine as he kissed me again. "I love you," he whispered.

I shivered violently, stunned and shaken. Adam slowly pulled out, a sensation familiar and yet somehow foreign. It left me oddly empty and sick. He discarded the condom and used his underwear to clean us up. Not even looking at his boxers, he threw them in my trash can. "Lost cause."

I curled onto my side, my bowels cramping and panic clutching my chest, but Adam took my chin and turned my head carefully, forcing me to look at him. Worry filled his eyes. "Was this okay, Peter?"

I nodded, words lost somewhere in all the whirling emotions and sensations. Adam spooned behind me, nuzzling the hair at the back of my neck, running his hands soothingly over my arms and stomach. I didn't respond, didn't say a word. Finally, I drifted into sleep, still shocked at what we'd done.

Chapter Thirteen

ADAM WOKE ME by kissing my eyelids and stroking my hair. I was sore all over, and I couldn't tell whether it was from being beaten up or from having sex. I decided it was both.

He pressed his cock into me again, this time from behind, on our sides. He fucked me slowly, whispering in my ear about how sexy I was, how he didn't want to wait anymore, and he was sorry if it hurt. It did hurt, but this time I was more relaxed, and he stroked my cock until I came, the aftereffects of my orgasm reducing the ache when he withdrew.

After, I found that if there was one uncomfortable truth about surprise anal sex, it was that it could be messy. I didn't want to even begin to think of a lie to explain the dark stains on the sheets, so I got rid of them by wadding them into a ball and stuffing them in a bag for Adam to dump in someone else's garbage can a few streets over.

Adam returned to stay for dinner. He sat at the kitchen table feeding Harry some scraps of his Lean Cuisine glazed chicken microwavable meal, the only thing I'd had the energy to make, when my dad came home from work.

Dad threw greetings to us both, heading for the fridge before drawing up short. "Well, Holy Mary Mother of God." Dad whistled, grabbing my chin to examine my face.

"You're a terrible Jew."

"The Catholics have the best exclamations, Pete." He frowned at the bruise on my jaw, my swollen nose, and his eyes wandered down to my neck, lingering for a long moment. "Did you get a punch in?"

I shook my head, taking a step back. "Nope."

"I'd hoped this was over. I thought at Kingsley—"

"It's not Kingsley, Dad. It's teenagers." I shrugged. "It's no big deal."

Dad looked ready to argue that point. His hands balled into fists and the veins in his temple throbbed. "What was it this time? Because you're a Jew? Because you lug that camera everywhere?" Dad's eyes cut over to Adam and then back to my neck. He swallowed hard and said, "Because you're gay?"

My heart skipped violently, my mouth going dry. It took me a couple tries to rasp out, "The guy called me a faggot, so I guess he thinks I'm gay." It wasn't exactly a yes, but not a no. Part of me wanted to scream, *Yes, yes! I'm gay! Clearly I'm gay!* But the words lodged in my bruised throat.

Dad nodded slowly and glanced at Adam again, his jaw clenching spasmodically. He closed his eyes and took a deep breath. I waited for the tirade to begin, but to my surprise he just said, "All right, son, so what do you want me to do about it? Do I need to call the school? Set up some kind of parent conference with the other—"

"No. Just—you know. Just forget about it. It's winter break and by the time I go back everything will probably be forgotten." I knew that wasn't true, but the last thing I wanted was my dad to get involved. How much of a sissy would I look like then?

Dad looked me over, eyes lingering on my throat again before asking, "What does your mother say?"

"Uh—" I turned back to my glazed chicken dinner and said around a mouthful, "She doesn't know yet."

Dad shook his head and pinched the bridge of his nose. "Great.

This is going to be a fun weekend." He pulled a dinner out of the freezer and popped it into the microwave, jabbing the keypad angrily to set the minutes and seconds.

"I'm sorry," I said.

Dad shook his head. "Not your fault, and I'm as upset as she's going to be."

He was angry, that was for sure, but Mom was going to lose her shit. She was going to be in bed on Valium or crying for the rest of the weekend. She might even mention my uncle's name again, like the first time I'd come home with a bruised face. It was the only time I'd ever heard her say it.

"I'm just—" Dad shook his head. "I'm just lost about how to handle this anymore." He suddenly turned to Adam. "What do you think we should do?"

Adam looked at me briefly. "I think Peter's probably right. Best to just let it go for now."

Suddenly Adam's eyes veered back and locked on to my throat, a deep flush rising to his hairline. My hand rose involuntarily to touch where he was staring, and Adam shook his head in a terse warning, but it was too late, Dad's gaze had followed.

"I'm going to go work in the study." He held my eyes. "Peter, I want you to keep me in the loop about this situation. If it's dangerous at this new school, we'll figure something else out."

"It's fine. It was a one-time thing," I promised.

He crossed to the table, pulled me into a hug, grabbed my head, and planted a wet kiss on my forehead. In the past, I'd have been embarrassed he'd done that in front of Adam, but I couldn't be more bare and vulnerable than I'd been when Adam had fucked me, so I didn't mind at all. Dad left the kitchen calling to Harry, and I sank down at the table, wincing.

"Peter?" Adam whispered.

"Yeah?"

"There is a huge, huge, *huge* hickey on your neck."

I nodded. "I figured."

"Yeah." Adam glanced toward the door. "Do you think your dad suspects? You know, about us?"

I shrugged. "I don't know. Maybe. Probably. He's smart and he used to tell me there was usually some truth behind every rumor. This is the fifth time this has happened now, so…" I let it trail off, exhaustion setting in.

I knew he'd seen the hickey. I also knew Dad was aware of my lack of a girlfriend. He'd put two and two together if he allowed himself to think about it, of that I was certain.

Suddenly I wanted nothing more than to lie down and go to sleep again for the next year. The idea that my dad knew, that he suspected what was happening between me and Adam should have been a relief, but it wasn't. I didn't feel up to facing even that much of my life.

Any minute my mom could come in and I'd have to endure her tears, her panic, and her rage. She really got angry when people beat me up. I guess I could understand that. It was the drop into depression and helplessness that I could do without.

"I want to go to bed, Adam. Uh—" I stood up slowly, my asshole throbbing with each beat of my heart. "I'll see you later?"

Adam frowned. "Are you okay?" He dropped his voice. "Did I hurt you?"

I laughed, my voice exhausted and thready. "Yeah, you hurt me. You rammed your huge, hard schlong up my ass, and it fucking hurt."

Adam's eyes grew wide with horror.

"Don't. Whatever you're thinking, don't. I'm okay. I was kidding. I just—" I sighed and groaned a little. "I've had a long day. I need a nap."

"Can I come upstairs for a little while?" Adam asked in a whisper.

I wanted to be alone to try to resurrect some of the barriers that'd been so thoroughly torn down when we had sex, but he looked worried, and the idea of being held by him was tempting. I always felt safe when he held me, and I wanted to feel safe again.

I nodded.

Adam followed me upstairs and climbed onto the bed. He pulled me down next to him, wrapping his arms around me and nestling into the curve of my body.

"Peter?"

"Yeah?"

"Do you—" Adam paused and snorted as though disgusted with himself, but then continued with a good dose of insecurity in his voice. "Do you love me?"

"No. I'll let just anyone fuck me. You know, I'm a slut. Totally easy." I twisted so I could see his eyes. Again, he wasn't kidding, so I said earnestly, "You know I love you."

"I just wanted to hear it. I just—" Adam kissed my temple. "I just wanted to make sure I hadn't ruined it."

"Nope," I murmured, floating in the space between awake and asleep.

"Okay." Adam sounded sleepy too, and it wasn't long before we both drifted off.

I'm not sure what woke me. Maybe I heard a noise, maybe I felt his eyes on me, but I scraped an eyelid open and saw my father standing in the doorway to my room, his face wrecked. I tried to wake up enough to understand why he looked that way, when suddenly I felt the warm arms around my waist, long legs twined with mine, and Adam's breath on my neck.

Oh.

Uh-oh.

Fuck.

Dad held my gaze for a moment and then slowly closed the door to my room, leaving me with my heart pounding in my throat.

✧　✧　✧

I DIDN'T KNOW what I expected to happen, but whatever it was, it didn't. Dad never mentioned seeing Adam and me napping. I almost thought I'd dreamed it, and he hadn't actually been in the doorway at all. It was only when I'd see him watching Adam over the dinner table with a speculative expression, or, even more revealing, *not* looking at us before we headed out for the night, I knew for sure I hadn't been dreaming.

As for Mom, she spent a day in her room on Valium, and then she ignored everything about the visible bruises on my face, like it'd never even happened. I didn't know if I was hurt or relieved about that.

The first week of break before the Algedis came into town, Leslie was on a ski vacation with her parents, and I spent all my free time with Adam and my camera. I convinced him to take me to North Knoxville to get some photos around the Fellini Kroger. The grocery was so nicknamed due to the unusual number of freaky characters working there, including a former prostitute with 666 tattooed across her forehead and a man with implanted horns poking out from his hair.

Adam parked the Mercedes in the back of the lot and lounged against it with his hands in his pockets while I loaded film into my camera. He followed me into the supermarket, pretending to shop while I surreptitiously snapped shots of the creepy customers and acne-pocked employees.

"Peter, get one of that guy over there," he whispered, studying the ingredients on a package of frozen burritos. He inclined his head toward the guy in a bodybuilding suit, striking poses in front of the freezers.

When a large woman sporting massive pink curlers got offended she'd been deemed a worthy subject, we left in a hurry. As we crossed the parking lot together, laughing and almost running, a voice called out, "Naughty Boy and Sweetie! Hold up!"

Adam and I looked at each other, startled and choking back another laugh. We slowed our jog and turned around.

A tall African-American man, looking to be in his late twenties, swaggered across the parking lot toward us, clutching a bag of groceries and smirking. He wore a pair of black dress pants, a rainbow button-down shirt open part of the way down his chest, and a giant smile.

"Well, well, well—" He ran a hand over his short afro. "If it isn't my naughty boy and his sweetie. Long time, no see." His voice was soft, but there was no other clue this tall, nice-looking man dressed up in women's clothes and danced around on stage every weekend.

"Uh, hey there." Adam grinned and put a hand out. "Good to see you, umm… Renée?"

His smile was slow and warm. "Robert. During the day I'm Robert Michaels."

"Dr. Michaels's son?" I gasped, suddenly knowing exactly who Robert's father was and how he knew my dad.

"Surprise, surprise!" Robert laughed. "Now you see why I wasn't about to tell on you this summer?"

"But your dad's—he's…" I trailed off, a little stunned.

"A Baptist minister. Well, *the* Baptist minister. Yes, I know."

Dr. Michaels was the pastor of the largest Baptist church in town, as well as a professor of biblical studies at the university. He was well known around Knoxville for his fiery sermons proclaiming hell and damnation for sinners great and small. He even had his own syndicated cable program all over the southern United States. My dad thought he was an ass.

I blinked and shook my head, trying to imagine his reaction to having a son who was not only gay, but a drag queen. "Oh, that's…oh."

"We don't talk a lot." Robert sniffed. "Obviously."

I nodded and lifted my camera. "Mind if I get a picture?"

Robert grinned and threw out a hip, striking a pose and laughing.

I took his picture as Adam asked, "How's Barry?"

"Ah, Barry's doing well. Why? Do you have a crush on him?" Robert winked.

Adam shrugged. "Huge, bald, handsome man? What's not to crush on?"

Robert slapped Adam's arm playfully. "I couldn't agree more. But, what about you two? I'm glad to see you're still together. Why haven't you been back to the club? It's eighteen-plus entry now— trying to bring in a bigger crowd. And I'm still in need of a reliable naughty boy to spank."

Adam laughed. "Well, Barry told me in no uncertain terms not to come back until we were both at least twenty-one."

"Why?"

"Because Peter got sick."

"Now why'd you go and do that, Peter?" Robert asked, turning to me and smiling flirtatiously.

"Me? You were the one sending me drinks by the dozen. Besides, I don't remember him saying that. I think Adam's just afraid of getting spanked again. He cried like a baby about it when we left."

Adam chuckled. "Yeah, right." He smiled slyly at Robert. "You know as well as I do how much I enjoyed the spanking."

Robert waggled an eyebrow and licked his lips. "Mm-hmm. Yes, I remember how very much you did."

Adam flushed, and I realized that he really must have come

when he was up there. I didn't know if that meant he'd had sex with Robert or not. Aside from their small smiles, neither of them seemed to see it that way.

Robert reached into his back pocket and pulled out his wallet, juggling his shopping bag to his hip. "Here, take my business card. It has my number on it. I'm having a party this Friday, and you little rugrats are welcome to come. It'll be fun, and Barry can't say who I can invite to our own home, now can he?"

"Cool." Adam grinned and pocketed the card. "We'll be there."

I pulled the card out of Adam's pocket and looked it over.

Robert Michaels
Producer
Outrageous Video

And then it listed all of Robert's phone and fax numbers. I slipped it back into Adam's pocket.

"All right, see you then." Robert turned with a wave and a swivel. "Oh, and Sweetie, don't puke on my carpet, okay?"

I grumbled as I climbed into the passenger seat of the car, "What is up with the 'sweetie' thing? Why does everyone call me that? Tina and now Renée, or Robert or whoever the hell he is."

Adam strapped his seat belt and used the rearview mirror to help him pull a loose eyelash free, saying nonchalantly, "Because you're sweet."

"I'm not sweet. I'm—" I paused. What was I? I couldn't think of anything. I looked at Adam, and he watched me with a slow smile.

"You're cute with your little crinkly frowny-face. It makes me want to fuck you."

We hadn't had anal sex since the last day of school. It'd hurt too much the first two times and I wasn't willing. Adam made it clear every single day that he wanted to do it again. As soon as possible.

"You always want to fuck me."

Adam laughed. "Once upon a time, you begged me to fuck you. You didn't even believe I truly wanted to, now you're sick of me wanting you."

"I'm not sick of it."

Adam started the car and pulled out. He stretched his arm across the seat so his fingers rested against my neck. "So, you don't want to be sweet, huh? Why not?"

"I don't feel sweet."

"You know what you're like? You're like your pictures."

"If you say my photos are 'sweet' then I'm going to jump out of this moving vehicle."

Adam laughed, letting his fingers twine into my hair. "Your pictures are *not* sweet. They're complicated. You're sweet to *me*, though. You even taste sweet."

"Bleh."

"So articulate. Dr. Landry would be impressed."

"Dr. Landry can suck my cock." I turned my head to look out the window, adjusting my glasses on my nose.

"Do you have a crush on Dr. Landry, Peter?" he teased. "Do you want him to suck your cock?"

I made a vague noise of denial. I kind of did think Dr. Landry was sexy in a weird way but I didn't want Adam to know that.

Adam laughed and asked, "Where to now, Mr. Paparazzi?"

I wished I knew.

Chapter Fourteen

I GROANED, THRUSTING into the heat of Adam's mouth, peering out the windows of the car, trying to see if anyone was around in the darkness. The lights from Robert's house were bright and inviting. A Christmas tree on the front porch blinked with multicolored lights, and we were in the car just across from it giving each other quickie blow jobs.

I grabbed his head and curled over him, coming with a hard grunt. I fell back against the seat, and Adam tucked my dick into my pants.

"Ready?" he asked.

I laughed shakily. "Let me catch my breath! Jesus!"

Adam leaned back and waited about five seconds. "Ready?"

I groaned and opened my car door. "Okay. Fine."

He rubbed his hands together gleefully and hopped out. We walked together toward the house, not touching because we didn't know who might be living in the houses around Robert.

The neighborhood, Fourth & Gill, was an older one set a few blocks away from the local homeless shelter. It was mainly occupied by university students and the elderly, but some of the bigger houses were being renovated, giving the area a pre-gentrification feel. A few vagrants from the shelter wandered the streets, begging money from the students as they headed out for the night.

A man in a red velour dress suit holding a plastic cup of beer opened Robert's front door as we approached. "Come in, come in!" he greeted us as though he owned the place. "Robert's in the kitchen. The food's in there too. And the keg."

Adam grabbed my hand and pulled me into the house. It was full of people, dressed in everything from T-shirts and jeans to full-costume Victorian period gowns. Adam guided me through the maze of bodies, somehow sensing the way to the kitchen. The sound of laughter and the scent of marijuana smoke hit me as we walked through the living room.

One wall of the kitchen was painted dark purple with giant silver swirls all over the walls, like an expanding galaxy. I was admiring the complexity of the mural when Adam said, "And here we go!"

"Naughty Boy and Sweetie!" Robert—no, Renée, crossed over to us, hands outstretched. She pulled us both into hugs and then motioned for beers to be brought over.

Barry showed up at her side, as big and bald as I remembered. "Don't you think you should learn from prior mistakes and not give these kids anything to drink?"

"You're no fun, Barry, baby."

He grimaced as beers were pressed into our hands.

Before we could even say hello in return, Renée was off and across the room, draping herself around another new arrival.

Barry eyed me. "Don't get drunk. Got it?"

I nodded. Barry stalked away, and I watched him put his arm around Renée's waist. Turning to Adam, I found him already talking to a guy with eyeliner and black lipstick. Adam rested his hand on my hip, and I sipped my beer, listening to them discuss the pros and cons of The Cure's latest album, while looking at the photos of Robert, Barry, and Renée hung on the wall. Apparently, they'd been together for at least a few years.

"*Disintegration* is the best record they've ever done," Adam said.

The guy flipped his dyed black ponytail over his shoulder. "You're just a kid. You can't appreciate good music."

Adam rolled his eyes. "Yeah, that's it. It isn't the fact that 'Plainsong' is breathtaking and 'The Same Deep Water As You' is fucking sexy as hell. No, it's not that at all."

"'Plainsong' totally rips off Joy Division, and you'd know that if you weren't, like, twelve."

I hated adult parties. I'd never been to a party like this one before, but I was already certain I hated them. I leaned back against the wall and closed my eyes, wondering how soon I could ask Adam if we could leave.

"The whole album is schlock and a complete sellout. 'Pictures of You' is lame and destined to be in some fucking Kodak commercial one day."

"Blasphemer! You slanderer! You—" Adam paused, turning to me. "'Pictures of You,'—wait, Peter, did you bring your camera in?"

My heart stuttered. In my hurry I'd left it in the car. I shoved off the wall, already in motion. It was always a bad idea to leave a camera in a car, but with the homeless shelter and the vagrants drifting up from it, I couldn't believe I'd left my Leica, my baby, my favorite, sitting in plain view in the back seat. Damn Adam and his stupid blow jobs.

Adam was on my heels as we exited the front door, but suddenly he dropped back, and I heard him exclaim, "Holy shit! What the fuck are you doing here?"

I didn't stop. I didn't care who was at the party from Kingsley or anywhere else. I just needed to make sure my camera was okay. I got to the car and was relieved to see it still sitting happily in the back seat, blissfully unaware that I'd deserted it. I yanked on the door, expecting it to be locked, and gasped when it opened easily. Pulling the camera strap around my neck, I took a few moments to get my heart under control.

Crossing the street, I saw Adam's outline in the doorway, arms thrown around some guy's shoulders, hugging him. I climbed the steps to the front door warily. It definitely wasn't someone from Kingsley. I didn't recognize the person.

"No fucking way! Peter, holy crap. This is—" Adam pulled the guy into another hug and said again, "No fucking way!"

Finally Adam let the guy go and turned to me, eyes shining, and one of the happiest grins I'd ever seen on his face. "Peter, this is Marcus! Can you fucking believe it?"

I really fucking couldn't.

"What are you doing here?" Adam asked again, smacking Marcus on the shoulder.

"You know Sean goes to UT. I hear he sells you weed."

"Sean's his brother," Adam said to me. "Yeah, but what are you doing *here?*"

"Sean knows the drag queen. He helps her with some TV show she does or something. I don't know."

Adam grabbed Marcus and hugged him again. "Why didn't you tell me you were in town? Why didn't you call?"

Marcus, much taller than I remembered from the Pantheon shots, his red hair a shade darker and no longer sporting glasses, laughed. "I was going to, but I just got here this morning. Besides, I wasn't sure if your dad was in town. I didn't want to upset things."

"He's not. Well, not yet." Adam turned to me. "Can you believe it, Peter? Crazy. Such a small world! It's been, what? Three years?" Adam's hands hadn't left Marcus's body since I got to the door.

I just stood there and smiled like an idiot, my heart a trip-hammer, my throat closing up. Not only did I have Leslie to deal with, but now Marcus had shown up. Marcus. Adam's *best friend* from Rome. Adam's *ex-boyfriend.* Maybe even his first love? Who knew? I'd never really asked those questions.

"Marcus, this is Peter." Adam waved at me, not taking his eyes off Marcus's face. "My best friend here."

Marcus's eyebrows went up in obvious recognition of the euphemism. "Ah, well, nice to meet you, Peter." He didn't seem very impressed.

I smiled tightly. "Yeah. Wow. Small world."

Adam laughed and hugged Marcus *again*. "How long are you going to be in town?"

"Just for the winter break and then it's back to Paris. Dad got transferred a year ago, you know?"

"Paris, huh? I hear the American school there is a huge party." Adam sounded envious.

"You should come visit."

"Absolutely. Hell, yeah."

I felt completely invisible, fading into the night. I sighed and the noise caught Marcus's attention.

"So, how long have you guys been 'best friends?'" Marcus asked, smiling at Adam with a knowing gleam.

Adam frowned and looked at me, suddenly dropping his hands from Marcus's shoulders and pulling me close to his side. He wrapped his arm around my waist and let his fingers drift under my long-sleeve T-shirt, brushing my stomach. "Did I say best friend? Peter is my boyfriend."

I felt a smile of triumph spread over my face. Boyfriend. Take *that*, Marcus. Boyfriend. He said *boyfriend*.

Marcus's eyebrows nearly hit his hairline. "And how does the Princess Sare-Bear feel about that? And your dad?"

"We're discreet," Adam said firmly. "You know, we do the best friends thing in school, in public, around the family. You know the drill."

"Do I ever," Marcus replied, a note of bitterness in his voice. "Well, wow. I'm happy for you." He smiled, but he didn't sound happy.

Adam grinned and grabbed my chin, angling in for a kiss that shocked me entirely since we were still standing half in the house and half out, surrounded by strangers whose affiliations had yet to be determined. Our noses bumped. I closed my eyes and kissed him back, astonished at how long the kiss lasted.

"Get in or out, lovebirds!" Renée's voice called over the crowd, and Adam reluctantly released my lips, nuzzling my neck for a moment before pulling me inside and shutting the door on the cold December air.

SEAN, AS IT turned out, was more Robert's friend than Renée's. They'd met during a filmmaking class and now spent their weekends creating television programs for the local public access station. They called their production company Outrageous Video. Marcus pointed out his brother sitting on a stool across the room playing foosball with some artsy-looking local rock-star types.

"He provides weed for those idiots too," Marcus said. "Makes a lot more doing that than making videos with the drag queen. He sinks a lot of that money into their business, though, buying new editing VCRs and stuff."

Renée pranced around the room refreshing drinks and doing little shimmying dance moves against the straight boys just to make them squirm.

Adam and Marcus hadn't shut up since we got back into the house. Their clipped, excited conversation consisted of things like, "Whatever happened to Lisa? Really? What about Edward?" Or, "Do you remember that time when—"

Renée had replaced the beer I'd lost when I abandoned it to get my camera, so I sipped it with a mixture of jealousy, frustration, and total boredom. I was disconnected enough from the room and the events going on to snap the occasional picture, but I really thought I'd punch Marcus if I had to smile one more time at something he said.

Adam kept me close. That was small consolation for the fact that we hadn't spent the evening at his house making out and playing Nintendo, far away from unexpectedly visiting ex-boyfriends.

Renée appeared at my elbow and pulled me onto the dance floor, setting my beer on a table on the way. I followed her reluctantly, muttering, "I don't really dance."

"I saw you and Naughty Boy dancing at Tilt-A-Whirl and your hips swivel just fine, baby."

I gave in, letting her pull me up against her as a slower song filled the room. I groaned, recognizing "Open Arms" by Journey. She rocked me back and forth, kind of petting my hair, and I followed her lead, glancing over her shoulder at Adam and Marcus from time to time.

"So, how do you know Sean's brother?"

"Huh?" I had to turn my head to keep my eye on Adam without looking like I was watching him.

"Marcus? Sean's brother?"

"I don't. Adam knows him from Rome."

"I thought Adam was from Jordan."

"Before that it was Rome."

"Small world, isn't it, Sweetie?"

"Yeah." It sure didn't feel like a world of laughter, more like a world of "someone upstairs has it out for Peter." Maybe I really needed to start believing in God.

"Hey, now. Don't fret. You live here. Marcus is just in town for the break. Possession is nine-tenths of the law or something like that. But, more importantly, Naughty Boy loves you. Any fool can see it." Renée stroked my back. "See how Sean looks at Jena?"

I lifted my head and saw Marcus's brother dancing a few feet away with a short, rather round girl with sparkling black eyes. "Yeah."

Renée leaned in closely, whispering in my ear, "Naughty Boy looks at you like that. I saw it that first night."

I smiled, warm hope from her words counteracting the burn of anxiety.

"Now—go over there and stake your claim." Renée shoved me toward Adam and Marcus.

I picked my way through the people until I could retrieve my beer from the side table. But then I thought better of it, remembering Afterschool Specials about people slipping drugs into drinks, so I left it behind. I moved empty-handed into the small space between Adam and the wall. Adam laughed spectacularly, his white teeth shining against his tan skin.

It seemed as though I stood there unnoticed for a minute or more, but suddenly he flung an arm behind him, hooked me with it and dragged me in close to his side. He leaned over and kissed my lips again, then whispered in my ear, "You are so fucking hot." Then he jumped right back into conversation with Marcus about the time they'd stolen markers from the art teacher and used them to deface the toilets in the school.

Renée caught Adam's eye from across the room and beckoned him over to dance with her. Passing his beer off to me, Adam went, and I watched as they did the YMCA with added hip-grinding.

"So, it's Peter, yeah?" Marcus asked, taking a sip from his glass.

I nodded, knowing damn well he knew my name. Adam had only said it fifty times in the last half an hour trying to get me to join in their conversation.

"How'd you guys meet?"

I shrugged. "During the orientation for our high school."

"Ah. Did he come up to you right away? Take you under his

wing and all of that?"

I pushed up my glasses, shrugging again.

"Adam is good at picking out the people who'll bend to his will. It's like his talent or something. Did you sleep with him on day one?"

"Why is that your business?"

"To be blunt, you should watch yourself, kid." Marcus's gaze followed Adam dancing in the living room with Renée before turning back to me. "I was you once. What's not to be crazy about when it comes to Adam, right? He's hot. He's smart. He treats you like you're special."

Marcus pulled a swallow from his beer. "Next thing you know he's dating some girl and the Princess Sarah is telling you to keep it hush-hush. Just take my word for it. He'll break your heart and leave without a backward glance when it's time for him to move on."

My throat clicked as I swallowed.

Marcus leaned over me. "Just ask yourself this—what does some kid like you from this redneck town have that I don't? What do you have to offer? Have you ever traveled at all? Have you been *anywhere* or done *anything?* He's passing time with you, and that's it. The same as he did with me. And we had *Rome.* You've got, what? The Sunsphere?"

"You're a jerk."

"I'm telling you this because I'm actually a nice guy."

Nice guy, my ass. I drank Adam's beer, trying to look like I wasn't rattled, but my hands were shaking. Marcus had just named every one of my secret fears. I sipped and refused to even look at him.

Adam spun away from Renée and glided over to me, grabbing his beer and squeezing my shoulder affectionately. "She's crazy. She wants us to come to the show next weekend for some Christmas thing. She's going to dress up as a sexy Mrs. Claus or something."

Adam registered my flushed face, my shaking hands and looked between me and Marcus, his eyes growing dark. "Did I *miss* something here?"

"No," I said softly.

Adam turned to Marcus. "What did you say to him?"

"Adam, listen, shut up. He didn't say anything. Okay?" I found a place to put down the beer. "Can we just get out of here? Get his number or whatever so we can just go, all right?"

Adam glared at Marcus with a look I'd only seen when he'd held Eric by his throat. "I don't think I need his number. Do I, Marcus?"

Marcus sneered. "It's not like you'd use it anyway."

"Oh, so that's what this is about? Have you been telling him how I'm going to leave and never call or write just because that's what I did when I left you?"

"Someone's got to warn a nice guy like Peter."

"Yeah, well that was two years ago, and I was sixteen years old. I wasn't ready for a long-distance relationship. Fuck, why am I even explaining myself to you? Come on, Peter." Adam grabbed my arm and then turned back around. "I was excited to see you and you just act like some fucking *bitch*. You knew—you *always* knew I didn't love you. I never said I did. What the *fuck* did you expect from me? We were just kids."

He pulled me across the room toward the front door, muttering under his breath and shaking his head. The winter air burned my throat as we crossed the street to his car. I didn't say anything, just climbed in and pulled on my seat belt, then secured my camera between my feet, lens up just in case the cap popped off.

Adam maneuvered the car from its parallel-parked position and jerked onto the road, gripping the steering wheel with white knuckles.

"What the fuck did he say to you?"

"Nothing," I said wearily, not wanting to review it all, not want-ing to listen to the truth again and, especially, not wanting to hear it from my own lips.

"Peter, whatever he told you is crap. The fact is, he and I didn't end on good terms. I thought he'd be over it by now, but obviously he isn't."

The lights from passing cars illuminated Adam's face in profile before leaving it shadowed again. "You sure seemed happy to see him at first."

"He was my best friend, but he wasn't the love of my life or anything."

"Were you the love of *his* life?"

"I don't really fucking care if I was. I don't know what his game was tonight, trying to upset you, trying to make you doubt me—that *is* what he was doing, wasn't it, Peter?"

"Why would he?"

"I don't know. I really don't." Adam ran a hand through his hair and sighed. "Sarah always said Marcus was trouble. She is always, *always* right."

I pondered this and then asked evenly, "What does Sarah say about me?"

Adam frowned. "Sarah likes you."

We rode in silence for a few minutes, Adam driving with angry, jerking movements.

"What did you see in Marcus?" I asked.

Adam sighed. "Well, he was nice, in the same grade, and I like guys with glasses." He flashed a "so-sue-me" expression. "We clicked. He played D&D, and he was always up for an adventure. We were horny and things happened. One day we gave each other hand jobs. The next it was blow jobs, and it went from there. Until Sarah found out and then it was all intrigue and bullshit—just like now."

"Aren't you sick of it?" I crossed my arms, feeling vulnerable and exposed.

"I am. I'm fucking tired of it. Sometimes I just want to take you to Kingsley, drag you up on the stage during assembly, and kiss you until we both pass out from lack of oxygen."

My stomach clenched. "Remind me why you don't do that?"

Adam laughed, some tension draining from his voice. "Because I don't want any more scenes like with Eric Morgan—especially if you aren't even going to fight back."

He had a point. I still had bruises on my shin, stomach, and hip.

"I'm thinking of getting contacts," I said, picking at a hangnail. "If I do, I won't have glasses."

Adam caressed my thigh. "If you think I just like you for your glasses, Peter the Eater, you're wacko, bonkers—"

"What about my ass?"

Adam frowned. "Are you asking if I like your ass? Because I do. A lot. But if you're asking if I like you *just* for your ass then I'm going to lean over, open the car door, and shove you out."

"Romantic."

"That's me." He smirked.

I leaned back and watched the buildings of downtown slip by as we merged with the interstate off Broadway. The Sunsphere loomed on the left, and I glared at it. Marcus had Rome. I had the Sunsphere.

"What'd that big gold disco ball ever do to you?" Adam asked, catching my expression in the glow of a passing tractor trailer's lights.

"It's not Rome," I whispered.

Adam massaged my neck. "Thank God for that."

When we got back to Adam's house, we found Mo on the sofa

with a bag of cookies and a porn flick on the television.

He barely glanced at us. "Mom and Dad'll be at the airport by noon. I'm picking them up. Get all your bad behavior in before that. Sarah's at Mike's getting her last round of sex. I've got my porn. You guys go do your thing, but keep it down because I'm still living in denial about you, okay?"

Adam ignored him and shuffled down the hall, clasping my arm and dragging me.

Mo called out, "I'm serious, Tad. I don't want to hear *any-thing*."

With the door locked, chair under the handle, the towel along the crack and the window open, Adam flopped onto the bed and stared up at the ceiling. "What a fucking night."

I stood by the door, fidgeting.

"Peter, get over here."

I shucked my shoes and crawled onto the bed. Laying down on my back, I was careful not to touch him, crossing my hands on my stomach and counting the stick-on stars. Twenty-nine of them, just like always.

"What's up?"

I shrugged. I didn't want words; they made things so complicated and messy. They had all kinds of meanings. Some true, some false. I wanted photos. Why couldn't Adam give me some photographs showing how he felt? Why couldn't he hand over a stack of Polaroids spelling out his feelings loud and clear? Celluloid that would give me complete understanding of his feelings and motivations?

But I knew the answer to that anyway.

Even if he did have the capacity, I wouldn't necessarily be able to interpret the photos any better than I could the words. Why did communication have to be so hard?

"Have you done Dr. Landry's assignment about the meaning of

love yet?" I asked, fiddling with the hem of my sweater. Dr. Landry had given us journal entries to complete for each day of the break so we didn't lose our "wordy-rhythm," he'd said.

"Yes," Adam answered, rolling onto his side, propping up on an elbow and looking down at me.

"What did you write?" I pulled off my glasses to rub at my eyes.

"I wrote a poem."

"Yeah?"

"Yeah." Adam went to his desk, jerking out a journal from the side drawer. "Do you want to read it?"

Duh. I played it cool and settled my glasses back onto my nose when he returned to the bed with the journal. "Okay."

<u>where you end, where I begin</u>
by Adam Algedi

he could still feel him inside

deep beneath his skin

swimming along in his bloodstream

streaming from his pores in sweat

spurting from his dick under warm covers

never gone

always there

there were days

when he wanted to be rid of him

the intense, vibrant undercurrent

that colored the meaning

of everything in his life

there were days when he wanted

to be alone in his body

alone in his mind

but he was starting to recognize
he was fused tight
soldered, welded, molded
—marked
it would be easy to say
"here's the park bench
where he first kissed me"
or
"we sat in that corner booth once
and he almost choked
on a hot tamale"
better yet
"I can't find any safe spaces"
but there's no escape from
the occupation of his body
even in his coffin
any empath would know
he's not alone in there.

I read it over several times before setting the journal on the night table.

"Well?" Adam asked.

I nodded slowly.

Adam took off my glasses, putting them next to the book. He pulled me into a hug, and, starting with my neck, pressed gentle, open-mouthed kisses up behind my ear, over my cheeks, and to my lips. The kiss intensified and I let him push me back to the mattress.

I tried to ignore it, but I could feel it inside my body, the poem and Marcus making everything feel precipitous. I knew exactly what that poem said about the meaning of love. It was secret, it was shameful, and it was doomed to be forever a private joy and an endless despair. Is that what Adam had in store for me? For us?

And then, as Adam tongued behind my ear, it hit me—he'd come out to Dr. Landry. There was no way he'd turn in that poem as his assignment unless Dr. Landry knew.

"Wait," I gasped.

"Why?" Adam licked and sucked, making me squirm.

"Dr. Landry knows about us?"

"Mm-hmm."

"You told him?"

Adam kissed the hollow of my throat. "Yeah. Well, no. Just about me. I think he knows, though, Peter." I stiffened, and Adam lifted up. "He's not going to say anything."

"How can you be sure?"

"He'd be completely irresponsible to do something like that, and besides, I trust him. Don't you?"

I nodded. Yeah, I trusted Dr. Landry completely. "What did he say when you told him?"

"He said he'd be there whenever I wanted to talk, to use the journal to work things through. He said it'd be okay. He made me feel better."

"Did he mention Leslie?" I hated talking about her when we were alone, but I wanted to know.

"He said I wasn't being fair to her or to myself." Adam sighed and rolled off me, staring at the ceiling. "He said to think it over. He'd support me no matter what I choose."

"That's good." I held my breath. *Choose me.*

"But I'm going to keep dating her. I care about her. She cares about me. We're a good fit. And she's—" Adam broke off.

"She's what?"

"She's good at what she does, okay?" Adam sounded defensive.

"I can forget I'm not with you, and that's something at least."

Leslie was good in bed. Just what I needed to know. Anxiety exploded into bitter anger. "Does she give a better blow job than me?"

"Peter!"

"I'm sure she's got more experience than I do." Bile rose in my throat. I sat up and flung my legs over the side of the bed. "Does she do things for you I can't? Is her cunt that fucking great?" I stood, reached for my glasses, and bent for my shoes.

Adam sat on the bed, anger lifting from him in waves. He stared at me, his eyes black with rage. In an instant, the mood had turned. He—or I—had ruined the night.

Disgust and anger bubbled in my gut. "I've got a great idea. Why don't you fuck Marcus until Leslie gets back in town? Then since she's so good in bed, I'm sure you can find a way to make up for my absence with her. You could probably get her to let you do her up the ass, so you won't be missing out on anything at all."

Adam bit out, "We did that once. *Once.*"

I pulled on my shoes and threw the chair away from the door. "You and me? Twice actually, but yeah." I whirled around and flung open the door. I didn't even see it coming, but suddenly I was thrown up against the wall.

Adam pressed against me, hands holding me in place. "You are such a little shit. A fucking jealous *bitch.* I don't know how I could give any more than I've given you. I love you more than my own fucking life. Fuck you, Peter. Fuck you."

He shoved me down the hallway and I stumbled. I caught myself on the wall and looked up to see Mo with his arms crossed.

"I told you to keep it *down*, Tad."

"Shut the fuck up, Mo."

Turning to Adam, I said, "Actions speak louder than words, *friend.*"

I made sure the front door slammed behind me.

✧   ✧   ✧

I WASN'T ASLEEP. How could I sleep? And, really, what did I want from him? Why did I have to love him so fucking much? And why did it all make so much sense when I wasn't so angry? Why did I have to remember exactly what it felt like when Eric's fists met my flesh? How could I blame Adam for what he was doing? He was protecting us. Both of us.

I almost called him, but then I was too proud to pick up the phone. I'd behaved just like he said, like a jealous bitch, and I was humiliated. I climbed out of bed, wearing nothing but boxers, and went down to the kitchen. Maybe I'd make a pan of brownies or something and eat them while sitting by the phone. Just in case it rang.

I'd nearly fallen asleep slumped on the stool at the counter with the entire pan mostly eaten beside me when I heard the soft tap at the window. I jolted and turned toward it, half expecting to see a hockey mask or some other horrible sight. Instead it was Adam, face tense and eyes still blazing.

I padded over to the door and let him in, the icy air from outside making me shiver. He stood in the pale light of the kitchen, rubbing his gloved hands together and staring at my face.

Finally, he said, "You were a real prick tonight."

I shut the door and turned to him, crossing my arms and waiting.

"My parents—look, I wanted tonight to be special. I wanted to go to the party and have fun. I wanted to come back home and be with you all night." Adam sighed. "I know actions speak louder than words, but you have to understand. You have to *know* I'm doing this because I love you. I don't want either of us killed. I don't want to see you hurt ever again. I look at the bruises you still have and—I get so fucking angry. I'm speaking as loud as I can with my actions, Peter."

"I know." I shivered again, holding my arms tight around myself. "I mean, at least, I should know."

Adam smiled feebly. "Peter the Eater? Can we just forget about all that yelling stuff and skip to making up?"

He moved forward and I fell against him, shaking harder when my skin came into contact with the chill of his jacket.

"I'm sorry. I shouldn't have flipped out like that," I whispered.

"It probably seemed like I was taunting you. I wasn't. I mean, she's good at what she does, but so are you."

My stomach churned. "*Please.*"

"I'm sorry."

"I'm cold."

Adam laughed. "Yeah? Well, can I stay and get you warm?"

My reasons for letting him fuck me weren't the best, all tied up in jealousy and contrition, but I didn't care—because soon I was on my elbows and knees on my bed, hands knotted in the sheets, trying not to hyperventilate as Adam slid into me from behind. That took up all the space in my mind.

I bit down hard on the pillow and tried not to cry out. My parents might be on the other side of the house, but the air ducts carried sound. Somehow, it was different this time. Getting fucked still hurt, but it felt good too. The delicious friction made my skin prickle as Adam shoved in. I quivered, and my dick throbbed, hard and eager against my stomach.

When he took a strong hold of my hips and rocked into me gently, I moaned, squirmed, and threw my ass back for more. He chuckled. "Slutty tonight. I like it."

I couldn't reply because if I opened my mouth I wasn't sure what kind of sound might come out. It might have been the angle of my hips, or the angle of penetration or both, but the pain faded quickly and the pleasure mounted fast. I felt stretched tight, and my nipples tingled. I dug my fingers into the sheets as Adam moved. It was so damn *good*. Adam thrust against my prostate nearly every time he went in, and it was so powerful I stopped breathing, straining with my whole body for *more*, and *harder*.

"Peter, fuck," Adam said, slamming into me hard enough that the sound of skin slapping together penetrated the rush of blood in my ears. "So tight. Fuck."

I gripped the sheets, shoving back to meet his thrust and then scrabbling to get away from it, overwhelmed by the strong sensations. Each stroke over my prostate made me break out in chills and sweats. I'd never felt anything so amazing. I chewed the pillow to keep from screaming as the world started to swim with black and purple dots.

"Breathe," Adam coaxed.

I burrowed my head under my pillow, using it to muffle the urgent noises in my throat, and arched back for more. I was going to pass out if I didn't get some air. I keened softly as Adam pulled all the way out. He added more lube before slamming in again. I tensed around him for a painful moment, and then I relaxed, his cock sliding in and out with squelching noises that were unbearably arousing.

My cock jerked with every thrust, aching and thudding with my pounding heartbeat. I wanted to beg him to touch it, plead with him to get me off, but I couldn't open my mouth or I'd be *loud*. I was already moaning like crazy, and if I got any louder we might wake my parents. I took in a little more air, my lungs burning and my heart racing, the blue and purple dots swimming in my eyes.

"Peter, breathe, dammit."

I wriggled one of my hands down to jerk my cock, and it made everything even better. I surged back to meet his next thrust, and my whole body convulsed from acute pleasure. Adam groaned behind me, low and soft, and then gripped my hips hard, holding me in place as he pummeled my ass, fast and rough.

I jerked, shaking all over with each thrust, still not breathing, holding it in, until the world narrowed, tightened, and then *exploded* as I came harder than I ever had. The air I'd been holding released in a shout, and my body collapsed into spasms.

Adam followed me down to the bed, fucking me still as I gasped and surrendered to prolonged aftershocks almost as strong as the orgasm itself. He bit the back of my neck, rutting into me firmly. I clenched around his cock, tightening my hole, and he moaned, grabbed my wrists, and squeezed them hard.

His cock thudded in my ass, and he whimpered, "Best thing ever." He slumped onto me, twitching and jerking as his cock pulsed.

As I shivered and squirmed on his dick, drifting in post-orgasmic relaxation, I thought he'd summed it up perfectly. I wasn't sure what we'd done wrong the first two times, but *that* was the best thing *ever*.

MOM HANDED ADAM some pepper for his eggs, then she sat at the counter, wrapped in a blue robe and some lacy, old-fashioned gown thing she liked to wear when she was writing period pieces. Dad stood at the stove cooking more eggs for himself and humming Christmas carols under his breath. "God Rest Ye Merry Gentlemen" and "O Holy Night" were his clear favorites, though he didn't have the voice for the high notes.

Adam and I sat at the table. I'd already made our breakfast before Mom and Dad stumbled into the room. Dad was cheerful and Mom was upbeat, and they were being touchy-feely with little kisses here and touches there.

I rolled my eyes at Adam, whispering, "Looks like other people got laid last night too."

He laughed and winked at me. "Bet it wasn't as good."

"Adam, honey," my mom said with a sweet smile. "Didn't you tell me the other day your parents would be coming to town for the holidays?"

Adam swallowed and wiped his mouth. "Yes, Mrs. Mandel. They'll be here this afternoon. Sarah is really excited to see our mom."

"I bet you're excited too," Mom said.

Adam smiled. "Sure. Yeah. It's been nearly four months. That's a long time to be on our own."

"Well, you've become such a fixture around here we'd love to meet your folks and let them know what a great kid they've raised." Mom smiled at Adam. "Wouldn't we, Abe?"

Dad nodded, but didn't say anything and didn't look at Adam.

"Abe?" Mom prompted.

Dad took a beat, and then said, "Maybe we should invite them over."

"That's the perfect idea!" Mom exclaimed. "After all, Adam's starting to feel like one of the family around here."

Dad dropped his gaze before looking to me. "Yep, one of the family. Or something like that." Dad actually turned red and turned his back to grab a plate for his eggs.

Mom looked between us in confusion before settling her attention back on Adam.

Adam had trouble meeting anyone's eye, and he mumbled, "That'd be nice. But I'm not sure what their schedule is like."

Mom waved her coffee mug in the air, turning to her romance paperback sitting next to her plate of buttered toast. "Oh well, it's the thought that counts." She was already distracted from her own suggestion, drawn into the fantasy worlds she preferred to inhabit.

Adam pushed away from the table. "I guess I really should get going. Mo will be back from the airport with Mom and Dad before long."

Butterflies let loose in my stomach. Something, I wasn't sure what exactly, felt off. I picked up our plates and carried them to the sink. "I'll walk you home."

Adam nodded, kissed my mom on the cheek, and waved good-bye to my dad. I followed him out the door, pulling my coat on over my sweater. We traipsed across the sidewalk and then started down the driveway to the street.

"My dad knows about us."

Adam nodded. "Yeah. Did you tell him?" He swallowed hard and ran his hands through his hair nervously.

"No. He saw us sleeping in my bed the day Eric…" I trailed off. I didn't want to remind him too vividly of the fight. He always got upset all over again. "I woke up and saw him in the doorway. I guess we forgot to lock the door."

"Oh. What did he say?" Adam stuffed his hands in his pockets and pulled out his gloves, putting them on and not meeting my eye.

"Nothing. It's been kind of awkward, but he hasn't said a word."

"You're lucky."

I studied Adam, and suddenly I knew why he was so anxious. "How'd he find out? Your dad, I mean. How'd he find out about you liking boys?"

"He found a letter I was writing to Marcus." Adam dropped his head and laughed bitterly. "The truth is I didn't just turn my back on Marcus when I left Rome. Sure, I never loved him, but he was my friend, and he'd been there for me when—" Adam broke off and looked at me. "There's a lot I've never told you about my life over there. It isn't that I didn't want to tell you; it just never came up." He stopped and turned to me with a quickly expelled breath. "Like I said, I've been with two guys. Marcus wasn't my first."

I frowned. "But you were only sixteen when you were with him."

"Yeah. I was fifteen when…" Adam shook his head and closed his eyes. "It was stupid. I totally fell for this guy's line. He was older; his name was Jamie and he was really hot. He was eighteen and a senior. I don't know whether he just likes 'em young, or if it was something about me, but he really made a play for me. I was shocked at first, you know? Surprised. I didn't even know I could *maybe* be into guys. All I knew was this guy kept treating me like I was something really special, paying attention to me and stuff."

Adam started walking again, and I fell into step next to him. His hands made sharp gestures as he talked, and he kept chuckling a little like it still cut him to think about it and he was trying to laugh off the pain.

"So, you know, I totally fell for him. You asked me if Marcus was the love of my life, and I said no. Well, until I met you, I would've said Jamie was the love of my life. I didn't know I even liked guys, you know? And here he was opening these doors I hadn't realized were there, making it all seem so hot and cool and amazing. First kiss, first blow job, first anal, first everything was with Jamie."

Jealousy sliced through my gut, but I nodded sympathetically.

"I was shocked as hell when he kissed me one night at a party. He'd called me to a bedroom in the back of the flat and locked the door behind us. I was nervous, but he just grabbed me and…" Adam paused for a long moment before going on. "We kissed. He blew me. I blew him. I was fucking wowed, you know?"

Yeah, I knew.

"So, long story short, he wasn't into me, really. He left for college in the States, and he never contacted me again. Broke it off with me just before he left. 'It's been fun.'" Adam shrugged. "I don't know why it still hurts. Now that I'm with you I can see I didn't really love him."

"Yeah?"

"Yeah."

"So, you started with Marcus then?" I drifted closer to Adam, my hands shoved deep into my jeans pockets and my shoulders hunched. I brushed against him deliberately and he bumped me in return.

"Yeah. And it was just friends stuff, you know? Kissing, hand jobs, then more. No big deal, but I did care about him." Adam sighed heavily. "So, when I left for Jordan, I really did intend to keep in touch. But then Dad found my letter." Adam swallowed hard. "It had—stuff in it, you know? About how I missed sucking and fucking him. It was stupid for me to put it in writing. It was way more detailed than it should have been."

He fell silent, and we walked for a few minutes. His house drew closer, the gray December light glinting on the windows.

"So, what happened?"

"Dad tore up the letter and said I couldn't be friends with Marcus any more. I was forbidden to contact him and then—"

"Then?"

"He hit me."

I gasped. "What?"

"It wasn't a big deal. I mean just some stripes across my back with his belt, but it was enough to scare me away from trying to contact Marcus. I've never seen my father so angry. His eyes were fucking scary." Adam looked ashamed and didn't meet my gaze.

I walked close beside him and tried to think of something to say. Adam snuffled and I looked over in time to see him wipe his nose with his sleeve. I didn't know if it was the cold or if he was crying. He focused on his sneakers.

"What'd your mom do?" I finally asked.

"She cried but then she came into my room that night and sat on the bed. She told me my father was wrong and if I liked boys she'd get used to it. But then she asked me not to mess around with guys until I went away to college, for her sake, for the peace of the house, to keep Dad from going apeshit."

"Oh."

We'd reached his house. I looked up, studying the windows and the green, flaking front door, suddenly feeling like I wasn't at all welcome there. He glanced over at me. "I want you to meet my mom."

"All right. You sure that's a good idea?"

"Yeah. I think so."

"Okay."

"Peter, I know you were hoping that with Leslie gone we'd see a lot of each other this break, and I should have said something before, but I was scared." Adam stood so close to me his frosted breath rushed over my cheeks. "But, the thing is, we can't."

"Because your dad will know."

"He'll suspect." Adam bit his lip. "I'm sorry, Peter. I spend so much time apologizing. Maybe I'm not good for you."

I'd never seen Adam look so unsure and alone. I threw my arms around his neck and hugged him in the driveway, not caring if the neighbors saw.

Adam pulled away, looking at the hill his brother would be driving over any minute with his parents. "I guess you should go, Eater."

I nodded and backed away. The sun broke through the winter haze and brightened Adam's hair so the red highlights stood out. I turned to go and heard him call for me to wait.

He jogged up and put his hand on my shoulder. "I want to hear your story, you know."

"My story?"

"About when you first knew you were gay." Adam hugged me

hard and whispered in my ear, "It's weird because you seem so sure about it. No doubts." Then he brushed a kiss on my cheek and, in his patented move, used a hand on my shoulder to shove me away. "Later, gator."

I pulled my coat tight and walked home alone, with a hollow uncertainty aching inside.

Chapter Fifteen

MOM STILL SAT at the kitchen counter, flipping through a holiday catalog and humming under her breath. Apparently Dad's Christmas songs had infiltrated her mind. She smiled at me. "Adam's such a great kid. I'm glad you made friends with him, honey."

I shrugged out of my coat and hung it over a kitchen chair. "Me too."

She flipped through a few more pages, turning down a couple of corners, marking items that caught her attention. Without looking at me, she asked, "What do you want for Christmas?"

I pushed up my glasses. "Contacts."

With a grin, Mom slid off the stool and came over, taking off my glasses and tousling my hair, just like Sarah did every day before school. "Oh, you'll be a lady-killer, Peter. You'll knock all the girls dead."

"The glasses get in the way of my camera."

Mom threw her arm around my shoulders and drew me in for a hug, my face shoved close to her bosom and her cheek resting on my head. "Peter, when did you grow up?"

"While you were writing hot sex scenes," I sniped.

Mom just hummed and petted my hair. "You'll be getting married before long. Having kids of your own."

"Sorry, Mom. No kids."

Mom clucked her tongue. "Just you wait, honey. Someone always wants kids and the other person gives in. That's just the way it goes."

"That doesn't sound very healthy." I pulled away from her, but let her keep her hands linked at my neck. "I guess Dad wanted kids?"

Mom kissed my cheek. "You were such a good baby, such a good child, such a sweet, sweet boy."

I groaned, pushing past her and opening the fridge. "Sweet. Why am I not surprised?"

She smiled distantly, like she hadn't really heard me. "Is there anything else you'd like this year? I got a good bonus for the next book, and I was thinking I'd get something special for you. A car, maybe? I could make the down payment as a present."

"What about the monthly payments and insurance?"

She shrugged. "You'll get a job."

I pulled out the carton of orange juice, pondering her suggestion. Finally, I took a deep breath and said, "How about a darkroom?"

"A darkroom instead of a car?" Mom sounded surprised.

"Yeah." I grabbed a glass and poured the juice.

"Well…" Mom frowned. "Where would we put it?"

"The downstairs guest bathroom? No one ever uses it. We never have guests." I'd given it a lot of thought and there were only two feasible places.

Mom pursed her lips and seemed to actually consider the idea. "I don't know, Peter. I'll have to think about that. Right now, my gut is saying no."

"What about in the garage then? The deep sink out there? All we'd have to do is put up some drywall and make a little room—"

"That would be a lot of trouble, and then we wouldn't be able to get both cars into the garage."

I gripped the glass harder. "I could build it. Adam would help me. And it wouldn't hurt the Camry to sit outside. You and Dad could switch out parking in the garage every other night."

Mom shook her head. "I don't know. Can't you use the darkrooms at school? If you had a car then you could use them whenever you liked."

"You asked me what I wanted, and I told you."

She opened her purse and fished out her bottle of Valium. "I think you'll be much happier with a car, Peter. You won't have to rely on your dad and me to take you places. You'll have independence. Freedom."

"I'll have a part-time job at some hellhole."

She shook out a pill. "You'll have an opportunity to learn time management and responsibility."

I gaped at her. "Do you even listen to me?"

"Of course I listen to you." She swallowed her pill down and took off for her writing den.

I knew I'd be getting a car.

✧   ✧   ✧

DAD CROONED THE Janis Joplin tune about a Mercedes Benz and the friends who drive Porsches as we walked around the car lot.

Truer words were never sung. I imagined myself parking in the Kingsley student lot with all the Mercedes, Jaguars, and Porsches. My car in the vision altered with each vehicle we inspected—an older Lincoln, a Ford Taurus, a beaten-up Dodge truck.

Dad clapped me on the shoulder as he pointed out a baby blue Volvo in the back of the lot. "Like in that movie, Petey. 'Volvo. They're boxy but good.'" He laughed and dragged me over to look at it.

It was okay. Pretty solid and a reasonable price. I opened the door and peered inside. It was in good shape.

Dad nodded slowly. "I have a great feeling about this one." He turned to yell across the lot at my mom. "Jessica, this is the one! Right here!"

Mom abandoned the Honda she'd been looking over and joined us next to the Volvo. She hummed and pursed her lips, taking in the car, looking at the interior, lifting the hood and looking underneath. "We'll need a mechanic to check it out, but if this is the one you like, Peter, I think it looks like a good purchase."

"I'd *like* a darkroom," I said for the tenth time. "But if I have to have a car, this one is fine."

I truly liked the car. Still, I had to keep up the pissed appearance about the darkroom just for the principle of the matter. Asking someone what they want and then forcing something else on them, even something they'd like better, just wasn't right.

I ran my hand over the top, the cold, hard metal sucking the heat out of my fingers. Mom dug around in her purse, pulling out her Chapstick. She smeared it on her lips while eyeing the car and then grabbed the back of my head and, laughing, forced Chapstick over my lips too. I struggled a little, but she had a grip on my hair and held me fast. I tried to act indignant, but I'd actually just been getting ready to ask for some. Mom leaned in and kissed my cheek, leaving a greasy mark there.

"You make me laugh, Peter," Mom said as she tucked the tube back in her purse.

Dad just rocked on his heels, grinning at the interaction. He threw his arm around my shoulder. "Okay, who do we talk to about getting this hunk of junk inspected so Santa can put it under the Hanukkah bush?"

I rolled my eyes. My parents thought they were so funny.

Mom motioned toward the office. "I'll go talk to them. You stay here, Abe."

Dad nodded amiably and kept his arm around my shoulder,

steering me all around the car, examining it from every angle while humming carols under his breath. "Petey-boy, I haven't seen Adam around lately," he said nonchalantly. "Did you two have a fight?"

"Nah, he's just busy with his parents." I leaned back against the car.

Dad stood next to me, his arm still around my neck. "So, do you love him? Or is this just experimentation?"

I swallowed and looked around the car lot, surprised he'd choose here and now to have this conversation.

"I love him."

Dad blinked slowly. He clutched my shoulder in a hard, but loving, squeeze. "Are you, uh—" I'd never really seen my dad stumble with words. "Are you, uh, sexually active?"

I didn't know the right answer to that question, so I just stared at him.

Dad nodded as though I'd replied. "Okay. Are you being careful? I know there's no way to stop you. You're a teenage boy and I know—" he broke off again and swallowed thickly, squeezing my shoulder again. "Are you being careful, Petey?"

His fearful tone brought tears to my eyes, and I bit my lower lip, my chin trembling. "Yeah," I croaked.

"Good boy. I figured you were. I wanted to be sure, though. If you need money for condoms, just ask."

I felt the roots of my hair burning.

"Adam's a good kid. Does he treat you well?"

Fuck. And how did I answer *that* question? Did I say, *"Yeah, Dad, great, except for the girlfriend he fucks?"* And did that still count as being treated poorly when you knew it was one of the few things that'd kept that incident with Eric and his fists from happening months earlier?

I nodded my head and whispered, "Yeah, he does."

"I wish you'd talked to me, Petey. I love you, and I wish you'd have come to me."

I lost it. I didn't know what it was or why, but I started to cry like I hadn't since I was a kid. My dad pulled me into his arms and patted my back. "It's okay, Petey. It's okay."

✦ ✦ ✦

IT WAS AFTER Christmas and just before New Year's Eve before I finally got to talk to Adam again.

"Hi, this is Adam. How are you today?" That instead of the usual, *"Hey, it's me."*

"Well, hello, Adam. This is Peter. I'm doing quite well, and yourself?" I teased.

"Great. I, uh, wanted to ask you over for dinner tomorrow night. I was telling my mom about you, and she'd like to meet you. She said she'd like to see some of your photographs. Sarah said to bring the photos of her and Leslie in the woods behind Kingsley? The ones where they're wearing those white dresses?"

"Um, okay. Does Sarah want me to bring the cheerleading photos too?" I asked.

"Yeah! Yes! Bring those too." Then he whispered, "Maybe some football shots. Some nice, you know, heterosexual selections?"

I cracked up. "Heterosexual selections? Did you just say that? Are you listening to yourself?"

"Yes. I am. Please, Peter."

"Okay. I swear I won't bring over the photos of you naked on my bed stroking yourself off."

Adam gasped. "Shut up."

"What? Is someone around? Should I bring the pictures of you making love to me in the bathroom? Or what about the pictures of—"

"Shut up." Adam's voice was strained. "Please."

"Okay. Jeez. I'm sorry."

"No. It's okay. Listen, can you come over around six?"

"Sure!" It'd be the first time I'd seen Adam in over a week.

"Great."

I heard Adam's mother's voice in the background and then Adam said, "Okay, sure, Mom. You guys have fun." There was a long beat and then he sighed heavily. "They're gone. She's taking Sarah to the mall for a few hours."

"Cool. So we can talk like normal now?"

"Sorry about that."

"It's fine." I held the phone in the cradle of my shoulder as I stirred the powdered cheese into the Kraft Macaroni and Cheese I was making myself for dinner. "So, guess what? My dad flat-out asked me about us the other day."

Adam sucked in a breath. "What'd you say?"

"The truth."

"Holy shit."

"Yeah. He asked if we were being careful. He told me he loved me."

Adam was silent for a long moment before he whispered, "You're lucky, Peter. I'm happy for you."

I nodded, even though I knew Adam couldn't see me. "So, where's your dad right now?"

"At the grocery store. Mom said we eat like animals, and she sent him off with a list of supplies, and to get meat for the freezer. Sarah's pissed because somehow or other Mom is making it her fault we usually survive on chips and salsa or hot dogs. You know, 'cause she's a girl and she should cook for us, I guess." Adam clucked his tongue. "Mom can be old-fashioned sometimes. Speaking of, what did *your* mom say?"

"About what?"

"About us."

"Oh." I stirred faster. "I don't think Dad's told her." I pulled the mac and cheese off the heat and poured it into the bowl I had waiting. "She said something on the way back from picking out my new car—oh, and I should tell you about that too—about how I would be able to date girls now that I can drive them. Dad just started to sing the 'Dreidel Song.' I didn't say anything either. I don't think she can handle hearing it."

I'd still never told Adam about my mother's issues. It hadn't seemed important.

"Grandkids," he said.

"Huh?" I sat down at the kitchen table and started eating.

"Your mom probably counts on grandkids. Most moms do."

"Why would she want grandkids when she barely wanted me?"

"Grandkids are different. They're only there when you want to see them, and they're proof your life will go on after you're dead. I actually wrote this cool story about aliens on another planet who can't have kids, so they clone themselves to reproduce. Adult clones, you know?"

I hummed to let him know I was listening and ate more mac and cheese.

"Anyway, so they come to earth, right? And they see the babies and children, and they get jealous of that purity, all of that primal instinct preserved in their little bodies. I mean, kids are just wild, growing, little animals, you know?"

"Yeah."

"So, they're jealous and angry because they realize they don't have anything equivalent to leave behind. They decide to try to reproduce. They do some experiments on their physiology and it turns out with a few tweaks they *can* reproduce with humans. But, here's the irony, the kicker—all of their offspring are sterile. Like mules. You know, 'cause it's cross-species breeding."

"Cool."

"Yeah."

"Did you show that to Dr. Landry?"

"Not yet. I just wrote it last week. I'll drop a copy of it in your mailbox if you want to read it."

"Yeah. Absolutely."

"Okay. Hey, Peter?"

"Mmm?" I hummed around a mouthful of food.

"I miss you."

My heart clenched. "Me too."

"By the way? At dinner? Leslie will be here. She's home from her trip, and Mom wanted to meet my girlfriend."

I bit my tongue and felt my happiness fade. "Oh. I don't think I can come after all."

"You can, Peter. I want you to. Six o'clock. Promise me."

I sighed. "Fine. Six o'clock. Is Leslie going to get all touchy-feely?"

"Not with my mom here. You'll see. No one wants to be touchy-feely with a mom around."

"If you say so."

"My dad just got home. I have to go. Six. Be here."

✦　✦　✦

THE ALGEDI HOUSE was warm and bright when I was ushered in by Mo at six on the dot. My mom had sent along a frozen pumpkin pie for dessert, and Mo eagerly relieved me of it.

Adam peeked around the corner from the dining room and broke into a wide grin. "Come on in, Peter!" he called.

I eased my way through the kitchen and past Mo, who was already defrosting the pie in the microwave. Ambushed by Sarah in the doorway to the dining room, she wrapped me up in a hug. "I've missed you!" she exclaimed happily.

I hugged her back with one arm, trying to hide my confusion and protect my portfolio from being crushed.

Mo looked over at us and grunted. "I didn't miss him." Then he added, "Well, maybe I missed him a little. Tad's a prick when he's not around."

Sarah grabbed my hand and dragged me into the dining room. Adam stood behind Leslie, who was seated across from his mother. He smiled anxiously and his eyes looked tired.

I had to drag my gaze away when Leslie piped up, "Hey, where are your glasses?"

"Contacts." I smiled shyly and leaned over to hug her hello.

Guilt and shame ricocheted inside me. Leslie was a good person. We were the assholes who kept lying to her. In any other situation, I'd love her without reservation, without pain. As it was, my affection for her sucked as much as my jealousy.

"How was your trip?" I asked her.

"It was cool. We skied and hung out at the resort. It was perfect actually."

"Good. I'm glad." I shared a smile with her, my gut clenching awkwardly, and then my eyes swung to Mrs. Algedi.

Her hair was a terrible bleached-blond color, and she wore thick glasses that made her eyes loom large. I wasn't surprised because I'd seen pictures, but it was hard to understand how she'd given birth to children as beautiful as Adam and Sarah.

She stood and put out her hand, and I shook it firmly, just as my father had taught me, making sure I didn't squeeze too hard, but also letting her know I respected her just as much as any man. None of that limp-handed stuff.

"So, you're Peter? Sarah and Adam told me all about you. It seems like you've been a good friend to them. I appreciate that." She smiled, but it was cold.

"They've been good friends to *me*, actually." I swallowed nervously and looked to Adam, who gave me a close-lipped smile in return.

Mrs. Algedi said, "Well, sit down. I was just asking Leslie some questions about her life. Getting to know her."

"Harassing her," Adam countered.

I dropped into the chair next to Leslie, and Adam sat on the other side. Sarah sat next to me and Mo stayed in the kitchen with the pie. I wasn't sure where Adam's father was, and I looked around nervously for him. I placed my portfolio carefully on its side beside my chair and, after determining Mr. Algedi was nowhere in sight, I turned my attention to Mrs. Algedi. She examined me like I was a hunk of meat she was considering feeding to the lions. I adjusted my sweater just to have somewhere else to look.

"Leslie was saying she wants to go to Princeton or Oglethorpe."

Leslie nodded enthusiastically, grabbing Adam's hand. "Oglethorpe has a great writing program, and I think Adam would be really happy there."

Adam hugged her and kissed her head. I managed to keep my face placid. It wouldn't be long until school began again, and I'd be submitted to daily and ongoing doses of Adam and Leslie touching.

Mrs. Algedi asked, "What about you, Peter?"

"I'm going to UT. My dad is a professor there so we'll get a big discount and that's important." I shrugged. "Budget is the biggest consideration."

Adam said, "I think education is all what you make of it, anyway. If you apply yourself, you can get just as good an education at UT as anywhere else." He pulled his hand away from Leslie, and I saw his mother notice his withdrawal. "I've been thinking about UT myself. I kind of like Knoxville, you know?"

"Knoxville is too hick for you," Leslie said. "You'll be happier in Atlanta with me. Oglethorpe has a gorgeous campus, and you'll be in a big city where there is *culture*." She smiled at him and bumped him with her shoulder. "Come on, don't you miss culture?"

Adam caught my eyes briefly and then dropped his gaze to the table. "Maybe, but Knoxville is cool too. I guess we'll just wait and see."

Mrs. Algedi turned her focus on me, and I felt pinned under her gaze. "Mandel is a Jewish name. Are you Jewish?"

"I was raised in a mixed household. I've occasionally attended Temple Beth-El and First Presbyterian Church. I don't go to either regularly."

"Ah. Something you and Adam have in common."

"Yes, ma'am."

"No 'ma'am'-ing, please."

I swallowed and nodded. Mrs. Algedi studied me silently for a long moment, then ran her gaze over Leslie, met Adam's eyes and raised her brow. I glanced his way in time to see him look down, and she nodded slowly. Then she stood. "My husband won't be joining us tonight. He's been detained by a work-related meeting downtown."

"Oh, I'm sorry to hear that," Leslie said. "I wanted to meet him."

Mrs. Algedi ignored that. "Peter, please help Adam set the table. Girls, help me in the kitchen."

Dinner was over quickly, and I helped Adam with the dishes while Sarah and Leslie went to Sarah's room. Mrs. Algedi supervised and blatantly listened in on our conversation.

"Taken any good pictures lately?" Adam asked.

"Yeah. They're hard to describe. But I didn't bring the new ones tonight. I'll have to show you later."

Adam shifted uncomfortably, wrongly misinterpreting my comments to mean the photos were somehow sexual. They weren't, but they hadn't seemed appropriate for "show the mom" either. He scrubbed at a spot on the bottom of the frying pan with great concentration.

"Is Sarah still dating Mike? She didn't mention him at dinner tonight, and that's weird."

Adam glanced over at his mom. "Oh, they aren't that serious. You know, just the occasional date. She's not as interested as when she first met him."

I was flabbergasted. Apparently, not only were they hiding my relationship with Adam from his parents, but also trying to hide Sarah's relationship with Mike. Yet, they weren't hiding Leslie. I tried to figure out what was going on.

Mrs. Algedi snorted. "You can cut the ruse, Adam. Your father isn't home, and Sarah's told me all about her boyfriend."

"Oh." Adam smiled and looked over his shoulder at his mom. "I figured, but—yeah. Well."

Mrs. Algedi drifted up behind us until I could feel the heat of her body and smell her perfume. Something floral. Soft. "Does your girlfriend know about Peter? Is she a willing accomplice in this or is she as clueless as I think she is?"

Adam remained silent, looking more ashamed than I'd ever seen him before.

"That's what I thought. I didn't raise you to be duplicitous, Adam."

She moved away, leaving me with my breath stuck in my throat and my gaze seeking out Adam's. His face stayed shuttered and ashamed. Then Mrs. Algedi called from the living room, "Peter! Why don't you bring your portfolio over? I'd like to see what kind of talent you have."

I dried off my hands in silence. Joining Mrs. Algedi on the sofa in the den, I showed off the "heterosexual selections" I'd chosen just for her.

And when it was time to leave, I couldn't wait to get out of there.

✧　✧　✧

THE NEXT DAY there was a letter from Adam in my mailbox.

Dear Eater,

I'm really confused. Mom's right. You've been right all along. Someone's going to get hurt, and I don't want it to be you. But, I don't want it to be Leslie either. I've never told you this because I knew you'd take it the wrong way, but I do love her, you know? Actually, I love her a lot.

Mom says I have to decide between you, or tell Leslie, or do something to make things right. My mind keeps going in circles. I keep thinking about you on the ground about to get the shit kicked out of you. I keep thinking about Les knowing just what to say to me when I'm losing my mind, even when she doesn't know I'm upset about you, or about losing you, about being— gay? Bi? Not straight. About being in love with you both.

I'm not all that good at being honest with myself or others about how I feel or about who I am. I've given it a lot of thought. I'm not good for you. I hurt you, and I hurt Leslie, even if she doesn't know it. I want you to walk away from me. I want you to leave and never look back because I can't get the balls to do the right thing.

You'll have to be strong and do what's right. I'm not going to break up with Leslie. She'll make a good wife one day if I don't ruin it.

Mom was right. She didn't raise me to do these things or to be the kind of person who would. I'm just as bad as Jamie. Maybe worse.

Please, Peter, this is not a breakup note. That's going to have to be up to you.
Adam

I stared at the note. I read it again. My heart pounded in my ears and my breath came in quick, rapid bursts. I threw on my coat and sprinted out the door toward Adam's house as fast as I could. My mind spat random phrases of what I'd read at me as though I'd somehow memorized the whole thing just by reading it twice.

Fuck him. Fuck him and his fucking bullshit. I stormed onto the Algedi front porch and pounded on the door, forgoing the doorbell for the satisfaction of banging both of my fists against the wood. I held Adam's letter still crumpled in one hand.

The door flew open and a large man stood before me. His black, thick eyebrows drew low and a scowl weighed heavily on his face. "May I help you?"

"I need to speak with Adam." I tried to peer over and around him. I wanted to shove him aside, stomp up the stairs, blaze down the hall and kick down Adam's door. Instead, I held my ground, hands clenched at my sides. "Please," I gritted out in an attempt at civilized speech.

I heard Sarah's voice from somewhere behind Mr. Algedi. "Who is it, Daddy?"

"Someone for Adam." Mr. Algedi's voice was deep and layered with his Iranian accent. His eyes narrowed as he looked me over.

Sarah's head ducked under Mr. Algedi's arm. "Peter! Oh, hey." Sarah bugged her eyes out at me in warning. "This is Adam's friend, Dad. I think Adam borrowed something of his, right? And you want it back?"

I clenched my jaw and held up the crumpled paper in my hand. "Actually, I have something to give back to *him*."

Adam appeared at his father's shoulder, his expression wary and nervous. He pushed at his father's arm, which was blocking the doorway, and said, "It's okay, Dad."

Mr. Algedi eyed me warily.

Adam shoved past him, zipping up his coat and tucking his hands into his pockets. "Come on, Peter. Let's take a walk."

I spun on my heel and took off down their sidewalk at a pace that forced Adam to jog to catch up with me. I didn't look back, but I heard the sound of the door shutting behind us. Adam followed at my elbow, just out of my line of vision, but close enough that I knew he wasn't going anywhere. Five minutes later we'd reached the neighborhood playground, and I was still really fucking pissed off.

I climbed onto the industrial-sized tire and dropped into the doughnut hole in the middle. When I heard him drop in behind me, I kept my back to him, taking deep breaths, trying to think of anything to say other than—

"What the *fuck* is this shit?" I spun around and threw the crumpled letter in his face. "What the *fuck* am I supposed to do with *that?*"

"Peter—"

"No, you shut up! You just shut the hell up for a minute." I was shaking all over, and I could feel my lips trembling. "What kind of cop-out is that, huh? *You* hit on *me.* *You* took *me* out. *You* started the sexual shit. *You* told *me* you love me. *You* forced me to deal with this bullshit with your goddamn girlfriend, and then you just fucking *cop out* on me? You just stuff this goddamn letter into an envelope and put it in my mailbox and wash your fucking conscience clean? Is that it? Because it doesn't fucking work that way, Adam. It isn't going to work like that at all."

I poked his chest hard, forcing him to step back against the rim of the huge tire. "You're going to deal with your fucking actions. *You're* going to make the tough calls. If you can't handle the duplicity, as your mother put it, then *you* break up with one of us. I'm not taking your goddamn bullshit. I'm *not* letting you take the easy way out. You don't get a clean slate just because you put this all on me. Do you understand me? Are you listening to what I'm saying?"

Adam's eyes were huge, and his mouth fell slightly open as I raged.

"Adam—" I clenched my jaw. "Are you fucking listening to me?"

"You are so *hot* when you're pissed," Adam whispered, licking his lips.

"*What?*"

"Oh my God, Peter, you are!" Adam took a step forward, hands reaching out toward me. "You are so unbelievably hot right now. Your face is all flushed, and you look like you're going to kick my ass, and I'm so turned on I think all the blood left my brain for my dick. I'm sorry, but that's all I can think about right now."

"You're a fucking bastard."

"Yeah. I am. I really am. But you're so sexy."

I rolled my eyes. "You send me this letter and you think I'm fucking putting out?"

"You sound like Leslie."

"What? You sent her a letter too?" I kicked at the dirt hard, wanting to kick him in the shins. "No. Of course you didn't. You wouldn't lay this shit on Leslie, just on *me*." I shoved him backward as hard as I could. He stumbled a little.

He held up his hands in supplication. "Peter, I'm an idiot. I shouldn't have written that letter. I'm stupid and impulsive."

"No shit. Tell me something I don't know."

"I'm sorry. I don't know what to say. I mean, you're right. It was a cop-out. But—" Adam pulled his hands through his hair. "My mom's been telling me how wrong all of this is, and she's right. She's right, Peter."

"Of course she's right, dumbass. *I'm* right. Your mom and me? We're right. Someone's going to get hurt. But, you know what? I don't fucking care. And what the fuck is this bullshit about marrying Leslie? You're eighteen. So give me a break. You're only here for a year and *fuck it all* if I'm going to walk away from you because you're too scared to do the right thing. Why am I going to punish myself for your fuck-ups? I'm not. I'm going to take what I can, while I can, and you're *going* to give it to me."

I could hear myself saying the words, and I knew I meant every single one of them, but I was still taken aback by myself.

Adam stared down at me in shock. I had to close my eyes to clear my head. Rage cooled into an adrenaline high that made me feel reckless. I shoved him back against the tire and kissed him hard, hands roaming down to cup his balls and grip his erection.

"You know what, Peter?" Adam said breathlessly between kisses. I released his groin and shoved him harder against the tire and wedged my leg between his. I ignored his question, but Adam licked his way to my ear and whispered, "I think you must be like Superman. Shy and retiring in glasses, man of steel without them." He gasped when I bit his neck. "Contacts make you aggressive. I like you aggressive."

"You don't think your stupid-ass letter had anything to do with it?" I growled.

"Maybe. But, you should make me believe it's the contacts, unless you want me to send you a letter like that once a week. I'm so hot for you right now. God, you need to be angry more often."

"Shut. Up." We were humping each other like mad against the tire, and I was having a hard time with the fact I'd basically thrown aside my resolve to make Adam grovel at the first sign of sex.

Adam moaned.

I closed my eyes and stilled my thrusts against his leg, thinking about how much I wanted to fuck him. I'd never fucked him before; he'd never wanted it.

"And you talk a lot when you're mad. Mad or high. Both make Peter chatty."

"Shut up." We moved against one another frantically. I was too close to coming, and I didn't want to come in my jeans, so I pushed back from him and unfastened my pants, pulling my cock free. "Get on your knees."

Adam's eyebrows hit his hairline, but he dropped immediately.

"Suck me."

He closed his eyes and took me in while scrambling to open his fly. He stroked himself as he blew me. Wet, hard suction had me coming in seconds. He swallowed and then nuzzled my groin as he finished jerking himself off.

We were quiet as we pulled our clothes together. I refused to meet his eye. I was still furious and hurt. I couldn't believe he'd written that letter. I couldn't believe I was willing to put up with his shit. And for what? For sex? For his "friendship?" I looked at him and sucked in a breath. His cheeks were flushed and his eyes glassy. For the way he made me feel just by existing?

"I'm going to break up with Leslie."

"No you're not."

Adam stood up and leaned back against the tire, gazing at the hills in the distance. "Maybe just for a while. I still think she'd be a good wife for me one day."

"Except you're gay."

"I'm bi. I guess. I don't like labels."

"Right. Whatever." I ran a hand through my hair. "You're eighteen. What the fuck are you thinking about marriage for?"

"I don't know. It's like this *feeling* I have when I look at her." Adam turned to me. "It's like when I look at you, and I know I want you with me forever."

"Forever?" My heart pounded in my throat. "You feel that for her?"

"In a different way. I just feel like there's *something* I'm supposed to do with her. Something we're going to be together."

"And when you look at me?"

"It's like—" Adam's shoulders bowed. "It's overwhelming."

"And what about your family?"

Adam sobered. "My dad—shit. What am I going to say to my dad about this?"

"Tell him you had to go suck me off and see what he has to say about that."

"Very funny. So funny. See how hard I'm laughing? Ha. Ha."

"You'll figure it out." I was still too pissed to give him anything more than that.

"Peter?"

"What?"

"Do you forgive me?"

I shrugged. "I will. Tomorrow."

Adam smiled a little sadly. "Okay. I can wait until tomorrow."

"Good. Because you'll have to." I climbed over the side of the massive tire and took off across the park, yelling over my shoulder, "Call me later!"

"Tomorrow?"

"Yeah. Tomorrow."

If I believed in God, I'd have begged him to help me, because in the face of Adam, I was helpless.

Chapter Sixteen

THE VOLVO SHOWED up in our driveway two days after New Year's. I sat at the wheel, running my hands over the dash and down the seats. I turned the ignition and pulled out of the driveway, pretty thrilled to have my own car, despite my initial protestations. And it was a good car at that, not something I'd be embarrassed to park next to Adam's Mercedes and Van's Lexus. A good solid car.

I turned on the stereo as I turned out of the neighborhood, heading toward Baxter Avenue. The opening wind chimes of "Plainsong" by The Cure came through the speakers. Adam's Christmas present to me had been deposited in the mailbox yesterday—a set of mixtapes for driving.

I pulled into the shopping center, which housed a new multiplex theater as well as a great photography store. I tried to push my frizzed-out hair into some semblance of order and climbed out of the car to go ask a man about a job.

After having been turned away from three other camera shops, I entered Foxx Photo with my head high. It wasn't an ideal location—thirty-five minutes from home and a tank of gas a week—but it was my last hope for a job at a photography store.

My mom had bargained and gotten a good deal, so the car payments were pretty cheap, but the insurance on top of it brought the total up enough to make me gulp. If I was lucky I might still have some money left to spend on film, movies, and sundries.

Five minutes later, I left without even filling out an application. *"Sorry, kid, no openings. Try this summer when John goes back to Utah. We might be needing someone then."*

The blush was off the rose. I no longer loved my car. I hated it. And I no longer loved my mom. I hated her too. And my dad got lumped in with her because he hadn't insisted she let me have a darkroom. I stood next to the Volvo, my back to the door, arms crossed, watching cars streak past. A bitter winter wind blew through my worn navy sweater, my jeans feeling too thin as I bit my cheek and glared into the distance.

"Sweetie?"

I jumped a mile.

Whipping around, I chuckled and grinned at the handsome man next to me. Robert wore a bright red and green Christmas sweater and black jeans, and, as always, a radiant smile.

"Oh, Sweetie, I'm sorry I startled you!"

"No problem. I was thinking hard, I guess. My brain was in extra slow gear."

Robert touched my arm and laughed, his head falling back. "I know what that's like!"

I grinned. "What are you doing here?"

He shook a small bag in my direction. "Picking up my photos, darling. Brand-new shots of me in my latest couture for the show. Would you like a peek?"

"Sure. I didn't see you in there," I said, going through the photos one by one, giving each shot attention. There were some really interesting new outfits, including one with a mermaid tail.

Robert's chuckle was soft. "Well, I was in the back *visiting* a friend, if you know what I mean."

I paused on a shot of Robert, well, *Renée* with her hip out, wearing a satin dress with a slit up to the thigh. "Barry works here too?"

Robert blinked. "No, silly. Renaldo works here."

"Renaldo?"

"Yeah, a guy I screw sometimes."

"You broke up with Barry? I thought you guys were living together."

Robert's eyes softened, and he put his arm around my shoulder. "You are so sweet, Sweetie. My God, you're so sweet. Never you mind, just look at the pictures. And for the record, no, Barry and I are still together."

"I'm not sweet," I muttered under my breath, turning back to the shots. I flipped through several more, irritated that Robert was treating me like a kid. So apparently he didn't only sleep with Barry. Why didn't he just say that?

"These are pretty good," I said after I'd gone through most of them. "Who took them?"

"Sean, my business partner. You met him at the party, right? Naughty Boy's friend's brother? It's not really Sean's thing, but he does a pretty good job with it."

He leaned in. I could smell his cologne. It was nice—sharp, woodsy in a way. I looked into his dark eyes and felt myself relaxing. I liked Robert without his makeup.

"Speaking of Naughty Boy, you looked like you were going to shoot laser beams out of your eyes when I walked up earlier. What's wrong? Is he treating you right? Do I need to talk to that young scoundrel?"

I couldn't help but smile. "No, that's not it. Well, that's not it today, anyway."

Robert laughed and touched my arm again. "What is it today?" Then he flipped a hand in the air, saying with an affected deep Southern accent, "Pshaw, don't mind me. I'm just nosy. But, tell me anyway."

I patted the car. "This is my new car. My Christmas present."

"Oh, very nice. I give it two thumbs up."

"I agree. The problem is my parents made the down payment, but I have to make the monthlies, and insurance too. I wanted a job I wouldn't hate, you know?" I glanced back at Foxx Photo. "I'm a photographer, so I thought—"

"Ah, I see. Unless they catch me giving Renaldo a blow job in the back, I'm guessing they aren't hiring, right?"

"Right," I sighed, leaning back against my car. "And neither are any of the other photography shops in town, which means with my luck I'm going to be stuck working at some greasy dump of a fast-food restaurant."

Robert gave me a long once-over. "How do you look in a dress?"

"What? No!" I laughed and shook my head adamantly. "Thanks, but I'm not interested. Besides, I'm too young to even drink at Tilt-a-Whirl, much less perform there."

"Tsk, tsk, tsk. The youth of today, they just talk and talk, they never listen. I wasn't going to suggest you do drag shows, Sweetie. I was just curious about how you look in a dress." Robert started laughing. "Oh, my. Yes, well, you think you can take better pictures than Sean?"

"Sure. Would you like me to help you next time?"

Robert ignored the question. "Can you sew?"

"Sew? Uh, no."

"Hmm, can you type?"

"Yeah," I answered, starting to wonder what was going through his mind.

"What about running video equipment? Know anything about that? Sound editing too?"

I shook my head.

"Want to learn?" he asked, smiling. "I need an assistant to help with all the projects we have going at Outrageous Video, and I need help with my drag show costumes and dances. *And* I desperately need help with the promotion of my show. I'm thinking of trying to guest-star at the Nashville clubs this summer."

"Are you offering me a job?"

"Are you interested in a job, Sweetie?"

"How much would you be paying?"

Robert wrapped me in a huge hug, his arms strong around my back and his masculine scent surrounding me. "Why don't we go back to my place, out of this cold weather, and talk about it?"

Robert's house was warm and still decorated for the holidays. I drank a cup of tea while we looked over his collection of costumes, shuffled through the various designs he had for new clothes, then checked out a few of his past projects for Outrageous Video. Most of them were bizarre comedy sketches he filmed and then broadcast on public television, but a few were serious documentaries, including one unfinished project about local drag queens. It had some really interesting footage of Robert preparing for the stage.

"I'd be willing to pay you eighty-five dollars a week if you think you can help me," Robert said, indicating a stack of papers that needed filing, phone calls that needed returning, and agents to contact regarding his show. "What do you say?"

"I say hell yeah."

Talking to Adam on the phone later, I paced around the kitchen in excitement as I outlined the whole thing. "Isn't this cool? I'm going to learn about making films, and how to make contacts with agents, and maybe even how to sew, though that isn't all that exciting to me, but—"

"Eater, are you on drugs?"

"What? No. Why?"

"Because you're talking up a storm."

"Fuck you."

"So eloquent."

"I've got such a cool job," I crowed.

"Fine, but I need to talk to you."

I took a deep breath, grabbed a jar of peanut butter, and started to make a sandwich, determined not to let whatever Adam had to say bring me down. "Okay, what's wrong?"

"My parents go home tomorrow."

"I know you'll miss them, but that's good in a way, isn't it? We can see each other again."

"And I've been rethinking taking a break from Leslie."

I rolled my eyes, held the phone to my ear with my scrunched-up shoulder, and added more peanut butter to the bread before adding honey to the other slice. I smashed them together, turned to the fridge to pull out some juice, and didn't say a word.

"Peter?"

I poured the juice and made a noise into the phone to let him know I was still listening.

"Did you hear me? I don't want to break up with—"

"I heard you," I interrupted. No need to hear the words twice. They weren't going to sound any better the second time around.

"Maybe I'll do it when the school year is over instead."

"I don't care when you do it or if you do it at this point, Adam."

He was silent for a moment before he said, "I know you care, Eater."

I didn't reply and simply took a bite of my sandwich. It was rude to talk with my mouth full anyway.

"Well, I think you should at least hear my reasons."

I kept chewing.

"We have the rest of the year to get through and after what happened with Eric—"

"Fuck Eric."

"But Peter—"

"I said *fuck Eric*."

Adam started to reply but suddenly said, "Yeah, Les, that sounds good. I love you too. Bye," before hanging up on me.

Obviously his dad had come into the room. Or his mom. Who knew if he'd told her we were going to continue seeing each other or if he'd just let her believe it was over. I didn't care one way or another.

It wasn't her business anyway. It was his and mine. And Leslie's.

Guilt hit and I had to fight hard to swallow my bite of sandwich. What we were doing to her sucked, but I didn't see why I always had to be the one to lose.

For once in my life, I wanted to win. Even if I was tired and I wasn't even sure what that meant anymore.

Part IV

Mid-January, 1991

Chapter Seventeen

O N MY FIRST day of work with Robert, I arrived just after breakfast and ran into Barry on his way out the door, heading to his second job at the university library. He winked at me, saying to Robert, "I trust you won't be liquoring him up during the day, right? No puking on my carpet." Then he was gone.

Robert asked to see some of my work and when I showed him the portfolio of portraits I'd brought, he clapped his hands and insisted we set up a photo shoot for the next month. I was a little uncertain because some of the photos he had in mind seemed difficult to pull off in the middle of winter, but I was getting paid to take pictures, so I couldn't complain.

He took me into his office, a repurposed bedroom with light blue walls and coral accents. There were two desks piled with various pieces of paper and costumery, and a vanity crowded into a corner and covered in makeup. In the walk-in closet, he showed off his "editing room." At the back of the long, narrow space was a small, square TV and multiple VCRs for editing videotape.

"Let's get you started on filing. Oh, and maybe you can help me brainstorm a new marketing plan for Renée's spring shows!"

The only blight on my first day at the new job was the return of Marcus. Sean dropped by Robert's place to help out with some last-minute sound editing on one of the comedy sketches. He'd brought his brother and a tall, nicely built, hot blond guy around the same age named Daniel.

After brief introductions, Sean, Daniel, and Robert disappeared behind the door to the walk-in closet/editing room. It wasn't a huge space, and with three grown guys in there, it had to be tight. There was no room for Marcus.

He sat next to me as I sorted through Robert's older photographs, picking out the best ones to choose between for a new flyer promoting the drag show. Marcus said nothing, but he watched my every move.

Finally, exasperated with his presence, I asked, "When do you go back to Paris?"

"Next week," he answered, shoving a thick hank of red hair off his forehead. "Still letting Adam dick you over?"

I ignored him as I flipped through photos, pausing on a picture of Renée in nothing but a zebra-striped teddy.

"Did he tell you about Jamie?" Marcus asked.

I remained silent, slipping one of the better pictures of Renée in gold sequins into the stack of "maybes."

"Did he?" Marcus shifted into my personal space. I felt his breath on my cheek, he was that close, and I had to close my eyes for a second to get my impulse to punch him under control.

"Yes." I turned in my seat to get farther from him. Admitting it felt like a trap.

"Adam will use you just the way Jamie used him."

"Fuck you," I said softly, standing, not caring that a few photographs fluttered to the floor. "Shut up about him."

"Or what?"

"Or nothing. I just don't want to hear it."

And I didn't. I remembered a week ago in the park, the letter, the look on Adam's face when I'd told him I wasn't putting up with his shit, and I turned away from Marcus. I was done putting up with everyone's shit now. Crossing the room, I knocked on the "editing room" door.

When the door opened, Robert was seated by Sean at the television and he swiveled his head to look my way. "Everything okay, Sweetie?"

"I'm going to lunch." I could feel Marcus at my shoulder, but I refused to look at him.

Robert lifted a brow and shook his finger in Marcus's direction. I heard a guffaw from behind me. "Go on then. Have a good lunch. See you in an hour."

I drove down Broadway to the Fellini Kroger and bought a package of sliced cheese, a bag of Doritos, and a bottle of water. It was scavenger food, but I didn't feel like eating at a fast-food place, and Robert's house was too far from mine to go home to cook anything.

I pulled into the parking lot of a nearby apartment complex. It was old, made of bricks and stone, and beautiful in its own way. A young couple exited the building, hands entwined and the girl's head thrown back laughing. I wondered what their apartment looked like.

Sighing, I tried to picture the kind of furniture they might have—probably hand-me-downs from their parents, or cheap stuff from Goodwill. But it was theirs and they could have a life together without anyone looking twice. What would it feel like to be free together like that?

I ate slowly. It didn't take long before I came back to Marcus and his comments. The things Marcus believed about Adam weren't true. Not that things weren't fucked up, but Adam did love me, and I loved him.

Part of me felt like I should go back, try to explain to Marcus that Adam hadn't wanted to walk away from him, that he'd been forced into it by his parents. But most of me just wanted Marcus as far away from Adam and me as possible.

I remembered the dark eyes of Mr. Algedi glaring at me, and I shuddered. I'd only seen him once, but it'd been enough to understand why Adam was frightened of him. I didn't have that kind of relationship with my dad, but my grandfather had been big and there was something terrifying about a large man towering over you in anger.

Once, I'd broken my grandmother's favorite porcelain teapot, and my grandfather had yelled at me for the first and only time in my life. He'd been strapping then, before cancer had left him as nothing but skin and bones and vacant eyes staring up at the nursing home ceiling, mouth obscured by tubes, gray hair dull with sweat.

Granddad, who'd been so strong and handsome, had died weak and sick. Life wasn't fair and the truth wasn't in the way things ended, or even how they began. The truth of a person, of a relationship, was in the parts between. The stories told later were all that lasted, and those stories were almost never completely true. It sucked, but everyone had to learn to live with that. Even Marcus. Even me.

I shoved the trash into the plastic Kroger's bag and started back to Robert's house. Marcus and Sean were gone when I arrived, but Daniel was still there. He and Robert sat at the kitchen table with a large set of blueprints spread between them.

Pausing in the doorway from the living room, I stared. The light from the south-facing window covered them both in a rosy radiance, like a painting. Robert, with his rich, dark skin and white polo shirt, shone in the afternoon light, and Daniel's sun-burnished, dark blond hair and light, sand-colored skin glowed alluringly, set off by a seafoam green sweater.

I reached instinctively for a camera that wasn't there. I wanted them to never move so I could exist in this divinely lit moment forever, away from pain, anger or jealousy. The glimmer of light in

Daniel's long, blond lashes and the stubble around his strong chin captivated me. A flush prickled my cheeks, as unexpected as it was embarrassing.

I cleared my throat, announcing my presence.

"Hey there, Sweetie," Robert said, waving me over from the doorway.

Daniel's clear brown eyes caught mine. I licked my lips and tried to make myself look only at Robert, but my eyes didn't obey. Daniel's brows twitched, and his lips curved slightly in a handsome smile.

"Daniel, love, this is Peter. My new assistant. You didn't get to meet him properly before."

"Hey," Daniel said, jerking his chin up in a casual greeting. He leaned back in his chair, his jeans-clad legs spread wide with a sexy confidence I envied—especially when I nearly tripped over my own feet walking to the empty chair Robert scooted out for me.

Daniel's smile grew warmer as I sat down. "Peter, huh?"

"Yeah. Good to meet you."

"You too. So you just started today?"

I bit my lower lip and felt the flush creeping up my neck. "Yeah. Robert's got a lot of filing for me to do."

Robert glanced between us and cocked his eyebrow. If I'd had any doubt Daniel was gay, it was cleared up with Robert's next words. "Down boy, Peter's only eighteen."

I kicked him under the table, though I didn't know why. It didn't matter if Daniel was hot. Nothing could happen anyway. I had a boyfriend.

Who has a girlfriend.

I was annoyed to think of Leslie, as if she justified my flustered reaction to Daniel's sexiness.

"Eighteen is legal," Daniel said, laughter lining his voice.

"Eighteen is young," Robert replied.

"Twenty-one isn't exactly old," Daniel said defensively.

"Maybe not," Robert allowed with narrowed eyes.

"I'm right here," I said, gritting my teeth. They both laughed and Robert winked at me. I rolled my eyes. "Anyway, what are you guys looking at?"

Daniel grinned, and I blinked at the brightness of his smile. Marcus's obnoxious presence earlier must have blinded me to Daniel's light brown eyes, broad forehead, strong arms and big hands. I wasn't blind anymore.

Robert tutted softly, and I forced my gaze over to him, my face hot again. "Well, *I'm* looking at blueprints for the house Barry and I might build next year, but I think Daniel is looking at something else."

"You're building a house?" I asked, refusing to engage with the rest of his statement.

"Barry's grandfather left him some land. We thought it might be a good idea to stop renting." He patted Daniel's hand. "Daniel here is an architecture student. He's being a doll and offering advice on the plans for free." Robert sounded proud, like he was showing off a particularly pretty photo of Renée instead of the credentials of a friend.

Daniel hadn't taken his eyes off me. In my peripheral vision, I could see him checking me out from head to toe, and it was making me sweat. I resisted the bizarre urge to sniff my armpits to make sure I didn't stink, refusing to allow myself a fast glance down to see what I was wearing. I couldn't remember if I'd chosen the good jeans that made my ass look great or the ratty ones that hung all wrong, and *why did it matter anyway?*

"So, what are you studying?" Daniel asked, leaning toward me with an earnest expression that made my stomach flip.

"Sweetie's still in high school."

"Oh," Daniel said softly, his face falling just enough I was sure

I'd truly piqued his interest—and now that interest was gone.

Ignoring the wave of disappointment, I answered him. "Photography. When I start at UT next fall, that'll be my major."

"Peter's a good little photographer," Robert said, and now he sounded proud of *me*. Maybe he collected people in his life so he could present them to others for admiration.

"Interesting," Daniel said. "Got a career plan for that? Seems a hard way to make a living." He put an elbow on the table and rested his chin on his hand, gazing at me kindly.

I wanted to tell him something impressive to gain back some of his romantic interest after losing it to the "still in high school" revelation, but I hadn't given my future career options too much thought. Life after college seemed pretty far away. So I winged it and hoped I sounded impressive enough.

"Freelance, mostly. But Robert's going to teach me some videography, so maybe I could work with a local firm making commercials eventually. I'm not sure. I've got some time to figure it out." I swallowed back the urge to add, *"I'm only eighteen."* He didn't need the reminder. I was sure any attraction to me had evaporated.

"So, you'd be behind the camera shooting Big Bob Rusty out on Alcoa Highway? You know, for Big Bob Rusty's Refurbished Wrecks?" Daniel grinned again.

Don't look at him. He's too handsome.

My heart lurched. "Sure. If they pay me, I'd be happy to film it for them."

"I've heard of worse jobs." Daniel glanced at his watch. "I've got somewhere I have to be. But did you get what I was saying, Robert? About the loads? That beam needs to be reinforced."

"Re-in-forced." Robert jotted the word down on the blueprints next to the beam in question. "Now I'm thinking of rear forced-entry and that's only good if you're playing pretend."

Daniel's laugh was infectious. "Don't scare this kid too much. He has the right to grow up without having his innocence ruined by your mouth."

I wanted to protest the "kid" and the implication that I was innocent, but I just said, "Robert doesn't scare me much, but Renée? She's another story."

Robert cackled at that, obviously delighted.

As we all walked toward the front door, I kept my eyes from straying to Daniel's ass after the first time, but I did get enough of a look to confirm he was as hot on bottom as he was on top.

Robert's eyebrow was up again, having caught me looking, but I waved it off and rolled my eyes.

Daniel shook my hand at the door. "Nice to meet you, Peter. Good luck working for Robert, and I hope you find a way to make photography work out for you." His hand was big and firm. I ran my fingertips over his palm as I let go, and his eyes sparked with surprise.

I cleared my throat. "Nice to meet you too."

Robert hugged Daniel and walked out onto the porch to wave as he drove off. Back in the house, Robert smiled as he clucked his tongue at me. "Flirting with the boss's friend on your first day. Unexpected, but charming. Color me surprised, Sweetie, that anyone other than Naughty Boy can catch your eye."

I shrugged. "It's no big deal. I can look, can't I?"

"Sure. Look and look some more. More than look for all I care, but cheating isn't something I especially condone."

I snorted under my breath as I followed him toward the office, ready to learn about the work.

"Oh, no. What *I* do isn't cheating because Barry knows all about it and so long as my heart is his, he doesn't care." Robert flipped the lights back on in the office, put his hands on his hips and gazed around the room with a small frown. "What a mess.

Filing is so boring, isn't it? Let's start with some video work."

I followed him into the closet/editing room and sat beside him on a folding chair in front of the TV and the dual set of editing VCRs. I watched him flip the power buttons on and choose out several VHS tapes to work with. As he made his choices and prepped the tapes, I worried my bottom lip between my teeth.

"Can I ask you something?" I asked after a few minutes.

"Of course."

"What's it called when the guy you're with is also with a girl who doesn't know about you?"

Robert's fingers paused over the play button on the VCR without pushing it. I felt oddly proud to have surprised him. I wasn't as pure and sweet as he thought I was. I was kind of awful actually, and so was Adam. A wave of immense relief washed over me. I'd told someone. I wasn't alone with the truth anymore. Adam had Dr. Landry, and now I had Robert.

"How long has that been going on?" Robert asked softly, his voice slipping into a tenderness I'd not heard from him before.

"A long time. Since before Christmas. October, I guess?"

"Wow." Robert looked sad, like he might cry, and I put my arm around his shoulders. I didn't expect to be comforting *him* after my revelation. "Fucking small town," he muttered. "This damn city. The damn South."

"He says he loves her."

Robert snorted a little. "He does, huh?"

"Yeah. And he says he loves me too. I don't know what to do, Robert. I don't want to lose him."

"Because you love *him*."

"Yeah." Of course I did. Well, I thought I still did.

Sometimes, in little whispers in the back of my head, ones I studiously ignored, I wasn't sure anymore. Being with Adam hurt as much as it felt good. I didn't think there was any other choice, though, and letting go of him didn't seem like the right thing to do either. Or at least it wasn't something I wanted to do, whether it was right or not.

Robert shook his head and turned to hug me hard. I relaxed with my cheek on his shoulder while he rubbed my back.

"You want to know what that's called?"

"What?"

Robert squeezed me and then pulled back, looking right into my eyes. "Baby, that's called 'fucked up.'"

✧ ✧ ✧

THE DAY WE returned to Kingsley, I drove myself to school in the new Volvo. I missed seeing Adam first thing in the morning, neatly scrubbed and still smelling like soap, but the freedom of driving my own vehicle had some advantages. Such as not having to worry about transportation issues interfering with my after-school job with Robert.

I parked in the senior lot before walking up the hill to the classrooms and my locker so I could drop off some books.

"Hey, faggot." It was a whispered sneer accompanied by a push.

I looked over my shoulder but couldn't determine just who'd said it. I knew it was one of the four football jocks standing by the entryway, but they were looking pointedly innocent. They started cackling as I turned away.

My heart hammered.

"Hey, Peter," Tina said, sidling up next to me. "Want to walk with me down to assembly?"

I smiled in relief at a friendly face and shoved my books inside my locker. "Yeah, hold on. Let me just get my English folder."

"I missed you over break, Peter." Tina leaned against the locker next to mine, smiling cheerfully up at me. "You know? I've been thinking—we should give that dating thing a try again. I mean, we're the only ones in the group without someone."

I blinked, wanting to ask her if she had amnesia, because surely she hadn't forgotten she was talking to the guy who'd been beaten up just before winter break for being a *fag*, right?

"Did Sarah put you up to this?" I asked.

She giggled. "No. Why would Sarah want us to date?" Tina put her hand on my arm as I slammed my locker shut and twirled the lock. "Oh my God. You have a crush on Sarah!"

I couldn't stop the guffaw. "Um, no."

"Well, what then? I mean, are you…" Tina looked toward the jocks by the entryway. "Are you, you know?"

"Gay?" I asked under my breath.

"Yeah."

I looked into her eyes. She was really asking in earnest. "I like someone else, that's all. Really, it's nothing personal."

Tina nodded and dropped her eyes to the ground. I pretended I hadn't seen them well with tears. God only knew what she saw in me that she kept coming back for more bad excuses.

We walked down the hill together. I put my arm around her shoulder, leaned down, and whispered, "Besides, my parents are really strict, like I said. They don't want me dating anyone."

She wrapped her arm around my waist. We took a few steps like that until I pulled away.

"Tell me, Peter," she said, her voice soft and sweet. "Tell me who you like."

Part of me felt like she knew the truth, no matter what it was she told herself, or wanted to believe, and part of me really wanted to just come clean. Instead, I said the first name that came to mind, a likely suspect who was outside of Tina's crowd. "Susan Morris."

"Susan? The redheaded lisper?" Tina covered her mouth, as if embarrassed by her comment. "Um, I'm sorry, Peter. That wasn't nice. But…Susan? *Really?*"

I smiled, holding the door open for her as we crossed into the auditorium. "Yeah, really. I think she's, um, cute? But don't say anything because I can't date her anyway. You know—"

"Strict parents," we said together.

Adam sat in his usual spot too many rows down from me. I studied the back of his head. He hadn't looked around since I came in, and I was anxious for him to notice me. Susan sat on my right, and Sarah sat on my left. Sarah whispered furtively with Mike, pushing his hands away from trying to get up her skirt.

She hissed, "Stop. We'll get caught. *Stop it.*"

Adam craned his neck around, caught my eye, and smiled before facing forward again. My heart sang in relief at his acknowledgment. I tried to hide my reaction by asking Susan how her break had been. She broke into a grin and told me about visiting her grandparents in Michigan. I didn't really listen, but I did notice Tina smiling knowingly, and I seriously questioned my sanity in telling her I had a crush on Susan. What had I been thinking?

After Mr. Waverly, the headmaster, began to talk, I shoved a piece of gum in my mouth and counted the ceiling tiles. After a third conclusive count, I refocused my attention on the front of the auditorium. Leslie sat a few rows in front of Adam, and she kept turning around to make faces at him while Mr. Waverly droned on about the upcoming semester.

Dr. Landry was in charge of her row, and finally he said, in an overly loud voice, "Miss Howard, end the flirting with Mr. Algedi, or I'll have to give you demerits. I'd hate to see you actually forced to *study* during your break period."

The area around them tittered, but Mr. Waverly didn't stop talking.

A student from each class, clutching a sheaf of papers with a moderately desperate look on their faces, sat on the stage behind

Mr. Waverly. Every day four students gave a speech to the rest of the school. Freshmen were required to speak for three minutes, sophomores for five, juniors eight, and seniors ten.

The day's senior was Jane Holland, who'd probably talk about something boring and mathematical. The junior was Mark Bush, an average guy who spent his weekends camping with a small group from his church. I figured he'd probably talk about hiking and Jesus. I didn't really know the sophomore or the freshman, so I couldn't begin to guess their topics. I just hoped they didn't say or do anything that would brand them negatively for the rest of their Kingsley careers.

I leaned back in my seat, took a deep breath, and closed my eyes.

Thirty-five minutes later, assembly was over, and Adam, Leslie, and I were walking up the hill together. Leslie grabbed my arm, peering at me with her big, blue eyes. "Peter, Tina says you have a crush on Susan Morris."

I choked on my gum.

"What?" Adam laughed. "Tina said *what?*"

Leslie whapped Adam on the chest with her hand. "Don't laugh, Adam. Peter has a crush on Susan, and I think it's sweet."

I coughed, trying to dislodge the gum. Adam thumped me on the back and the piece flew out, hitting the sidewalk ahead of us. "I don't have a crush on Susan Morris."

"Tina said you do. You don't have to be shy, Peter," Leslie said, grabbing my arm excitedly. "Susan is in my Women's Chorus class. I could totally ask her if she likes you."

"No!"

Adam was still laughing, his shoulders shaking. I wanted to kick him.

"No," I said more calmly. "I can't date. You know that. And I don't want anyone to tell her what I said to Tina. Okay? Please,

Leslie. Promise me."

Leslie looked disappointed but she sighed and agreed. "If you really feel that way, okay. But it's a shame because you'd be such a cute couple."

Adam laughed again. Leslie started hitting his arm with her open palm, and he took off, running up the hill.

She followed, yelling, "Don't make fun of Peter!"

I shook my head, wondering how many more lies I'd have to tell just to make it through the year. Maybe Adam was the one who was right. Maybe I should pick some girl to use as a shield. But just the thought made my stomach turn—for more reasons than one.

I wasn't living honestly, but I couldn't bring yet another person into the web of lies. It was bad enough Leslie was caught in it and didn't even know.

✧　✧　✧

"MR. MANDEL, HOW were your holidays?"

I looked up from racing to write the final sentences in the journal we'd been required to keep over winter break. One page for every day. It'd been miserable for me to accomplish, and I was still short by half a page. "Um, great, sir."

Dr. Landry said, "Good. I'm glad to hear it. Did you bring any photos for me to look over?"

I patted my portfolio propped up against my desk, and he nodded. Then he turned his attention to the back of the classroom. "Mr. Morgan, rumor has it you have a way with your fists."

I froze in my seat.

"Uh, not really, sir," Eric mumbled in reply. "Not really. No."

Dr. Landry clambered up onto his chair, sitting backward, as was his way. He scratched his chin and eyed Eric. "In *Hamlet,* act three, Shakespeare wrote, 'The lady doth protest too much, methinks.'"

Eric stared at Dr. Landry, saying nothing. I glanced at Adam, who had his eyebrows drawn low, and Leslie shifted her gaze between me and Eric.

"Or, if that one doesn't speak to you, Mr. Morgan, how about Emerson's quote: 'The louder he talked of his honor, the faster we counted our spoons?'"

"Excuse me, sir?" Eric asked.

Dr. Landry scratched his chin again. "Think it over. And I encourage the rest of the class to do so as well." He stood and wrote on the board, *Journal topic: Honor and spoons.*

He looked over the class one more time, then pulled a dusty book off a shelf behind his desk. "Today we'll skip our planned discussion of Keats and turn to a more modern poet, Alan Ginsberg, and his poem 'Howl.'"

After class, as I was standing up to leave, I dropped my pencil.

Behind me, Eric muttered, "Yeah, bend over, boy."

Leslie grabbed him by the arm, saying sweetly and so softly Dr. Landry couldn't hear, "I get the impression you want to be fucked up the ass with some spoons, Eric."

The guys around her hooted, and Eric blushed bright red. I really wished Leslie wasn't so amazingly *awesome.* Guilt slithered through me, sticky and uncomfortable.

Chapter Eighteen

FOR THE REST of the semester, the word "spoons" became a code word on campus not just for bad behavior but for any behavior other kids weren't comfortable with.

Mike, talking about the basketball game, said, "That was a foul, man. The ref should've called it. Nothing but spoons."

Tina said at the lunch table, "Yeah, Michael Dobbs cheating on that test was totally spoons."

Dr. Landry seemed to find it all quite amusing, handing out spoons in class instead of demerits. "I see you didn't do your homework again, William Henry. Have a spoon to help you eat what's left of your honor." Everyone laughed, the point was made, and the spoon was returned at the end of the period.

I was worried the entire situation would turn Eric into someone to be even more feared. But as the weeks wore on and nothing came of it, I worried about Eric less and less. Mainly because juggling my part-time job, my homework, and my duties for the yearbook left me with little time to spare. And Adam didn't like how all of it cut into our time together.

"You're the one who got me involved with the yearbook to begin with," I countered, eating a peanut butter and jelly sandwich on the go. It was six-thirty in the evening, and I was just leaving Kingsley campus to go to Robert's house to help with a new dress he was making. I was in charge of the sequins.

Adam followed me out of the building where we'd been covering a chess tournament for the yearbook. Sadie Sanders had taken her ever-loving time moving her final piece to victory. I took bites of the sandwich I'd made the night before as I walked toward the Volvo. It was really soggy, but I was too hungry to care. Adam dogged my steps.

"I miss you. It's been forever since we did our homework together. Don't you miss that?"

I glanced around, making sure we were alone, swallowed my last bite of sandwich, and pulled out my car keys. "Yeah, I miss that. But I've got stuff I have to do, Adam. You can come to Robert's if you want. Help with the sequins?"

Adam rolled his eyes. "Eater—"

It irritated me that he was complaining and yet refused to make it easier for us to see each other. I wanted to be with him, but if he wouldn't come up to Robert's then that was his problem. He knew as well as I did Robert wasn't a taskmaster, and we'd find a way to spend some time alone—probably even half-naked—before we had to go home. But he was being stubborn just to make a point.

He crossed his arms over his chest. "What's going on with you and Robert?"

I laughed. "Seriously?"

"Yeah, you're always with him now."

"Because he's my boss, you idiot. What the hell, Adam? Are you accusing me of something?"

Adam narrowed his eyes, and I almost opened my mouth to insist that one, Robert was too old for me, and two, absolutely not my type, but I didn't. Adam of all people wasn't allowed to act like monogamy was something I owed him. Even if it was something I gave him anyway.

I went back to trying to get the keys in the car door. "Listen, I've got to go. I'm already late."

Adam grabbed my jacket and pulled me around. For a second I thought he was going to kiss me, and my heart stuttered. The parking lot might be dark, and it might look empty, but it was still a really bad place for us to lock lips.

Instead, he just studied me.

I pulled my arm free. "Come to Robert's?"

Adam shook his head, so I got into my car. What could I do about it if he was going to act like an asshole? In my rearview mirror, Adam stood stock still where I'd left him, watching me drive off.

Later, Robert demonstrated a new dance routine while I tried to sort through the mess of legal papers he'd been reviewing with an attorney. Apparently, some agent out of Nashville was interested in working with him, so the sequins had been shelved for a later date.

I took a sip of the beer Robert had pressed into my hand and glanced up in time to see him do a bizarre arabesque move in his high heels. I nearly cracked up. A six-foot tall Black man in running shorts, a T-shirt, and three-inch heels dancing around in a kitchen with a universe painted on the walls was pretty damn funny, no matter how I looked at it.

"Then I'll toss it, like this—" Robert twirled his hand in the air and pretended to throw a scarf into the audience.

I was trying not to choke on my beer from all my laughing when the front door opened and Barry's deep *hello* boomed through the house.

Robert ignored him, kicking up his heels, continuing to describe the costuming aspect. "And after a few more moves like this, I'll rip the panties off—"

"Good God, woman," Barry said. "You'll traumatize the kid. Go put on your girly things if you're going to do this nonsense. No hot-blooded boy wants to see a man in heels. Put on your dress."

Robert grinned and thrust out his hip. "I can't. It's not finished yet."

Barry ran a hand over Robert's ass, pinching him at the juncture of thigh and butt. "Well, makeup at least."

"Nope."

"Have it your way. We've got a visitor."

My heart thumped hard once, hoping Daniel would walk around the corner. I hadn't seen him since we'd met, but I knew he was still helping Barry and Robert with the house designs. His name was dropped into the ebb and flow of their conversations, along with an array of other people I hadn't met, on a fairly regular basis. I focused on the legal paperwork again with determination. I wasn't going to be caught in my desire to see him. I schooled my face to look as disinterested as possible.

"Hey." Adam's voice was quiet, and I turned in surprise.

"Oh." I stood up, cold disappointment that he wasn't Daniel washed over me, but I smiled quickly to cover it up. I crossed over and started to hug him, but he pulled back. "You're here," I said, awkwardly.

"Yeah. What's up?"

"I was helping Robert with some stuff," I waved at the table, where Barry looked through the piles of papers. "I'm glad you're here."

"Naughty Boy," Robert greeted him happily enough, though I detected a touch of distance in his tone. His opinion of Adam had changed since my revelation. "Come in, and I'll show you my new routine. You can tell me what you think." He lowered his lashes in faux flirtation. "Maybe you'll even come see the show this week? You keep promising and not delivering."

"Well, I would but—" Adam looked back at me, his eyes dark and angry. They reminded me of his dad's. "I need to talk to Peter. Outside, if that's okay."

Robert thrust out a hip and frowned, but he said, "Go on if you want, Peter." He narrowed his gaze on Adam. "Don't make me have to send Barry out there to whoop your ass, though. You hear me, Naughty Boy?"

Adam's chilly smile was like cold fingers down my back. I had a hard time locating my jacket, even though it was right where I always left it, slung over the back of a kitchen chair. I pulled it on and led Adam toward the front door, saying over my shoulder, "I'll be right back."

I shivered immediately in the winter darkness and shoved my hands in my pockets, turning to face Adam with my teeth chattering. We stood between the Volvo and the Mercedes, Adam's face dark and blank and my stomach twisted in knots.

"We need to break up," Adam said quietly.

I swallowed but said nothing. We'd done this song and dance before.

"It's not working out anymore. We never see each other. You'd rather be here—"

I scoffed. "It's my *job* to be here."

"It's your *job* to watch Robert dance around in running shorts?"

"Yes. I have to pay for my car, Adam. That's insurance and the monthlies too. I'm not like you, okay? My parents don't have a million dollars they can just spend on nice cars for their kids, and a house for them to live in."

"Peter—"

I cut him off. "Stop. We aren't breaking up. If I can put up with Leslie, then you can put up with my job. Fuck. Are you really such a selfish bastard?"

Adam's eyes narrowed dangerously. "There's something going on. Ever since you started working here, you're different."

I threw up my hands. "Different how?"

"I don't know. But you've met someone or something because you're not the same. I feel it. You're not as in this with me as you were before, and if that's the case, then we should just end it."

I pushed him back against the car. "Shut up. Stop being a dick."

I didn't say I hadn't met anyone, and I didn't argue that I was the same as ever, because I *was* different. Working for Robert and telling him our secret had changed how I felt about myself and about Adam. I wasn't alone with my truth anymore. I had someone on my side. And, yes, I'd met a guy who'd found me attractive.

Even though nothing could ever happen with Daniel, I realized that just knowing someone else aside from Adam saw me that way had opened the world up a little.

But I didn't tell Adam any of that. Instead, I kissed him.

At first he seemed intent on staying angry, but soon we were in the back of the Mercedes, rutting against each other, and he seemed content to deal with our problems the way we always did.

Adam raked his fingernails up my back and it hurt, but I didn't tell him to stop. I bit his neck, hoping to leave a mark he'd have to find a way to explain to Leslie. He moaned, and we humped harder, grappling with each other.

Finally, I let him shove his hand down the back of my pants, rubbing the pad of his finger against my asshole until he worked the tip of it in, rough and dry. I groaned, the burning pain adding to my pleasure, and I shoved my cock against his hip until I came.

He wriggled his finger inside me through the contractions, and I cried out when they pulsed on longer than usual. Adam's climax came shortly after, and we both clung to and panted against each other, until I said, "I've gotta get back inside. I have work to do."

Adam helped me clean up my pants with some baby wipes he kept in the glove compartment, and then he nuzzled my face. "I'm sorry."

"S'okay."

"I miss you."

"I kinda got that message."

Adam snorted. "I was a dick."

"Yeah, you really were." I kissed the top of his head. "Feel better now?"

He nodded, and I shoved away. "Then I've got to go."

Despite using the baby wipes to clean up, and the car mirrors to check our hair wasn't insane, we were both still pretty disheveled when we went back into the house.

Barry and Robert took one look at us and laughed. "Get out of here. Go have fun with your man," Robert said. "I'm going to have fun with mine. You've inspired me. Barry, baby, want to do it in the car?"

Barry laughed at Robert, a deep, throaty sound, then pulled him close and kissed his nose. "No, woman, I don't."

Chapter Nineteen

I RAQ HAD INVADED Kuwait. That much I knew from the bits of
television news I caught on my visits to Dad's study. Adam was
in Knoxville because of that invasion. He'd told me that at the
beginning, but what I hadn't understood was how personally he
took it, how much he wanted US intervention, and how worried he
was about the outcome. There were some things about Adam I
wondered if I'd ever fully grasp.

But January sixteenth left no doubt in anyone's mind where
Adam stood on the issue of Operation Desert Storm. He skipped
classes to stay in the senior lounge, glued to the television set,
pointing out again and again that Jordan was *right there* next to
Kuwait, and his parents were there, and Saddam Hussein was a
vicious dictator, a pig who massacred his own people, and should be
brought to justice.

I'd only seen Adam that angry one other time—on the day Eric
had beaten me up. I didn't know what to do, so I went to my classes
and took extra notes in the one I shared with Adam. No teachers
wanted to bother him when they heard why he was missing.
Though Dr. Landry skipped classes too, sitting in the lounge with
Adam, saying nothing, just drinking coffee and offering silent
support.

Sarah was unusually quiet, but didn't stay glued to the set like
Adam. She said reasonably, "We'll know they're okay when they

call. I'm sure they'll call tonight."

They didn't call for three nights, but it wasn't for lack of trying. There'd been some issues getting them into Rome, ridiculous hang-ups that should have been sorted out more easily than they were. Adam had been in a near-panic about it. Once he heard they were safe, he calmed down. Instead, he started talking almost incessantly about the war and the Middle East's problems in general.

"Israel isn't that big, you realize," Adam said during lunch alone with him in the cafeteria.

"Yeah," I replied quietly, eating a bite of apple.

"I mean, it'd be like people in Knoxville fighting against the people in Lenoir City."

"I don't really think about it being so small." I chewed, considering it. "I guess the creation of the Israeli state really, um, stirred up shit."

Adam looked at me, eyes wide. "You could say that, yeah. I mean, seriously, Peter, how would you like it if the government cordoned off Knoxville, and said it was now a different country, and people started moving in, running you out of your home?"

"Hmm." I frowned.

"Would you fight? Would you fight to keep your home?"

"Me?" I swallowed my bite of apple. "Um…probably not. No. I guess not." I was kind of ashamed, but I couldn't see myself taking up arms and risking my life for some land.

"Would other people fight?"

"Well, yeah. Especially the good old boys. They'd fight for sure."

Adam raised his hands in a "there you have it" gesture. "And it never ends."

"So you don't think there'll ever be peace in the Middle East?"

Adam smiled, a little patronizing in his answer. "Do you think there will ever stop being good old boys in Tennessee?"

"I doubt it."

"Yeah, well, I doubt it too."

I took another bite of my apple, thinking about our conversation. Finally, I asked, "What about you? Would you fight for your home?"

Adam gazed at my face for a long time, his brows lowered in thought. "I don't know. I haven't decided."

I waited for him to say something more, but he turned back to his sandwich, settling into a gloomy silence.

I hadn't mentioned to Adam that the thing *really* suffering from all the time I spent on my new job, doing homework, or working for the yearbook wasn't our relationship, but my photography.

I hadn't been able to spend any quality time with my camera in nearly two weeks, and I was going insane. I didn't have any new material to show Dr. Landry after I'd exhausted all my holiday pictures. He continually harassed me about letting my creative outlet get lost in the shuffle.

But it was worse than that. I felt like I couldn't think if it wasn't in photos. Without a picture to tell the story, then I couldn't begin to understand the events in my life. If I didn't have a photograph to express the emotion, it was bottled up inside of me.

All the sexual desire that raced in my veins whenever I saw Adam just continued to flow there, not spent in the blow jobs and hand jobs we managed to sneak in various closets, the darkroom at school, or the hurried suck-fests late at night after I left Robert's but before I went home.

Not to mention, without photography, I didn't know how to deal with Adam's intensity regarding the war. Most of the time I tried to pretend it wasn't happening, but Adam was incapable of maintaining that façade. He wrote war stories, shared journal entries with me about his fears, and stayed late after Dr. Landry's class to discuss it. When we did find time together, he sometimes spent an hour with me in silence, staring moodily out the window. Other times, he'd scribble in his notebook, frowning, and I knew it was about the war again.

The anxiety of keeping all my fears inside and my inability to express myself built steadily until I pulled my hair and gritted my teeth, trying to let some of it out. Robert found me that way on Friday evening, hunched over the editing equipment. I was shaking and so tense I felt like I might explode. Robert's gentle hand stroking through my curls brought me back around.

"You're working too hard. Go home, Sweetie. And don't come here tomorrow. You need a day off."

He moved his hand through my hair. It was soothing, sweet, gentle—like looking through a diffusion filter on my camera lens. I sighed, letting his hands relax me, and then he rubbed my shoulders, his thumbs digging in. When his hands ran over my hair again, he grabbed a handful and pulled my head back. I opened my eyes in time to see his painted lips dropping to kiss my forehead. He was halfway to Renée.

"Go home. You've done a great job, and I'd be willing to pay you the same even if you cut back your hours. What do you think?"

I blinked at him. I didn't want to take advantage. "I think you need to put on the rest of your outfit if you're going to make that bachelorette party on time."

"Should I wear the blue? Or the green?"

"The pink. Be outrageous."

It was Friday night, and I wanted to find Adam, but I didn't know where he'd be. I decided to hit the Old City while I was still on the north side of town to see if the group might be at Beans. No such luck.

I checked Swansea Station, home of dirty magazines and specialty condoms. They weren't there either. I patted my pockets, found a quarter, and used a pay phone to call the Algedi house.

Mo picked up. "Yeah?"

"Hey, it's Peter. Adam around?"

"No. He's out with Sarah and that slew of brats they hang out with."

I ran a hand over my hair, the wind picking up and whipping around the corner to sting my cheeks. "Um, got any idea where they went?"

"I think Tina's dad's having a winter cookout on his houseboat, or some shit like that."

I kicked at the phone booth. "Okay, well, tell him I called."

Frustrated, I started to drive back home, but found I'd detoured into the city, driving toward the river. The lights on the water beckoned, and I got out of the car, worked the camera's settings, and took some photos of the Tennessee River at night.

I drove over to the abandoned World's Fair Park, taking shots of the Sunsphere in its nighttime glory. I focused on those lines that made Knoxville unique, if somewhat ugly—the low concrete buildings, an abandoned railroad station, and the twin peaks of the outdoor auditorium.

I got back into the Volvo and headed for the UT campus. I walked up to the top of the Hill, snapping shadowy, almost ghostly shots of Ayres Hall, and then climbed the massive oak tree in front of it, leaning back against a branch, staring up at the stars.

The dense night felt different than any other I'd known. I was alone in it, but not. I was surrounded by the rumble of traffic on Cumberland Avenue and the screams of laughter from drunken college students as they stumbled between parties. Several couples roamed up over the Hill in search of seclusion for some semi-romantic making out, yet I was the only one *here*, the only one who would ever know this exact time and place. I felt huge, the size of a universe, and tiny too. Less than a speck in the scheme of things.

I sat up and angled the camera to take a photo of myself. I

wanted to remember the way I felt. I sighed, tilted my head up, and looked at the stars again. There was only one thing wrong.

I didn't want to be alone.

When I got back to the Volvo, it wouldn't start. I wasn't too surprised. It'd been slow to start the last few mornings, and my father had suggested it needed a new battery since the one we'd bought the car with was already about three years old. I cranked the engine a few times before slamming my hand on the steering wheel.

Looking out the windshield across the parking lot on the Hill, I could see a small clot of college kids stumbling around near the Psychology building. One person in particular seemed to be either a very strangely shaped girl or a guy wearing a long, flowing dress. Four other guys followed behind.

I got out of the car. I heard the group of students laughing, and I thought one of them screamed something about the moon. Uncertain of approaching strangers in the night, I looked around for a phone booth but realized I didn't have any change left to make a call anyway. I'd have to ask to borrow some.

As I neared, I saw the person in the dress was indeed a boy, but not a drag queen like Renée, just a twenty-something blond guy wearing a long, sleeveless dress and what seemed to be a garland of dead leaves on his head. It was way too cold to be walking around like that, but his well-bundled friends didn't seem worried. They appeared more concerned about keeping him out of the tree I'd just climbed down several minutes earlier.

"You're high, idiot. You'll get hurt."

"The sky is made of moonbeams," the scrawny, blond guy in the dress said meaningfully.

"Yeah, I know," one guy in a green puffer coat said and laughed. "But Minty, you can see it just as well from down here."

"You'll tear your dress, princess," a dark-haired one called.

"Moonbeams!"

I cleared my throat. "Excuse me. I'm sorry to bother you. I'm just—" I jerked my thumb toward my car. "My battery stalled and I'm out of change to call my folks."

The one called Minty came toward me, his hands outstretched and white-blond hair glowing in the moonlight, a sharp contrast to the wreath of dark-brown dead leaves on his head. "Have you seen the moon?" His blue eyes sparkled, and he looked the insane kind of mad. "It's made of moonbeams. And they're everywhere. They're in your eyes!"

"Ignore him," the friend in the green coat said, stepping forward to grab him before he could touch me. "He's high."

"Okay." I stood there staring at Minty, not sure what to do, hoping someone would give me a quarter already. It was cold, and this was too strange, surreal even. "I'm sorry, but could I borrow some change? Please?"

"Hey aren't you Robert's employee? Peter, right?"

I placed the laugh I'd heard earlier, and a strange thrill of excitement shot through me. Daniel wore a bulky navy-blue coat and a dark blue baseball cap. He held a much smaller purple women's coat in one hand. I realized it must be his friend's—Minty's.

"Oh, hey," I said, affecting nonchalance that sounded ridiculous in comparison to the way I'd pleaded for a quarter only moments before. Heat rose through me. "Daniel? The architecture student or something?" I tried to say it like I hadn't been wondering off and on for weeks whether or not I'd ever see Daniel again.

"That's me." Daniel turned to Minty, grabbed hold of him, and strong-armed him into the coat. "Okay, merman-turned-moonboy, we've got a crisis to deal with that isn't you and your trip."

"There are moonbeams in your skin," Minty said to him.

"They're everywhere," Daniel agreed.

"In *everything*."

"Yes." He turned to the other guys he was with, all of whom

seemed perfectly okay with Minty being in a dress and tripping out of his mind. "I'm going to help Peter get his car started. Go ahead and herd this asshole back to his dorm. Show him that Brian Eno film I brought over, *Thursday Afternoon*. That should trip him out for a while."

Daniel grabbed Minty by his collar and pulled him into a tight hug. "Go with Antonio and Windy, okay?"

"And Linden?" Minty asked.

"Yeah, and Linden. They're going to show you a movie about a girl made out of moonbeams."

"Now you're *shitting* me."

"Maybe. You'll have to see for yourself."

Minty kissed Daniel's cheek with a wet smack and then took off running toward the east side of the Hill with Daniel's other friends in quick pursuit. "I'm made of moonbeams!" he screamed as they reached him and grappled him into a slower pace.

"Wow," I said. "Is he on LSD or something?"

"Got it in one." Daniel gently punched my shoulder, and I didn't rub it even though it kind of hurt.

"Is he your boyfriend?"

Daniel cracked up, shaking his head, his handsome face nearly split with his wide, shiny grin. "Hell, no. Not my type."

"Oh."

He pulled off his baseball cap, ran a hand through his dark blond hair, and resettled the hat on his head. "Babysitting a tripping friend is always an exercise in frustration, but Minty requires a whole new level of patience."

"I wouldn't know."

"It's probably best if you don't." Daniel grinned at me, eyes sparkling in the moonlight and looking a deeper brown than I remembered. I noticed the stubble I'd admired at Robert's had grown into a soft-looking shadow—an almost-beard. Daniel rubbed his gloved hands together. "Now let's have a look at your car."

I wanted to blurt out, "*I have a boyfriend!*" like that would protect me from the weird way my stomach tumbled over itself when I looked at him. Instead, I headed toward the Volvo and popped the hood.

"I think it's the battery," I said, looking at the engine with him. I wasn't entirely sure where the battery even was. I'd never had much interest in cars or in what made them run. Not like my mother.

"Hmm." He poked at a few things. It felt intimate underneath the hood, our breath puffing and mingling in clouds between us as he worked. He grunted and then nodded. "Try to start it."

I was reluctant to leave his side, but I couldn't think of any reason to delay, so I got into the driver's seat and tried to start the car. It cranked a few times, but wouldn't turn over. I climbed out and returned to the small shelter under the hood. A moist cloud of his exhalation glided over my face, and I tried to breathe it in.

"Well, damn," he muttered.

"Battery?"

"Looks like. Got any jumper cables?" His eyes were hard to see in the shadow, but I could make out their glistening shape in the low light. I licked my lips and wondered what it would be like to kiss someone who wasn't Adam.

"You know, to jump the battery?" he added.

"Oh, yeah. Of course. In the trunk."

"Have a first aid box back there too? And antifreeze and an ice scraper?"

I laughed softly. "Maybe."

"It's pretty much the standard safety kit parents put in every well-loved teenage kid's car. And you look well-loved to me."

Before I could stop myself, I said, "Is that a nice way of saying I have baby fat?"

Daniel chuckled. "No. In fact, I'm trying to forget you *have* baby fat."

The space between us was so small and yet so big. I shouldn't breach it. I didn't know him, and there was no reason to touch him. No reason at all.

I put my hand on his shoulder and brushed at it. "You had a leaf," I lied.

Daniel went still, his eyes drifting to my mouth. Everything narrowed to a tight awareness of his gaze on my lips. My fingers itched to touch his unshaven face. As if compelled by some internal force, my head tilted and my hand came up so my fingers were only a few inches from his cheek. I couldn't breathe.

He took a few steps back and put his hand on the hood to close it. "My car's parked at the University Center. Come on."

The disappointment stung. I moved out of the way and wiped the back of my hand over my mouth, obliterating the kiss I'd wanted him to take.

I didn't feel ashamed by my near-betrayal, and I knew why: Leslie, and Adam's declaration that he loved her. Did sharing a kiss with a guy I found attractive mean anything when Adam asked me to share his *heart?*

"It's not far from here." Daniel said quietly.

My hand shook as I rubbed it over my lips again.

He grabbed hold of my elbow, stilling the movement. "Hey, it's not that I don't want to. Hell, I've wanted to from the minute I saw you at Robert's house."

"Are we—are you—what are you talking about?"

Daniel gave a small laugh and touched my chin. "Kissing you. I'm pretty sure you're as attracted to me as I am to you, but you're in high school. And I can't go there."

"I have a boyfriend," I said.

His eyes grew tender, and he sighed. "Another good reason not to kiss you, then." He waved in the direction of a well-lit path leading toward the main sidewalk near the rushing cars of Cumberland Avenue. "It's cold, Peter, and I don't know about you, but getting your car started sometime in the next year seems like a good idea."

My name in his mouth was a thrill, and I wanted to have a few minutes to tamp down my reactions. I could walk with him to the UC, get in his car, and ride with him, all the while knowing that he knew I'd wanted to kiss him, and knowing that he wanted to kiss me too, and knowing that he wasn't going to actually do it. It seemed like a recipe for more humiliation and arousal, which didn't seem exciting or fun, just disappointing and miserably tempting.

I closed my eyes, called to mind Adam's smile, his eyes, his hands, and his expression when he was fucking me. It should have worked to dispel whatever I found exciting about Daniel, but when I opened them again and met his gaze, the attraction was still there.

"I'll wait here." It seemed a safer choice.

"Look, I'm not leaving you alone."

"I'm fine. I was here alone for a long time before you came."

"Right, well, now you're not alone, and friends don't let friends sit by themselves in a broken-down car at night." He motioned to my keys. "Lock it up. Renée would stab me in the eye with one of her heels if I let anything happen to you out here."

"I'm not a kid."

"Maybe you're not. But I just sent my little posse off, and now all I've got is you for back-up. What if I get attacked on my way over there? You're making it really hard for me to do this favor for you."

"I'm sorry."

"Nah, *I'm* sorry. I shouldn't have brought up kissing you. Would it be better or worse if I just did it? Got it over with so we could move on and get your car started so you can get home?"

A zip of arousal shot up my spine so hard and fast that I gasped, and my dick responded like Daniel had dropped to his knees in front of me. "What? No. No kissing." This time I said it like it was a protective mantra.

Daniel's laughter was warm and easy. "Okay. Rumor is you're a sweetheart and loyal to your man. I'm sorry if I upset you."

"Robert told you that?"

"It was Renée, actually, but yeah."

"So you knew about my boyfriend?"

"Yeah. And his girlfriend."

My lust cooled under an icy embarrassment. "Renée told you all of that?"

"Well, I asked her about you, and she was drunk as a skunk. But, for the record, she's really bad at keeping secrets. Robert's a little better at it, but since they're the same person, well, I think you see what I mean."

I felt shaky inside. "She told you about Adam's girlfriend?"

"Hey, listen, it's okay. I shouldn't have said anything. I'm messing this all up with you. I just want to help you with your car."

"Wait, you asked Renée about me?" My body didn't seem to know how to react, swinging between hot prickling embarrassment and giddy wild excitement in seconds.

When and why? Maybe it was at Tilt-a-Whirl if it was Renée who'd told him. Why would Daniel think about me at a gay club where there were plenty of really sexy guys to think about instead? At least there had been last fall.

"Yeah, I did. But like I said, you're in high school, so my interest has been put on layaway."

"Layaway? Like a bike?"

He chuckled. "A really sleek bike I'd like to ride."

I flushed.

"I asked Renée about you because you're hot, and I wanted to know more. I'm sorry if I crossed a line."

"You didn't. She did."

Daniel shrugged. "She's gossipy, but she's got a good heart."

"The fact that she told you all that kind of sucks since I don't know anything about you."

Daniel took off his cap again and then put it back on. "So, walk with me to the UC to get my car, and you can learn something about me to make up for it."

"Yeah?"

"I'll make it worth your while."

I hoped the thing I'd learn was what it was like to kiss him. I grabbed my camera, locked up the Volvo, and fell into step beside him.

We cut through the grass toward Cumberland. The night was crisp and old leaves crunched underfoot until we reached the sidewalk. I fiddled with my camera settings while I tried to figure out how angry I was with Renée.

"Have you ever been in my situation?" I asked.

"What? Dated a guy who had a girlfriend?"

"Yeah."

Daniel shook his head and looked down at me with a small smile. "Nope. But I've been in some bad situations, some worse than what you've got going on."

"Like what?"

"There's so much to choose from." Daniel's strides picked up speed. "Hmm, okay. I lost my virginity when I was fifteen. To my best female friend."

I hustled quickly beside him and tried to imagine having sex with a girl. I shuddered and hoped he thought it was from the cold. "You used her as a beard?"

"She thought I did. Once she found out. But that wasn't my motivation. Mostly, I just didn't *want* to be gay. I thought if I liked doing it with her enough, then I could make it work."

"But you were wrong?"

"Obviously." The lights from an oncoming car illuminated Daniel's face, and I could see the sadness in his eyes. "To make it worse, she was in love with me, and she felt used. She ended up going into therapy for self-image issues."

The cars on Cumberland whipped by at high speeds, and almost every driver looked like they were college age or younger. A car swerved over the white line and Daniel grabbed my arm, pulling me away from the road. He turned and flipped off the driver.

"Wow."

"Asshole," Daniel muttered, guiding me back onto the sidewalk. "Anyway, it's wrong to mess with other people that way." He sighed. "I got a letter from her last year telling me she was getting married."

"That's good, right?"

"I don't know. I haven't met the guy, and she's not known for having good taste in men. She fell for me, didn't she?" Daniel put his hand on my shoulder and squeezed. "Not that I'm blaming *her*. All of it—everything—was on me."

I didn't say anything because we'd reached the parking lot beside the UC, and Daniel pointed at his car—a small blue Honda with a large dent in the side.

"Betty Blue," he said and made a hand gesture as though introducing me to his car.

"Uh, nice to meet you, Betty Blue."

Daniel popped the locks and I climbed into the passenger side. The radio was tuned to the college station and the new song by R.E.M., "Losing My Religion," played quietly. The drive back to the Hill only took a couple of minutes, and I listened as Daniel sang along, his voice creating a harmony with Michael Stipe's warble.

I glanced at him out of the corner of my eye, his long throat tense as he sang, and his unshaven face absorbed in the lyrics.

We pulled up next to the Volvo, and Daniel showed me how to hook up the jumper cables, explaining that red went with red, and black with black, and to never mix the two unless I wanted to end up crispy and very dead. Then he started his car again, calling out his open door, "Crank the engine for me."

The Volvo started easily, and Daniel stayed in his car, letting it juice up for a few minutes. I half wanted him to come over and sit with me while we waited, but I knew it was probably best if he didn't.

In the confines of my car, if he offered to kiss me again? I wouldn't say no.

When Daniel was sure the Volvo would carry me all the way home, he removed the jumper cables, lowered the hood, and passed them to me through my open window.

"Thank you," I said.

"No problem." He touched the bill of his hat and nodded goodbye.

I called out, "Wait!"

Daniel turned, his eyes questioning.

"Can I take your picture?" I held up my camera.

Daniel looked baffled but he shrugged. I was relieved when he didn't slap on a cheesy grin, but just stood there with his hands in his pockets and a bemused expression on his face.

My hands shook a little as I focused on him. I snapped the shot, and he turned to go.

"One last thing," I said.

"Yes, Peter?" A mixture of amusement and frustration layered his voice.

"What was her name?"

"Who? Margaret?"

"The girl from high school."

"Yeah, Margaret. She was a good person. Deserved a hell of a lot better than me."

"You're a good person, Daniel," I realized I hadn't said his name aloud in all the time we'd talked. It sounded loud in my ears, and I wanted to say it again. "You helped me even though I was a jerk tonight, so thanks."

"No problem. See you around."

I watched him walk away toward the dorms, his ass filling out his jeans and his shoulders stretching broad under his coat. He took off his cap and rubbed a hand through his hair, tousling it, before setting the cap back on. I took a photo of his back as he went.

He didn't look over his shoulder once. I finally put the Volvo in gear and drove home.

Chapter Twenty

THE NEXT MONDAY shouldn't have been as horrible as it was. First off, it had snowed the night before, leaving a light dusting of white over everything. Kingsley wasn't closed, although the public schools were out, and the entire campus had a festive feel from the moment I arrived. Guys chased each other down the hill, throwing horribly small snowballs at retreating backs, and girls twirled in the still-falling flurries, trying to catch flakes on their tongues.

I smiled, hitching my bag up on my shoulder as I walked away from the Volvo, my spirits lifting at the shenanigans around me. Susan Morris stood with Tina and Leslie at the edge of student parking, her red hair bright in the crisp winter sun. Tina beckoned me. I noticed the grin on Leslie's face, as well as the expression on Susan's, and I swallowed hard. My heart pounded as I resolutely turned away from them, any trace of snow-day happiness vanishing. I booked it toward the building that housed my locker.

It was just my luck that the combination jammed, trapping me there ten seconds longer than necessary, so I had no choice but to smile when I was suddenly surrounded. Susan's sweet, if slightly common, face was red from the cold, her nose glowed, and her eyes were half-lowered in obvious embarrassment.

"Peter? I know you didn't want me to say anything," Tina began.

"Listen, I need to, um… I need to speak to Dr. Landry before class. I can't talk right now." My locker finally pulled open, and I exchanged my Geometry notebook for my English notebook, tossed it into my backpack next to my journal, and carefully placed my camera on the top shelf of my locker.

Leslie grabbed my arm. "Peter, Susan is really nice, and since you like her, we talked to her about your parents not letting you date. She's okay with that, right Suz?"

I blinked. Oh my God, I could *not* believe what was happening.

"Right," Susan said softly. "I'm so excited, Peter. I've liked you from the beginning. You're so nice and smart." Her lisp tripped along sweetly.

"And cute," Tina supplied.

"And cute," Susan agreed.

I shook my head. "I, um, well, you're smart and nice too, but I can't date anyone."

"It's okay, Peter. We can just see each other at school for now, and when summer starts and you don't have so much work, we can start going out then." Susan shyly touched my hand, and somehow I found I was holding her cold fingers. "Leslie and Tina said I could start hanging out with you guys as a group, and then we could see each other at parties—"

My eyes must have grown wider as Susan talked, because Tina squealed and grabbed Leslie's arm. "Look how excited he is."

I pulled my hand away from Susan, smiled in what I hoped was a kind way, and said, "I really have to see Dr. Landry. See you later."

As I walked away, I glanced back to see them all holding hands and gibbering to one another.

Susan didn't take no for an answer. More than once I tried to explain to her I couldn't date, and told her I wasn't comfortable calling myself her boyfriend, especially when we didn't do anything remotely like what people do in a relationship, but Susan didn't mind. She ignored my concerns entirely at worst, and at best she laughed them off.

Quickly, I realized she had more to gain from the situation than I realized at first. After all, I was part of the "popular" crowd due to Sarah and Adam's friendship, and if Susan was my girlfriend that meant she was part of the crowd too.

She hung out with the group during lunch or went with us all to the movies. She sometimes held my hand, and more than once I was tricked into a kiss by turning my head at the wrong moment. But she never used tongue and didn't seem concerned about going any further. She didn't even have my phone number, so she never called me at home. But she was always there at Kingsley to greet me first thing in the morning. I honestly didn't know what to do or what to think.

I was surprised Susan even *wanted* to hang out with us given the way Sarah had treated her the first day. But over the months, they'd reached a strange kind of peace. Susan shared several classes with Sarah, and she'd ended up being instrumental in helping Sarah reach a new height of understanding in Geometry. Now, with Susan acting as my girlfriend, Sarah was even friendlier with her.

For his part, Adam seemed amused by the situation, but he also made it clear he thought it was a good thing. "See, Eater?" he said when Eric and his friends walked by, double-taking at Susan sneaking a kiss on my cheek before class. "No more need to call spoons."

I rolled my eyes, waving after Susan's retreating form. "If this isn't spoons, I don't know what is."

One Saturday night after I'd left Robert's house, I headed over to Allison's. Her parents had gone to Albuquerque for the weekend. I knew Adam, Leslie, Sarah, Mike, Van, and Susan would all be in attendance, as well as a few other people Allison had invited. Tina was sick with the flu, but otherwise the gang was mostly all there, so I wanted to be there too.

Allison's place was big, loud, and crowded, but I found Adam and Leslie. I took the beer Adam pressed into my hand and drained it quickly. It wasn't that I hated parties like this one, because I didn't. But I preferred the smaller ones consisting of just our group. All the extra people made me a little nervous, so I grabbed a second beer and started in on it.

Almost as soon as I'd finished, I had to pee. I excused myself, stumbling through the house looking for an unoccupied bathroom. I finally had to settle on the one outside by the pool house. Despite the cool weather, the area around the pool wasn't empty. Mike and Sarah were on one of the lounge chairs, both of them with their shirts off, kissing in the moonlight. I wasn't surprised that they'd found a private place, because they always sneaked away at parties to make out. I *was* surprised to see Susan standing quietly against the doorjamb of the pool house, with her mouth open and eyes glazed, watching Sarah writhing on Mike's lap.

That's when I knew I wasn't the only one living a lie.

Catching me watching her stare at Sarah, Susan blushed to the roots of her hair. I mouthed, "No big deal," as I approached. She touched my arm and looked into my eyes. "Seriously," I whispered. "It's okay."

Susan blinked back tears and rushed past me. I used the facilities, my heart hurting for both of us.

Mike and Sarah were still going at it hot and heavy when I headed back inside the main house, so I pulled the blinds on the French doors leading out to the pool so no one else would get treated to an accidental live porn-show.

Over the next few weeks, Susan and I worked out an arrangement of covering for each other without ever directly talking about it. I wasn't sure how much Susan suspected or guessed about me and Adam. I assumed she thought I suffered unrequited lust for him, like she did for Sarah. But I admitted to myself that she might know more than she let on. Like most gay kids, Susan was good at keeping secrets.

As February thawed, I was drowning in them.

I couldn't tell people at school that I was a drag queen's personal assistant. I spoke about Outrageous Video only in veiled terms, for fear my friends would decide to watch the public broadcasting station to see what I'd been up to.

And I'd carefully crafted a lie for my parents to explain how I'd met Reverend Michaels's son and how he'd offered me a job helping him with his video productions. I didn't tell them Robert was gay, or a drag queen, or that I was learning the art of making man-sized dresses.

On top of those lies, my dad still hadn't told my mom about me being gay. Adam theorized that my father hoped it was something I'd grow out of and eventually I'd find a nice girl, like Susan, and settle down to make a lot of babies. But I knew the real reason was Dad didn't think she could handle it because of what had happened to her brother.

Then there was the secret I kept from Adam: my preoccupation with Daniel. I hadn't seen him since the night on campus, but I'd thought about him. A lot. Both photos I'd taken came out blurry. But alone in my room, I studied every detail anyway. I ran my finger over the fuzzy outline of his face and the cap covering his dark blond hair, wishing I'd gotten a clearer shot.

The fact that I kept Daniel a secret from Adam told me everything I needed to know about my motivations.

Secrets and lies felt like my whole life.

At least my schedule wasn't as hectic as it had been. Robert insisted I only work four days a week, which, on the downside, limited my opportunities to run into Daniel again, but, on the upside, gave me Sunday to spend with Adam and some free hours for my photography.

I shoved aside thoughts of lies as I lay fully clothed on Adam's bed, watching him scribble a story in a notebook at his desk. His hand flew over the page, backtracking to scratch out and rework a phrase. It fascinated me how he drew with words.

He looked up and caught my eye. "You never told me, you know."

"I never told you what?"

"How you knew you were gay." Adam put aside his pen and pushed away his notebook.

I sighed, leaning against the wall behind the bed. "I guess I was about ten when I realized most other guys didn't want to kiss Han Solo."

"Uh-huh."

"Like, I *really* wanted to kiss Han Solo."

Adam laughed, crawled onto the bed, and pushed on my shoulders until I was on my back. He covered me with his body, starting a gentle roll of his hips that had me hard in an instant.

"I thought you wanted to hear my story."

"I do. Talk."

I sighed, licked my lips, and tried to keep my train of thought despite his dick digging into me.

"Um, so, I uh—" I shook my head. "Okay, so I wanted to kiss Han Solo." I shifted, and my cock was stroked by each thrust of his hips. "Then I tried to kiss my babysitter—a boy who lived down the street. He told other people. That's why at my old school they, uh, Adam, uh—"

"Go on."

"Why they called me a fag at my old school." I threw back my head and began to rut against him hard. It wouldn't take much. Adam's hand on my zipper seemed to promise he was going to—

But it was too late. I moaned and came in my jeans.

Adam laughed against my hair. "Oh, Eater, I love when you do that. You're so easy."

I sighed, ran a hand over my face, and let him try to clean the cum out of my jeans with baby wipes.

"Tell me more," he said.

"So, I kissed my babysitter," I continued. "And when I started jerking off, it was always while thinking about guys. I just knew."

"What guys?"

"Guys! You know, lots of guys!"

Adam kissed me, and I tasted his tongue. He shifted on the bed and grabbed my hand, pulling it to his erection. I unzipped his pants, wrapped my fist around his cock, and thumbed the head.

"Tell me more," Adam whispered.

"I jerked off looking at male underwear models in the Sears catalog. Sometimes I got hard at school fantasizing about every cute boy in my class. I'd imagine them sucking my cock. And when I'd masturbate, I'd put a finger in my ass. I'd pretend it was someone's dick."

Adam shook when he came, and I licked his cum from my hand.

"Fucking hell, Peter. That's so fucking hot."

I pushed his jeans down all the way. He was still panting from his orgasm when I rolled him over, palmed his firm ass cheeks, and spread them wide.

"And somehow, I just knew it wasn't very straight to want to do *this* to another guy either."

Adam grabbed his pillow and stuffed a corner of it in his mouth as I bent to swirl my tongue all around his puckered hole. He twisted and moaned, stifling his noises, and I pushed my tongue until it gained entrance, and his tight anus squeezed the tip of it hard.

When I started to push a finger in next to my tongue, he flipped over, grabbed my wrist, and pulled me up for a kiss.

"Get your pants off and ride me," he said, reaching for a condom, already getting hard again.

As I slid down on his cock, feeling stretched and achingly horny still, Adam smiled up at me. "If I could, I'd fuck you forever. Your ass is the best thing I've ever been inside."

I felt a weird swell of pride as I lifted up and down, loving the long drag of his dick in my hole. My ass was better than Leslie's pussy. I closed my eyes and rode him hard, reveling in that knowledge.

When he came, I came again too, collapsing on his chest. Adam wrapped his arms around me, and I let him hold me as a vague dissatisfaction fell.

Being better than Leslie wasn't enough. It didn't make up for all the secrets and lies in my life. I didn't know how much longer I could stand being a person I couldn't respect.

✧ ✧ ✧

MID-MARCH, ALL OF the other seniors started talking about acceptance letters. I knew where I was going, and I knew I'd get in, so none of it was a big deal for me. Still, it was important to everyone else, and shouts of "I got into Harvard!" echoed in the corridors.

Girls squealed when they found out they'd be going to the same university, and some fought off tears more or less successfully when their friends got into their first-choice school when they hadn't.

Adam never said a word. He'd been annoyingly secretive all year about his college plans, always claiming that he wanted to wait and see what offers came in first.

"What's he down in the mouth about?" Mike asked Leslie, nodding toward Adam as we all sat at a round table in Beans.

"He got in everywhere he applied," she answered.

My stomach twisted. So she knew things I didn't. "And where was that?"

"Oglethorpe and UT."

Adam stared at his coffee morosely. "I haven't decided yet."

I remained silent and so did Leslie. She met my eyes, though, and made a pouting face. It was clear she wasn't pleased with Adam's answer either.

Mike said, "Oglethorpe is a good school, and Sarah and I will both be there."

"And me," Leslie said.

I bit my lip. I hadn't known Mike and Sarah were also going to Oglethorpe. The chances of Adam leaving Leslie *and* Sarah were slim to none. Bitterness settled in my gut.

"I like Knoxville," Adam said stubbornly. "I don't understand what's so hard to grasp about that concept."

Van and Mike exchanged glances, the kind I was becoming familiar with, and I took a sip of my coffee to avoid their eyes.

Susan said, "I might take a year off to do Habitat for Humanity. If I don't do it now, when will I ever have the chance?"

I sipped my coffee in silence as Susan changed the topic from schools to what everyone would do if they took a year off. I didn't listen; instead, I parceled out the months in my mind. One and a half more until Adam left for Europe for the summer. And then he'd go to Oglethorpe. And then—maybe he'd be gone for good.

I had little optimism that Adam and I might make a future together. Not in the face of everything else. Like college. Like Sarah and his mother. Like Daniel and my attraction to him. Like the fact that Adam was kissing Leslie's cheek and whispering in her ear. Like the fact that I wanted so much more than this, so much more than Adam was willing to give.

Adam didn't have to be my future. He could be my for now.

And I'd take whatever I could for as long as I could because, despite everything, I loved him, and it wasn't going to last. We didn't stand a chance.

"Mom wants him to go to Oglethorpe," Sarah said, looking directly at me. The subject had apparently swung back to Adam. "She's adamant he should at least give it a shot."

Adam shrugged. "It's not Mom's life, it's my life, and I'll do what I want to do."

I didn't have any faith in that. Between his mom, Sarah, and Leslie all pushing for him to go to Oglethorpe, there was no way he'd end up staying in Knoxville. No way at all. My brain buzzed and something loosened inside me, like a knot untangling from the huge mess of my lies.

A way out.

✧   ✧   ✧

THE NEXT DAY, Leslie and Adam passed notes back and forth while Dr. Landry talked about Sylvia Plath and her unfortunate love affair with the gas stove. I closed my eyes and lost myself in the memory of seeing Daniel at Robert's the night before.

The moment I'd spotted Betty Blue in the driveway my heart had started pounding. By the time I'd let myself into their house, my mouth had gone dry, and I was hyperaware of everything about myself—my clothes, the stubborn pimple on my chin, and even the way I walked.

I'd found them sitting at the kitchen table.

"Hey." Daniel jerked his chin up like when we'd been introduced.

I stuffed my hands in my pockets and tried to sound casual. "Hey. Long time, no see."

"Not that long." The light from the window shone bright against the side of his face. He'd shaved, and I noticed the line of his jaw, the

way it led down to his long neck and strong shoulders. He looked so good in a brown, blue-flecked sweater that skimmed over his nicely shaped chest and turned his eyes a dark umber. His blue jeans hugged his package nicely, and I stared at it a little too long. Admittedly, he didn't seem to mind, but it made my cheeks flush when he caught me.

Smirking, he asked, "Did you get a new battery?"

"Uh, yeah. The next morning. Thanks again for the help."

"Anytime."

An awkward silence fell, and Robert's annoyingly expressive eyebrows went up. My cheeks got hot, and I cleared my throat, trying to appear nonchalant. Daniel's mouth twisted in a small smirk, but he kept his eyes averted, staring at the tile floor.

I couldn't stop gazing at his face until my fingers again itched for my camera. This time it was around my neck, and this time the picture wouldn't be blurry. I could feel Robert's eyes on me but the opportunity was too good to let pass. I raised the camera and took three fast shots.

Hearing the snicks, Daniel jerked his eyes up. The calm force of his gaze, even through the lens, felt like a touch. I gasped and stepped back.

Barry came in from the garage with a five-pack of blank cassette tapes. He handed them to Daniel as I fiddled with the settings on my camera to avoid looking at anyone.

"Just put what you think I'd like on two or three of them," Barry said. "Keep the rest for yourself or whatever."

I motioned toward the office. "I guess I'll get to work."

"It's okay, I'm leaving." Daniel stood, tucked the cassettes under his arm, and shook Barry's hand. "Thanks, man. I'll get you some good stuff." He hugged Robert.

"You don't have to go yet," Robert said.

"Yeah, I kind of do."

I swallowed as he approached, pausing right in front of me. I couldn't breathe as I stared up into his eyes.

"See ya," he said and then swerved by me to leave from the kitchen

door instead of the front.

Barry frowned. "What was that about?"

"He's hot for Sweetie. Can you blame him?"

"Shut up," I said.

Barry cackled. "Ah, I see. And Puker's hot for him?"

"I am not hot for him."

"Look at him blush," Robert said.

"What? I'm not! I'm just…oh, fuck it. You know what? Screw you both."

"If you insist!" Robert preened.

I hesitated, thinking of denying it again more vehemently but instead stomped toward the office in protest.

Barry chuckled. "Drama queens," he said. "Surrounded by damn drama queens."

"Can't live with us and can't live without us, baby," Robert called as he followed me.

I played the scene over again, remembering the way Daniel had leaned toward me before he'd started out the door. A phantom touch tingled on my arm as I imagined him grabbing hold of me and dragging me up for a kiss. I bit my lip and closed my eyes, hoping I didn't pop an erection.

Dr. Landry's chalk screeched on the board as he wrote SYLVIA in capital letters. He hadn't finished the A before my mind drifted back to Daniel, and thinking about how he'd left as soon as I'd arrived. Was being around me really that hard? Did I have that kind of effect on him? If I were older, if I weren't with Adam, who knew what might happen between us?

Suddenly, William Henry shouted out, "Like *Twin Peaks?* Right? Like Laura on *Twin Peaks!*"

I turned around to stare at him, along with everyone else in the classroom. His face was lit up in a way I'd never seen.

"I get it! She was overwhelmed by the darkness within!"

Dr. Landry blinked, then burst into a grin, turned to the chalkboard, and wrote, *Laura = Sylvia*. "That, William Henry, will be the topic of your term paper. I look forward to reading your genius."

He then gazed around the room, letting his eyes fall on me. "Is anyone having a hard time coming up with a theme for their term paper? Mr. Mandel, perhaps?"

I blinked, startled to have been singled out from the entire class. "I, uh, guess I—"

"Don't have any good ideas?"

"I guess not, sir."

"Let me suggest you come up with one lickety-split. No time to lose. They're due in just a few weeks, after all. Time has a way of sneaking up on you, pouncing at the last minute."

"Yes, sir," I agreed.

"How about you, Mr. Algedi?"

"I was thinking of doing a paper comparing the relationships of Ruth and Naomi to Jonathan and David in the Bible and looking at them from the perspective of literature."

Dr. Landry's eyebrow went up. "Ah, an exploration of the meaning of love in the earliest literature, so to speak?"

"Maybe?" Adam replied, suddenly losing his surety.

"Good choice, Mr. Algedi. Interesting, and no doubt the research will serve you well in your History of Religious Philosophy class too."

Adam grinned. "I'm a busy guy. It doesn't hurt to do double duty."

Dr. Landry looked at Adam meaningfully. "No, indeed it does not. Unless of course it *does*." He turned to the board, scrawling quickly as he spoke. "Journal topic: the casualties of double duty. Class dismissed."

✦   ✦   ✦

SPRING BREAK CAME up fast, with the end of the year looming just behind it. Leslie's parents had rented a condo for us near Ft. Myers, Florida. We were all invited but only Mike, Sarah, and Adam had been able to go. Well, and me.

I didn't want to though. Me, Leslie, and Adam at the beach? With no adult supervision? It seemed like a recipe for torture, or disaster, or both.

Adam insisted. "Eater, what the hell? It's senior year spring break. You have to go. I want you there."

"I need to work," I lied.

"You can work something out with Robert. I'll talk to him myself. You know he's always going on about not wasting your youth and—"

"I'm afraid to fly." It was a half-truth. I'd never flown and the idea of it made me ill, and if it worked for getting me out of the trip, then it was worth exaggerating my phobia.

I turned away from Adam's gaze and toward Robert's designs for a new corset. "So, go on. Have a good time. It's okay, really."

Adam put his hands on my shoulders, turning my body to force eye contact. "You know it's a lot more likely you'd die in a—"

"Car wreck. Yes, I know." I crossed my arms.

"Well, how will you ever go with me to see the Leaning Tower of Pisa? Or Paris in the springtime? Or the Great Wall of China? Or—"

"I'd be willing to be sedated for that." And those trips were never going to happen because all I had with him was the rest of this year and then he'd be gone. "But I'm not getting on a plane to go to *Florida*. Period."

Adam studied my face and broke into a grin. "I love it when you put your foot down."

Relief mixed with jealousy rippled through me. The idea of him enjoying spring break with Leslie while I stewed about it at home wasn't awesome either. But it had to be better than going along for the ride. Even so, some spite slipped through. "I'll see you when you get back, right? It's just a week. You'll be gone for three months over the summer, and then you'll be at Oglethorpe, and we'll never see each other, so it shouldn't be that big of a deal."

"We'll see each other. I'll make sure of it."

I noticed he didn't deny that he was going to Oglethorpe.

"And I want you to come on spring break, Eater."

"You can't always get what you want," I sang under my breath, turning back to Robert's new designs. The breathless pain in my chest pissed me off. I was okay with being his for-now guy, but sometimes I wanted to rip the bandage off and be done with it almost as much as I wanted to wring every last blow job or moment of affection out of our crumbling relationship.

Adam touched my hair gently, letting his fingers card through my mop of curls. "We'll drive down, then. You and me. Just the two of us. We can meet up with the gang at the beach."

In a flash, I pictured the two of us alone in the car for hours, stopping for blow jobs and ice cream. Temptation snuck in. "Really?"

Adam grinned. "Really. And I could make sure we had a few nights to ourselves too. A road trip, Peter. Think about it: just you and me in roadside motels? Heat, sand, sun. Fuck, it'll be hot."

I tried to fight my baser instincts but I couldn't. The temptation of having Adam naked and alone in a hotel room while the Florida sun baked the streets outside our windows was beyond my ability to fend off. I felt a little ashamed of myself as I folded. "Just you and me?"

"You're in?"

I swallowed hard and let go of my last shred of dignity. "Yeah. I'm in."

Chapter Twenty-One

WE LEFT KNOXVILLE in the wee hours in Adam's Mercedes. The trip was uneventful, and I spent it in the passenger seat, happily listening to Adam talk about his ideas for a fantasy novel while The Cure and The Smiths played.

When we crossed the Florida state line, I could smell seawater in the air, like an olfactory beacon floating amidst the torrid billboards advertising strip clubs to lonely truckers. Adam pulled over to buy some fruit at one of the roadside stands next to a gas station and called Leslie from a nearby pay phone.

"Yeah, we're stopping for the night. The car's making weird noises. I think I need to have it checked out."

I paused midway through peeling my orange and stared at him. The car wasn't making any weird noises I knew about.

"I'll call you tonight to let you know what's going on. I love you too." Adam hung up the phone and grinned. "Whaddya think, Eater? Just like I promised. Two days with only you and me?"

"I think I love you."

Ignoring the old lady running the fruit stand, Adam hugged me close. "I think I love you too."

The highways of northern Florida were sprinkled with small towns, each of them unique and yet the same, and every tiny town had at least one old-fashioned motel with a name like "Motor Inn of St. Augustine." Ours was called Hacienda Court.

I stood by the car in the dusty, hot parking lot, waiting for Adam to arrange our room. I snapped a few photos of the flashing, arrow-shaped vacancy sign and a few more of the Spanish moss dripping from the trees and telephone lines. I relished the scent of the ocean in the air even though we were miles inland.

Adam walked lightly from the office. "C'mon, let's check out the room."

Given how banged up the outside of the place looked, I expected the inside to be kind of seedy, but it was actually pretty nice. The light was blue-tinged, which would make photographs tricky, but it was nothing I couldn't fix in the developing process.

Our room had two double beds with stiff, rough coverlets in a riot of floral color, tightly patterned industrial carpet, a television with cable promising the latest blockbuster releases, and a small writing table with two upholstered chairs to match the beds.

I put my luggage down next to the mirrored closet and checked out the bathroom, just as my father always did, deeming it clean enough. Adam stood with his back against the door, watching in amusement as I pulled the coverlets off both of the beds.

"What are you doing?"

"You never know, okay? One time my folks were staying in this pretty nice place. But I pulled back the bedspread and there was this big, fresh wet spot in the middle of the mattress. The maid had been fucking the janitor or something."

Adam snorted but came over to inspect the bed with me. "Oh, yeah? And where was this?"

"Hospitable Inn in Nashville."

The beds passed my inspection, so I dropped onto one of them, stretching out. "Oh God, I'm so tired."

Adam pulled his shirt over his head. He sniffed his armpits and wrinkled his nose. I laughed at his face as he took a deep whiff of his shirt before tossing it aside. He sat next to me, his fingers kneading into my thighs. "Wanna shower together?"

"Only if it's going to lead to sex," I said, already working to get the buttons of my jeans undone.

Adam headed into the bathroom. "I'm not sure. You'd better come see."

We fucked in the shower, watched cartoons in bed, and fell asleep in each other's arms. The next morning, I resisted going across the street to the Waffle House for breakfast, arguing we should just stay naked instead. But Adam said, "Man cannot live on semen alone," and tickled me until I agreed to go eat.

That afternoon, we swam in the pool, horsing around and getting a little too turned on for public propriety. We napped on separate pool chairs in the shade, drying off until clouds rolled in and a cold downpour started.

Back in the room, wet towels around our shoulders, laughing and completely soaked, Adam slammed the door shut behind us. I grabbed a dry towel from the back of one of the chairs and rubbed it over my body, my teeth chattering.

As the thunder cracked again, I turned around to find Adam leaning back against the door, dripping wet. His eyes had gone dark and intense, and his mouth was slightly open. His nipples were erect, and he was covered in goosebumps.

I dropped my towel to the floor and moved toward him as if pulled by a string. Falling to my knees in front of him, I tugged down his wet swim trunks, licking his flesh. It tasted of chlorine, salt, and rain. He wrapped his fingers in my hair as I took his cock in my mouth. Feeling the blood pulsing under the soft skin of his shaft, I welcomed the nudge of the crown against the back of my throat.

My own dick was hard and throbbing, uncomfortable in my wet swimsuit, but when I reached for it, Adam pulled out of my mouth and drew me up into a kiss. Breathlessly, he whispered,

"Peter, I want you to fuck me."

My heart pounded and the rush of blood in my ears was a dull roar. I let him steer me to the bed, shaky and unsure but eager too. I hadn't ever expected him to volunteer for that. I licked my lips, tasting the mix of pool water and rain as the back of my knees hit the edge of the bed.

"Come on, Peter," Adam whispered. "Be in charge here. Please."

I drew in a deep breath, wanting to take what he was offering. I didn't want to let him down. I stood on my toes to even our heights, grabbed his hair, and kissed him hard. He moaned into my mouth and his knees went weak as I guided him down to the bed.

His skin was soft. Dark, coarse hair covered his legs and peppered his chest. I covered him with my body, grinding our hips together, pushing my dick against his. He grabbed my ass and urged me on, but I held back, hoping to last long enough to fulfil his request.

My cock flexed with every beat of my heart while I searched out the condoms and lube from the bedside drawer where we'd stuffed them. I put one on and slicked it liberally.

"Are you sure?" I asked, crouching between his legs to push a well-slicked finger into his asshole, running a soothing hand down his leg when he hissed.

"Yes." He moved his hips gingerly.

I kissed his thighs, licked his balls, and sucked on his cock as I worked to open his ass. He gazed at me the whole time, eyes wide, hands in my hair, running down over my neck, clenching my shoulders.

I couldn't wait any longer, or I was going to come just thinking about what we were doing. I lifted his legs to press the thick head of my cock against his asshole. I caught his eyes, which burned into me, hot and dark. I trembled. I didn't want to hurt him, and it was my first time topping. I didn't want to push too hard, go too fast, or damage him.

"Peter—" Adam reached up and touched my face. "Do it."

I breathed in, and Adam did too. On our exhale, I pushed and gasped when the head of my cock was squeezed and then enveloped in the hottest, tightest grip I'd never known to imagine.

"Oh," I gasped. "Oh, fuck!"

Adam broke out in a sweat all over, and his thighs shook. His gaze bored into me. "Do it," he grunted.

I moaned, and pushed forward a little more, shocked and amazed when my dick sank into him slowly, the tight muscle of his anus squeezing along my shaft. I tried to keep my eyes open to make sure he was okay, but I couldn't. The spasming heat of his hole on my cock was incredible, and my lids fell shut as I tried not to come immediately.

"Fuck," I whispered. "Oh fuck!" As I moved into him, I leaned forward, hooking Adam's knees with my elbows to hold him open. "Oh my God."

I tried not to thrust. I wanted to give him time to adjust, the way he always did for me, but I couldn't stop one roll of my hips. I whimpered again at how good it felt—hot, tight, amazing.

"Peter," Adam whispered. "Look at me."

I met his eyes and shuddered. He was beautiful. His cheeks red and flushed, eyes dilated, huge. I took deep breaths and held as still as possible. I bit my cheek against the urge to pump my hips and shuddered at the thrum of his heartbeat against my cock.

"Okay," Adam breathed, sounding in control and sure. "Fuck me now."

I lunged forward to taste his lips. The movement was all my body needed to start thrusting, rocking in and out, deep and long, short and fast. I had to close my eyes again, water dripping down my face from my hair as I fucked him. I kissed his lips, moved down and sucked on his neck, and felt the end coming way too soon.

"Adam, fuck, fuck—"

"S'okay," he whispered. "Come on. It's okay."

I thrust into him four more times, my whole body quivering with the effort, and then I shuddered all over, coming hard with long, drawn-out jerks. Adam ran his hands over my back and whispered in my ear. I didn't know what he said, but I felt the sensation of his mouth moving against my skin.

Shuddering, I moaned and shook, amazed that I was *inside* him. I dropped down to his chest, hiccupping small noises of pleasure against his neck.

Eventually, I pulled out, and Adam made a small hissing sound. I checked his anus, worried he might be hurt, but aside from a slight gape I knew would tighten up quickly, there was nothing out of the ordinary. I pulled off the condom, threw it away—and realized Adam hadn't come. He wasn't even hard anymore.

I felt a hot coil of humiliation in my stomach. I'd failed as a top.

Adam chuckled. "Don't worry, Peter. I lost it when you pushed in. Never came back. It wasn't you. You were great, okay?" He pulled me down, forced me into a cuddle position, and kissed my forehead. "*You* were fucking amazing."

I didn't know if I believed him, but I was too touched he'd let me inside and was defending my performance to even care. I turned into his arms, buried my face in his neck, and whispered, "I love you."

He held me closer. "I love you too."

At that moment, I didn't care what might happen later. I didn't care what anyone might think, or how anyone might feel if we were ever found out. He loved me. I *knew* he did. And *for now* that was good enough.

✧   ✧   ✧

AFTER WE LEFT the motel to join the group in Ft. Myers, Adam was quiet. I stared out the window, sometimes putting my camera to my eye and rolling the window down to get a clear shot of some of the passing scenery. Adam slowed whenever he saw me getting ready to take a picture.

After about forty minutes of unusual silence, Adam finally said, "I'll be sleeping with Leslie, you know."

I snorted. If that was what he was moody about, I didn't know what to say. It wasn't as though I'd expected anything else.

"Peter—"

"I don't want to talk about it." I turned the stereo up a little. Morrissey crooned my pain better than I could.

"I just wanted to warn you."

"I already knew." I looked out the window and held on to the image of Adam's face when he'd asked me to fuck him.

"Okay, well…okay." Adam's hand sneaked across the gear shift and rested on my thigh. I turned it over and ran my fingers over the lines in his palms.

"It's no big deal. I'll be fine."

Adam squeezed my hand and smiled like he didn't entirely believe me.

✧   ✧   ✧

ASIDE FROM THE obvious drawbacks, it was every high school kid's dream of spring break—the sun, the sand, the weary feeling in my limbs after a day in the waves. I spent half of the time high on relaxation or beer, taking photograph after photograph, and the other half trying to remember I shouldn't kiss Adam just because he looked hot and sweaty in the sun, and I shouldn't flinch when Leslie pounced on him, and I should pretend to be sad that Susan wasn't there too.

But on the plus side, there were sand dunes, starfish, and Leslie's hair in the sun. There was Sarah's skin growing darker and shining with sweat, Adam's hair glinting with red highlights, and Mike's arms, bunched with muscles, throwing Sarah into another wave.

During the day, the beauty of the world was too much for me to resist, and I managed something close to happiness. It was easy enough, almost like when we were at school, but night was something else entirely.

There were two couples and two bedrooms, so I was relegated to the sofa bed. It only made sense, but after the first miserable night in the condo, I took to sleeping with my headphones on, because there were noises coming from the bedrooms.

Sex noises.

The first night, I sweated and twisted on the lumpy mattress, tears in my eyes and my chest aching so hard I could barely breathe as the sound of my boyfriend making love to his girlfriend filtered into the living room. I blinked at the ceiling, nausea churning, my heart crawling up my throat and lodging there painfully. I tried to be a grown-up about it but I couldn't. That first night I covered my head with the pillow and cried quietly.

Adam wasn't too loud, but I could still hear his grunts of pleasure when he came, and I could definitely hear Leslie's breathy gasps and little cries as he screwed her. And if *they* weren't fucking, then Mike and Sarah definitely were, and they didn't even *try* to keep it down. Grunts, screams, laughter, the works. It was alternately horrifying and kind of a turn-on, so the second night I drowned it all out. Loud music blaring through my headphones seemed to do the trick.

In the middle of the third night, I woke suddenly, startled by someone sitting on my pullout bed. I tore off my headphones, heart racing.

"Shh, Eater." Adam whispered, "Calm down. Be quiet."

My pulse thundered in my ears. "What the fuck are you doing?"

Adam clamped his hand over my mouth. "Shh! You'll wake someone up!" He sat there in pajama pants and nothing else, a strange expression on his face.

I breathed hard through my nose, snorting, still trying to get over being scared half to death. Adam didn't move his hand, but climbed on top of me. I grunted in shock, but he just tightened his hand and murmured, "Uh-uh, be quiet."

Then he rubbed against me, shoving his other hand under my T-shirt, his mouth by my ear, whispering, "God, I want you so much. All day. In your bathing suit. So fucking hot. And you're so cute putting all that sunscreen all over. Makes me insane. Want you *so* much, Peter. Fuck, you make me crazy."

I bit the palm of his hand, and he released my mouth, kissed me, and started thrusting against my thigh.

I managed to say, "Are you fucking *nuts?*" before he put his hand over my mouth again.

Adam shoved both of our pajama bottoms down, our cocks dragging against each other. I realized I was hard and had been since he woke me up.

"Peter, can you be quiet? I want to suck you. Please be quiet, please." He slid down my body, letting his hand glide down from my mouth, over my chest, and down to grasp my balls. I bit my lip hard because he was sucking my dick like he'd taken home the Olympic gold medal for blow jobs.

His hand cradled my balls, and his middle finger extended into the crack of my ass to brush against my hole. Adam sucked hard and fast, bobbing his head feverishly. I shuddered under him, finally clenching my fists in his hair and shaking all over as I spurted into his mouth.

He shimmied up to kiss me, and then moved up even closer, with his knees on either side of my head to push his cock between my lips. I opened my throat and let him fuck my mouth. He thrust in and out at a rapid pace, sometimes gagging me, but I tilted my head back and managed to let him push down into my throat. When he came, he pulled out so just the crown of his cock was in my mouth, and I swallowed his cum while he shook silently through his orgasm.

Then he kissed me, quick and dirty, pulled up his pajama pants, and, without another word, went back to Leslie and their bed.

✧　✧　✧

I WOKE SLOWLY, hearing the rest of the group moving around, the rumble of the sliding glass door to the balcony and the crashing of the waves from the beach four stories down.

Suddenly the bed dipped, and I opened my eyes to see Leslie grinning at me. She ran a hand over my hair, which was no doubt sticking up everywhere. "Get up, sleepyhead!"

I groaned and covered my head with the closest pillow, but Leslie pulled it off, laughing. "Come on! It's time to play, play, play!" She started bouncing on the bed, shaking me.

"Fine," I grumbled, rolling away from her and off the other side of the bed. My mouth was rancid from Adam's surprise visit the night before, and I wanted to brush my teeth before getting too close to anyone at all. Plus I hated how bright her innocent smile was. The guilt chewed at me. "Fine. I'm up."

Mike, Sarah, and Adam were at the kitchen table eating. Adam looked chipper, even merry, as he downed a bowl of Frosted Flakes, reading a battered copy of *Medea* for extra credit in Dr. Landry's class.

"Get up, Eater!" Adam called out.

"I'm *up!*" I stalked toward the bathroom, halfway there before I realized I'd forgotten my clothes to change into after my shower. I rubbed sleep from my eyes as I crossed the living room, but caught Mike's eye as I passed him.

My stomach froze up and my heart beat wildly. I turned away from him and carefully gathered up some clothes, avoiding his gaze as I walked back to have my shower. I turned on the hot water and pulled off my pajamas.

Mike knew.

He'd heard, or seen, or something. His piercing eyes said it all. He knew *something*. It was no longer a suspicion. Mike had certain knowledge.

I soaped up, my mind whirling. *Fuck.*

After breakfast, we put on bathing suits and went to the beach as a group. Nothing seemed different, except for a coldness to Mike's smile when he talked to me. I was quieter than usual that day, but no one seemed to notice because I didn't normally say much anyway. I took long walks alone with the camera, taking pictures of shells and seagulls. It was almost easy to forget I was trying to avoid a confrontation with Mike.

Part of me just wanted to get it over with. But I'd learned by being my mother's son that avoidance often led to an antianxiety pill being taken, or a new novel getting started, and the entire problem got pushed aside or totally forgotten. So I hoped maybe I was wrong, and the look Mike had given me was just…gas or something.

It wasn't.

Mike found me kneeling in wet sand about half a mile away from the little camp our group had set up on the beach down from the condo. I was photographing a sea urchin when Mike's shadow fell over the intended subject.

I pushed my messy hair out of my eyes and fumbled the Minolta, nearly dropping it in the water, managing a last-minute save.

"Um, hey." I cradled the camera to my chest. "Is it time for dinner already?"

Mike stood with his arms crossed, a serious expression on his face. "What's going on with you and Adam?"

I swallowed, looked away, and stared out to sea. "What are you talking about?"

"I saw him leaving your bed last night. Are you two queer or something?"

I choked on a fucked-up laugh. "What? Adam's with Leslie. I'm with Susan. He just came out to talk, that's all."

Mike narrowed his eyes.

"Ask Adam," I said.

"Yeah, like that would get me anywhere. Listen, I know him, okay? And I know Sarah. If he lies anywhere near as well as she does, then he'd have me believing I saw aliens leaving your bed last night, and I'd been brainwashed to imagine it was him."

"Mike—"

"Listen, Peter. I like you, okay? And I like Adam. I love Sarah, and I don't want to do anything that's going to jeopardize that. But if you guys are fucking with Leslie and Susan, that'd just be spoons like I can't even say."

"*What?*" I twitched, forcing my face into an expression of offense. "Mike, hey—" I tried to remember how Sarah did it. I thought about her best lies, what made them really work. "Okay, yeah. I guess it won't come as a big shock to you that I'm gay." I said, lowering my eyes and hoping to God he didn't hit me.

Mike shifted but didn't say anything.

I took a shaky breath and gave a little more truth. "And, yeah, maybe I feel something for Adam." I leaped off the cliff of hope, praying I could pull off the lie. "But it's nothing reciprocal, man. He just likes me as a friend. He's in love with Leslie. Everyone knows that. *I* know that. I mean—"

"So what about Susan?"

I sighed. The truth worked for me again. "She knows."

"Really?" Mike seemed unconvinced.

"I swear to God."

He stared into my eyes, measuring me, before sighing. "Yeah. Okay." Another few moments of contemplation before he asked, "So you're a fag?"

I fiddled with the on/off switch of my camera. "Don't act so surprised. I mean, I've only been beaten up for it how many times in my life? Are you going to tell Adam? Please, Mike—don't tell him. I don't want to lose his friendship." I bit my lip, shame welling inside me as I pushed the lie forward. "He's my best friend, and I don't want him to drop me when he finds out I'm gay. Please."

Mike studied me, his eyes intense. "Okay. For now. Just—you know, be careful, man. I don't want to see you get hurt."

I smiled in relief. "Thanks, Mike."

"Okay, well, let's get back." He walked a little stiffly next to me, all of our usual casual contact held back.

"Um, Mike? You can relax. I'm not going to jump on you."

He chuckled a little, visibly shaking himself. "Sorry. Maybe I'll figure out where I dropped my sense of humor on the way back. I'm sure I had it earlier today."

"You probably left it in Sarah's—"

Mike laughed loudly, clapping a hand on my shoulder. "Don't even go there, man."

That evening, Adam tried to light the charcoal on the grill while Leslie and Sarah got the hot dogs and hamburgers ready, and I read a book. I didn't usually read a lot, but it was something to keep me occupied and quiet.

Unnerved by what had happened with Mike, I turned it over and over in my head, wondering when I'd gotten so good at lying. I wondered how he saw Adam leaving the bed. Maybe he'd gotten up for some water? I tried to imagine what would have happened if he'd seen us a few seconds earlier. There would've been no way to talk our way out of it.

"Adam!" Mike yelled from the kitchen where he was getting in the way of Sarah's work. "What did the hippo say to the one-eyed giant?"

"No more stupid jokes!" Adam answered, bending over to try another match. "Fuck!"

Mike started out to help him, but the charcoal caught fire as soon as Mike stepped over the threshold to the balcony. He and Adam clinked beers, leaning over the railing, gazing out to the ocean, and talking in voices too quiet for me to hear.

I huddled down on the sofa to read. It was Adam's book from earlier. *Medea* by Euripides. Greek. Tragic. I slid my eyes over Jason's justification for his actions, read about Medea's disintegration into rage, and the slaughter of their children.

"Hell hath no fury," Leslie said, suddenly next to me.

I jumped, shaken at the sound of her voice by my shoulder. "What?"

"Shakespeare. Hell hath no fury like a woman scorned." She grinned. "Or two-timed in the case of Medea."

I cleared my throat, licked my lips, and shoved my glasses up my nose. I'd put them on earlier after my eyes started burning from a small sandstorm. "Yeah?"

"Yeah."

"So, you think it's true?"

"If I found out Adam was fucking around on me, I'd cut off his dick and feed it to him."

My eyebrows shot up. "Yeah?" My voice definitely squeaked.

"You know how everyone always blames the other woman for 'stealing her man?' Ha!" Leslie scoffed and shook her blond hair. "Not me. I mean, really, the guy is the one to blame for cheating, you know?"

I made a noncommittal noise. Why were we having this conversation? I stared at the book in my hands, feeling like it had an indictment on the cover, a glowing accusation spelling out everything Adam and I had ever done together. My stomach clenched, and I swallowed hard.

As quickly as the bizarre conversation started, it was over. "I'm sorry Susan couldn't come," Leslie said.

"S'okay, Les. I'm having a good time, anyway," I whispered, feeling like a piece of shit.

"You're not really that interested in her, are you?"

I blinked, shoved at my glasses again, and fingered the spine of Medea. "Why would you say that?"

Leslie's dimples flashed; she leaned close and whispered, "You don't have to pretend, Peter. I know you didn't want to hurt her feelings, but why you told Tina you were interested in the first place is beyond me."

"I thought I was?" I offered, confused and wanting the conversation to stop.

"Well, I guess the fact she's moving to Michigan soon means you won't actually have to go through the awkward issue of breaking up with her, am I right?"

"Um, huh?"

Apparently, it wasn't going to be long until I *didn't* have a girlfriend.

"She didn't tell you?"

I cleared my throat and remained silent.

Leslie's eyes grew concerned. "I'm so sorry, Peter. I didn't know she hadn't told you. With her parents getting divorced, she and her mom are moving back to live with her grandparents for a while. She said she was going to tell you."

"Oh." I didn't really feel any sense of loss. She and I weren't even close friends.

"So that'll be that, huh?" Leslie leaned forward and pushed her forehead against my temple, a kind of friendly nuzzle. "You lucked out."

I snorted.

"Hey!" Adam called from the doorway. "Keep your grubby paws off my woman!"

Leslie threw her arms around my neck, put her hand over my mouth, and pretended to kiss me passionately. I blinked and struggled until Adam pulled her off my lap, tickling her until they fell to the floor laughing.

I hated everything about us all, and shame ate at my insides.

That night, I waited up for him, careful not to fall asleep so I could tell him about Mike. The night was thick with heat, and I only wore my pajama bottoms, not using the covers either. I wished there was a fan in the living room like the big ones I'd seen over the beds.

All was quiet. There were no sounds of grunts or groans, or box springs squeaking. Apparently the day in the sun and surf had worn everyone out, or my snide little comments throughout the evening had paid off and everyone was doing their best to keep their orgasms quiet.

I didn't know what time it was, probably close to three in the morning, when Adam came out of the bedroom he shared with Leslie.

I sat up on the pullout bed before he could pounce on me, whispering, "Go back to your room."

Adam sneered like I'd lost my mind and sank down beside me, his arms already moving to hold me.

I pushed his hands away. "No, seriously. Mike asked a bunch of questions today. You need to go back. He might come out."

"I know." Adam smirked, running a hand down my chest,

tweaking my right nipple. "He asked me a lot of questions too."

"What did you tell him?" I shoved away Adam's still-wandering hands.

"I told him you're my best friend, and I came out to talk to you because you always have good advice."

"I do?"

Adam laughed softly. "Not really, but you're cute, so that makes everything better."

I rolled my eyes and leaned to the side, trying to get away from his fingers. "You need to stop. He'll come out here."

Adam shook his head. "Peter, calm down. Everything is copacetic. Just chill out." He ran his thumb over my bottom lip. "If I promise to keep an eye out, will you please let me touch you?"

I gazed toward Mike and Sarah's room.

"Eater, I told Sare-Bear to keep him occupied, okay?" His hand was already sliding into my pajama bottoms. "I promised her some good weed in exchange. All is well."

"What about Leslie?"

"Dead to the world."

He kissed me quiet and grabbed my dick, jerking me with strong, sure strokes. When I was close, breathing hard and scrabbling at his back and shoulders with my fingers, he bent down and sucked me in, just in time to swallow my cum.

✧   ✧   ✧

I TOOK PHOTOGRAPHS of sea crabs, sand dollars, and seaweed. I raised my camera because Sarah's skin and sun-streaked hair made her look more like a tiger's-eye than ever. She smiled and flipped me off just as I took the shot.

I walked down the beach with Leslie and Sarah while Adam and Mike tried to surf on the Gulf of Mexico's puny waves. Light and dark, the girls held hands and skipped, hamming it up for me, playing at being models.

I took too many photos of Adam that afternoon. There was one with a shovel, bucket, and sandcastle, and one of him gazing off into the distance, the sun seeming to set his hair on fire. And one of him smiling at me with that look in his eye, the one that said he needed me, wanted me. A look that was gone by the time I took the camera away from my face.

We went to a seafood place right on the beach the last night. Nothing fancy, just some picnic tables on the patio with the waves crashing in as high tide came up.

"Peter, get a picture of us," Leslie said, leaning into Adam's arms, smiling. The sunset backlighting them was all orange, yellow, and red, and I worked to get the exposure right. Sarah and Mike wanted a picture too, and then I took a group shot of the sunset behind all the proper, heterosexual couples.

Later, lying in bed and staring at the sliding glass doors out to the balcony, I thought about Adam's arm around Leslie's shoulder, the casual way he walked with her, kissed her, and pulled her possessively close. And then I remembered his mouth on my cock and his desperate noises in my ear as he'd rubbed himself off. I curled on my side, the ugliness of our situation stabbing through me.

I was glad Adam didn't come to me that night. My conscience was raw and I hated who we'd become.

✧　✧　✧

ADAM AND I left Ft. Myers a day earlier than the others to give us plenty of time to drive home. Leslie gave Adam a playfully passionate farewell by the Mercedes, throwing her arms around him and laying a huge kiss on his lips. He pretended to waver under her weight, falling back and letting the hood of the car catch him.

Leslie laughed, gave him a quick kiss, and pushed away. "Okay, drive safely," she said, walking around to give me a hug. She whispered in my ear, "I adore you, Peter. I understand why Adam loves you."

I swallowed, ashamed at how innocent she was and what lying assholes we were.

Sarah came over and punched me in the stomach. I pretended it hurt. She grinned and wrapped her arms around my neck, hugging me too. "Don't let him fall asleep at the wheel, okay?"

I agreed as she kissed my cheek.

Adam talked my ear off about everything under the sun as he drove us north. More ideas he'd had for short stories, a plan to try to get the old one he'd written about the human clones published, and his thoughts on keeping in touch while he was in Rome during the summer.

"I'll call when I can, but I'll mainly write. But I promise I will. I *promise*."

"Okay," I said, shrugging. As much as I dreaded it, summer couldn't come quick enough. I wondered what it would be like to breathe without Adam in my life. Who I might be without him now.

"I won't be able to say things like, 'I want to suck your cock,' even though I'll want to do that, Peter. I always want to do that."

I laughed, pushed my glasses up on my nose, and cupped myself through my jeans. "Mmm, tastes great."

"Don't make me pull over." Adam's eyes gleamed in a way that told me he'd have no problem doing just that.

"And what about this fall?"

He still didn't say the words, but what he did say told me everything I needed to know about where he'd chosen to attend college.

"I'll see you every weekend. *Every* weekend. I promise."

I sighed. "Don't make promises you can't keep."

"Peter, if I say I'll see you every weekend, then I mean I'll see you every goddamn weekend."

I pulled off my glasses and rubbed my eyes. I needed a new prescription. Since I'd been wearing contacts, my sight seemed to have improved.

Adam changed the topic back to Dr. Landry's class and the yearbook assignments we still had to get done by the end of the year. I let him because I didn't want to argue. I only had a few weeks left with him now, and I wasn't going to waste them fighting.

We stayed that night in a Hospitable Inn two hours outside of Atlanta. The air-conditioning unit was broken, blowing full blast no matter what we did. It was late, and it was the only available room. We got under the covers and cuddled together.

We were both exhausted, but not too tired to take advantage of our time alone. Before long, I lay flat on my stomach, the scratchy motel linen under my cheek with Adam heavy on my back. He took his time fucking me, savoring it, and I didn't rush him. Who knew when we would be so entirely alone again? Who knew what the future might bring?

I ignored the little voice hissing that, when it came to Adam, I knew all too well.

Chapter Twenty-Two

MY ASSEMBLY SPEECH was set for the last week of school, and I felt sweaty and nauseous just thinking about it. I didn't know what on earth I was going to talk about for ten whole minutes.

Dr. Landry held me back after class a few days beforehand, offering to help me out if I needed it. I thanked him, but how was he going to help me stand up in front of an auditorium full of people and make words come out coherently? Unless he knew how to body-switch, that just wasn't going to happen.

I said as much to Adam one Saturday when we were both at Robert's, sewing sequins on a new mermaid tail, and his only response was, "I wrote this story about body-switching where this straight guy found himself in a gay guy's body, and the body wouldn't get it up for girls, you know? 'Cause it was hardwired to be gay."

I blinked at him then turned back to the green and blue sequins. "Dr. Landry said I should stick with what I know. I guess he means photography."

Robert and Barry were huddled over by the new, tiny television at Robert's desk, looking at some other drag queen's promotional video. I glanced over at them, but they didn't seem to be paying any attention to us.

"So, the guy ended up having gay sex, because he was so horny, you know? And he liked it."

"I could do a slideshow of my best pictures and talk about how I got the different effects."

"When he switched back to the straight body, he was bi."

I hunched over and worked the sequins carefully. "Are you listening to me?"

"Sure, I'm listening, Eater." Adam held up a long string of blue and green sequins, pondering it. "You don't know what to talk about. Nothing new there."

I sat back, crossed my arms, and glared at him. "Well, some people aren't word-sluts, you know. Some people conserve their energy for more important things."

"Yeah? What's more important than words?"

"Giving head."

Adam smirked. "Are you saying you give better head than I do?"

"Yes, I am." I smiled wickedly. "I do."

Barry interrupted us with, "I'm sure Robert would be willing to let you guys put this to the test." He pulled out his wallet. "I'm putting my money on Puker."

I laughed. "Um, nope, sorry. I don't have sex with my boss."

Adam winked at Robert. "And I only have sex with Renée in public. You know, I still have wet dreams about that spanking."

Robert's mouth twisted into a smirk. "I'll have to get Sweetie here a little riding crop. I'm sure he'd be happy to use it on you."

I tried to imagine smacking Adam's ass with a riding crop. It wasn't an unsexy idea. I wasn't sure if I had it in me, though. Maybe if Adam pissed me off enough—which he was *bound* to do again before too long.

Putting aside my angst about the speech and my handful of sequins, I climbed into Adam's lap, straddled his waist, and kissed him. He rested his hands on my thighs and fluttered his long lashes at me. "Would you hit me with it?"

"I'd make you cry."

Adam swallowed hard and kissed me again. Robert laughed and half-heartedly chastised us for making out on the job.

That evening, as the sunset turned the mountains on the horizon orange and red, we ran from his house down to mine, breathless and laughing. My folks were gone for the night on an anniversary trip to Asheville, and we were going to have a night alone for the first time since our spring break trip.

As we collapsed naked onto my bed, both of us already hard, he turned to me and said, "Do your speech on photography, and I know you'll do great."

"I really don't think I've got a choice on the subject matter."

"Dr. Landry would say you have a choice, you always have a choice, but sometimes it's just better to take the path of least resistance. It's not always evil, you know."

I rolled on top of him and kissed his jaw. *The path of least resistance.* It sounded like a relaxing way to go. In the beginning, being with him seemed like the easiest thing, the right thing, the path of least resistance. As time went on, the path had grown covered in thorns.

"It'll have to be photography," I said, shoving my thoughts aside.

"Like I said," Adam teased, sliding his hands down to grip my ass. He smiled bashfully and licked his lips. "Hey, so, what did you think about that spanking idea? Would you be up for it?"

I shrugged. "Maybe. Why?"

"We don't need a crop. I mean, you have a belt." Adam's cheeks were red but he looked at me intently, gauging my reaction.

"True." I cleared my throat. "Would you... I mean, do you want me to spank you?"

He flushed even more, and his eyes went dark.

"I could do that. Let me just—" I started to get up, and he

pulled me back down against him.

"Nah. It's silly. Never mind."

I ran my finger over his lips and kissed his soft mouth. "Adam, we can try it."

He shivered, and when I got up, he didn't stop me. I went to my closet, pulled out a medium-sized belt, and showed it to him. He swallowed hard and nodded. I brought it back to the bed and sat beside him.

His eyes never left the belt as I folded it in half. "You're so hard," I said. His cock strained up from his stomach with a bead of pre-cum already on the tip, begging me to lick it or touch it. Or slap it with the belt.

"Tell me how you want me to do this."

His breath came in shallow pants now, and his eyes remained on the leather in my hand. "On my ass. And tell me why you're doing it. You know, while you hit me."

I was confused. "I'm doing it because you want me to. What do you mean 'why I'm doing it?'"

He looked embarrassed. "Never mind. It's nothing." He licked his lips, smiled tremulously, and rolled onto his stomach. "Oh, and Peter?" he said, with his face jammed against the mattress. "Do it hard. Make it hurt, okay?"

I nodded, and when I realized he couldn't see me with his eyes scrunched shut and his face in the blankets, I opened my mouth to say okay, but found I couldn't. I got off the bed and tugged on his ankles. He got the message, scooting down until his feet were on the floor and his ass was right on the edge of the bed and tilted up—a tight, fleshy target.

My heart hammered, and I felt a little awkward and uneasy. When I'd woken up that morning, I'd never imagined I'd be standing over Adam with a belt. I studied his shaking body, flushed all over. His cock leaked drops of stringy pre-cum onto the floor from where it hung down. He truly wanted this.

He was tall, and the position was clearly awkward. I remembered him bent over Renée's legs, his ass up and red from her palm prints. *This is for being gay,* she'd said. *This is for being dirty.* The reasons why. I remembered Adam's face crumpling with pleasure as she'd reached the climax of that perverted little show, and I understood what he wanted from me.

I rubbed the fold of the belt against his ass, and he juddered, chuckling nervously into the mattress. I slid it slowly down his legs, and then between them to loop the belt around his cock. I pulled a little, and he moaned, lifting his ass up more, eager for whatever I was going to do to him.

I slid the belt back around, lifted it, and took a deep breath. Finally, I let the belt fall with a loud smack on his ass. He jerked, and a faint line appeared on his skin, not nearly as red on his darker tone as it would've been on my paleness, but a line all the same. I bit into my lip, surprised by the jolt in my own cock. I lifted the belt and smacked it down on him again.

Adam shifted on the bed, his dick slipping up underneath him, and he rubbed it on the edge of the mattress.

"This is for being a liar, Adam," I said in a quiet voice, and I raised my belt high.

Crack.

He jerked and cried out, lifting his ass, begging for another. This time the line was a lot darker on his skin, but I knew I could hit even harder.

"This is for thinking you could get away with it."

Crack.

"Peter!" he cried, his fingers clenching the sheets.

"This is for lying to your mother."

Crack.

"This is for lying to Leslie."

Crack.

My cock ached, and I stroked it between strikes. I watched his ass cheeks clench in anticipation when I raised the belt, but I brought it down on the bed just to see him jump. He twitched and lifted his ass higher, whispering, "Please."

"This is for lying to me and your father and everyone else you know."

Crack.

"This is for making me a liar too."

He moaned, twisting on the bed, his face buried in the mattress again. I wielded the belt against his ass four more times, watching the red lines grow darker and darker. I slowed the hits long enough to kneel between his legs, reach up and pull his cock down again so I could see it hanging over the edge of the bed. Sure enough, it was still hard, and the head was slick with how turned on Adam was from all of this.

I gripped my cock and jerked it, my balls tightening in a coil of pleasure. I'd never thought I'd get off on this, but here I was aching to shoot my load on his red ass cheeks. I leaned close, rubbing my dick on his skin, smearing pre-cum where his flesh burned hot from the belt's strikes. Adam reached back to spread his ass cheeks wide, exposing his asshole to me.

I shivered, not sure what he was offering, but I knelt to blow lightly on his hole and see it twitch. I leaned in and gave it a tender, closed-mouth kiss, and then sat back on my heels to run my index finger over it, watching it flex and relax with each pass.

"Peter, Peter," he whimpered.

I quickly grabbed his hands and pushed them away, spread his ass cheeks myself, and licked his pucker, feeling it give under my tongue. When I pushed it inside, he cried out, jolting on the bed.

"So, so good!" he whimpered, rutting his hard cock against the edge of the bed again, before pushing his ass back on my tongue. I drilled it into him, twisting it inside, and then I pulled back, Adam's taste filling my mouth.

I stood and raised the belt. "This is for being a faggoty slut who likes my tongue in your asshole."

Crack.

He shook, and I could tell, by the way he was humping the bed and how his breath came in short, shaky gasps, that he was close to coming. I bit my lip, narrowed my eyes, and summoned the anger I had deep inside me—the resentments I felt every day, that both of us tried to pretend weren't there.

"This is for sticking your cock in my ass, and then turning around and sticking it in your girlfriend's cunt."

Crack.

"And this—" I thought of the meanest thing I could say that was true. "This is for being a piece-of-shit cheater. Not just on me, but Leslie too."

Crack.

Adam howled. He reached beneath him and grabbed his cock, squeezing it once before convulsing hard as he came. With his other hand, he tore at the sheets, pulling them free at the corner. He cried out, jerked, and twisted on the bed. His cum smeared all over his stomach and the blankets as he kept on shooting for what seemed like a very long time.

I stood over him, jerking my cock as hard and as fast as I could. As he writhed in his orgasm, my own rose up and pumped through my groin with pleasure that took my breath away. I threw my head back, and before I unloaded bursts of white cum onto his bright red ass cheeks, I managed to hiss, "This is for making me love you."

I collapsed on his back, smearing my jizz between us. We panted together for a long moment. Adam flipped me over, staring down at me with hot, wild eyes, and kissed me like he'd only just remembered why he loved me so much and, now that he had, he was never going to let me go.

My heart slammed, the drug of orgasm not taking the edge off what I'd just done. My mind grasped for meaning, a desperate, drowning sensation taking me over as I flailed emotionally, trying to keep from going under, trying to understand. What had I done? What did it mean? A sob wrenched me. Grief and anger, hatred and love all swelled inside me, and they heaved from my throat in waves.

Adam stroked his fingers over my cheek, smearing the wetness of my tears. "It's okay," he whispered. "I deserve it. It's okay."

I squeezed my eyes closed so I wouldn't have to look at him.

Nothing about us was okay. It never had been, and it never would be. This was what he made me feel, this was what we'd turned into, and I hated it and myself. I wanted out. I wanted a future where Adam didn't want me to hit him and it didn't satisfy me so much.

"We're okay, Peter."

I shook my head, tears squeezing from my eyes.

"I love you," he said, voice trembling. "Do you love me too?"

"Yes." My throat spasmed, and he held me while I cried.

✧   ✧   ✧

THE AUDITORIUM LOOKED different from the stage. I sat gripping my papers as row after row of seats filled with Kingsley's uniformed students. I took deep breaths, trying not to pass out. I watched Adam and Leslie walk in holding hands, and when Leslie saw me, she waved, jumped up and down, and clapped for me. I waved back, stomach roiling.

Dr. Landry climbed up onto the stage, knelt beside me, and whispered, "Mr. Mandel, look on the bright side. This isn't Vietnam. There's no chance of your guts being sliced open by automatic weapons. When the speech is over, you won't look down and find your intestines on the floor in front of you."

I stared at him, wide-eyed.

"At least there's that." He patted my shoulder and walked back down to take attendance in the rows he governed.

It seemed to take forever and also only two seconds for Mr. Waverly to give the day's announcements. I mentally begged Van and the drama club to please, please, please choose today for the Kingsley Pirates to overthrow assembly with a surprise skit, but no such luck.

I sat through a freshman boy's three-minute talk on being a Christian, a sophomore girl's five-minute talk about the Habitat for Humanity project she'd worked on over the summer, a junior going on endlessly about soccer, and then, finally, it was my turn. My ears rang as I walked up to the podium, my mouth went dry, and my throat clogged. I tried to force myself to gaze out at the audience, but the number of eyes staring back at me made my legs weak, so I stared down at the wrinkled sheaf of papers I held in my hand and read straight from my notes.

"I started taking pictures when I was just a kid. My first camera was a Polaroid, but I pushed my parents into buying me a nice Minolta. It came with autofocus and auto flash."

I talked some more about my first cameras, noticing that my voice trembled. I motioned, without lifting my head, for the guys in the theater control booth to lower the lights. "Now I'll show you some pictures I've taken over the years, and explain how I got some of the effects."

When the lights went down and the first slide came up, I breathed easier. It was a picture I'd taken with my Polaroid. "That's Harry. He's my dog, and this was my very first picture. As you can see, there's nothing special about it." The audience tittered a little, and I laughed too. "The next picture was taken with my first Minolta. It's a photo of an abandoned tree house in my neighborhood."

I went through twenty-eight pictures, briefly explaining each one, and was amazed to find the time passed quickly. As the lights came back up, I thanked everyone for their attention and offered lessons in developing to anyone who wanted to learn. The applause was obviously obligatory, and I sat back down on the folding chair I'd been sweating in only ten minutes earlier.

My body sang with release. I'd done it. And I'd survived. Sure, I might not have given as thrilling a talk as when Lissy Egbert told us about her father's arrest and trial for possession of peyote, or the girl who talked about her brother's mental illness complete with descriptions of his hallucinations, but I'd lived through it, and that was all that mattered.

Millar Johansson was the second senior speaker since we'd had to double up. I wasn't paying much attention to what he said at first, but slowly the words started to filter through my lingering adrenaline rush.

"My parents are here today, and I want to take the opportunity to thank them for their support. I also want to thank Dr. Landry for helping me find the courage to give this particular speech."

I blinked and looked up. The back of Millar's blond head was the only thing I could really see, except when he turned to look at the left side of the audience and the edge of his profile came into view.

"My name is Millar Johansson, and I'm gay."

The audience gasped, and my mouth fell open.

"I thought about beating around the bush, talking about it via euphemisms, giving you all a bunch of words about how hard it is to live a lie, but then I decided to just be upfront. So there you have it. I'm gay."

Millar gestured with his hands, spreading them wide. "I don't expect most of you to understand what it's like to live through high school as a gay guy. I don't expect most of you will have any sympathy for what I've been through. But the time for lies is past, and I'm looking forward to a future clear of deceit. By coming out, even at this late date in my high school career, I'm hoping I'll be able to reach one of you out there who's still hiding in the closet, still living in fear. If I'm able to make things easier for any of you, then I'll know I did the right thing today."

I heard murmuring, and several teachers issued demerits to people who were talking.

Millar continued, "I know I'm supposed to speak for ten minutes, and I know I'll lose points for not doing just that, but I'm going to open the floor for questions instead. Anyone?"

I stared at the back of his head. Silence reigned. I scanned the audience, but there wasn't a single raised hand. The moment wore on, and everyone started to shift in their seats uncomfortably.

"So be it," Millar said, his voice a little sad.

That's when I noticed Leslie standing up. Her voice was strong and clear when she said, "I don't have a question, Millar. I just want to thank you for being so brave."

"Thank *you*," he said.

The auditorium remained silent as Millar stepped back from the podium. I twisted my papers in my hands as he walked off the stage, watching as his parents and Dr. Landry hugged him.

I peered down into the audience, searching for the one face I really wanted to gauge. I finally found it.

Adam shook his head. I lifted my eyebrows, hoping he'd understand—*if Millar could do it…couldn't we?* Adam pressed his lips into a thin line and looked away.

I sighed and stood, following the other students from the stage. What was the difference between Millar and us that allowed him to have such balls? What did that kind of courage feel like?

Judging by the grin on Millar's face, it looked like it felt amazing.

✧　✧　✧

"ARE *YOU* GAY, Leslie?" Eric Morgan sneered, leaning low as he passed by our lunch table. "Are you a rug-muncher?"

"Back off, or I'll shove some spoons up your ass," Leslie countered. She sighed and pushed her hair out of her eyes. "Bastard. He's a little too worried about who's gay and who isn't, don't you think?"

Susan sat next to me, being my "girlfriend," her salad half-eaten and her eyes averted. "You're not gay," she said softly.

Leslie laughed. "Of course not. That doesn't mean I'm not really proud of Millar. He's so brave. I wish no one had to live hiding who they are."

Mike and Van joined us at the table, and soon Tina, Sarah, and Allison arrived. Adam sat with his arm around Leslie's shoulders, still not meeting my eyes.

"Do you know anyone else who's gay?" Susan asked, keeping her gaze averted.

Mike looked over at me but said nothing.

"Oh, sure," Leslie said nonchalantly. "My cousin's a lesbian, and a guy in my church youth group came out last summer. But here at school? Nah. It's sad, really. There's nothing wrong with being gay, you know. It's just the way they're made. It's like—I don't know, being left-handed or something."

I sipped my water and pushed the chicken casserole around on my plate, struck anew by how thoroughly Leslie didn't deserve to be lied to. Adam didn't look at me.

"Sometimes it's a choice," Adam said softly. "You know, if someone's bisexual or something."

I narrowed my eyes. *A choice. What he feels for me is a choice? Bullshit.*

"That's not true," Leslie said. "Bisexuality is just as valid as any other sexuality and just as involuntary."

"You're such a typical child of psychologists," Van jumped in. "Even if bisexuality isn't a choice, it *is* a choice whether or not you stick your dick in something, right? I mean, you can choose if you stick it in ass or pussy."

Leslie rolled her eyes. "Whatever, Van. It's not that simple."

"It *is* that simple," Van countered. "Monogamy is a choice."

Adam's tan skin had a green cast as he stood up, muttering, "I've got to go. I forgot some stuff for my next class back in my locker."

Leslie grabbed his hand and kissed it. "See you later."

Adam still avoided my gaze as he walked away.

"By the way, Peter, good talk this morning," Van offered.

I thanked him, even though he was just being uncharacteristically nice. After waiting a suitable amount of time and avoiding Mike's searching looks, I made my excuses and headed for the darkroom.

Chapter Twenty-Three

GRADUATION WAS HELD on a Saturday on the front lawn of the school with white folding chairs set up for the audience. Families arrived, dressed in their Sunday best and smiling from ear to ear. Hands were shaken and exclamations of recognition exchanged.

Dad and Mom sat near the back, and Dr. Landry approached, his head tilted toward the sky, eyes mostly closed, and somehow magically avoided walking into anyone.

"Mr. Mandel, won't you introduce me to your family?"

I'd been looking forward to this moment all year. I knew my dad and Dr. Landry would hit it off, and I watched happily as I was proved right. Dr. Landry had read some of my father's articles and a couple of his books. I held my breath, hoping my mother wouldn't tell Dr. Landry she wrote romance novels, but she was so distracted by all the bustle around us that she seemed oblivious to the fact my dad had made a friend.

The band started to play. I left my dad and Dr. Landry talking and gave my mom a kiss on the cheek before heading to the main building to join the rest of the graduates.

"Hey, Eater, you're almost late," Adam said as I passed him. The alphabetical line of seniors, with Adam and Sarah near the front, stretched all the way down the hall. Everyone was fiddling with their caps or shoving each other around.

I shot him a smile and waved at Sarah as I jostled my way back through the line to my position. My curly hair was unruly from the humidity and my cap wouldn't stay on. I messed with it for a while, but it was no use, and eventually I had to kneel down for Katie McGowan to put a few clips in my hair to hold it in place.

I'd never really talked much to Katie through the year, but when I stood, she hugged me and said, "Congratulations, Peter. We made it, huh?"

Everyone seemed jolly, and for the first time ever the cliques dissolved. It was just us, just individuals who'd gone through something formative together, and were about to embark on the new and unknown. Any social barriers between us disappeared in the face of nerves and exhilaration.

Mr. Waverly, dressed in a nice suit, stepped to the front of the line, cupped his hands, and yelled, "Ladies and gentlemen, it's nearly time. Settle down! Settle down a minute."

Silence fell, and Mr. Waverly clasped his hands behind his back, rocking on his heels and smiling. "It's been an honor and a privilege to witness your growth over these last four years. It's been a wild ride for some of you and a smooth one for others. A lot of you I saw far too much of in my office, and others never darkened my door. Each of you, though, has made an indelible stamp on this school, and none of you will ever be forgotten. March into your future with your heads held high. You're Kingsley graduates and you'll always have a home here."

I grew oddly choked up considering I'd been at Kingsley for only a year, but what a year it had been. I felt like I'd lived a lifetime since I'd first seen Mr. Waverly during the orientation, and now, somehow, it was all over.

I'd been so nervous that first day, so anxious and ready to find out just what the year ahead would bring. I never could have imagined it would have brought me Adam or Sarah or Robert. I couldn't have imagined I'd have friends like Leslie and Mike, or I'd have a boyfriend and a lot of sex. I never could have known it would bring me up so high and down so low. I'd discovered so much about myself—things I was proud of and things I didn't like. And I'd found out that love wasn't all it was cracked up to be. Not when the world is against you.

I wasn't ready for what the future held for us, but it was here. It was now, and we were heading out into it, and all I knew was it had to be different. Our life after Kingsley couldn't stay the same. The span of time ahead was a vast roll of film for me to fill, and I'd be damned if it was going to be more of this pain, this heartache.

With or without Adam.

I shivered despite the heat.

"And now we begin," Mr. Waverly said, and motioned for us to follow. As we exited the building and started toward the rows of folding chairs now filled with our family, "Pomp and Circumstance" began to play. I put my chin up, like I wasn't afraid at all, and let the excitement of the unknown future rush over me and fill me up.

I smiled broadly as Sarah and Adam collected their diplomas. Mike was the next of our group to pass by, then Allison and Leslie. Leslie caught my eye as she walked to the front, and then it was my turn before I knew it. I took the rolled-up paper, shook Mr. Waverly's hand, and walked off the stage, grinning.

Now the world would change. Now I'd be different.

When it was over, Dad and Dr. Landry chatted, getting animated about *The Gnostic Gospels*, while Mom and I waited for Adam to break away from Leslie's family.

When Adam reached us with Sarah in his wake, he let my mom kiss his cheek before giving me a brief and manly hug. "Well, Eater," he said. "You graduated. What are you going to do now?"

"I'm going to Disneyland!"

He laughed and shoved me. I shoved him back, and we grappled together in our gowns, knocking off each other's hats and laughing like idiots.

"I know your Y chromosomes make you stupid, and you can't help it, but just *stop*," Sarah said.

I lunged at Sarah instead, and she kneed me hard enough in the shin I collapsed to the ground, half-laughing and half-moaning. "Crap, Sarah. What the hell?"

"I told you to stop." She knelt beside me. "I didn't really hurt you, did I?"

I laughed and looked up at her, feeling the lump on my shin growing. "Yeah, you really did."

"Welcome to the family," Adam said, and reached down to haul me up. "She's violent, and now she loves you enough to hurt you. Aren't you a lucky guy?"

Mom smiled at Adam, Sarah, and me like we were the cutest things she'd ever seen, and I rolled my eyes at her. Dad and Dr. Landry rocked on their heels, two peas in a pod, chuckling under their breath.

"None of you care if she beats me up?" I asked, still laughing.

"Love hurts," Adam said. "Everyone knows that. Hey, Mrs. Mandel, rumor has it you have a graduation gift for me."

My mom put her arm through Adam's and handed him the package. He bent his head low, listening to her tell him how grateful she was he'd come into our lives. Then he opened it, revealing a black Montblanc pen.

"For writing your first book," Mom said, and Adam grinned, kissing her cheek again. I was pleased with the gift too. I took it out of Adam's hand to feel the solid weight of it in my palm.

"Thank you, Mrs. Mandel," he said, taking it back from me. "You have no idea how much this means to me, and how much being welcomed into your lives has meant. Thank you. You're the best."

"I'm sorry your parents couldn't see you graduate," Mom said to Sarah, shaking her hand.

"It's not a big deal," Sarah replied. But even with her game-face on, we could all see she was hurt by their absence.

"Mom wanted to be here," Adam said, squinting in the sun. "But Dad needed her to stay and help him with some briefs he's working on."

"It's good she can be with him," my mother said politely.

"I guess. Oh, there's Mike and his family," Sarah said, pulling off her cap. It wasn't tradition at Kingsley to toss them, mainly because it was such a pain in the ass to clean up afterward. "I should go over."

As Sarah walked away, Dr. Landry offered his congratulations. "Mr. Algedi, it's been a pleasure and a privilege to have you in my class this year."

Adam grinned and hugged him. Dr. Landry returned the embrace with a fond smile.

"Thanks, Doc."

"You're a good kid," Dr. Landry said as he pulled away. His eyes met mine for a moment before turning back to Adam. "Think about doing the right thing, okay?"

Adam's expression fell, but before a frown could set in, Dr. Landry patted his arm again. "Keep in touch. I'll want to know what's going on in your life. The same goes for you, Mr. Mandel." He patted my arm too and said goodbye to my parents.

Adam punched me in the shoulder, and I groaned, rubbing where his fist had made contact. "Seriously?" I asked.

"Love hurts," he said again, grinning before following after Sarah to say hi to Mike's parents. I looked over to find the gift Mike's mother had given Sarah had left her all smiles and happiness. When Mike slung his arm around Sarah's shoulder and gave her a sound kiss on the cheek, envy stabbed low and sharp.

In another world, Adam and I could be like that. But then Leslie ran up to them and Adam swung her up into his arms like a bride, and I knew we never could. Not with how he felt about her. Not when he didn't want to give her up.

"Are we ready, Jessica?" Dad asked.

"Peter?"

I nodded. "Go on to the car. I'll meet you there in just a minute."

I raised my camera and took a few photos of the campus. I snapped shots of two little girls in white dresses hugging Levi Sorensen, and was taking pictures of Millar's family when the camera was smacked out of my hands, and the strap around my neck tightened painfully. A stripe of hot, burning pain sliced into my skin, jerking me back. For a moment I couldn't breathe and grabbed at the strap, struggling.

Just as suddenly, the pressure stopped, and I swung around, crouching down to protect myself from whatever might happen next. It was Eric Morgan, his eyes dark with menace.

"What the *hell?*" I asked, stunned he would dare to attack me in broad daylight, in front of dozens of people, at our graduation.

"You got off easy, faggot. You'll get what you deserve in college. When you're dying from AIDS you'll think the beating I gave you was angel kisses."

I rubbed my throat, and he stared at me. There was nothing soft in his look, no shame, no sorrow, only hot hatred, and then he turned to walk away, slow and steady like nothing had happened.

I kept my eyes on him until he was halfway across the parking lot, not daring to look away. As I glanced around at happy, laughing families, I realized that somehow the attack had gone unobserved.

Adam walked a hundred feet from me with Leslie's father's arm around his shoulder. I stood alone as they strolled through the parking lot together. Adam nodded his head at whatever Mr. Howard was saying, and my stomach ached as if I'd been punched. I was alone in this. Adam's place under Mr. Howard's arm protected him from people like Eric.

I wanted Adam safe. I did. I wanted us *both* safe. Yet my hands trembled with rage when Adam moved out from under Mr. Howard's arm to kiss Mrs. Howard's cheek just like he'd kissed my mother's.

Climbing into my parents' car, all the bittersweet joy of the day was replaced with a sick, lonely anger throbbing in my chest, making it hard for me to breathe.

"Pull over and get some ice cream, Abe," my mom said on the way home, pointing toward the Kroger by our neighborhood. "To celebrate."

"Want some ice cream, Petey-boy?"

"Sure," I answered, staring out the window, simmering on the inside, on the verge of boiling over. Maybe ice cream would cool me down.

Dad left Mom and me in the car as he ran into the grocery.

For once my mother noticed my mood, asking, "Why so sullen, Peter?"

"I'm just tired."

She looked at me using the car's vanity mirror, skepticism all over her face. She stared at me a long time, and I tried to ignore her, hoping Dad would get back with the ice cream so we could just go home.

"That doesn't explain why your neck is so red."

"Some asshole jerked on my camera."

"Uh-*huh*, and why did he do that?" Mom asked.

"Because I'm gay," I said.

I hadn't planned it. I just said it. I opened my mouth, and the words came out.

Mom laughed. "What nonsense."

My pulse raced. "Mom, I'm gay."

"No, you're not. You have a little girlfriend." Mom laughed again.

I swallowed and took a deep breath. "Mom, I'm *gay*. Do you understand? I'm gay. Like your brother."

Mom stared at me in the vanity mirror and then she turned around to study my face. Her eyes bored into me before her mouth crumpled. She pressed her fingertips to her eyes and faced the front in a silence so complete that it felt like a denial.

My heart jerked like it was going to stop. The atmosphere in the car was too dense to breathe. She was silent for so long I couldn't take it anymore.

"Did you hear me, Mom? I said I'm gay. I'm just like you. I like boys."

More silence, and vomit rose into the back of my throat.

"Mom? Will you say something?"

"I heard you," she said, turning the air conditioner up higher and angling the vents to blow directly at her face.

Now she was supposed to tell me she loved me. She was supposed to say everything was okay. She was supposed to get out of the car, pull me out too, and hold me tight. Why wasn't she doing any of those things?

Dad returned and tossed the bag in the back seat next to me. "Chocolate for Petey and mint chocolate chip for you," he said cheerfully.

Mom said nothing.

Dad stopped with one hand on the ignition, his face grew pale as he looked between us. "What'd I miss?"

Mom just stared straight ahead.

Dad adjusted the rearview mirror and focused on me. "Peter? What did I miss?"

My heart stuttered, but I stated the truth loudly. "I told Mom I'm gay."

Dad's eyes half closed, then he nodded, pushed the mirror back into place, and started the car. "Let's go home."

When we arrived, Mom went to their room and shut the door. In the silence, Dad shoveled out ice cream for both of us, and we sat at the kitchen table with Harry at our feet.

"I wish you'd had let me handle telling her," Dad said after he ate his entire bowl and had gotten up for more.

I shrugged and ate another spoonful. After I swallowed, I asked, "Why didn't you, then?"

"The time was never right."

Heaviness crushed my chest despite my studied nonchalance. I ate my ice cream, pushing it past the painful lump in my throat. "Is this going to be a problem?"

Dad's lips thinned, and he ran a hand over his head. "No, of course not, Peter. Your mother loves you very much, and this doesn't change anything."

"If it doesn't change anything, why is she hiding out in her bedroom? Probably knocking herself out with Valium?" I wondered if he would bring up my uncle now. I wondered if he would finally tell me the whole truth.

"She needs time to process the information."

"If she needs so much time, why hadn't you told her before now?"

"It isn't about you, or about you being gay. It isn't even about gay people in general," Dad said, reaching down to scratch Harry's ears. "Son, there are things I should've explained to you a long time ago about all of this."

"Then why didn't you?" I clutched my spoon tighter, blood rushing in my ears.

"I didn't want to scare you."

"Well, believe me, Dad, I've been scared for a long time, and not talking to me hasn't helped at all."

He rubbed his face. "I know I failed you. I'm sorry."

"Don't do that. Don't make me feel sorry for you. Mom's turned her back on me, and no one tells me anything."

Dad leveled me with a hard look. "Now, don't exaggerate. Your mother could handle this better, but give her time. You've had a lot of time to get used to the idea that you're gay, so give her a minute or two."

"How can this be news to her? How?"

"Son, she's got damage."

"Her brother. I know."

Dad stared at me. He licked his lips and then nodded slowly. "So you know about him?"

"Grandma Robbins mentioned him a few times. I've overheard things. He got beaten up for being gay, and Mom's messed up about it."

"Your mom's fragile."

"I'm fragile too."

Dad put his hand over mine, and I tugged it away. "I know, Petey. That's why I didn't want to tell you. I wanted to keep your heart safe, but I can't do that. No parent can."

"Tell me now." I rattled the spoon against the edge of my bowl, anger raging in me with fear.

Dad measured me for a long moment. "All right. Your uncle's name was George Robbins, and he and your mom were really close growing up. She was his baby sister, late-born and spoiled. He was her protector and hero."

I motioned for him to continue.

"When your mom was twelve, George got married. It was the year he graduated high school, which was young, but not uncommon back then. Your mom was crazy about his wife. Her name was

Beth. Beth Harsnip. She was a real sweet girl. I always liked her. She died a few years back of breast cancer."

"I remember. You and Mom went to the funeral."

"Yes. Well, George married her when they were both quite young. And, as it turned out, George wasn't really suited for married life."

My huffed. "Right. Because he was gay."

"I'm not sure if he understood what he was then. It was very hush-hush at that time, especially in rural towns, and despite his…desires, he tried to be a good husband. When your mom was about fifteen, George was caught with another man, a stranger passing through, in a compromising position." Dad touched my hand. "It was nineteen-sixty-five, and the man who found him was Beth's cousin."

"What happened?"

"The next night they beat the hell out of him, tied him to the back of a truck, and dragged him until he was dead."

I dropped my spoon, my stomach rebelling. I'd known they'd killed him, I'd gleaned that much, but like *that?*

"They dumped his skinned body in the front yard of your grandma's house. Your mom found him."

"I didn't know."

Dad took a slow breath. "She never got over it. And all these years, I've wondered…" He turned his attention to Harry, his lips pressing together like he was trying to keep his words in.

"Wondered what?"

His lips trembled as he met my eye. "If deep down she's known about you, and it hurts too much for her to accept it. That she's dropped out like she has because it's too terrifying for her to be the mom to you that she could've been to someone else."

Sickness and hurt pushed the ice cream into the back of my throat. I shoved the bowl away and stared at my dad.

"She loves you too much to let herself know you."

I shook my head, confusion tumbling inside me. "It was her job. As my mom, it was her *job*."

"I know." Dad rubbed a hand over his face. "She's been in and out of therapy over it. It probably doesn't make sense to you, but it took a lot of years for your mom to forgive George."

"Forgive *George?*"

"I know how that sounds. Believe me. But keep in mind your mom was so young, and it was so painful to find out this unspeakable—back then—thing about her brother whom she'd worshiped like a Catholic worships the saints."

I wanted him to stop talking. My hands shook and I was going to be sick.

"George's death was a massive scandal. Your grandmother was disgraced, your grandfather enraged, and your mom was deeply humiliated on top of her trauma and grief. The kids tormented her when the news got out. Not to mention, she loved Beth so much. She'd seen her more as a sister than as a sister-in-law. The suffering they all went through, all that pain and humiliation. And for what? A quick sexual encounter with a stranger?"

"It wasn't just that. It wasn't just *that* for him."

"She knows that now as an adult, but, back then she only saw how that one act tore her own mental health apart, how it destroyed Beth, her parents, their marriage, and their lives."

I was shaking all over, hot and cold racing over my body. "Does she still blame him? Even a little?"

"Of course not."

"Are you sure? Maybe she blames me for being gay? It feels like that."

"No." He reached out to touch me again, but let his hand fall short when I drew back. "When we decided to have you, Petey, she told me everything about her brother, and she said if something happened, if you turned out gay, she'd feel guilty because it would be her fault." Dad's fingers stretched toward me, and I avoided them. "We both believe it's a genetic trait. Something born in a person that can't be changed."

"Why is the way I love so awful that someone has to be called out to blame for it?" My eyes burned. "Am I that horrible? Was he?"

"Peter, no. You're not awful or horrible and neither was your uncle. What happened to him is horrendous and disgusting. It was wrong, and the men who did it should have rotted in jail."

"They didn't?"

"There was no proof who was involved. No witnesses to speak up."

I shook my head and a small sob burst out of me.

Dad reached for me again, but I backed my chair away from the table. I wanted nothing to do with his comfort, or this story, or a world where these men lived out their lives and my uncle died a horrible death that my mother had once blamed him for. I shook my head again and tried to fight down another sob.

"Being gay isn't something to be ashamed of, Petey. I told your mother that when we got married. But right now, she's wrestling with old demons. Guilt, fear, horror, and a kind of grief we'll never understand."

"I just wanted her to be my mom for once."

"She's scared for you."

"I get it. I'm scared for me too."

Dad looked like he might cry for a moment. He got up, pulled me into his arms, and whispered into my hair, "You're brave. I'm proud of you."

I let him hold me, a mess of feelings slamming into me again and again, until I felt weak.

"Your uncle was a good man, but if he'd lived his truth, if he'd left town and gone to the city…"

"You can't know what would have happened to him."

"Given the events of the last ten years, maybe AIDS would have gotten to him in the end." Dad sounded sad and a little scared about that. "But he'd have had ten or twenty years, maybe. Surely that would've been better than what happened to him?" He sounded certain. "Being gay is hard."

"I know that. Firsthand."

"I'm not blaming the man for what happened to him or even for his choices, Peter. But I'm telling you to listen to your heart and live your truth. Do better than I've done with your mother and with you."

"I don't know what you mean."

"Clinging to lies and denying reality is a dangerous and hurtful way to live. We did wrong by you. I'm going to try to make up for that. And I know your mother will too, once she's recovered from this shock. I'm sorry I've been a coward."

Finally, Dad pulled away, kissed my head, and put our bowls in the dishwasher. "I need to go to her now. Just know we love you. No matter what. No matter who you love or what you do. We both love you."

After he kissed my head again and walked out, I stared at the wallpaper in the kitchen as hot tears rolled down my cheeks. I didn't know how to believe him, and, for the first time in my life, I felt like an alien in my own home.

I sat down that night with a mass of photographs from my senior year, picking through them and choosing the best ones of each person who'd played a pivotal role. As I found them, I tacked them up on my bulletin board over my desk.

First, I chose a photo of Leslie. I found one where her blue eyes sparkled and her smile shone bright like a summer day. I saw so clearly why Adam loved her. The next photo I chose had three people in it. Van, smart, witty, and never quite satisfied, Allison, dark and shallow but ultimately loyal, and Mike, one of the best guys I'd ever met.

Next I pulled out a photo of Susan gazing over a cup of steaming coffee at Java. She looked like the subject of a Pre-Raphaelite painting, her cheeks flushed and her red, curly hair wild around her face. Sarah, the object of her adoring stare, had been completely oblivious to both her beauty and her unrequited love.

I carefully sorted through snapshots of Sarah and settled on the first one I'd ever taken of her—sharp, ruthless, and somehow soft at her core. I wasn't afraid of Sarah anymore, but I could see why I had been.

Then I hunted for just the right one of Renée. I chose a shot of Robert instead, a casual picture with his arm slung over Barry's shoulder on the front porch of their house. I hung it up next to the picture of Leslie.

As I scouted for the right photo of Adam, I came across a group shot taken during spring break—a bonfire on the beach, Leslie in Adam's lap, Sarah leaning against Mike, and all of them glowing from the light of the fire.

I sighed and put my head down on the desk. It was hard to love people and lie to them. I thought of my mom's brother and wondered—what had it been like for him? Had he loved the man? How much must he have longed to be something he wasn't? So much that he'd married a woman to try to make it work. So much he'd died horribly for it.

I rubbed my eyes and tacked the photo on the board before starting back through the stack for a good shot of Adam from the trip. When I found the one I was looking for, I leaned back in my chair and studied the shape of his mouth, the mess of his hair, and the way his eyes scrunched when he laughed.

I'm gonna miss you.

The words felt shot into my mind, as though from a cannon of inevitability. So final, so deep, and there wasn't room in me for it to hurt anymore.

I stood to tack the photo at the top of the board.

Love was like honey—a little was good, a lot was amazing, and too much? Well, too much made a big, sticky mess, a sweet mire I was drowning in, alone and more exhausted by the minute.

I went back into the stack and looked for the photos I'd taken of Daniel. The ones from Robert's house were the best, but the hot expression in his eyes was too much for me to look at for long. It made my heart tumble in ways that screwed me up inside.

In the end, I pulled out one of the blurry photos of Daniel from the night he helped me on the Hill. I tacked it in the bottom corner, away from the other pictures.

Falling back on my bed, I waited. I didn't know for what exactly. Maybe something that would make everything all right. I waited for my mother to come to my room to say she was sorry, to tell me she loved me. I waited for Adam to come over and make love to me, to kiss my heartbreak away. I waited for our friends to call and ask if I wanted to go out to celebrate graduation, to be together one last time.

Nothing and no one came.

I fell asleep with my clothes on. Alone.

Chapter Twenty-Four

THREE DAYS LATER, my mother hadn't left her room, and my father was out of apologies for her. I hadn't seen Adam either because he'd been invited on a last-minute trip up to the mountains with Leslie and her parents. He was leaving for Rome the morning after he got back. I felt both devastated and relieved by that. The idea of being away from him ached, but I didn't see an end to our situation otherwise. It would be a clean break.

It was all happening just in time and too soon all at once.

Ever since I'd talked to my father about my uncle and my mom, I'd been thinking about what I wanted and how I wanted to live my life. Who I was with Adam wasn't someone I was proud of, and in some sick way, I both wanted to stay with him and wanted him gone. It was a push and pull that had escalated over months and now culminated in me being almost relieved he was leaving. A summer where I could breathe easier and figure out what I wanted—without him muddying the waters with sex and promises he'd never keep.

The morning he left was mundane and bizarre. The sun was shining, the roses blooming, and it could have been any other day, except we were packing up his suitcases.

"Summer won't last forever," Adam said, a quiet promise, touching my arm and kissing me when Sarah and Mo weren't looking. "I'll be back before you can even miss me."

I tried to smile, but it felt wobbly and wrong.

"I promise, Peter. You won't regret waiting for me."

I opened my mouth to say something, I didn't know what, but just then Leslie arrived. Her eyes were puffy from crying, and her mouth was twisted in suppressed sobs. Adam left me to go to her, pulling her into his arms and making promises.

They sounded a lot like the promises he'd just made to me.

Leslie's grief brought into focus the reality of his leaving, but unlike Leslie, I had no outlet for my tumbling feelings—one minute relieved I was finally ridding myself of a painful tumor, and the next hurting like my soul had been cut free of my body. Leslie's tears were loud and abundant, and mine were stuffed deep inside for later, if I ever shed them at all.

As the morning wore on, I found myself comforting her more than once, hugging her and giving reassurances. It was surreal.

Before he left, Adam and I didn't get any real time alone to say any intimate goodbyes or have sex or be *us*. A few minutes before he was scheduled to leave, Adam pulled me into his bedroom, which looked horribly empty all boxed up. He shut the door, held me tight, and kissed me fast.

"This is goodbye?" I asked, my heart flipping, a shiver of sadness passing through me.

He nodded. "I love you, Peter. Don't forget me while I'm gone. I'll be back for you. I promise." He put his hand on the doorknob, kissed my lips again, and looked into my eyes. "I love you. Tell me you'll wait for me. Please, promise."

A lump came to my throat. I couldn't speak. I didn't know what to say, and yet I found myself nodding.

"You promise?" he asked again.

"I love you," I forced out through my tight throat. It was all I could say, but he took it for the promise he wanted and kissed me hard again.

Shaking, I followed him down the hallway to the basement. He was storing a few boxes of things down there for safekeeping until the fall.

"Tad! It's time!" Mo yelled from the driveway.

I stood by their car for a minute, watching Leslie cry in Adam's arms until I couldn't deal with it anymore. I turned to go, but not before Sarah grabbed me in a hug and whispered in my ear, "I never expected to like you so much." She kissed my cheek, pulled back, and said, "Take care this summer."

Leslie and Adam didn't seem to notice when I left, both of them absorbed in their long, sad goodbye. I wanted to scream. *She* got to flaunt her grief, and I had to suck mine up and save it for a private place and time. I had to make false promises. I had to hide.

I ran the rest of the way home and up the stairs to my room.

An hour later, when I knew for sure he was gone, *gone*, on a plane and *gone*—the pain of it hit me hard. I cried, clutching my pillow and wondering if I would ever again get to smell Adam's hair, hold him in my arms, or kiss him. Wondering if I even wanted to anymore. Wondering why it all hurt so damn much. I curled up in my bed, determined to stay there until I understood the meaning of my own heart.

That plan was derailed only a few hours later when Adam called. "I'm in New York. We board in thirty minutes for the flight to Rome. I'll write when I get there."

"Okay. I'll stand by my mailbox until I get the first letter." I scrubbed at my face and sat on the kitchen floor, petting Harry and letting him lick the salt from my cheeks.

"Better wear sunscreen or you'll fry." Adam was silent for half a beat. "I wanted to tell you, Peter—you're the best thing that's ever happened to me."

I didn't know what to think. Had he said the same to Leslie?

"I thought we needed a code word, so when I'm someplace

where Dad is listening, we can say it, and we'll know that it means I love you."

"Adam, I know you do," I said softly. That was part of the problem. If he didn't, then we could have just ended this now or months ago, before the lying had ever really started.

"The Sunsphere. Okay? If I mention the Sunsphere, it means—"

"I love you."

"Yeah."

I opened my mouth to tell him the truth. I wanted him to know I wasn't going to wait for him, or maybe I was, but not if we just went back to the same old lies and games. I didn't want to be the guy who lied to a friend and slept with her boyfriend. I didn't know how to be a gay man, but I knew it didn't have to look like that.

Something in me had broken over our months together. It hadn't been an instant break, more of a slow shatter. I could point back to moments and say, "This crack started there, and this one there," but now I was a mess of barely-held-together glass, and it was only a matter of time until I fell apart completely.

Until we both did.

I heard Sarah's voice in the background, and Adam had to go. The moment had passed, and I'd stayed silent. He believed I was waiting for him and maybe I was. All I knew was I needed this break like I needed air to breathe.

When I turned around, my mom was sitting at the kitchen counter, sipping orange juice, and looking at me with strange eyes.

My heart couldn't take it, so I just shook my head and went back up to my room. I flipped on the radio, found the college station, and turned up the volume loud enough to block out any sound from downstairs before flopping onto my bed to stare at the ceiling.

An unrecognizable song ended and the opening chimes of "Pictures of You" skittered into the room, as real as if they were just outside my window. In my mind, I started at the beginning, recalling every photograph I'd ever taken of Adam, every significant moment of our time together. The song trailed off before my memories did, and the voice of the disc jockey took up the silence.

When I'd satisfied myself that I'd brought to mind the whole of me and Adam, all that was meaningful and true, sans lies, sans hurt, sans Leslie, I got out of bed and stood by the bulletin board, looking at the photos of Adam there.

After the DJ introduced the next song and the jangle of mandolin and drums poured into the room, my eyes fell to the corner and Daniel's blurry shape. I remembered him singing softly as he drove me back to the Volvo, the same song that was playing now. I remembered him saying that if I wasn't in high school, he would have kissed me.

I unpinned Daniel's picture and shoved it into my desk drawer. Then I snapped off the radio, turned and grabbed my Leica from my nightstand. Adam was gone, and he'd taken with him the need to lie. It was time to get back to my truth, back to my photographs.

In the doorway, I stopped.

I went back and pinned Daniel's photo up again. My heart skipped, and I lifted my chin. I wasn't in high school anymore. Things were different now. Adam was gone, and I was on my own.

I held my chin high as I walked steadily down the stairs. It was time for a new start. A summer of me without Adam. A summer to find out who I wanted to be.

I stepped out my front door and into the golden afternoon sunshine.

END OF BOOK ONE

Read more about Peter in **You Are Not Me**
('90s Coming of Age, Book 2)

Gay Romance Newsletter

Leta's newsletter will keep you up to date on her latest releases, sales and deals, future writing plans, and more from the world of M/M romance. Join Leta's mailing list today.

Other Books by Leta Blake

Contemporary

Will & Patrick Wake Up Married
Will & Patrick's Endless Honeymoon
Cowboy Seeks Husband
The Difference Between
Bring on Forever
Stay Lucky

Sports

The River Leith

The Training Season Series
Training Season
Training Complex

Musicians

Smoky Mountain Dreams
Vespertine

New Adult

Punching the V-Card

'90s Coming of Age Series
Pictures of You
You Are Not Me

Winter Holidays

North's Pole

The Mr. Christmas Series
Mr. Frosty Pants
Mr. Naughty List
Mr. Jingle Bells

A Boy for All Seasons
My December Daddy

Fantasy

Any Given Lifetime

Reimagined Fairy Tales

Flight
Levity

Paranormal & Shifters

Angel Undone
Omega Mine

Horror

Raise Up Heart

Omegaverse

Heat of Love Series
Slow Heat
Alpha Heat
Slow Birth
Bitter Heat